A Singular Life

A Singular Life

Elizabeth Stuart
Phelps

MINT EDITIONS

A Singular Life was first published in 1894.

This edition published by Mint Editions 2020.

ISBN 9781513279930 | E-ISBN 9781513284958

Published by Mint Editions®

 MINT
EDITIONS
minteditionbooks.com

Publishing Director: Jennifer Newens
Design & Production: Rachel Lopez Metzger
Project Manager: Micaela Clark
Typesetting: Westchester Publishing Services

Contents

I

There were seven of them at the table that day, and they were talking about heredity. At least they were talking about whatever stood for heredity at the date of our history. The word had penetrated to religious circles at the time; but it was still interpreted with a free personal translation.

Perhaps there is no greater curiosity of its kind than that of a group of theological students (chiefly in their junior year) discussing science. It is not certain that the tendencies of the Seminary club dinner are not in themselves materialistic. The great law of denial belongs to the powerful forces of life, whether the case be one of coolish baked beans, or an unrequited affection. That the thing we have not is the thing we would have, neither you nor I nor the junior may deny; and it is quite probable that these young men set an undue value upon a game dinner and *entrées*, which was not without its reactionary effect upon their philosophy.

Jaynes, for instance, had been reading Huxley. Jaynes was a stout man, and short, with those round eyeglasses by which oculists delight in deforming round people. He confessed that he was impressed by the argument. He said:—

"Varieties arise, we do not know why; and if it should be probable that the majority of varieties have arisen in a spontaneous manner"—

"A little vinegar, Jaynes, if you please," interrupted Tompkinton gently. Tompkinton was long and lean. His hair was thin, and scraggled about his ears, which were not small. His hands were thin. His clear blue eye had an absent look. In cold weather he wore an old army cape of his father's. He studied much without a fire, for the club board at the "short price" cost him two dollars and seventy-five cents a week. His boots were old, and he had no gloves and a cough. He came from the State of New Hampshire.

Then there was Fenton: a snug little fellow, who took honors at Amherst; a man who never spent more than five hundred a year in his life, yet always wore clean linen and a tolerable coat, had a stylish cut to his hair, and went to Boston occasionally to a concert. It was even reported that he had been to see Booth. But the Faculty discredited the report. Besides, he had what was known as "a gift at prayer."

Fenton was rather a popular man, and when he spoke in answer to Holt (who observed that *he* considered Huxley's Descent of Man an infidel book) he was listened to with marked attention.

Holt was in the Special Course. He was a converted brakeman from the Hecla and St. Mary's, a flourishing Western railway. Holt, being the only student present who had not received any undue measure of collegiate culture, was treated with marked courtesy by his more liberally educated fellow-students.

"We are reading Darwin up at my room, two or three of us, after dinner," observed Fenton kindly. "We should be happy to have you join us sometimes, Holt."

Holt blinked at the speaker with that uncertain motion of the eyelids which means half intellectual confusion, and half personal embarrassment. Not a man of these young Christians had smiled; yet the Special Course student, being no natural fool, vaguely perceived that something had gone wrong.

But Fenton was vivaciously discussing last November's ball games with his *vis-à-vis*, a middler whose name is unknown to history. It was some time before he said, looking far down the long table:—

"Bayard, who is it that says it takes three generations to make a gentleman?"

"Why, Holmes, I suppose," answered he who was addressed. "Who else would be likely to say it?"

"Any of the Avonsons might have said it," observed a gentlemanly fellow from the extreme end of the table; he returned his spoon to his saucer as he spoke. There were several students at the club who did not drink with their spoons in their teacups, and even laid the knife and fork in parallels upon the plate, and this was one of the men. He had an effective and tenderly cherished mustache. He was, on the whole, a handsome man. It was thought that he would settle over a city parish.

"I doubt if there was ever an Avonson who could have said it, Bent," replied Bayard. The Avonsons were a prominent New England family, not unknown to diplomacy and letters, nor even to Holt of the Hecla and St. Mary's.

"But why, then?" persisted Bent.

"They have believed it too thoroughly and too long to say anything so fine."

Bent raised an interrogative eyebrow.

"You won't understand," returned Bayard, smiling. All the fellows turned towards Bayard when he smiled; it was a habit they had. "You aren't expected to. *You* are destined for the Episcopal Church."

"I see the connection less than ever," Bent maintained. "But I scent heresy somewhere. You are doomed to the stake, Bayard. That is clear as—as the Latin fathers. Have an apple,—do. It's sour, but sound. It's Baldwin year, or we shouldn't get them except Sundays."

Bayard mechanically took the apple, and laid it down untouched. His eye wandered up the cold length of the long table decorated with stone china. Somehow, few aspects of the theological life struck his imagination so typically as a big vegetable dish piled with cold, unrelieved Baldwins, to be served for after-dinner fruit on a winter day. In the kind of mental chill which the smallest of causes may throw over a nature like his, Bayard did not exert himself to reply to his classmate, but fell into one of the sudden silences for which he was marked.

"My father," observed the New Hampshire man quietly, "was a farmer. He dug his own potatoes the day before he enlisted. Perhaps I am no judge, but I always thought he was a gentleman—when I was a little boy."

Tompkinton shouldered himself out of the conversation, asked one of the fellows what hour the Professor had decided on for eternal punishment, and went out into the wintry air, taking long strides to the lecture-room, with his notebook under the old blue army cape, of which the northwest wind flung up the scarlet side.

"Has the Professor tea'd you yet, Bent?" asked Bayard, rousing, perhaps a little too obviously anxious to turn the channels of conversation. Genealogical problems at best, and in picked company, are unsafe topics; hence peculiarly dangerous at a club table of poor theologues, half of whom must, in the nature of things, be forcing their way into social conditions wholly unknown to their past. Bayard was quicker than the other men to think of such things.

"Oh yes," said Bent, with a slightly twitching mustache. "Ten of us at a time in alphabetical order. I came the first night, being a B. Madam his wife and Mademoiselle his daughter were present, the only ladies against such a lot of us. I pitied them. But Miss Carruth seemed to pity us. She showed me her photograph book, and some Swiss pickle forks—carved. Then she asked me if I read Comte. And then her mother asked me how many of the class had received calls. Then the Professor told some stories about a Baptist minister. And so by and by we came away. It was an abandoned hour—for Cesarea. It was ten o'clock."

"I was in town that night," observed Bayard. "I had to send my regrets."

"If you were in town, why couldn't you go?" asked the middler.

"I mean that I was out of town. I was in Boston. I had gone home," explained Bayard pleasantly.

"You won't come in now till after the Z's," suggested Fenton quickly; "or else you'll be left over till the postgraduates take turn, and the B's come on again."

The Baldwin apples were all eaten now, and the stone china was disappearing from the long table in detachments. Jaynes and the Special Course man had followed Tompkinton, and the middler and Bent now pushed back their chairs. Bayard remained a moment to ask after the landlady's neuralgia,—he was one of the men who do not economize sympathy without more effort than its repression is usually worth,—and Fenton waited for him in the cold hall. The two young men shoved their shoulders into their overcoats sturdily, and walked across the Seminary green together to their rooms.

Strictly speaking, one should say the Seminary "white." It was midwinter, and on top of Cesarea Hill. From the four corners of the earth the winds of heaven blew, and beat against that spot; to it the first snowflake flew, and on it the last blizzard fell. Were the winters longer and the summers hotter in Cesarea than in other places? So thought the theologues in the old draughty, shaking Seminary dormitories dignified by time and native talent with the name of "halls."

Young Bayard trod the icy path to his own particular hall (Galilee was its name) with the chronic homesickness of a city-bred man forced through a New England country winter under circumstances which forbade him to find fault with it. His profession and his seminary were his own choice; he had never been conscious of wavering in it, or caught in grumbling about it, but sometimes he felt that if he had been brought up differently,—like Tompkinton, for instance, not to say Holt,—he should have expended less of that vitality necessary to any kind of success in the simple process of enduring the unfamiliar.

"How was the gale round your room last night?" inquired young Fenton, as the two climbed the frozen terraces, and leaped over the chains that hung between rows of stunted posts set at regular intervals in front of the Seminary buildings. For what purpose these stone dwarfs staggered there, no one but the founders of the institution knew; and they had been in their graves too long to tell.

"It made me think of my uncle's house," observed Bayard.

"By force of contrast? Yes. I never lived in Beacon Street. But I can guess. I pity you in that northwest corner. My mother sent me a soapstone by express last week. I should have been dead, I should have been frozen stark, without it. You heat it, you know, on top of the base-burner, and tuck it in the sheets. Then you forget and kick it out when you're asleep, and it thumps on the fellow's head in the room below, and he blackguards you for it through the ceiling. Better get one."

"Are you really *comfortable*—all night?" asked Bayard wistfully. "I haven't thought about being warm or any of those luxuries since I came here. I expected to rough it. I mean to toughen myself."

In his heart he was repeating certain old words which ran like this: Endure hardness, as a good soldier of Jesus Christ. But they did not come to his lips. He was as afraid of cant as too many young theologues are of sincere simplicity.

"Oh, come, Bayard!" urged the other. "There's where you miss it. Why not be comfortable? I don't see that Christianity and misery need be identical. You are certain to have a tough time if you go on as you begin. Talk about election, foreordination, predestination! You take the whole set of condemnatory doctrines into your hands and settle your own fate beforehand. A man doesn't leave Providence any free will who sets out in life as you do."

"Do I strike you that way?" asked the young man anxiously. "If there is anything I abhor, it is a gloomy clergyman!"

"There you are again! Now I'm not finding fault with you," began Fenton, settling his chin in his comfortable way. "Your soul is all nerves, man. It is a ganglion. You need more tissue round it—like me."

The two young men stood at the foot of the bare, wooden stairs in the cold entry of Galilee Hall, at the dividing of their ways. It was the usual luck of the other that he should have a southwest room, first floor. But Bayard climbed to his northwest third-story corner uncomplainingly. It occurred to him to say that there were objects in life as important, on the whole, as being comfortable. But he did not. He only asked if the lectures on the Nicene Creed were to be continued at four, and went on, shivering, to his room.

It was a bitter February afternoon, and the wind blew the wrong way for northwest corners. Bayard had spent the day in coddling his big base-burner, which now rewarded him by a decent glow as he entered his study. He had no chum, and thanked God for it; he curled into the shell of his solitude contentedly, and turned to his books at once, plunging headlong into the gulf of the Nicene Creed. At the end of two hours he got up, shivering. The subject was colder than the climate, and he felt congealed to the soul. He flung open his bedroom door. An icy breath came from that monastic cell. He thought, "I really must get some double windows." He had purposely refrained all winter from this luxury lest he should seem to have more comforts than his poorer classmates.

The early winter sunset was coming on, and Cesarea Hill was wrapping herself in gold and purple and in silver sheen to meet it. Bayard went to his window, and stood, with his hands locked behind him, looking abroad.

The Seminary lawns (old Cesareans spoke of them as the Seminary "yard"), encrusted in two feet of snow, took on the evening colors in great sweeps, as if made by one or two strokes of a mighty brush. The transverse paths that cut across the snow, under rows of ancient elm-trees, had the shape of a cross. The delicate, bare branches of the elms were etched against a blazing west. Above, the metallic sky hung cold and clear. A few students were crossing the lawns, tripping and slipping on the paths of gray and glittering ice. In the wide street beyond, a number of people were breasting the blast, valiantly prepared for a mile's walk to the evening mail. The night threatened to be very cold. Across the street, the Professors' houses stood in a serious row. Beyond them, the horizon line ran to Wachusett, undisturbed; and the hill and valley view melted into noble outlines under snow and sun.

Emanuel Bayard stood at his window looking across to the hills. The setting sun shone full in his face. I see no reason why one should hesitate to give a man full credit for personal beauty because one chances to be his biographer, and do not hesitate to say that the attractiveness of this young man was extraordinary.

He was of slender build, but tall, and with good square shoulders that sturdily supported his head. He had the forehead of a student, the carriage of a man of society, and the beauty of a myth, or a saint, which may be the same thing. His complexion was a trifle fair for a man; his brown hair, shot with gold, curled defiantly all over his head; when he first decided to study theology, he used to try to brush it straight, but he might as well have tried to brush Antinous out of fable. He had bright, human, healthy color, and, as has been intimated, a remarkable smile. His lips were delicately cut; they curved and trembled with almost pitiful responsiveness to impressions. Thought and feeling chased over his face like the tints of a vibrating prism cast on a white surface. It was in his eyes that the extreme sensitiveness of his nature seemed to concentrate and strengthen into repose. His nearest friend might have said of Bayard's eyes, They are hazel, and said no more. Some stranger in the street, to whom the perception of the unusual was given, might have passed him, and said, That man's eyes are living light. Indeed, strangers often moved back and looked again at him; while people who knew him best sometimes turned away from him uncomfortably, as if he blinded them. This power to dazzle, which we often see in merely clear-minded persons with a well-painted iris, may not be associated in the least with the higher nature, but even the contrary. It was the peculiarity about Bayard that his eye seemed to be the highest as well as the brightest fact in any given personal situation. Neither a prophet nor a cut-throat would for an instant have questioned the spiritual supremacy of the man.

In Paris, once, he was thrown in the way of a celebrated adventuress, and she confessed to him, sobbing, as if he had been her priest, within an hour. Rank is of the soul, and Bayard's was unmistakable. Beauty like his is as candid, in its way, as certain forms of vice. It is impossible for him to conceal his descent who is born a spiritual prince.

But the young man was thinking nothing of this as he faced the cold and gleaming sky, to see the sun drop just to the north of Wachusett, as he had done so many winter nights since he took possession of the northwest corner of Galilee Hall. If his musing had been strictly translated into words, "I must prove my rank," he would have said.

As he stood mute and rapt, seeming to bestow more brilliance than he took from it on the afterglow that filled the grim old room, his eye rested on the line of Professors' houses that stood between him and his sunset, and musingly traveled from ancient roof to roof till it reached the house behind which the sun had dropped. This house was not built by the pious founders, and had a certain impertinent, worldly air as of a Professor with property, or a committee of the Trustees who conceded more than was expected by the Westminster Catechism to contemporaneous ease and architecture. It was in fact a fashionable modern building, a Queen Anne country house, neither more nor less.

As Bayard's glance reached the home of his theological Professor it idly fell upon the second-story front window, where signs of motion chanced to arrest his attention. In this window the drawn shade was slowly raised, and the lace drapery curtains parted. A woman's figure stood for a moment between the curtains. There were western windows, also, to the room, and the still burning light shot through from side to side of the wing. In it she could be seen clearly: she stood with raised arm and hand; there was something so warm and womanly and rich in the outlines of that remote figure that the young man would have been no young man if his glance had not rested upon it.

After a moment's perceptible hesitation he turned away; then stepped back and drew down his old white cotton shade.

II

More than thirty years before the day of this biography, a blue-eyed girl sat in her brother's home in Beacon Street, weighing the problem which even then had begun to shake the social world every year at crocus time, Where shall we spend the summer?

When Mary Worcester's gentle mind, wavering between the hills and the shore with the pleasant agitation of a girl who has never known any compulsion severer than her own young choice upon her fate, turned in the direction of the mountain village which her mother used to fancy, it seemed the least important of acts or facts, and was so regarded by her brother; for Hermon Worcester was a preoccupied young man, more absorbed in adding to his fortune, inherited in wool, than in studying the natural history of an attractive orphaned younger sister, left, obviously, by Providence upon his hands.

So, properly chaperoned and luxuriously outfitted, to the hills went Mary Worcester that conclusive summer of her life; and the village of Bethlehem—a handful then, a hamlet, if one should compare it with the luxurious and important place of resort known to our own day—received, as unconsciously as she gave, the presence of this young visitor whose lot was destined to become so fair a leaf bound in with the village history.

They are not usually the decisions to which we give the most thought that most control our lives, but those to which we give the least; and this city girl glided into her country holiday as unaware as the rest of us are when we cross the little misty space that separates freedom from fate.

She was not an extraordinary girl; unless we should consider extraordinary a certain kind of moral beauty to which the delicacy of her face and form gave marked expression. Such beauty she assuredly possessed. Her head had a certain poise never to be found except in women to whom we may apply the beautiful adjective "high-minded." Her eyes and the curve of her lip bore this out; and she had the quality of voice no more to be copied by a woman of the world than a pure heart is to be imitated by a schemer.

She was not an intellectual woman in our modern sense of the word. She was a bright, gentle girl; more devout than her mates who rode with her on picnics from the hotel, but as ready to be happy as the rest; she had a certain sweet merriment, or merry sweetness, peculiar to herself, and of which life and trouble never entirely robbed her. If we add to this that she had the angelic obstinacy sometimes to be found in unobtrusive and amiable people, her story, so far as it concerns us, need not be the enigma that it always remained to many of those who knew her best. In this summer of which we speak, when Miss Worcester had been for a couple of weeks among the hills, it befell that her party, for some cause not important enough to trace, moved into lodgings across the road from the hotel, where they commanded a cottage otherwise occupied only by the proprietor or tenant of the house. The cottage, after the fashion of its kind, was white of surface, green of blinds, and calm of demeanor. Its low front windows swept the great horizon of Bethlehem without obstruction, and when one drew the green-paper shade of the upper chamber in the rear, a tall pine—one of fourscore, the picket of a rich and sombre grove—brushed into one's face, and eyed one like a grave, superior rustic who knew his worth and one's own, and was not to be distanced.

Mary Worcester, in a white, thin dress, was sitting by this window one July day, looking down on the long fingers of the pine bough, when she was disturbed by a sudden agitation in the green heart of the tree. The boughs shook and parted, and the branch that lay over upon her window-sill trembled, yielded, started, gave a smart, stinging blow upon her bending cheek, and swept aside. She sprang back to save her eyes, and, in doing so, perceived the top round of a ladder rising from the tree.

She was startled for the instant; but observing that the ladder continued to rise steadily, and had evidently higher aspirations than her window-sill, she remained where she was. At this moment a voice from below delicately suggested that if any of the ladies were upstairs they might like to draw the shade, as some repairs were necessary upon the roof. The speaker was sorry to incommode anybody, and would withdraw as soon as possible.

Owing, perhaps, to that kind of modesty which feels an embarrassment at being recognized, the young girl did not draw her shade, but moved into the adjoining room while the carpenter climbed the ladder. The doors and windows were open through, and she stood for a moment uncertain, her light dress swaying in the draught. Then, turning, she looked back at the mechanic. At that moment his face and shoulders were on a level with her window. To her surprise, she recognized the man as their host, the owner of the cottage.

ELIZABETH STUART PHELPS

In a few moments a stout arm struck the roof over her head, and resounding blows shook the cottage sturdily, while a few old shingles flew past her window and troubled the pine-tree, which, shivering at the indignity, cast them to the moss below.

To escape the clamor, Miss Worcester tossed on her straw hat and fled below stairs. Her friends were all out and the house was empty. She wandered about such of the lower rooms as she had the right to enter, for a few moments, and then strolled out aimlessly into the grove. She flung herself down on the pine needles in the idle reverie of youth and ease and health; no graver purpose in life than to escape the noise of a shingler's hammer appeared to her. When the blows upon the roof had ceased she rose and went back. At the foot of the pine-tree, with his ladder on his shoulder, unexpectedly stood the man.

He was a well-built man, young and attractive to the eye. He did not look as rugged as his class, and showed, proportionately, more refinement. His eyes were dark and large, and had the sadness of a misunderstood dog. He raised them in one swift look to the young girl. She drifted by in her white dress with her straw hat on her arm; her hair was tumbled and bright; a little spot on one cheek, where she had rested it upon her arm, burned red. She smiled and said something, she did not know what. The mechanic lifted his old straw hat: the little act had the ease of town-bred gentlemen; something about it surprised the young lady, and she lingered a moment.

"And so you mend the roof for us?" she said, with her merry sweetness. "We thank you, sir."

"It is my business," replied the mechanic a little coldly. But his eyes were not cold, and they regarded her with deferent though daring steadiness.

"You are then the carpenter. Are you sure?" she persisted audaciously.

"That," replied her host, after a silence in which she heard her own heart leap, "is for you to determine." He bowed, shouldered the ladder which he had let drop, and passed on into the shed with it. His lodger, with burning cheeks, fled to her room, and drew down the green-paper shade.

The following day was Sunday, and the city lodgers in a party attended the village church. Mary Worcester, daintily dressed and devoutly inclined, sat with her head bowed upon the rail of the pew before her. When the village choir recited the opening fugue she did not move; but when the minister's voice broke the pleasant silence that followed, and the invocatory prayer filled the meeting-house, she lifted her eyes to the pulpit, and behold, he who had shingled the cottage yesterday was the preacher of to-day.

The services took their usual course. The scent of lilacs came in at the open windows of the country church. The rustic choir sang. The minister had an educated voice and agreeable manner. He did not preach a great sermon, but he spoke in a manly fashion, read the Bible without affectation, and prayed like a believer. It was not until the close of the service that he suffered his glance to rest upon the pew occupied by his lodgers, and thus he perceived the deepened color and the gentle agitation of her face. Their eyes met, and the fate of their lives was sealed.

At first they read their idyl with terror in their joy. She by her experience of the world, he by his inexperience thereof, knew what it meant for them to plight their troth. But Almighty Love had laid its hand upon them: not the false god, nor the sorcerer, nor the worldling, nor the mathematician, that steal the name,—none of these masqueraders moved them.

MARY WORCESTER AND JOSEPH BAYARD sat under the pine-trees of the grove behind the minister's cottage and faced their fate.

"I am a country parson," said the young man proudly, "and a carpenter, as your brother will remind you. I learned the trade to put myself through college,—a fresh-water college up in Vermont. Never mind the name. I doubt if he has ever heard of it. My father was the schoolmaster of our village. He was poor. My mother was an invalid for twenty years. It cost us a good deal to take care of her. After he died, you see it fell to me. I did the best I could for her. She died this spring. I never could go very far away from her. She liked to see me often, and it cost a good deal to get suitable nurses. She needed other things, of course. I was in debt, too, for my education. I've been paying that off by degrees. Take it all, I've got run down, somehow. Mother used to say I had her constitution. The people here called me to supply awhile, but they said I had too poor health to settle without trial. I don't wonder. They don't want a minister to die of consumption on their hands."

He stopped abruptly, and cast a bitter look at the young girl's drooping face to see how these blows struck that gentle surface. She did not lift it, but by the space of a breath she seemed to stir and tremble toward him.

"I love you," said the young man, flinging his thin hands out as if he thrust her from him. "A carpenter-parson, without a dollar or a pulpit he can call his own, and some day doomed to be a sick man at that! Go! I will never ask you to be my wife. Beacon Street! Do you think there is a man in Beacon Street who will ever love you as I do? Try it. Go and try. Go back to your brother. Tell him I scorned to ask you to marry me—for your sake, oh my Love!"

His voice fell into the whisper of unutterable passion and sacrifice, and he covered his face and groaned. Then Mary Worcester lifted her unworldly eyes and looked upon him as a woman looks but once in life, and upon but one.

"But if," she said, "*I* should ask *you*?"

He gasped, and sprang to his feet. Then he saw how she trembled before him. And she stretched up her arms. So he took her to his heart; and before the snow fell upon the hills of Bethlehem she had become his wife.

Life dealt with them as the coldest head on Beacon Street might have predicted. Her brother fell at first into burning anger, and then into a frozen rage. When the thing became inevitable, he treated her civilly, for he was a gentleman; more than that she never sought from him, and did not receive. She married her country parson intelligently, deliberately, and joyously, and shared his lot without an outcry. She knew one year of blessedness, and treasured it as a proof of paradise to come. She knew one such year as the saddest of us would die to know, and the gladdest could not look upon without a pang of divine envy. She knew what love, elect, supreme, and unspotted from the world, as the old words say, can give a woman, and can do for her. And then she reached the chapter where the plot turns in the beautiful, delirious story, and she read the sequel through,—a brave, proud woman, calling herself blessed to the end.

The minister's health failed, as was to be foreseen. He could not keep his parish, "as she might have known," said Hermon Worcester to the lady (her name was Rollins, by the way) who had chaperoned that summer party, and whom the brother had never succeeded in forgiving. Joseph Bayard descended from his pulpit to his carpenter's bench, and his high-born wife did not protest. "A man must feel that he is at work," she said. She mentioned the circumstance to her brother proudly when she acknowledged the last check; for she received her mother's inheritance duly, and spent it rapidly. She supplied the ailing man with such comforts as Bethlehem had never seen. She lavished all the attainable luxuries familiar to her youth upon the invalid in the frozen mountain home. Nothing and no one could restrain her. It was her way, and love's. That divine compassion which takes possession of a woman's soul when passion subsides from it swept a torrent of pity and tenderness about the enfeebled man. She persuaded him at last out of the mountain cottage which had watched their courtship and known their honeymoon, and carried him to Italy, where she played the last desperate chances in the game of life and love and death that thousands of women have staked and lost before her.

In the midst of this experiment the two returned abruptly to America, and hid themselves in the Bethlehem cottage; and there, in the late and bitter mountain spring, their boy was born.

The baby was a year old when his father died. Mary Bayard looked at the frozen hills across the freezing grave. In all the world only the mountains seemed to understand her. Her brother came up to the funeral, and politely buried the carpenter, whose widow was civilly invited to return to the home of her youth; but she thanked him, and shook her head.

"I will stay here among our people. They love me, some of them. They all loved him. I have friends here. There is no kindness kinder than that in the hearts of country neighbors. I've found that out. Beacon Street has forgotten me long ago, Hermon. There is nothing left in common between us now."

"At least there is your birth and training!" exclaimed her brother, flushing hotly. "I should think," glancing around the white cottage, crowded with little luxuries that love and ingenuity could hardly convert into comforts (by his standard of comfort) in that place and climate,— "I should think you would like to come back to a good Magee furnace and a trained maid!"

"There have been times"—she began slowly, but checked herself. "Those are gone by now. This is the place where I have been a happy woman."

"There is something in that," replied the man of business in a softer tone. He looked at her a trifle wistfully.

A certain tenderness for her returned in his heart after that. He cared for her as he could, sometimes taking the chilly journey to see her in winter, and spending a part of every summer in the Bethlehem cottage.

ELIZABETH STUART PHELPS

Thus he came to discover in himself a root of interest in the boy. When the child was three years old, he induced his sister to come to Boston to consult a famous physician.

"She is dying of no disease," he told the doctor irritably. "She had fine health. That ailing fellow wore it all out. He was a heavy burden. She carried everything—for years. She spent almost all her property on him: it was not trusteed; it is nearly gone; I couldn't help it. She has spent herself in the same way. She is that kind of woman."

"I have seen such," replied the physician gently, "but not too many of them. I may as well tell you at the outset that I can probably do nothing for her."

Nor could he. She lingered, smiling and quiet, in her brother's house for a few months; then begged to be taken home. Fires were kindled in the mountain cottage, and the affectionate villagers brought in their house-plants to welcome her; and there, on the morning after her return, they found her with her cheek turned upon the soft curls of the child's head. The boy was asleep. But he waked when he was spoken to. It was his uncle who took him from his mother's arms.

They buried her beside her husband; and her husband's people wept about her grave, for they had loved this strange and gentle lady; and they cut their white geraniums and heliotrope to bring to the funeral, and sighed when they saw the cottage under the pine grove stripped and closed. For the boy was taken to the home of his mother's girlhood, and reared there as she had been; delicately, and as became a lad of gentle birth, who will do what is expected of him, and live like the rest of his world.

III

I t had always been considered a mistake that the Professors' houses stood on the "morning side" of the street. But this, like many another architectural or social criticism, was of more interest to the critic than to the criticised. In point of fact, the western faces of the dwellings consecrated to the Faculty received the flood tide of the sea of sun that rose and ebbed between Cesarea and Wachusett. A man's study, a child's nursery, a woman's sewing-room, fled the front of the house as a matter of course; and the "afternoon side" of the dwelling welcomed them bountifully.

As Professor Carruth had been heard to say, that side of the street on which a man is born may determine his character and fate beyond repeal. The observation, if true, is tenfold truer of a woman, to whom a house is a shell, a prison, or a chrysalis.

The Professor's daughter, who had not been born in Cesarea, but in the city of New York, took turns at viewing her father's home in one of these threefold aspects. On that winter day of which we have already spoken, she might, if urged to it, have selected the least complimentary of the three terms. The day had been bleak, bright, and interminable. She had tried to take the morning walk to the post-office, which all able-bodied Cesareans penitentially performed six days in the week; and had been blown home in that state just so far from adding another to the list of "deaths from exposure" that one gets no sympathy, and yet so near to this result that one must sit over the register the rest of the morning to thaw out.

After dinner she had conscientiously resumed her study of Herbert Spencer's Law of Rhythm, but had tossed the book away impatiently,— she was metaphysical only when she was bored,—and had joined her mother at the weekly mending-basket. The cold, she averred, had struck in. Her brain was turning to an icicle—like that. She pointed to the snow-man which the boys in the fitting-school had built in front of the pump that supplied their dormitories with ice-water for toilet uses; this was carried the length of the street in dripping pails whose overflow froze upon one's boots.

There had been a rain before this last freeze, and the head of the snow-man (carefully moulded, and quite Greek) had turned into a solid ball of ice.

This chilly gentleman rose, imposingly from behind a desk of snow. Manuscripts of sleet lay in his frozen hand. An old silk hat, well glazed with drippings from the elm-tree, was pitched irreverently upon the back of his head.

"They say," replied Mrs. Carruth complainingly, "that the snow-man is meant to take off one of the Professors."

"Do they? I should think he might be. Which one?" answered the Professor's daughter. Her languid eyes warmed into merriment. "I call that fun."

"I call it irreverent," sighed the Professor's wife. "I call it profane."

"Now, Mother!" The young lady laid a green, theological stocking across her shapely knee, and pulled the toe through the foot argumentatively. "Don't you think that is a little over-emphasized?"

Mrs. Carruth lifted her mild, feminine countenance from that shirt of the Professor's which she always found absorbing,—the one whose button-holes gave out, while the buttons stayed on. She regarded her daughter with a puzzled disapproval. She was not used to such phrases as "over-emphasis" when she was young.

"Helen, Helen," she complained, "you do not realize what a trial you are to me. If there is anything sacrilegious or heretical to be found anywhere, you are sure to—to—you are certain to find it interesting," ended the mother vaguely.

"See, Mother! See!" interrupted Helen. Her laugh bubbled merrily through the sewing-room. "Just look out of the window, and see! The boys have stuck a whisk broom for a feather in the snow professor's hat! And now they're giving him spectacles and a fountain pen. What delicious heresy, isn't it, Mother? Come and look!"

But after these trifling and too frequent conflicts with her mother, Helen never failed to feel a certain reaction and depression. She evaded the mending-basket that afternoon as soon as possible, and slipped into her own room; which, as we have said, was in a wing of the house, and looked from east to west. She could not see the snow professor here. Nobody now accused her of heresy. The shouts of the boys had begun to die away. Only the mountains and the great intervale were peacefully visible from the warm window. Through the cold one the Theological Seminary occupied the perspective solidly.

Nature had done a good deal for the Christian religion, or at least for that view of it represented by our Seminary, when that institution was established at Cesarea, a matter of nearly a century ago. But art had not in this instance proved herself the handmaid of religion. The theological buildings, a row of three,—Galilee and Damascus Halls to right and left of the ancient chapel,—rose grimly against the cold Cesarea sky. These buildings were all of brick, red, rectangular, and unrelieved; as barren of ornament or broken lines as a packing-box, and yet curiously possessed of a certain dignity of their own; such as we see in aged country folk unfashionably dressed, but sure of their local position. Not a tremor seemed ever to disturb the calm, red faces of these old buildings, when the pretty chapel and the graceful library of modern taste crept in under the elms of the Seminary green to console the spirit of the contemporary Cesarean, who has visited the Louvre and the Vatican as often as the salary will allow; who has tickets to the Symphony Concerts in Boston, and feels no longer obliged to conceal the fact that he occasionally witnesses a Shakespearean play.

Helen Carruth, for one, did not object to the old red boxes, and held them in respect; not for their architectural qualities, it must be owned, nor because of the presence therein of a hundred young men for whose united or separate personalities she had never cared a fig. But of the Cesarean sunsets, which are justly famous, she was observant with the enthusiasm of a girl who has so little social occupation that a beautiful landscape is still an object of attention, even of affection. And where does reflected sunset take to itself the particular glory that it takes on Cesarea Hill?

The Professor's daughter was in the habit of watching from her eastern window to see that row of old buildings take fire from the western sky behind her; window after window, four stories of them, thirty-two to a front on either side, and the solemn disused chapel in the midst. It would have been a pleasant sight to any delicate eye; but to the girl, with her religiously trained imagination and unoccupied fancy, it was a beautiful and a poetic one. She had learned to watch for it on sunny days in her lonely Cesarea winters,—between her visits to New York or Boston. Now Damascus Hall, and now Galilee, received the onset of flame; now this floor reflected it, and now that; certain windows became refracting crystals, and flung the gorgeous color back; certain others drew it in and drank it down into their glowing hearts. One—belonging to a northwest corner room in Galilee Hall—blazed magnificently on that evening of which we tell. It attracted her eye, and held it, for the fiery flood rolled up against that old sash and seemed to break there, and pour in, deep into the unseen room, deeper than any other spot could hold. That window breathed fire as martyrs do, in ecstasy. It seemed to inhale and exhale beauty and death like a living thing whose doom was glory, and whose glory was doom. But the splendid panorama was always swift; she had to catch it while it lasted; moments unrolled and furled it. She stood with uplifted arm between her lace curtains; her eyes smiled, and her lips were parted. The old Bible similes of her childhood came inevitably even upon her lighter moods. It was not religious emotion, but the power of association and poetic perception which made her say aloud:—

"And the city had no need of the sun. . . to shine in it, for the glory of God did lighten it."

As the words fell from her lips the sun dropped beyond Wachusett. The fire flashed, and ran, and faded. Cold, dull, delicate colors replaced the glory on Galilee Hall; the burst of gold had burned out and melted; the tints of cool precious stones crept upon the window whose display had pleased her. She passed her hand over her eyes, for she was blinded by the dazzling effect. When she looked again, she noticed that the old white shade in the northwest corner room was drawn.

She turned away, feeling an unreasonable sense of discomfort, as if she had been rebuffed in an unconscious intrusion. At that moment she heard her father moving about his study, which was below her room. The sound of flying slippers and the creak of his whirling study-chair indicated that his work was over for the day, and that he was about to take his evening pilgrimage to the post-office. His daughter ran down to see him.

He glanced up from the arctic overshoes which he was tugging on over his boots, with a relieved and pleasant look.

"Ah, Helen! You are just in time. I need you, my child. Just write out some invitations for me, will you?—in your mother's name. She seems to be too much absorbed in some domestic duties to attend to it, and I *must* have those omitted men to tea this week. Your mother says she can't have them to-morrow on account of—I have forgotten the reason, but it was an important one."

"She has some preserves to scald over. Yes," said Helen, with ripples in her eyes, "I think they are quinces. At any rate, it is of national importance. Friday, did you say? Certainly. I will have them written by the time you have selected your cane, Father. Who are these? The A's? Or the C's?"

"They are the B's," answered the Professor, looking over his assortment of handsome canes with the serious interest of a sophomore. If the

Professor of Theology had one human weakness, it was for handling a fine cane. This luxury was to him what horses, yachts, and dry wines may be to different men. His daughter was quite right in assuming that the notes of invitation would be written before he had suited himself out of a dozen possibilities to his delicate Oriental grapestick with the heavy ivory handle.

"They are the B's," he repeated abstractedly. "Two B's, and—yes, one C. One of the B's I would not overlook on any account. He is that B who was preëngaged, for some reason, in the autumn. He must be invited again. His uncle is one of the Trustees. There's the catalogue; you'll find the address—Galilee Hall, Bayard, Emanuel. Don't make a mistake, my dear; and I hope you will take pains to be at home and help us entertain them."

"I was going in to the concert," said Helen disappointedly, pausing with her pen suspended. "I meant to spend the night with Clara Rollins. But—no, I won't, Father, if you care about it."

"Thank you, my dear," he said gently. He kissed her as he went out, and Helen smiled contentedly; she was deeply attached to her father. In his home the Professor of Theology was the most loving and beloved of men.

There came up a warm storm that week, and by Friday Cesarea Hill swam in a sea of melted snow. The two B's and one C waded their way to their Professor's house to tea that evening, across rills and rivers of ice-water, and through mounds of slush. Bayard sank over rubbers amid-stream more than once; he wore the usual evening shoe of society. He was always a well-dressed man, having never known any other way of living. It was different with his fellow-students. That one C, for example, who strode across the Seminary green in comfort and rubber boots, had provided, it seemed, no other method of appearance within doors. His pantaloons were tucked into the rubber boots at the knees, and had the air of intending to stay there.

"Look here, man!" gasped Bayard, as the young men removed their overcoats in the large and somewhat stately hall of the Professor's house. "You have forgotten your shoes!"

"I have some slippers in my pockets, if you think them necessary," replied the other. "You know more about such things than I do."

The speaker produced a pair of slippers, worked in worsted by his sister; a white rose ornamented the toe of each. As he stooped to put them on, Bayard observed that the man wore a flannel shirt of the

ELIZABETH STUART PHELPS

blue-gray tint at that time preferred by day laborers, and that he was guiltless of linen.

The three guests entered the drawing-room, headed by the flannel shirt. The one C sat down on the largest satin easy-chair, stretching his embroidered slippers on the Persian rug with such dignified unconsciousness of the unusual as one might go far to see outside of Cesarea, and might not witness once in a lifetime there. Occupied with the embarrassment of this little incident, Bayard did not notice at first that the daughter of the house was absent from the parlor. He fell to talking with his favorite Professor eagerly; they were deep in the discussion of the doctrine of election as taught in a rival seminary, by a more liberal chair, when Mrs. Carruth drew the attention of her husband to the gentleman of the flannel shirt, and seated herself by Bayard.

"I hope you are not very hungry?" she began in her literal voice. "We are waiting for my daughter. She attends the Symphony Concerts Fridays, and the coach is late to-night from the five o'clock train."

"Oh, that coach!" laughed Bayard. "I walk—if I want my supper."

"And so did I," said a soft voice at his side.

"Why, Helen, Helen!" complained the Professor's wife.

The young lady stood serenely, awaiting her father's introduction to the three students. She bowed sedately to the other B and the C. Her eyes scintillated when she turned back to Bayard. She seemed to be brimming over with suppressed amusement. She took the chair beside him, for her mother (who never trusted Cesarea service to the exclusion of the old-fashioned, housewifely habit of looking at her table before her guests sat down) had slipped from the room.

"You *walk* from the station—a mile—in this going?" began Bayard, laughing.

"No;" she shook her head. "I waded. But I got here. The coach had nine inside and five on top. It hasn't come yet. I promised Father I'd be here, you see."

Bayard's quick eye observed that Miss Carruth was in dinner dress; her gown was silk, and purple, and fitted her remarkably well; she had a sumptuous figure; he reflected that she had taken the time and trouble to dress for these three theologues as she would have done for a dinner in town. He saw that she gave one swift glance at the man in the flannel shirt, who was absorbed in the Professor's story about the ordination of somebody who was rejected on the doctrine of probation.

But after that she looked at the student's head, which was good. Upon the details of his costume no eye in the drawing-room rested that evening, again. That student went out from Cesarea Seminary to be a man of influence and intellect; his name became a distinguished one, and in his prime society welcomed him proudly. But if the Professor's family had been given the catalogue and the Inquisition to identify him, it may be questioned whether thumbscrews would have wrung his name from them. It being one of the opportunities of Christianity that it may make cultivated gentlemen out of poor and ignorant boys, Cesarea ladies take pride in their share of the process.

At tea—for Cesarea still held to her country tradition of an early dinner—Bayard found himself seated opposite the Professor's daughter. The one C sat beside her, and she graciously proceeded to bewitch that gentleman wholly out of his wits, and half out of his theology. Bayard heard her talking about St. Augustine. She called him an interesting monomaniac.

The table was served in the manner to which Bayard was used, and was abundantly lighted by candles softly shaded in yellow. In the pleasant shimmer, in her rich dress, with the lace at her throat and wrists, she seemed, by pretty force of contrast with the prevailing tone of the village, the symbol of beauty, ease, and luxury. Bayard thought how preëminent she looked beside that fellow in the shirt. He could not help wondering if she would seem as imposing in Beacon Street. After a little study of the subject he concluded that it would not make much difference. She was not precisely a beautiful woman, but she was certainly a woman of beauty. What was she? Blonde? She had too much vigor. But—yes. Her hair was as yellow as the gold lining of rich silverware. She was one of the bright, deep orange blondes; all her coloring was warm and brilliant. Only her eyes struck him as inadequate; languid, indifferent, and not concerned with her life. She gave the unusual effect of dark eyes with bright hair.

While he was thinking about her in the interludes of such chat as he could maintain with her mother, who had asked him twice whether he graduated this year, Miss Carruth turned unexpectedly and addressed him. The remark which she made was not original; it was something about the concerts: Did he not go in often? She had not asked the one C if *he* attended the Symphony Concerts. But Mrs. Carruth now inquired of that gentleman if he liked the last preparatory lecture. The Professor was engaging the attention of the other B. And Bayard and

Helen Carruth fell to conversing, undisturbed, across the pleasant table.

He felt at home despite himself, in that easy atmosphere, in that yellow light. The natural sense of luxury crept around him softly. He thought of his northwest room over there, rocking in the gale, and of the big dish of apples at the club table. He thought of the self-denials and deprivations, little and large, which had accompanied his life at Cesarea; he tried to remember why he had chosen to do this or suffered that.

His ascetic ideals swam and blurred a little before the personality of this warm, rich, human girl. There was something even in the circumstance of eating quail on toast, and sipping chocolate from a Dresden cup in an antique Dutch spoon, which was disturbing to the devout imagination—in Cesarea.

Over his sensitive face his high, grave look passed suddenly, like the reflection thrown from some unseen, passing light.

"I had better be at my room and at work," he thought.

At that moment he became aware of a change in the expression of the Professor's daughter. Her languid eye had awaked. She was regarding him with puzzled but evident attention. He threw off his momentary depression with ready social ease, and gayly said:—

"You look as if you were trying to classify a subject, Miss Carruth; as if you wanted to put something in its place and couldn't do it."

"I am," she admitted. "I do."

"And you succeed?"

"No." She shook her head again. "I do not find the label. I give it up." She laughed merrily, and Bayard joined in the laugh. But to himself he said:—

"She does me the honor to investigate me. Plainly I am not the one C. Clearly I am not the other B. Then what? She troubles herself to wonder."

Then he remembered how many generations of theological students had been the subject of the young lady's gracious and indifferent observation. She was, perhaps, twenty-five years old, and they had filed through that dining-room alphabetically—the A's, the B's, the C's, the X's and the Z's—since she came, in short dresses, to Cesarea, when her father gave up his New York parish for the Chair of Theology. It occurred to Bayard that she might have ceased to find either the genus or the species theologus of thrilling personal interest, by this time.

Then the Professor mentioned to the other B a certain feature of the famous Presbyterian trial for heresy, at that time wrenching the religious world. Bayard turned to listen, and the discussion which followed soon absorbed him.

The face of the Professor of Theology grew grave as he approached the topic of his favorite heresy. Stern lines cut themselves about his fine mouth. His gentle eyes darkened. He felt keenly the responsibility of the influence that he bore over his students, even in hours of what he called social relaxation, and the necessity of defending the truth was vividly present to his trained conscience. Bayard watched his host with troubled admiration. It was with a start that he heard a woman's voice sweetly breaking in upon the conversation. She was speaking to the guest of the flannel shirt.

"Oh, have you seen the snow professor since the rain? He's melted into such a lovely slush!"

"Helen!" rebuked her mother plaintively. "Helen, Helen!"

But the Professor smiled,—a warm smile peculiar to himself. He shot a tender look across the table at his daughter. He did not resume the subject of the Presbyterian trial.

"The trouble with the snow professor," suggested Bayard, "is that he had the ice in his head, but the sun at his heart."

Helen Carruth turned quickly towards him. Her glance lingered into a look distinctly personal and indistinctly grateful. She made no answer, but her eyes and the student's understood each other.

IV

I t is manifestly as unfair to judge of a place by its March as to judge a man's disposition by the hour before dinner. As the coldest exteriors may conceal the warmest loves, so the repelling Cesarean winter holds in store one of the most alluring summers known to inland New England. The grass is riper, the flowers richer, the ranks of elms are statelier, the skies are gentler, and the people happier than could be expected of Cesarean theology. Nay, theology itself unbends in April, softens in May, warms in June, and grows sunny and human by the time the students are graduated and turned loose upon the world,—a world which is, on the whole, so patient with their inexperience, and so ready to accept as spiritual leaders men whose own life's lessons are yet to be learned, and whose own views of the great mysteries which they dare to interpret are so much more assured than they will be ten years later.

Emanuel Bayard and Helen Carruth walked together beneath the ancient trees that formed the great cross upon the Seminary green.

The snow professor was melted out of existence; head of ice and lecture of sleet had vanished months ago. Dandelions glittered in the long grass. Sparrows built nests under the awful chapel eaves. It was moonlight and warm,—a June night,—and the elms cast traceries of fine shadows, like a net, about the feet of the young people; they seemed to become entangled in the meshes, as they strolled up and down and to and fro, after the simple fashion of the town; which pays no more attention to a couple sauntering in broad day, or broad moonlight, in the sight of gods and men, across the Seminary "yard," than it does to the sparrows in the chapel eaves.

They were not lovers, these two; hardly friends, at least in the name of the thing; she was not an accessible girl, and he was a preoccupied man. A certain comfortable acquaintance, such as grows without drama in the quiet society of university towns, had brought them together, as chance led, without distinct volition on the part of either. He would graduate in three days. He had called to say good-by to the Professor's family, and had taken Miss Helen out to see the shadows on the cross where the paths met—the mild and accepted form of dissipation in Cesarea; for Professors' daughters. They walked without agitation, and talked without sentiment. Truth to tell, their talk was serious, above their years, and beyond their relation.

The fact was that Emanuel Bayard had that spring with difficulty received his license to preach. There was a flaw in his theology. The circumstance was momentous to him. His uncle, for one thing, had been profoundly displeased; had rebuked, remonstrated, and commanded; had indeed gone so far as to offend his nephew with threats of a nature which the young man did not divulge to Miss Carruth, for his natural reserve was deep. She had noticed that he did not confide in her as readily as the other students she had known. But he had told her enough. The Professor's daughter, too well used to the ecclesiastical machinery and ferment of the day, was as familiar with its phases and phrases as other girls are with the steps of a cotillion or the matrimonial chances of a watering-place. She knew quite well the tremendous importance of what had happened.

"I understand," she said in her deep, rich, almost boyish voice, "I understand it all perfectly. You wouldn't say you did, when you didn't."

"How *could* I?" interrupted Bayard.

"You couldn't, and so they stirred up that fuss. You were more honest than the other fellows. And you were punished for it."

"You are good to put it in that way, but what right have I to take it in that way?" urged Bayard wistfully. "The other fellows are just as good men as I; better, most of them. Fenton passed all right, and the rest. I don't feel inclined to parade my ecclesiastical honesty and set myself above them,—in my own mind, I mean. I have dropped below them in everybody else's; of course I know that."

"Whom do you mean by everybody else?" demanded Helen quickly. "Your uncle, Mr. Hermon Worcester? The Trustees? The Faculty? And those old men on the council? Oh, I know them! Haven't I dined and breakfasted on Councils and Faculties ever since we came here? Haven't I eaten and drunken and breathed Trustees and doctrines, and what is sound, and what isn't, and—Don't you tell, but I never was afraid of a Trustee in my life—never! I don't know another soul in Cesarea who isn't,—not even my father. When I was a little girl, I used to ruffle up their beaver hats the wrong way, out in the hall, so they would look dissipated when they went over to the chapel. Then I hid behind the door to see. But I never told of it—before. You won't tell your uncle, will you? I hid a kitten in his hat, once, and when he came out of the study the hat was walking all over the hall floor, without visible means of locomotion."

Bayard laughed, as she had meant he should. The tense expression of his face relaxed; she watched him narrowly.

ELIZABETH STUART PHELPS

"Come," she said in a changed tone, "take me home, please. The house is full of Anniversary company. I ought to be there."

He turned at her command, and took her towards her father's house. They walked in silence down the long Seminary path. She was dressed in light muslin with a violet on it, and wore ribbons that matched the violet. She had a square of white lace thrown over her bright hair. The meshes of the tracery from the elm-trees fell thickly under her quick tread. At the stone posts which guarded the great lawns, she hesitated; then set her feet resolutely out from the delicate net into the bright spaces of the open road.

"Mr. Bayard," she said in her clear voice, "you *are* an honest man. It is better to be that than to be a minister."

"If one cannot be both," amended Bayard. "But to start in like this, with a slur attached to one's name at the beginning,—I don't suppose you understand how it dooms a fellow, Miss Carruth. Its equivalent would be almost enough to disbar a man in law, or to ruin him in medicine."

"I understand the whole miserable subject!" cried Helen hotly. "I am sick to my soul of it! I wish"—She checked herself. "Let me see," she added more calmly. "What was it they tormented you about? Eternal punishment?"

"I managed to escape on that," said Bayard. "I don't know anything about it, and I said so. I think, myself, there is a good deal of cheap talk afloat on that subject. Our newspapers and novels are full of it. It is about the only difficult doctrine in theology that outsiders understand the relations of; so they stick on that, and make the most of it. It is an easy way of making the Christian religion intolerable—if one wants to. My difficulty was rather with—I see you know something of our technical terms—with what we call verbal inspiration."

"Oh yes." Helen nodded. "Whether 'The Lord will have war with Amalek from generation to generation' was inspired by Almighty God; or 'Shadrach, Meshach, and Abednego,—Reuben, Gad, and Asher, and Zebulun, Dan, and Naphtali,' and all that. I know. . . Inspired moonshine! I am a little bit of a heretic myself, Mr. Bayard; but I'm not—I'm not as honest as you; I'm not pious, either."

"I hope you don't think *I* am *pious*!" began Bayard resentfully.

But she laughed sweetly in his frowning face. They stood at her father's high stone steps. The Anniversary company were chatting in the parlors.

"Good-night," she said in a lower tone; and then more gently, "and good-by."

He started slightly at the word; turned as if he would have said something, but said it not. He took her hand in silence; then perceived that she had withdrawn it suddenly, coldly, it seemed, and had vanished from him up the steps of stone.

He walked back to Galilee Hall slowly. His bent eyes traced the net of shadows around his reluctant feet. What was that? Inspired moonshine? Inspired moonshine! He lifted his face and looked abroad on Cesarea Hill.

His head was heavy, and his heart throbbed. Perhaps at that moment, if he had been asked which was the greater mystery, God or woman, this honest man could not have answered.

With sudden hunger for solitude, he went to his room. But it was full of fellow-students. Fenton was there, and Tompkinton, Jaynes, Bent, and Holt, and the middler. They received him noisily, and he sat down among them. They related the stories current in denominational circles,—ecclesiastical jokes and rumors of sectarian conflicts; they interchanged gossip about who was called where, and what churches were said to lack supplies, the figures of salaries, the statistics of revivals, and the prospects of settlement open to the senior class.

Bayard listened silently. His heart was not with them, nor in their talk. Yet he criticised himself for criticising them. Besides, *he* had received no call to settle anywhere.

Almost alone among the intellectual men of his class, he found himself, at the end of his preparatory education, undesired and unsummoned by the churches to fill a pulpit of them all.

He had done his share, like the rest, of that preliminary preaching which decides the future of a man in his profession; but he stood, on the eve of his graduation, among his mates, marked and quivering,—this sensitive fellow,—that most miserable of all educated, restless, and wretched young men with whom our land abounds, "a minister without a call."

He had said nothing to Helen Carruth about this. A man does not tell a woman such things until he has to.

Something in his face struck the students quiet after a while, and they dropped away from the room. His friend Fenton made the move.

"It is said," he whispered to Tompkinton, as they clattered down the dusty stairs of Galilee Hall, "that his trouble with that New Hampshire Council has followed him. It is reported that his license did not come easily. It has got abroad that he is not sound. Nothing could be more unfortunate—or more unnecessary," added Fenton in his too cheerful voice. There had been no doubt of *his* theology. *He* had received three calls. As yet he had accepted none. He expected to be married in the fall, and looked for a larger salary.

Suddenly he stopped and clapped his hands to his head.

"Bayard!" he called loudly. "Bayard, come to the window a minute!"

The outline of Bayard's fine head appeared faintly in the third-story window, against the background of his unlighted room. The moon was so bright that his face seemed to be a white flame, as he looked down on his classmates from that height.

"I brought up your mail," said Fenton, "and forgot to tell you. You'll find a letter lying on your table behind the third volume of Dean Alford. You keep your room so dark I was afraid you mightn't see it."

Bayard thanked him, and groped for the letter; but he did not light the lamp to read it; he sat on in the moonlit room, alone and still. His heart was hot within him as he remembered how the students talked. That vision which sets a man apart from his fellows, and thus makes him miserable or blessed, or both, beckoned to him with distant, shining finger. His face fell into his hands. Great God! what did it mean to take upon one's self that sacred Name in which a Christian preacher stands before his fellow-men? What had common pettiness or envy, narrow fear or little weakness, to do with the soul of a teacher of holiness? How easy to quibble and evade, and fall into rank! How hard to stand apart, to look the cannon in the eye, alone!

It is not easy for men of the world, of ordinary business, pleasure, politics, and those professions whose standards are pliable, to understand the noble civil war between the nature and the position of a man like Bayard; and yet it might be worth while to try.

There is something so much higher and more delicate than our own common standards of ethics that it is refining to respect, even if we fail to comprehend, the struggles of a man who aspires to the possession of perfect spiritual honor.

Bayard had not moved nor lifted his face from his hands, when a step which he recognized heavily struck and slowly mounted the lower flight of the old stairs of Galilee Hall. It was his uncle, Trustee of Cesarea Seminary, and of the faith of its founders, returning from the home of the Professor of Hebrew, where he had been entertained on Anniversary week.

Bayard sighed and groped for a match. This interview could not be evaded, but he winced away from it in every nerve. It is easier to face the obloquy of the world than the frown of the man or woman who has brought us up.

Hermon Worcester was bitterly mortified that Emanuel had received no "call." He had not said so, yet, but his nephew knew that this well-bred reserve had reached its last breath. As Bayard struck the light, he perceived the forgotten letter in his hand, and, perhaps thinking to defer a painful scene for a moment, said, "Your pardon, Uncle," and tore the envelope.

The letter contained a formal and unanimous call from the seaside parish whose vacant pulpit he had been supplying for six weeks to become their pastor.

"HELEN! HELEN!"

The mild, cultivated whine of the Professor's wife complained through the hot house.

Helen ran in dutiful response. It was late, and the Anniversary guests had scattered to their rooms. The girl was partly undressed for the night, and stood in her doorway gathering her cashmere wrapper about her tall, rich form. Mrs. Carruth looked through the half-open door of her own room.

"I cannot get your father out of his study, Helen," she urged plaintively. "He has one of his headaches at the base of the brain—and those extra Faculty meetings before him this week, with all the rest. Do go down and see if you can't send him up to bed."

Helen buttoned her white gown to the throat, and ran softly downstairs to the study. The Professor of Theology sat at his study table with a knot between his eyes. A pile of catalogues lay before him; he was jotting down statistics with his gold pencil on old-fashioned foolscap paper. He pushed the paper aside when he saw his daughter, and held out his hand to her, smiling. She went straight to him as if she had been a little girl, and knelt beside him, crossing her hands on his knee. He put his arm around her; his stern face relaxed.

"You are to put the entire system of Orthodox theology away and come to bed, Papa," she said, with her sweet imperiousness. "Mother says you have a headache at the base of something. It is pretty late—and it worries her. What are you doing? Counting theologues? Counting theologues! At your time of life! As if you couldn't find anything better to do! What is this?" She caught up a stray slip of paper. "'Deaf—deaf as an adder: 10. Blind—stone-blind: 6.' What in the name of—Anniversary week does *that* mean?"

"That is a personal memorandum," said the Professor, flushing. "Tear it up, Helen."

"I know," said Helen, nodding. "It's a private classification of theologues. Which does it catalogue, their theology or their intellects? Come, Papa!"

"I'll never tell you!" laughed the Professor, shutting his thin, scholarly lips. And he never did. But the laugh had gained the point, as she intended. He took his German student lamp and started upstairs. Helen walked through the long, dim hall with her two hands clasped lovingly upon his arm.

"I *am* bothered," admitted the Professor, stopping at the foot of the stairs, "about one of my boys. He is rather a favorite with me. There isn't a finer intellect in the senior class."

"But how about his Christianity, Father?" asked the girl mischievously.

"His *Christianity* is all right, so far as I know," admitted the Professor slowly. "It is his theology that is the hitch. He isn't sound. He has received no call."

"Do I know him?" asked Helen in a different tone.

The Professor of Theology turned, and held his student lamp at arm's length above his daughter's face, which he scanned in silence before he said:—

"I am not prepared to answer that question, Helen. Whether you know him I can't say; I really cannot say whether you know him or not. I'm not sure whether I do, myself. But I am much annoyed about the matter. It is a misfortune to the Seminary, and a mortification to the young man."

He kissed his daughter tenderly, and went upstairs with the weary tread of a professional man at the end of a long day's work.

Helen went to her own room and shut the door. But she did not light the candles. She sat down at her open window, in the hot, night wind. She leaned her cheek against her bare arm, from which the loose sleeve fell away. The elms were in such rich leaf that she could see the Seminary buildings only in broken outline now. But there was wind enough to lift and toss the branches, and through one of the rifts in the green wall she noticed that a light was burning in the third-story northwest corner of Galilee Hall.

It was past midnight before she went to bed. As she closed her blinds, for the first time in her life, the Professor's daughter did deliberately, and of self-acknowledged intention, stoop to take a look at the window of a student.

"His light is still burning," she thought. "What can be the matter?"

Then she flushed red with a beautiful self-rebuke, and fled to her white pillow.

Night deepened into perfect silence on Cesarea Hill. The last light in Galilee Hall went out. The moon rode on till morning. In the deserted green the clear-cut paths shone wide and long, and the great white cross lay as if nailed to its place, all night, between the Seminary and the Professor's house.

V

G oshamighty, stand off there! Who in—are *you*?"
  This candid remark was addressed by a fisherman in blue
flannel shirtsleeves to a gentleman in afternoon dress. It was in the
month of September, and the fleets were busy in and off the harbor of
the fishing-town. The autumn trips were well under sail, and the docks
and streets of Windover buzzed and reeled with crews just anchored
or about to weigh. At the juncture of the principal business avenue of
the town with its principal nautical street—from a date passing the
memory of living citizens irreverently named Angel Alley—a fight was
in brisk progress. This was so common an incident in that part of the
town that the residents had paid little attention to it. But the stranger,
being a stranger, had paused and asked for a policeman.

The bystanders stared.

"There ain't none nigher'n the station," replied a girl who was watching
the fight with evident relish. She wore a pert sailor hat of soiled white
straw, set on one side of her head, and carried her hands in the pockets
of a crumpled tan-colored reefer. Her eyes were handsome and bold.
The crowd jostled her freely, which did not seem to trouble her. "There's
a fellow just arrested," she explained cheerfully, "for smashing his wife
with a coal-hod; they're busy with him down to the station. He fit all the
way over. It took four cops to hold him. Most the folks are gone over
there to see the other game. This fun here won't be spoiled just yet awhile."

Something in the expression with which the gentleman regarded
her attracted the girl's attention. She took her hands out of her pockets,
and scanned him with a dull surprise; then, with a motion which one
could not call abashed, but which fell short of her previous ease of
manner, she turned her back and walked a little away towards the edge
of the crowd.

The fight was at its hottest. Two men, an Italian laborer and an
American fisherman, were somewhat seriously belaboring each other,
to their own undisguised satisfaction and the acclamation of the
bystanders. Both were evidently more or less drunk. An open grogshop
gaped behind them. Similar places of entertainment, with others less
easily described, lined both sides of Angel Alley, multiplying fruitfully,
till the wharves joined their grimy hands and barred the way to this
black fertility.

It was a windy day; the breeze was rising, and the unseen sea could be heard moaning beyond.

Just as the stranger, with the indiscretion of youth and inexperience, was about to step into the ring and try to stop the row, a child pushed through the crowd. It was a boy; a little fellow, barely four or five years old. He ducked under the elbows and between the legs of the spectators with an adroitness which proclaimed him the son of a sailor, and ran straight to the combatants, crying:

"Father! Fa—ther! Marm says to please to stop! She says to ax you to *please* to stop, and come home wiv you' little boy!"

He ran between the two men, and put up his little dirty fingers upon his father's big, clenched hand; he repeated piteously, "Father, Fa—ther, Fa—ther!"

But more than this the little fellow had not time to say. The father's dark, red face turned a sudden, ominous purple, and before any person of them all could stay him his brutal hand had turned upon the child.

Cries of shame and horror rose from the crowd; a woman's shriek echoed from a window across the street, and the screams of the boy pierced the bedlam. The Italian, partly sobered, had slunk back.

"Stop him! Part them! Hold him, somebody! He'll kill the child!" yelled the bystanders, and not a man of them stirred.

"Why, it's only a *baby*!" cried the girl in the reefer, running up. "He'll murder it! Oh, if I was a *man*!" she raved, wringing her hands.

At that moment, before one could have lifted the eyelash to see how it fell, a well-aimed blow struck the brute beneath the ear. He fell.

Hands snatched the writhing child away; his mother's arms and screams received him; and over the fallen man a slight, tall figure was seen to tower. The stranger had thrown down his valise, and tossed off his silk hat. His delicate face was as white as a star. He quivered with holy rage. He trampled on the fellow with one foot, and ground him down; he had the attitude of the St. Michael in Guido's great picture. He had that scorn and all that beauty.

A geyser of oaths spurted from the prostrate ruffian. The stranger stooped, and pinned him skillfully until they ceased.

"Now," he said calmly, "get up. Get up, I say!" He released his clenched white hand from the other's grimy flesh.

"He'll thresh the life outen ye!" protested a voice from the increasing crowd. "You don't know Job Slip's well 's we do. He'll make short work on ye, sir, if you darst let go him."

"No, he won't," replied the stranger quietly. "He respects a good blow when he feels it. He knows how it ought to be planted. He would do as much himself, if he saw a man killing his own child. Wouldn't you, Job Slip?"

He stepped back fearlessly and folded his arms. The rapidly sobering sot struggled to his feet, and instinctively squared off; looked at the gentleman blindly for a moment, then dropped his huge arms.

"Goshamighty!" he said, "who in—are *you*?"

He took one of the stranger's delicate hands in his black and bleeding palms, and critically examined it.

"*That?* Why, my woman's paw is stronger 'n' bigger 'n *that*!" contemptuously. "And you didn't overdo it neither. Pity! If you'd only made it manslaughter—why, I could ha' sent ye up on my antumortim deppysition."

"Oh, I knew better than that," replied the stranger calmly, turning for his hat. He thought of the boxing-lessons that he used to take on the Back Bay, years ago. Some one in the crowd brushed off the hat with the back of a dusty elbow, and handed it respectfully to the gentleman. The girl in the reefer picked up his valise.

"I've kep' my eye on it, for you," she said in a softened voice.

"Well," said Job Slip slowly, "I guess *I*'ll keep my eye on *him*."

"Do!" answered the stranger heartily. "I wish you would. They don't fight where I'm going."

"Who be you, anyway?" demanded Job Slip with undisguised admiration. He had not made up his mind yet whether to spring at the other's throat, or to offer him a drink.

"I'm in too much of a hurry to tell you now," answered the gentleman quietly. "I've missed the most important engagement of my life—to save your child."

"He's goin' to his weddin'," muttered a voice behind him. The girl started the chorus of a song which he had never heard before, and was not anxious to hear again.

"You have a good voice," he said, turning. "You can put it to a better use than that."

She stared at him, but made him no reply. The crowd parted and scattered, and he came through into the main street.

"Sir! Sir!" called a woman's voice from a window over his head.

The young man looked up. The mother of the little boy held the child upon the window-sill for him to see.

"He ain't much hurt!" she cried. "I thought you'd like to know it. It's all along of you. God go with you, sir! God bless you, sir!"

He had put on his hat, but removed it at these words, and stood uncovered before the drunkard's wife. She could not know how much it meant to him—that day. Without looking back he strode up the street. The Italian ran out and watched him. Job Slip hesitated for a moment; then he did the same, following the young man with perplexed and sodden eyes. The Italian stood amiably beside his late antagonist. Both men had forgotten what they fought about, now. A little group from the vanishing crowd joined them. The mother in the window—a gaunt Madonna—shaded her eyes with her hand to see the departing figure of the unknown while she pressed the bruised and sobbing child against her breast. The stranger halted at the steps of the old First Church of Windover; then ran up lightly, and disappeared within the open doors.

"I'll be split and salted!" said a young man who had not been drinking, "if I don't believe that's the new parson come to town!"

The speaker had black eyebrows which met in a straight and heavy line.

"I'll be—!" said Job Slip.

THE CHURCH WAS THRONGED. CITIZENS and strangers jostled each other in the porch, the vestibules, and the aisles. It was one of those religious festivals so dear to the heart of New England, and so perplexing to gayer people. No metropolitan play could have collected a crowd like this in Windover.

The respectability of the town was out in force. The richest fish firms, the largest ship-owners, and the oldest families shed the little light of local glory upon the occasion. Most of them, in fact, were members of the parish. Windover had what an irreverent outsider had termed her codocracy. The examination—to be followed that evening by the ordination—of the new minister was an affair of note. Windover is not the only town on the map where the social leaders are fond of patronizing whatever ecclesiastical interests are dependent on the generosity of their pockets and the importance of their names. Nothing tends to the growth of a religious sect so much as the belief that the individual is important to it.

Upon the platform, decorated by the Ladies' Aid Society with taste, piety, and goldenrod, sat the Council called to examine and to ordain Emanuel Bayard to the ministry of Christ. These were venerable

ELIZABETH STUART PHELPS

men; they drove in from the surrounding parishes in their buggies, or took the trains from remoter towns. A few city names had responded; one or two of them were eminent. The columns of the "Windover Topsail" had these already set up in display type, and the reporters in the galleries dashed them off on yellow slips of paper.

As the minister-elect, panting with his haste, ran up the steps and into the church, the first thing that he perceived was the eye of one of his Cesarea Professors fastened sternly upon him. It gave him the feeling of a naughty little boy who was late to school. This guilty sensation was not lessened by a vision of the back of his uncle's bald head in an eminent seat among the lay delegates, and by the sight of the jeweled Swiss repeater, familiar to his infancy, too visibly suspended from Mr. Hermon Worcester's hand. The church clock (wearing for the occasion a wreath of purple asters, which had received an unfortunate lurch to one side, and gave that pious timepiece a tipsy air) charitably maintained that Bayard was but seven minutes late. The impatience of the Council and the anxiety of the audience seemed to aver that an hour would not cover, nor eternity pardon, the young man's delay. He dropped his valise into the hand of the sexton, and strode up the broad aisle. The dust of the street fight still showed upon his fashionable clothes. His cheeks were flushed with his fine color. His disordered hair clung to his white forehead in curls that the straitest sect of the Pharisees could not have straightened. Every woman in the audience noticed this, and liked him the better for it. But the Council was composed of straight-haired men.

Somebody beckoned him into the minister's room to repair damages: and as he crossed the platform to do so, Bayard stooped and exchanged a few whispered words with the moderator. The wrinkled face of that gentleman changed visibly. He rose at once and said:—

"It is due to our brother and to the audience to state that your minister-elect desires me to make his apologies to this parish for a tardiness which he found to be unavoidable,—morally unavoidable, I might say. And I should observe," added the moderator, hesitating, "that I have been requested *not* to explain the nature of the case, but I shall take it upon myself to defy this injunction, and to state that an act of Christian mercy detained our brother. I do not think," said the moderator, dropping suddenly from the ecclesiastical to the human tone, "that it is every man who would have done it, under the circumstances; and I do not consider it any less creditable for that."

A sound of relief stirred through the house as the moderator sat down. The audience ceased twisting its head to look at the tipsy clock, thus enabling the Ladies' Aid Association to get that aster wreath for the first time out of mind. Mr. Hermon Worcester's watch went back to its comfortable fob. A smile melted across the anxious face of Professor Haggai Carruth of Cesarea. The minister-elect reappeared with plumage properly smoothed, and the proceedings of the day set in, with the usual decorum of the denomination.

It is not a ceremonious sect, that of the Congregationalism of New England; and its polity allows much diversity upon occasions like these, whose programme depends a good deal upon the preference of the moderator. Bayard's moderator was a gray-haired, kind-hearted, plain country minister, the oldest man in the Council, and one of the best. It was not his intention to subject the young man to one of the ecclesiastical roastings at that time in vogue, and for the course of events which followed he was not responsible. This was a matter of small moment at the time; but Bayard had afterwards occasion to remember it.

He listened dreamily to the conventional preliminary exercises of the afternoon. His mind was in a turmoil which poorly prepared the young man for the intellectual and emotional strain of the day. That scene in the street flashed and faded and reappeared before him, like the dark lantern which an evil hand brings into a sacred place. The blow of the man's fist upon the child seemed to fall crashing upon his own flesh. Across the crescendo of the chorus of the hymn the cry of the little boy ran in piteous discord. The organ rolled up the oaths of the wharves. While the good, gray-haired moderator was praying, Bayard was shocked to find that the song of the street girl ran through his burning brain. The gaunt Madonna in the window of the drunkard's home seemed to be stamped—a dark photographic letter-head—upon the license to preach the Christian religion which he was required (with more than usual precision) to produce.

"Why," said a sour voice suddenly at his elbow, "why do you consider yourself a child of God?"

Bayard recalled himself with a start to the fact that the personal examination of the day had begun, and that the opening shot had come from the least important and most crabbed man in the Council. And now for three quivering hours the young man stood the fire of the most ingenious ecclesiastical inquisition which had been witnessed in that part of the State for many a year.

ELIZABETH STUART PHELPS

At first it rather amused him than otherwise, and he bore it with great good nature.

He was patient beyond his years with the small clergyman from the small interior parish, whose hobby was that theological students were not properly taught their Bibles, and who had invented a precious catechism of his own, calculated to prove to the audience how little they or the candidate knew of Boanerges, Gog and Magog, and the four beasts which are the chief zoological ornaments of the Apocalypse. Having treated these burning questions satisfactorily, Bayard fenced awhile with the learned clergyman who was alive only in the dead languages, and who put the candidate through his Greek and Hebrew paces as if he had been a college boy.

Bayard had felt no serious concern as to the outcome of the examination, a mere form, a husk, a shell, with which it was not worth a man's while to quarrel. The people of the church—he had already begun to call them his people—were enthusiastically and lovingly pledged to him. He smiled into their familiar faces over the heads of his inquisitors, and manfully and cheerfully stood his ground. All, in fact, went well enough, until the theology of the young man came under investigation. Then a cloud no bigger than a man's tongue, if one may say so, appeared to darken the interior of Windover First Church. The oldest and deafest men in the Council pricked up their ears. The youngest and best-natured grew uneasy. The candidate's people looked at him anxiously. His uncle flushed; Professor Carruth coughed sternly. The moderator ruled and overruled, and tried with troubled kindness to quench the warming flame of ecclesiastical censure in which many a bright, devout young life goes out.

Suddenly Bayard awoke to the fact that the smoke was curling in the fagots at his feet; that the stake was at his back, the chains upon his hands; that he was in danger of being precondemned for heresy in the hearts of those gray old men, his elder brothers in the church, and disgraced before the eyes of the people who had loved and chosen him.

The house was now so full and so still that a sigh could be heard; and when a group from the street pushed noisily in, and stood by the entrance, impatient expressions leaped from pew to pew. Bayard looked up at the disturbance. There by the green baize doors stood the Italian, Job Slip, and the young fellow (with the eyebrows) who did not drink, two or three other spectators of the fight, and the girl in the reefer. An uninvited delegation from Angel Alley, these children of the devil had crept among those godly men and women, and stared about.

"A circumstance," complained Mr. Hermon Worcester afterwards to Professor Carruth, "which might not happen on such an occasion in our New England churches once in twenty years."

Bayard had been singularly gentle and patient with his tormentors up to this moment. But now he gathered himself, and fought for his life like a man. Brand after brand, the inventions of theology were flung hissing upon him.

Did he believe that heathen, unacquainted with Christ, were saved?

What did he hold became of the souls of those who died in infancy?

If they happened to be born dead, what was their fate?

Explain his views on the doctrine of Justification by Faith.

State explicitly his conception of the Trinity. Had none? Ah—ah!

Were the three Persons in the Trinity separate as qualities or as natures? Did not *know*? Ah—ah.

State the precise nature, province, and character of each Person. Did not feel qualified to do so? Ha—hum.

What was the difference between Arianism and Socinianism?

Did the Son exist coördinate with, and yet subordinate to the Father?

What is the distinction between the attributes and the faculties of the Deity?

Did an impenitent person ever pray?

Describe the doctrine of Free Will.

Is a sinner ever able to repent, of his own choice?

Is he punished for not being able to do so?

Is the human race responsible for the guilt of Adam?

Why not?

Explain the process of sanctification, and the exact province of the Holy Spirit.

Carefully elucidate your views on Total Depravity.

Could a man—did we understand you?—become regenerate without waiting for the compelling action of the Holy Spirit?

Is there any Scriptural ground for belief in the possibility of a second probation? What? Please repeat that reply.

Did not the first sin of a child justly expose him to eternal punishment? *What?*

At this point in the trial, Bayard was acutely conscious of the controlled voice of Professor Carruth, who had asked no question up

ELIZABETH STUART PHELPS

to that moment. Dear old Professor! he was trying to haul his favorite student out of the fire before it was too late.

"But," he asked gently, "is not one act of sin an infinite wrong?"

"I believe it is; or it may reasonably become so."

"Is it not a wrong committed against an Infinite Being?"

"Yes, sir, it is."

"Does not an infinite wrong committed against an Infinite Being deserve an infinite punishment?" pleaded the Professor of Theology.

"You have taught me so, sir."

A rustle swept the house. The stern face of the Professor melted in its sudden, winning fashion. He drew in his breath. At least, the reputation of the Department was secured!

"Do you not believe what you have been taught?"

"Professor," said Bayard, smiling, "do you?"

It being well known that the now conservative Professor of Theology had been the liberal and the progressive of his first youth, this reply created a slight smile. But the Professor did not smile. The crisis was too serious.

"The candidate does not deny the doctrine," he urged. "He will undoubtedly grow into it as other men have done before him."

"Whether men are eternally damned"—began Bayard.

"Job," whispered the Italian back by the door, "he swear at 'em!"

"No, he ain't," said the sober fellow. "It's the way they talk in churches."

"What tongue is it they do speak?" persisted the Italian.

"Blamed if I know," whispered Job Slip with unusual decorum. "I think it's High Dutch."

"No, it ain't; it's Latin," corrected the sober fellow. "I can make out a word now and then. They translate parts as they go along. It's darn queer gibberish, ain't it? I guess the natives used to talk like that in Bible times."

"All this row," said Job Slip, whose befuddled brain was actively busy with the personal fate of a minister who could knock him down, "all this d—— row's along of me. It's because he was late to meetin'!"

The Italian nodded seriously. But the girl in the reefer said:—

"Shut up there! The second round's on, now."

"Explain the difference between verbal and plenary inspiration," demanded the small clergyman in a small, suspicious voice.

"There! I *said* it was High Dutch!" whispered Job Slip triumphantly.

"Explain the difference," repeated the small clergyman.

The candidate explained.

"Is every word of the Old and New Testament of the Scriptures equally inspired by Almighty God?"

"Please give me your definition of inspiration," said Bayard, wheeling upon his questioner.

The small clergyman objected that this was the candidate's business.

"It is one of the maxims of civil law that definitions are dangerous," replied Bayard with a smile. But it was no time for smiling, and he knew it. He parried for a little in the usual technicalities of the schools; but it was without hope or interest. He knew now how it would all end. But he was not conscious of a moment's hesitation. His soul seemed elate, remote from his fate. He looked out across the lake of faces upturned to his. He had now grown quite pale, and the natural fairness of his skin and delicacy of his features added to the effect of transparence which his high face gave. The dullest eye in the audience observed, and the coldest lip long afterwards acknowledged, the remarkable beauty of the man. With a sudden and impressive gesture of the hand, as if he cast the whole merciless scene away from him, he stepped unexpectedly forward, and in a ringing voice he said:—

"Fathers and brothers of the church! I believe in God Almighty, Maker of heaven and earth. I believe in Jesus Christ his Son, our Lord and Saviour. I believe in the sacredness and authority of the Bible, which contains the lesson and the history of His life. I believe in the guilt and the misery of sin, and I have spent the best years of my youth in your institutions of sacred learning, seeking to be taught how to teach my fellow-men to be better. I solemnly believe in the Life Eternal, and that its happiness and holiness are the gifts of Jesus Christ to the race; or to such of us as prove fit survivors, capable of immortality. I do not presume to explain how or why this is or may be so; for behold we are shown mysteries, of which this is one. If I am permitted to guide the people who have loved and chosen me, I expect to teach them many truths which I do not understand. I shall teach them none which I do not believe. Fathers and brothers, I show you my soul! Deal with me as you will!"

He stood for a space, tall, white, still, with that look—half angel, half human—which was peculiar to his face in moments of exaltation. His dazzling eyes blazed for an instant upon his tormentors, then fell upon his people and grew dim. He saw their uplifted faces pleadingly turned to him: troubled men whom he had been able to guide; bereaved women whom he had known how to comfort. Oh, his people! Tears were on their cheeks. Their faces swam before him. How dear, in those few months that he had served them, they had grown! To stand disgraced before them, a stigma on his Christian name forever, their faith deceived, their trust disappointed,—his people, to be his no more!

"God!" he said in his heart. "Was there any other way?"

An instant's darkness swept over him, and his soul staggered in it. Then, to the fine, inner ear of the spirit the answer came:—

"In honor, between Me and thee, thou hast no other way."

The troubled voice of the moderator now recalled him, using the quaint phrase of elder times for such occasion made and provided: "The Council will now be by themselves."

In three quarters of an hour the Council returned and reported upon the examination. Emanuel Bayard was refused ordination to the Christian ministry by a majority of five.

Now, the savage that lurks in the gentlest assemblage of men sprang with a war-cry upon the decorum of the crowded church. Agitated beyond self-control, the people split into factions, and resolved themselves into committees; they wept, they quarreled, they prayed, and they condemned by turns. The gray-haired moderator and the dejected Professor, themselves paler than the rejected candidate, sought to convert the confusion into something like order wherewith to close the exercises of that miserable day. Daring the momentary silence which their united efforts had enforced, a thick voice from the swaying crowd was distinctly heard.

Job Slip, who had somehow managed to take an extra drop from his pocket bottle during the electric disturbance of the last half hour, was staggering up the broad aisle, with the Italian and the sober man at either elbow.

"Lemme go!" cried Job, with an air of unprecedented politeness. "Lemme get up thar whar I ken make a speech. D—— ye, I won't cuss ye, for this is a meetin'-house, but I *will* make my speech!"

"Hush, Job!" said the girl in the sailor hat. She came forward before all the people and laid her hand upon the drunkard's arm. "Hush, Job, hush! You bother the minister. Come away, Job, come away. Mari's here, and the young one. Come along to your wife, Job Slip!"

"I'll join my wife when I get ready," said Job solemnly, "for it's proper that I should; but I ain't a-goin' to stand by an' see a man that licked me licked out'n his rights an' not do nothin' for him! No, sir! Gentlemen," cried Job pleasantly, assuming an oratorical attitude and facing round upon the disturbed house, "I'll stick up for the minister every time. It ain't *his* fault he was late to meetin'. You hadn't oughter kick him out for that, now! It's all along of me, gentlemen! I drink—and he—ye see— don't. I was threshin' the life out'n my little boy down to Angel Alley, and he knocked me down for't. Fact, sir! That there little minister, he knocked *me* down. I'll stand by him every round now, you bet! *I'*ll see't he gets his rights in his own meetin'-house!"

Half a dozen hands were at Job's mouth; a dozen more dragged him back. The Council sprang to their feet in horror. But Job squared off, and eyed these venerable Christians with the moral superiority of his condition. He pushed on towards the pulpit.

"Come on, Tony!" he cried to the Italian. "Come, Ben! You, Lena!" He beckoned to the girl, who had shrunk back. "Tell Mari an' Joey to foller on! Won't hear us, won't they? Well, we'll see! There ain't a cove of the lot of *them* could knock me down! Jest to save a little fellar's bones! Gentlemen! look a' here. Look at us. *We're the delegation from Angel Alley, Sir.* Now, sir, what are you pious a-goin' to do with *us?*"

But a white, firm hand was laid upon Job's shoulder. Pale, shining, frowning, Bayard stood beside him.

"Come, Job," he said gently, "come out with me, and we will talk it over."

The broad aisle quickly cleared, and the rejected minister left the church with the drunkard's hand upon his arm. The remainder of the delegation from Angel Alley followed quietly, and the soft, green baize doors closed upon them.

"Say," said Job Slip, recovering a portion of his scattered senses in the open air,—"say, I thought you said they didn't fight where you was goin'?"

The drunkard's wife stood outside. She was crying. Bayard looked at her. He did not know what to say. Just then he felt a tug at the tail of his coat, and small, warm fingers crept into his cold hand. He looked down. It was the little boy.

VI

The real crises of life are those that the stories leave untold. It is not the sudden blow, but the learning how to bear the bruise afterwards, that constitutes experience; not the delirium of fever, but the weariness of convalescence. What does one do the Monday morning after the funeral? How does one meet the grocery bills when the property is gone? How does a man act when his reputation is ruined by the span of an afternoon? Fiction does not tell us, but fact omits nothing of the grim details; spares not the least stroke of that black perplexity which, next to the insecurity of life, is the hardest thing about it.

You men of affairs, give a moment's manly sympathy to the position of a young fellow like yourselves, halting just over the line between education and a life's work, trained for a calling which the worldliest soul among you respects as nobler and higher than your own, tripped at the outset by one of its lower and more ignoble accidents; a man who will not lie to God or his own soul, who has scorned the consequences of being simply true, but must bear them for all that, like other men. For the holiest dedications in this world suffer the taint thereof; and it is at once the saddest and the healthiest thing about the work of a man of God that it is subject to market laws, to fashion, to prejudice, to envy, and to poor judgment, like other work.

It seems a little thing to write about, but at the time it was not the least aspect of the great crisis into which Emanuel Bayard had arrived, that, when he came out into the strong, salt breeze of Windover that afternoon, it suddenly occurred to the heretic minister that he had nowhere to spend the night. Alas for the bright and solemn festival in which his should have been the crowned hero's part! He heard the excited women of the parish asking each other:—

"Who is going to eat up that collation?"

"What is ever going to become of all that one-two-three-four cake?"

"Feed those old ministers *now*? Not a sandwich! Let 'em go home where they belong. If we're going to have no minister, they shall have no supper! We'll settle him in spite of 'em!"

Thus the Ladies' Aid Association, with flushed cheeks and shrill voices. But the deacons and the pillars of the disturbed church collected in serious groups, and discussed the catastrophe with the dignity of the voting and governing sex.

Sick at heart, and longing to escape from the whole miserable scene, Bayard walked down the street alone. His steps bent blindly to the station. When he had bought his ticket to Boston, it came to him for the first time to ask himself where he was going. Home? What home? Whose? Hermon Worcester's? That glance at his uncle's rigid face which he had allowed himself back there in the church recurred to him. The incensed and disappointed man had suffered his smitten boy to go forth from that furnace without a sign of sympathy. He had given Emanuel one look: the pupils of his eyes were dark and dilated with indignation of the kind that a gentleman does not trust himself to express.

"I cannot go home," said Emanuel suddenly, half aloud. "I forgot that. I shall not be wanted."

He put his ticket in his wallet and turned away. Some people were hurrying into the station, and he strode to a side door to escape them. The handsome knob of an Oriental grapestick touched his arm. The white face of the Professor of Theology looked sternly into his.

"Suppose you come out to Cesarea with me to-night? We can talk this unfortunate affair over quietly, and—I am sure you misapprehend the real drift of some of these doctrines that disturb you. I believe I could set you right, and possibly—another examination—before a different Council"—

Bayard's head swam for an instant. A girl in a muslin dress stood at the meeting of the arms of the great cross in the Seminary lawn. It was moonlight, and it was June, and this dreadful thing had never happened. He was in that state when a woman's sympathy is the only one delicate enough for a man's bruised nature to bear. He quivered at the thought of being touched by anything harsher than the compassionate approval, the indignant sorrow, the intelligent heart—

"No," he said, after a scarcely perceptible hesitation. "Thank you, Professor—I can't do it. I should only disappoint you. I am almost too tired to go all over the ground again. Good-by, Professor."

He held out his hand timidly. The thin, high-veined hand of the Professor shook as he responded to the grasp.

"I didn't know," he said more gently, "but you would be more comfortable. Your uncle"—the Professor hesitated.

"Thank you," said the young man again. "That was thoughtful in you. If your theology were half as tender as your heart, Professor!" added the poor fellow, trying to smile with the old audacity of Professor Carruth's pet student. But he shook his head, and pushed out of the door into the street.

There he stood irresolute. What next? He was to have been the guest of the treasurer of the church that night, after the ordination. It was a pretty, luxurious home; he had been entertained there so often that he felt at home in it; the family had been his affectionate friends, and the children were fond of him. He thought of that comfortable guest-room with the weakest pang that he had known yet: he felt ill enough to go to bed. But they had not asked the dishonored minister, now, to be their guest. It did not occur to him, so sore at heart was he, that he had given them no opportunity.

He was about to return to the station, with a vague purpose to seek shelter in some hotel in a village where nobody knew him, when a plain, elderly woman dressed in black approached him. He recognized her as one of the obscurer people of his lost parish. She had been comforted by something he had said one Sunday; she had come timidly to tell him so, after the fashion of such women; she had known trouble, he remembered, and poverty, it was clear.

"Ah, Mrs. Granite!" he said pathetically. "Did you take all the trouble to come to say good-by to *me*?"

"You look so tired, sir!" sobbed Mrs. Granite. "You look down sick abed! We thought you wasn't fit to travel to-night, sir, and if you wouldn't mind coming home with us to get a night's rest, Mr. Bayard? We live very poor, sir, not like you; but me and my girl, we couldn't *bear* to see you going off so! We'd take it for an honor, Mr. Bayard, sir!"

"I will come," said the weary man. And he went, at once. Certain words confusedly recurred to him as he walked silently beside Mrs. Granite, "He had not where," they ran,—"He had not where to lay his head."

The light burned late in the clean, spare room in the cottage of the fisherman's widow on Windover Point that night.

Early in the morning her mother sent Jane Granite running for the doctor; and by night it was well known in Windover that the new minister was ill. He was threatened with something with a Latin name; not epidemic in Windover, whose prevailing diseases are measles and alcoholism. Mrs. Granite found the minister's anticipated malady hard to pronounce; but Jane, who had been at the high school, called it meningitis.

But here again fact dealt with Emanuel Bayard as no respectable fiction could be expected to. An interesting delirium or deadly fever might have changed the whole course of his life. Had he fallen then and there a martyr to his fate, the sympathy of the town, the interest of the denomination, the affection of his lost parish, the penitent anxiety of Mr. Hermon Worcester, would—how easily!—have marked out his future for him in flower-beds that seemed forsooth to be the vineyard of the Lord; and he might have done a deal of pleasant hoeing and trimming there, like other men, till harvest time. But floriculture is small pastime for the sinew elected to cut thickets and to blaze forests; and he arose to tear and bleed at his self-chosen brambles as God decreed.

He had not meningitis; he suffered no mortal malady; he did but lie helpless for two weeks under one of those serious nervous collapses which seem ignominy to a young man. During these critical days his people elect and lost had plenty of time to quarrel over him, or to send him currant jelly. And the wife of the treasurer was reported to have said that he ought to be in her house. But Mrs. Granite and Jane nursed him adoringly, and as soon as the doctor permitted, Jane brought the patient his mail. It contained a curt but civil letter from his uncle, regretting to learn that he had been indisposed, and requesting an interview.

As soon as he was able to travel, Emanuel went to Boston.

An unexpected incident which happened on the morning that he left Windover gave back something of the natural fire to his eyes, and he looked less ill than Mr. Worcester had expected, when they met in the library on Beacon Street.

This circumstance checked the slightly rising tide of sympathy in his uncle's feeling; and it was with scarcely more than civility that the elder man opened the conversation.

"I wish to discuss this situation with you, Emanuel, once for all. You have for some time avoided the issue between us which is bound to come."

"I have avoided nothing," interrupted Emanuel proudly.

"It is the same thing. You have never met me halfway. The time has come when we must have it out. You know, of course, perfectly well what a blow this thing has been to me—the mortification—the. . . After all I have done for you"—

The cold, clear-cut features of Hermon Worcester's face became suffused; he put his hand against his heart, and gasped. For the first time it occurred to the young man that the elder, too, had suffered;

with a quick exclamation of sympathy or anxiety, he turned to reply, but Mr. Worcester got to his feet, and began to pace the library hotly.

"What do you propose to do?" he cried. "Seven years of higher education, and—how many trips to Europe? And all the—that—feeling a man has for a child he has brought up—wasted, worse than wasted! What do you propose to do? Thirty years old, and a failure at the start! A disgrace to the faith of your fathers! A blot on an old religious name! Come, now! what next? . . . I suppose I could find you a place to sweep a store," added Hermon Worcester bitingly.

Emanuel had flushed darkly, and then his swift pallor came on.

"Uncle," he said distinctly, "I think this interview we have been preparing for so long may as well be dispensed with. It seems to me quite useless. I can only grieve you, sir; and you cannot comfort me."

"Comfort!" sneered the other, with his least agreeable expression; for Hermon Worcester had many, in frequent use.

"Well," said Emanuel, "yes. There are times when even a heretic may need something of that sort. But I was about to say that I think it idle for us to talk. My plans are now quite formed."

"Indeed, sir!" said Mr. Worcester, stopping short.

"I have been invited by a minority of my people to start a new work in Windover, of which they propose that I shall become the leader."

"Not the pastor!" observed Mr. Worcester.

"Yes, the pastor,—that was the word. It will be a work quite independent of the old church."

"And of the old faith, eh?"

"Of the old traditions, some of them," replied Emanuel gently; "not of the old truth, I hope. I cannot hope for your sympathy in this step. I have decided to take it. It strikes me, Uncle, that we had better not discuss the matter."

"His mother before him!" cried Hermon Worcester, violently striding up and down the velvet carpet of the library, "I went through it with his mother before him,—this abhorrent indifference to the demands of birth and training, this scandal, this withdrawal from the world, this publicity given to family differences, the whole miserable business! She for love, and you for—I suppose you call it religion! I can't go through it again, and I won't! It is asking too much of me!"

"I ask nothing of you, Uncle," said the young man, rising.

"You'll end in infidelity, sir. You will be an agnostic in a year's time. You'll be preaching positivism! I will have nothing to do with it! I warned you before, Manuel,—back there in Cesarea. I am forced to repeat myself. Under the circumstances, you will not expect a dollar from me. I would as soon leave my property to an atheist club as to you, and your second probations, and your uninspired Bibles!"

Mr. Worcester snapped in the private drawer of his desk, and locked it with unnecessary force and symbolism.

"I don't forbid you my house, mind. I sha'n't turn you into the street. You'll starve into your senses fast enough on any salary that the rabble down in that fishing-town can raise for you. When you do—come back to me. Keep your latch-key in your pocket. You will want to use it some day."

"I must run my chances, sir," said Bayard in a voice so low that it was scarcely audible. Instinctively he drew his latch-key from his pocket and held it out; but Mr. Hermon Worcester did not deign to notice it. "I have never thought about your money, Uncle. I'm not that kind of fellow, exactly. You have always been good to me, Uncle Hermon!" He choked, and held out his hand to say good-by.

"But look here—see here—you'll stay to dinner? You'll go up to your room, Manuel?" stammered the elder man. "I explicitly told you that I didn't drive you out of your home. I don't desire any scene—any unnecessary scandal. I wish you to understand that you are not turned into the street."

"I have promised to be in Windover this evening, to settle this matter," replied Bayard. He looked over his uncle's head, through the old, purple, Beacon Street glass, upon the waters of Charles River; then softly closed the library door, looked for a moment about the dark, familiar hall, took his hat from the peg on the carved mahogany tree where he had hung his cap when he was a little boy in Latin School, and went down the long, stone steps.

It occurred to him to go back and tell Partredge and Nancy to look after his uncle carefully, but he remembered that he had no reason to give them for his indefinite absence, bethought himself of his uncle's horror of airing family affairs before servants, and so went on.

He walked up the street slowly, for he was weak yet. At the door of an old friend, he was tempted to pause and rest, but collected his senses, and struggled on.

He turned to look for a cab; then remembered that he had no longer fifty cents to waste upon so mere a luxury as the economy of physical strength. It was his first lesson in poverty,—that a sick man must walk, because he could not afford to ride. Besides, it proved to be a private carriage that he had seen. The elderly coachman, evidently a family retainer, had just shut the door and clambered to the box; he was waiting to tuck the green cloth robe deliberately about his elegant legs, when a low exclamation from the coach window caused Bayard to look back.

Helen Carruth had opened the door, and stood, irresolute, with one foot upon the step, as if half her mind were in, and half were out the carriage. She was richly dressed in purple cloth, and had that fashionable air which he could not conceive of her as dispensing with if she were a missionary in Tahiti. She looked vivid, vital, warm, and somehow, gorgeous to him.

"*You?*" she cried joyously; then seemed to recall herself, and stepped back.

He went up to her at once.

"I have been staying with Clara Rollins for a week," she hastened to say. "I am just going home. It's her afternoon at the Portuguese Mission, so she could not see me off. I did not know you were in town, Mr. Bayard."

"I am not," said Bayard, smiling wanly. "I am on my way to Windover; I am late to my train now."

"Why, jump in!" said the young lady heartily. "We are going the same way; and I'm sure Mrs. Rollins would be delighted to have you. *She*'s at the Woman's Branch."

"The Woman's who?" asked Bayard, laughing for the first time for many days. He had hesitated for a moment; then stepped into the carriage, and shut the door.

"I presume you've been in this vehicle before?" began Miss Carruth.

He nodded, smiling still.

"At intervals, as far back as I can remember. Miss Clara and I used to go to the same dancing-school."

"Mrs. Rollins was saying only yesterday what an age it was since they had seen you—Mr. Bayard!" she broke off, "you look ill. You are ill."

He had sunk back upon the olive satin cushions. The familiar sense of luxury and ease came upon him like a wave of mortal weakness. For a moment he did not trust himself to look at the girl beside him. Her beauty, her gayety, her health, her freedom from care, something even in her personal elegance overcame him. She seemed to whirl before his eyes, the laughing figure of a happy Fortune, the dainty symbol of the life that he had left and lost. The deliberate coachman was now driving rapidly, and they were well on their way over Beacon Hill. She gave Bayard one of her long, steady looks. Something of timidity stole over her vivacious face.

"Mr. Bayard," she said in a changed tone, "I have heard all about it from my father. I wanted to tell you, but I had no way. I am glad to have a chance to say—I am sorry for you with all my heart. And with all my soul, I honor you."

"Do you?" said the disheartened man. "Then I honor myself the more."

He turned now, and looked at her gratefully. This first drop of human sympathy from man or woman of his own kind was inexpressibly sweet to him. He could have raised her hand to his lips. But they were in Mrs. Rollins's carriage, and on Beacon Street.

"Oh!" cried Helen suddenly. "Look there! No, *there*! See that poor, *horrible* fellow! Why, he's arrested! The policemen are carrying him off."

They had now reached Tremont Street, where the young lady had an errand which had decided her direction to the northern stations. But for the trifling circumstance that Helen Carruth had promised her mother to bring out from a famous Boston grocer's that particular brand of olive oil which alone was worthy of a salad for the Trustees' lunch, the event which followed would never have occurred. Thus may the worry of a too excellent housekeeper lay its petty finger upon the future of a man or of an enterprise.

Bayard looked out of the carriage window, and uttered a disturbed exclamation. Struggling in the iron grip of two policemen of assorted sizes, the form and the tongue of Job Slip were forcibly ornamenting Tremont Row.

"I must go. I must leave you. Excuse me. Drive on without me, Miss Carruth. That is a friend of mine in trouble there."

Bayard stopped the coachman with an imperious tap, and a "Hold on, John!"

"A *what* of yours?" cried Helen.

"It is one of my people," explained Bayard curtly. He leaped from the carriage, raised his hat, and ran.

"Just release this man, if you please," he said to the police authoritatively. "I know him; I am his minister. I'm going on the train he meant to take. I'll see him safely home. I'll answer for him."

"Well—I don't know about that, sir," replied the smaller policeman doubtfully.

But the larger one looked Bayard over, and made answer: "Oh, bejabers, Tim, let 'im goa!"

Job, who was not too far gone to recognize his preserver, now threw his arms affectionately around Bayard's recoiling neck, and became unendurably maudlin. In a voice audible the width of the street, and with streaming tears and loathsome blessings, he identified Bayard as his dearest, best, nearest, and most intimate of friends. A laughing crowd collected and followed, as Bayard tried to hurry to the station, encumbered by the grip of Job's intoxicated affection. Now falling, now staggering up, now down again, and ever firmly held, Job looked up drunkenly into the white, delicate face that seemed to rise above him by a space as far as the span between the heavens and the earth. Stupidly he was aware that the new minister was doing something by him that was not exactly usual. He began to talk in thick, hyphenated sentences about his wife and home, his boy, and the trip he had taken to Georges'. He had made, he averred, a hundred dollars (which was possible), and had two dollars and thirty-seven cents left (which was altogether probable). Job complained that he had been robbed in Boston of the difference, and, weeping, besought the new minister to turn back and report the theft to the police.

"We shall lose the train, Job," said Bayard firmly. "We must get home to your wife and little boy."

"Go wherever y' say!" cried Job pleasantly. "Go to h—— along of you, if you say so!"

There was something so grotesque in the situation that Bayard's soul recoiled within him. He was not used to this kind of thing. He was no Christ, but a plain human man, and a young man at that. His sense of dignity was terribly hurt. Without turning his head, he knew when the carriage drove on. He felt her eyes upon him; he knew the moment when she took them off; Job was attempting to kiss him at that particular crisis.

Bayard managed to reach the last platform of the last car as it moved out of the station, and to get his charge to Windover without an accident. He had plenty of time for reflection on the trip; but he reflected as little as possible. With his arm linked firmly through Job's and his eyes closed, he became a seer of visions, not a thinker of thoughts. Her face leaned out of the carriage window,—faded, formed, and dimmed, and formed again. He saw the velvet on her dress, the little dash of gold color on her purple bonnet, the plain distinguished fashion of her yellow hair about her forehead. He saw the astonishment leap into her brown eyes, and that look which no sibyl could have interpreted, forming about her merry lips. He heard the coachman say, "Shall I drive on, Miss?" And the answer, "Yes, John, drive on. I must not miss the train."

He opened his eyes, and saw the sullen horizon of the sea across the marshes, and the loathsome face of Job leaning against the casement of the car window at his side.

By the time they had reached Windover, Slip was sleepy and quite manageable. Bayard consulted his watch. It was the hour for his evening appointment with the officers of the new parish.

"*Again!*" he thought. He looked at the drunkard wearily. Then the flash of inspiration fired his tired face.

"Come, Job," he said suddenly. "Never mind our suppers. Come with me."

He took Job as he was,—torpid, sodden, disgusting, a creature of the mud, a problem of the mire. The committee sat in the anxious conclave of people embarked upon a doubtful and unpopular enterprise. Emanuel Bayard pushed Job Slip before him into the pretty parlors of the ex-treasurer of the old First Church. For the treasurer had followed the come-outers. He had joined the poor and humble people who, in fear and faith, had tremblingly organized the experiment for which, as yet, they had no other name than that they gave it in their prayers. Christ's work, they called it, then. The treasurer was their only man of property. His jaw dropped when he saw Job.

"Gentlemen," said the young pastor, "gentlemen, I have brought you a sample of the material under discussion. What are we going to do with *this*?"

VII

J ane Granite stood at the foot of the steep, uncarpeted stairs. She had a stone-china cup filled with tea in her hand. She had hesitation in her mind, and longing in her heart. When the minister had sent word that he would eat no supper, it was plain that something must be done. Her mother was out, and Jane had no superior intelligence to consult. For Mrs. Granite was appointed to the doom that overtakes the women of a poor and struggling religious movement; she was ex-officio beggar for the new mission; on this especial occasion she was charged with the duty of wringing a portion of the minister's almost invisible salary out of the least unfriendly citizens of the town. The minister had observed her from his window, tugging at her black skirts as she sallied forth, ankle-deep, in the slush of the February afternoon; and his brows had darkened at the sight. For the good woman would trudge and soak five miles for—what? Possibly five dollars. How dreary the devices of small people to achieve large ends!

To the young man who had never had to think what anything cost, the cold, pecuniary facts of his position were galling past the power of these simple people to comprehend.

He did not care too much on his own account. He felt more surprise than impatience to see his coat turn shiny and frayed, and to know that he could not get another. He was learning not to mind his straw mattress as much as he did at first; and to educate himself to going without magazines, and to the quality of Mrs. Granite's tea. When a man deliberately elects a great personal sacrifice, he does not concern himself with its details as women are more likely to do.

But there were aspects of his chosen work to which his soul was as sore as a boy's. He could not accustom himself with the ease of a poor man's son to the fact that a superb, supreme faith like the Christianity of Christ must beg for its living. "It degrades!" he thought, looking up from his books. "Lowell was right when he said that no man should preach who hadn't an independent property." His Bible fell from his clenched hand; he picked it up penitently, and tenderly smoothed the crumpled leaf at which it had opened. Half unconsciously, he glanced, and read:—

"Take no scrip in your purse;" his burning eye followed along the page; softened, and grew moist.

"Perhaps on the whole," he said aloud, "He really knew as much about it as any American poet."

He returned patiently to his preparation for the evening service, for he worked hard for these fishermen and drunkards—harder than he had ever worked at anything in his life. To make them one half hour's talk, he read, he ransacked, he toiled, he thought, he dreamed, he prayed.

The only thing which he had asked leave to take from his uncle's house, was his own library. It piled Mrs. Granite's spare chamber from the old, brown carpet to the low and dingy ceiling. Barricades of books stood on the floor by the ugly little coal-stove; and were piled upon the stained pine table at which he sat to study in a hard wood chair with a turkey-red cushion. Of the pictures, dear to his youth, and to his trained taste, but two had come through with him in the flying leap from Beacon Street to Mrs. Granite's. Over the table in his study a fine engraving watched him. It was Guido's great Saint Michael. Above the straw mattress in the chilly closet where he slept hung a large photograph of Leonardo's Christ; the one from the Last Supper, as it was found in the ruined fresco on the monastery wall.

But Jane Granite stood irresolute upon the bare, steep stairs, with the stone-china teacup in her hand.

The minister had never concentrated his mind on Jane. He was a busy man. She was a modest, quiet girl; she helped her mother "do" his rooms, and never slammed the door when she went out. He felt a certain gratitude to her, for the two women took trouble for him far beyond the merits of the meagre sum allowed them for his bread and codfish. But for the life of him, if he had been required to, he could not have told anybody how Jane Granite looked.

When her timid knock struck the panel of his door, he started impatiently, put down his pen, and patiently bade her enter.

"I thought perhaps, sir—you would drink your tea?" pleaded Jane. "You haven't eaten a morsel, and mother will mind it when she comes home."

Bayard looked at her in a dazed way; trying to see the connection between forty-cent Japan tea and that beautiful thing said of Whitefield, that he "forgot all else about the men before him, but their immortality and their misery."

"It's getting cold," said Jane, with quivering lip. "I stood on the stairs so long before I could make up my mind to disturb you. Let me get a hot cup, now, sir—do!"

ELIZABETH STUART PHELPS

"Why, I'll come down!" said Bayard. "I must not make myself as troublesome as this."

He pushed away his books, and followed her to the sitting-room, where, in default of a dining-room, and in vague deference to the antecedents of a guest popularly reported not to be used to eating in the kitchen, the meals of the family were served.

"Maybe you'd eat the fish-hash—a mouthful, sir?" asked Jane, brightening, "and there's the stewed prunes."

Bayard looked at her, as she ran to and fro, flushed and happy at her little victory over his supperless intentions. Jane was a trig, neat body; small, as the coast girls often are—I wonder why? whether because the mother was under-fed or over-anxious when the fleets were out? Jane Granite wore a blue gingham dress, closely fitted to a pleasant figure. She had a pleasant face, too; she had no beauty, but that certain something more attractive than beauty to many men,—a kind of compactness of feature, and an ease of outline which haunts the retina; it is not easy to describe, but we all know it. Her mother had told the minister that Jane was keeping company—that is the Windover phrase—with some one; the details had escaped his memory.

He looked at her, now, for the first time attentively, as she served his tea. She flitted to and fro lightly. She sang in the kitchen when she saw him smile. When he said, "Thank you, Jane! You have given me a delicious supper," a charming expression crossed her face. He observed it abstractedly, and thought: How kind these good people are to me! The paper shades were up, and Jane wished to draw them when she lighted the kerosene lamp; but Bayard liked to watch the sea, as he often did at twilight. The harbor was full, for the weather was coming on wild. Clouds marshaled and broke, and retreated, and formed upon a stormy sky. The lights of anchored fleets tossed up and down in the violet-gray shadow. The breakers growled upon the opposite shore. The best thing about his lodging was its near and almost unobstructed view of the sea, which dashed against a slip of a beach between the wharves of Windover Point, within a thousand feet of Mrs. Granite's cottage.

As he sat, sipping his green tea, and making believe with his hash, to save the feelings of the girl; watching the harbor steadily and quietly, the while, and saying nothing—he was startled by the apparition of a man's face, pressed stealthily against the window-pane, and disappearing as quickly as it came. Bayard had been sitting between the window and the light. Jane was dishing out his prunes from a vegetable dish into a blue willow saucer, and had seen nothing. Wishing not to alarm the girl, he went to the window quietly, and looked out. As he did so, he perceived that the intruder had his hand on the knob of the front door. Bayard sprang, and the two met in the cottage entry.

"What are you doing here?" began Bayard, barring the way.

"I guess I'd better ask what are *you* a-doin' *here*," replied the other, crowding by the minister with one push of an athletic shoulder. "I'm on my own ground. I ain't so sure of you."

Little Jane uttered a cry, and the athletic young man strode forward, and somewhat ostentatiously put his arm about her waist.

"Ah, I see!" smiled the minister. "It is strange that we have not met before. We must often have been in the house at the same time. I am a little absent-minded. Perhaps it is my fault. A hundred pardons, Mr.—?"

Trawl. Ben Trawl was the name. Ben Trawl was not cordial. Perhaps that would be asking too much of the lover who had been mistaken for a burglar by another man; and the young minister was already quite accustomed to the varying expressions with which a provincial town receives the leader of an unpopular cause. He recognized Ben Trawl now;—the young man who had the straight eyebrows, and who did not drink, who had been one of the crowd at the fight in Angel Alley on the ordination day which never had ordained.

The pastor found the situation embarrassing, and was glad when Mrs. Granite came in, soaked through, and tired, with drabbled skirts.

She had collected six dollars and thirty-seven cents.

Bayard ground his teeth, and escaped to his study as soon as he could. There they heard him, pacing up and down hotly, till seven o'clock. Bayard had arranged one of those piteous attempts to "amuse the people," into which so much wealth of heart and brain is flung, with such atmospheric results. His notion of religious teaching did not end with the Bible, though it began there. The fishermen who had irreverently named the present course of talks "the Dickens," crowded to hear them, nevertheless. The lecture of that evening ("Sydney Carton," he called it) was a venture upon which Bayard had expended a good deal of thought and vitality.

Poor, wet Mrs. Granite waded out again, without a murmur, to hear it; she walked beside the minister, alone; it was a long walk, for the new people met in the well-known hall near the head of Angel Alley.

"Ben Trawl's kinder off his hook," she explained apologetically. "He

ELIZABETH STUART PHELPS

wouldn't come along of us, nor he wouldn't let Jane come, neither. He has them spells."

Jane Granite watched them off with aching heart. As he closed the door, the minister smiled and lifted his hat to her. Where was there a smile like *his* in all the world of men? And where a man who thought or knew so little of the magic which his beauty wrought?

For love of this radiance and this wonder the heart of the coldest woman of the world might have broken. Little Jane Granite looked after him till he was drowned in the dark. She came in and stood at the window, busying herself to draw the shade. But Ben Trawl watched her with half-closed eyes; and when bright, wide eyes turn dull and narrow, beware of them!

"Come here!" said Ben, in the voice of a man who had "kept company" with a girl for three years. In Windover, the respectable young people do not flirt or intrigue; breach of troth is almost unknown among them. To walk with a girl on Sunday afternoon, and to kiss her Sunday evening, is to marry her, as a matter of course. Ben Trawl spoke in the imperious tone of the seafaring people who call a wife "my woman," and who lie on the lounge in the kitchen while she brings the water from the well.

"You come here, Jane, and sit on the sofy alongside of me! I've got a word or so to say to you."

Jane Granite came. She was frightened. She sat down beside her lover, and timidly surrendered the work-worn little hand which he seized and crushed with cruel violence within his own.

"Mr. Granite wasn't never wholly satisfied about Ben," Mrs. Granite was saying to the minister as they splashed through the muddy slush. "His father's Trawl the liquor dealer, down to Angel Alley, opposite our place, a little below. But Jane says Ben don't touch it; and he don't. I don't know's I've any call to come between her and Ben. He's a stiddy fellow, and able to support her,—and he's that fond of Jane"—

"He seems to be," said Bayard musingly. His thoughts were not with Mrs. Granite. He hardly knew what she had said. He was not used to this petty, parish atmosphere. It came hard to him. He underestimated the value of these wearisome trifles, in the large work performed by little people. Nothing in the world seemed to him of less importance than the natural history of Ben Trawl.

"The wind is east," he said abstractedly, "and there's a very heavy sea on."

He cast at the harbor and the sky the anxious look habitual with the people of Windover; the stranger had already acquired it. He had not been a month in the fishing-town before he noticed that the women all spoke of their natural foe as "the terrible sea."

The hall which the new people had leased for their services and entertainments had long borne the grim name of Seraph's Rest; having been, in fact, for years, a sailors' dance-hall of the darkest dye.

"Give us," Bayard had said, "the worst spot in the worst street of this town. We will make it the best, or we will own ourselves defeated in our work."

In such streets, and in such places, news has wings. There is no spot in Windover where rumor is run down so soon as in Angel Alley.

Bayard had talked perhaps half an hour, when he perceived by the restlessness in his crowded and attentive audience that something had happened. He read on for a moment:—

"'Are you dying for him?' she whispered. 'And his wife and child. Hush! Yes.'"

Then, with the perfect ease which he always sought to cultivate in that place between speaker and hearer, "What is the matter?" he asked in a conversational tone.

"Sir," said an old captain, rising, "there's a vessel gone ashore off Ragged Rock."

Bayard swept his book and manuscript off the desk.

"I was about to read you," he said, "how a poor fellow with a wretched life behind him died a noble death. Perhaps we can do something as grand as he did. Anyhow, we'll try. Come, boys!"

He thrust himself into his coat, and sprang down among the audience.

"Come on! You know the way better than I do! If there's anything to do, we'll do it. Lead on, boys! I'm with you!"

The audience poured into Angel Alley, with the minister in their midst. Confusion ran riot outside. The inmates of all the dens on the street were out. Unnoticed, they jostled decent citizens who had flocked as near as possible to the news-bearer. Panting and white, a hatless messenger from the lighthouse, who had run all the way at the keeper's order to break the black word to the town, reiterated all he knew: "It's the Clara Em! She weighed this afternoon under full canvas—and she's struck with fourteen men aboard! I knew I couldn't raise nobody at the old Life-Saving Station"—

"It's t'other side the Point, anyhow!" cried a voice from the crowd.

"It's four mile away!" yelled another.

"Good heavens, man!" cried Bayard. "You don't propose to wait for *them*?"

"I don't see's there's anything we can *do*," observed the old captain deliberately. "The harbor's chockful. If anybody could do anything for 'em, some o' them coasters—but ye see there can't no boat *live* off Ragged Rock in a breeze o' wind like this."

"How far off is this wreck?" demanded Bayard, inwardly cursing his own ignorance of nautical matters and of the region. "Can't we get up some carts and boats and ropes—and ride over there?"

"It's a matter of three mile an' a half," replied the mate of a collier, "and it's comin' on thick. But I hev known cases where a cart—Now there's them I-talians with their barnana carts."

"You won't get no fog with this here breeze," contended a very ancient skipper.

"What'll you bet?" said the mate of the collier.

An Italian with a fruit cart was pushed forward by the crowd; an express cart was impressed; ropes, lanterns, and a dory appeared from no one knew where, at the command of no one knew who. Bayard suggested blankets and dry clothes. The proposal seemed to cause surprise, but these supplies were volunteered from somewhere.

"Pile in, boys!" cried the minister, in a ringing voice. He sprang into one of the carts, and it filled in a moment. One of the horses became frightened at the hubbub and reared. Men swore and women shrieked. In the momentary delay, a hand reached over the wheel, and plucked at Bayard's sleeve. He flashed the lantern in his hand, and saw a woman's strained, set face. It was Job Slip's wife, Mari, with the little boy crying at her skirts.

"Sir," she said hoarsely, "if it's the Clara Em, he's aboard of her—for they shipped him at five o'clock, though they see the storm a-comin'— and him as drunk as death. But it's true—he got it at Trawl's—I see 'em lift him acrost the wharf an' sling him over int' the dory."

"I'll do my best," said Bayard with set teeth. He reached over the wheel as the horses started, plunging, and wrung the hand of the drunkard's wife. He could not trust himself to say more. Such a vision of what life meant to such a woman swept through Angel Alley upon the wings of the gale, that he felt like a man whose eyes have beheld a panorama on a stage in hell.

Many people, as the carts rolled through the town, followed on foot, among them a few women whose husbands, or lovers, or brothers were known to be aboard the Clara Em.

"Here's an *old* woman with a boy aboard! Seems you might find room in one them wagons for her!" cried a young voice. It was the girl known to Windover only by the name of Lena; she for whom the "terrible sea" could have no horrors; the one woman of them from whom no betrothed lover could sail away; to whom no husband should return.

"She's right about that. We must manage somehow!" called Bayard. Strong hands leaned out and swept the old woman up over the wheel, and the horses galloped on.

There was neither rain nor snow; but the storm, in the seaman's sense of the word, was approaching its height. The wind had now become a gale, and blew southeast. The sky was ominously black. To Bayard's sensitive and excited imagination, as he looked out from the reeling wagon, the mouth of the harbor seemed to gape and grin; the lights of the fleet, furled and anchored for dear life, lost their customary pleasant look, and snapped and shone like teeth in the throat of a monster.

The wagons rolled on madly; the horses, lashed to their limit of speed, leaped down Windover Point. They had now left the road, and were dashing across the downs which stretched a mile farther to the eastern shore. The roughness of the route had become appalling, but a Cape horse is as used to boulders as a Cape fisherman; neither wagon overset, though both rolled like foundering ships. The lanterns cut swathes of light in the blackness which bounding wheels and racing heels mowed down before them.

Walls of darkness rose ahead, and at its outermost, uttermost margin roared the sea. It seemed to Bayard as if the rescuing party were plunging into eternal mystery.

The old woman whose son was aboard the Clara Em crouched at the minister's feet. Both sat in the dory, which filled the wagon, and which was packed with passengers. The old woman's bare hands were clenched together, and her lips shut like iron hinges. Bayard wondered at her massive silence. It was something primeval, solemn, outside of his experience. The women of the shore, in stress like hers, would weep, would sob, or shriek. But to the women of the sea this anguish was as old as life itself: to it they were born, and of it they were doomed to die; they bore it as they did the climate of the freezing Cape.

"That there saving service couldn't ha' done nothin' agin' a wreck on Ragged Rock if they wanted to," observed the old captain (they called him Captain Hap), peering from the wagon towards the harbor shore. "It's jest's I told ye; they're too fur—five mile across."

"But why is there no station nearer?" demanded Bayard with the warmth of inexperience. "Why is nothing put over here—if this reef is so bad—where it is needed?"

"Wall," said Captain Hap, with deliberation, "that's a nateral question for a land-lubber. Every seaman knows there ain't no *need* of gettin' wrecked on that there reef. It's as plain as the beard on your face. Windover Light to the west'ard, Twin Lights to the east'ard,—a fog bell, and a bell-buoy, and a whistlin'-buoy,—Lord! why, *everybody* knows how to keep off Ragged Rock!"

"Then how did this vessel happen to strike?" persisted Bayard. The men interchanged glances, and no one answered him.

"Hi there! Look, look! I see her! I see her spars!" yelled a young fellow on the front seat of the wagon. "It's her! It's the Clara Em! . . . Lord A'mighty! what in—was they thinkin' of? She's got on full canvas! See her! see her! see her! See her lights! It's *her*, and she's bumpin' on the reef!"

Cries of horror ran from lip to lip. The driver lashed his horses onward, and the men in the wagons flung their lanterns to and fro in uncontrollable excitement. Some leaped over the wheels and ran shouting against the gale.

"Clara Em, ahoy! Clara Em, aho—o—oy!"

But the old woman at Bayard's feet sat still. Her lips only moved. She stared straight ahead.

"Is she praying? or freezing? Perhaps she's out of her mind," thought Bayard.

He gently pulled her blanket-shawl closer over her bare head, and wrapped it around her before he sprang from the wagon.

VIII

There was but little depth of snow upon the downs and cliffs, but such as remained served to reflect and to magnify all possible sources of light. These were few enough and sorely needed. The Windover Light, a revolving lantern of the second power, is red and strong. It flashed rapidly, now blood-red and now lamp-black. Bayard thought of the pillar of fire and cloud that led the ancient people. There should have been by rights a moon; and breaks in battalions of clouds, at rare intervals, let through a shimmer paler than darkness, though darker than light. Such a reduction of the black tone of the night had mercifully befallen, when the staggering wagons clattered and stopped upon the large, oval pebbles of the beach.

The fog, which is shy of a gale, especially at that season of the year, had not yet come in, and the vessel could be clearly seen. She lay upon the reef, broadside to the breakers; she did not pitch, but, to a nautical eye, her air of repose was the bad thing about her. She was plainly held fast. Her red port-light, still burning, showed as each wave went down, and the gray outlines of her rigging could be discerned. Her foremast had broken off about five feet from the deck, and the spar, held by the rigging, was ramming the sides of the vessel.

The astonishing rumor was literally true. The Clara Em—one of the famous fishermen of which Windover was too proud to be vain; the Clara Em, newly-built and nobly furnished, none of your old-time schooners, clumsy of hulk and rotten of timbers, but the fastest runner on the coast, the stanchest keel that cleft the harbor, fine in her lines as a yacht, and firm in her beams as an ocean steamer—the Clara Em, fearing neither gods nor men nor weather, and bound for Georges' on a three weeks' fresh-fishing trip, had deliberately weighed anchor in the teeth of a March southeaster, and had flung all her clean, green-white sails to the gale. As nearly as could be made out from the shore, she had every stitch up, and not a reef to her face, and she lay over against the rock like a great eagle whose wings were broken. Even a landsman could comprehend the nature of this dare-devil act; and Bayard, running to lend a hand to slide the dory from the wagon, uttered an exclamation of indignant horror.

"How did this happen? Were they mad?"

"Full," replied the old captain laconically.

"Yes, I see she's under full sail. But why?" he persisted innocently.

The old captain, with a curious expression, flashed a lantern in the young minister's face, but made no reply.

Cries could now be heard from the vessel; for the wind, being dead off, bore sounds from sea to shore which could by no means travel from shore to sea. Ragged Rock was a rough spot in the kindest weather; and in that gale, and with the wind in that direction, the roar and power of the surf were great. But it should be remembered that the blow had not been of long duration; hence the sea was not what it would be in a few hours if the gale should hold. In this fact lay the only possible chance of extending rescue in any form to the shipwrecked crew.

"Clara Em! Aho—oy—oy!" yelled a dozen voices. But the united throats of all Windover could not have made themselves articulate to the straining ears upon the schooner.

"Where's yer crew? Show up, there! Can't ye do *nothin'* for yerselves? Where's yer dories? Hey? What? Clara Em! Aho—oy—oy!"

"They're deef as the two years' drownded," said the old captain. "An' they ain't two hundred feet from shore."

"Why, then, surely we can save them!" cried Bayard joyfully. But no man assented to the cheerful words.

The dory, a strong specimen of its kind, was now out of the wagon, and a score of arms dragged it over the pebbles. The surf dashed far up the beach, splashing men, boat, wagon, horses. Against the cliff the spray rose a hundred feet, hissing, into the air. The old captain eyed the sea and measured the incoming rollers with his deep-set eye.

"Ye cayn't do it," he pronounced. "There ain't a dory in Windover can live in *that*"—he pointed his gaunt arm at the breakers.

"Anyhow, we'll try!" rang out a strong voice. Cries from the wreck arose again. Some of the younger men pushed the dory off. Bayard sprang to join them.

"I can row!" he cried with boyish eagerness; "I was stroke at Harvard!"

"This ain't Charles River," replied one of the men; "better stand back, Parson."

They kindly withstood him, and leaped in without him, four of them, seamen born and bred. They ran the dory out into the surf. He held his lantern high to light them. In their wet oil-skins their rough, wild outlines looked like divers, or like myths of the deep. They leaped in and seized the oars with one of the wild cries of the sailor who goes to his duty, his dinner, or his death, by the rhythm of a song or the thrill of a shout. The dory rose on a tremendous comber, trembled, turned, whirled, and sank from sight. Then came yells, and a crash.

"There!" howled Captain Hap, stamping his foot, "I told ye so!"

"She's over!"

"She's busted!"

"She's smashed to kindlin' wood!"

"Here they be! Here they come! Haul 'em in!"

The others ran out into the surf and helped the brave fellows, soaked and discomfited, up the beach. They were badly bruised, and one of them was bleeding.

The pedestrians from the town had now come up; groups of men, and the few women; and a useless crowd stood staring at the vessel. A big third wave rolled over and smashed the port light.

"It's been going on all these ages," thought Bayard,—"the helpless shore against the almighty sea."

"Only two hundred feet away!" he cried; "I *can't* see why *something* can't be done! I say, something *shall*!—Where are your ropes? Where are your wits? Where is all your education to this kind of thing? Are you going to let them drown before your eyes?"

"There ain't no need of goin' so far's that," said the old captain with the aggravating serenity of his class. "If she holds till it ebbs they can clomber ashore, every man-jack of 'em. Ragged Rock ain't an island except at flood. It's a long, pinted tongue o'rock runnin' along,—so. You don't onderstand it, Parson. Why, they could eeny most *walk* ashore, come mornin', if she holds."

"It's a good pull from now till sun-up," objected a fisherman. "And it's the question if she don't break up."

"Anyhow, I'm going to try," insisted Bayard. A rope ran out through his hands,—shot high into the air,—fell into the wind, and dropped into the breakers. It had carried about ten feet. For the gale had taken the stout cable between its teeth, and tossed it, as a dog does a skein of silk, played with it, shook it to and fro, and hurled it away. The black lips of the clouds closing over the moon, seemed to open and grin as the old captain said:—

"You ken keep on tryin' long's you hev the inclination. Mebbe the women-folks will feel better for't; but you cay—n't do it."

"Can't get a rope to a boat two hundred feet away?" demanded Bayard.

"Not without apparatus,—no, sir! Not in a blow like this here." The

ELIZABETH STUART PHELPS

old seaman raised his voice to a bellow to make himself audible twelve feet away. "Why, it's reelly quite a breeze o' wind," he said.

"Then what *can* we do?" persisted Bayard, facing the beach in great agitation. "What are we here for, anyhow?"

"We ken watch for 'em to come ashore," replied the captain grimly.

Turning, in a ferment half of anger, half of horror, to the younger men, Bayard saw that some one was trying to start a bonfire. Driftwood had been collected from dry spots in the rocks—or had a bucket of coal-tar been brought by some thoughtful hand? And in a little cave at the foot of the cliff, a woman, upon her knees in the shallow snow, was sheltering a tiny blaze within her two hands. It was the girl Lena. She wore a woolen cap, of the fashion called a Tam o' Shanter, and a coarse fur shoulder cape. Her rude face showed suddenly in the flaming light. It was full of anxious kindliness. He heard her say:—

"It'll hearten 'em anyhow. It'll show 'em they ain't deserted of God and men-folks too."

"Where's my old lady?" added the girl, looking about. "I want to get her up to this fire. She's freezing somewheres."

"Look alive, Lena! Here she is!" called one of the fishermen. He pointed to the cliff that hung over Ragged Rock. The old woman stood on the summit and on the edge. How she had climbed there, Heaven knew; no one had seen or aided her; she stood, bent and rigid, with her blanket shawl about her head. Her gray hair blew back from her forehead in two lean locks. Black against the darkness, stone carved out from stone, immovable, dumb, a statue of the storm, she stared out straight before her. She seemed a spirit of the wind and wet, a solemn figure-head, an anathema, or a prayer; symbol of a thousand watchers frozen on a thousand shores:—woman as the sea has made her.

The girl had clambered up the cliff like a cat, and could be seen putting her arms around the old woman, and pleading with her. Lena did indeed succeed so far as to persuade her down to the fire, where she chafed the poor old creature's hands, and held to her shrunken lips a bottle of Jamaica ginger that some fisherman's wife had brought. But the old woman refused.

"Keep it for Johnny," she said, "till he gets ashore." It was the only thing she had been heard to say that night.

She pushed the ginger away, and crawled back to her solitary station on the cliff. Some one said: "Let be! Let her be!"

And some one else said:—

"Whar's the use?"

At that moment a voice arose:—

"There's the cap'n! There's Joe Salt, cap'n of the Clara Em! He's acrosst the bowsprit signalin'! He's tryin' to communicate!"

"We haven't seen another living figure moving across that vessel," said Bayard, whose inexperience was as much perplexed as his humanity was distressed and thwarted by the situation. "I see one man—on the bows—yes. But where are the rest? You don't suppose they're washed overboard already?—Oh, this is horrible!" he cried.

He was overwhelmed at the comparative, almost indifferent calmness of his fellow-townsmen.

The light-keeper and the old captain had run out upon the reef. They held both hands to their ears. The shouts from the vessel continued. Every man held his breath. The whirling blast, like the cone of a mighty phonograph, bore a faint articulation from the wreck.

"Oh!" cried the young minister. "He says they're all sunk!"

He was shocked to hear a laugh issue from the lips of Captain Hap, and to see, in the light of the fire, something like a smile upon the keeper's face.

"You don't understand, sir," said one of the fishermen respectfully. "He says they're all—"

"May as well out with it, Bob," said another. "The parson's got to get his initiation someways. Cap'n Salt says they're drunk, sir. The crew of the Clara Em is all drunk."

At this moment a terrible shriek rang above the roar of the storm. It came from the old woman on the top of the cliff.

Her eyes had been the first, but they were not the only ones now, to perceive the signs of arousing life upon the wreck.

A second man was seen to climb across the bows, to pause for an instant, and then to plunge. He went out of sight in a moment. The inrolling surf glittered in the blaze of the bonfires like a cataract of flame. The swimmer reappeared, struggled, threw up his arms and disappeared.

"I have stood this as long as I can," said Bayard in a low, firm voice. "Give me a rope! Tie it around me, some of you, and hold on! I'm going to try to save that man."

"I'll go, myself," said one of the fishermen slowly.

"Bob," replied the minister, "how many children have you?"

"Eleven, sir."

"Stay where you are, then," said Bayard. "Such things are for lonely men."

"Bring the rope!" he commanded. "Tie it yourselves—you know how—in one of your sailor's knots; something that will hold. I'm a good swimmer. I saved a man once on a yachting trip. Quick, there! Faster!"

"There's another!" cried the light-keeper. "There's a second feller jumped overboard—swimming for his life! Look, look, look! He's sunk—no he ain't, he ain't! He's bearing down against the rocks—My God! Look at him, look, look, look!"

Busy hands were at the rope about the minister's waist; they worked slowly, from sheer reluctance to do the deed. Bayard stamped the beach with divine impatience. His head whirled with such exaltation that he scarcely knew who touched him; he made out to perceive that Ben Trawl was one of the men who offered to tie the bow-line; he heard the old captain say, shortly:—

"I'll do it myself!"

He thought he heard little Jane Granite cry out; and that she begged him not to go, "for his people's sake," and that Ben Trawl roughly silenced her. Strangely, the words that he had been reading—what ages since!—in the hall in Angel Alley spun through his mind.

"'Are you dying for him?' she whispered. 'And his wife and child. Hush. Yes!'"

So! This is the "terrible sea!" This is what drowning means; this mortal chill, this crashing weight upon the lungs, the heart, this fighting for a man's breath,—this asphyxia—this conflict with wind and water, night and might—this being hurled out into chaos, gaining a foot, and losing three—this sight of something human yonder hurtling towards you on the billow which bears you back from it—this struggling on again, and sweeping back, and battling out!

Blessing on the "gentleman's muscle," trained in college days to do man's work! Thanks to the waters of old Charles River and of merry Newport for their unforgotten lessons! Thank God for that wasted liberal education,—yes, and liberal recreation,—if it teach the arm, and fire the nerve, and educate the soul to save a drunken sailor now.

But save? Can human power save that sodden creature—only wit enough left in him to keep afloat and drift, dashing inward on the rocks? He swirls like a chip. But his cry is the mortal cry of flesh and blood.

Bayard's strangling lips move:—

"*Now Almighty Father, Maker of Heaven and Earth*"—

There were mad shouts upon the beach. A score of iron hands held to the line; and fifty men said to their souls: "That is a hero's deed." Some one flung the rest of the pailful of tar upon the fire, and it blazed up. The swimmer saw the yellow color touch the comber that broke above his head. The rope tightened like the hand of death upon his chest. Caught, perhaps? Ah, there! It has grazed the reef, and the teeth of the rock are gnawing at it; so a mastiff gnaws at the tether of his chained foe, to have the fight out unimpeded.

"If it cuts through, I am gone," thought Bayard.—"*And Jesus Christ Thy Son, our Lord and Saviour.*"—

"Haul in! Haul in, I say! Quick! Haul 'em in for life's sake, boys!—She tautens to the weight of two. *The parson's got him!*"

The old captain jumped up and down on the pebbles like a boy. Wet and glittering, through hands of steel, the line sped in.

"Does she hold? Is she cut? Haul in, haul in, haul in!"

The men broke into one of their sudden, natural choruses, moving rhythmically to the measure of their song:—

> "*Pull for the shore, sailor,*
> *Pull for the shore!*"

As he felt his feet touch bottom, Bayard's strength gave way. Men ran out as far as they could stand in the undertow, and seized and held and dragged—some the rescuer, some the rescued; and so they all came dripping up the beach.

The rope dropped upon the pebbles—cut to a single strand.

Bayard was with difficulty persuaded to release his rigid clutch from the shoulder of the fisherman, who fell in a shapeless mass at his preserver's feet. The light of the tar fire flared on the man's bloated face. It was Job Slip.

"Where's the other?" asked Bayard faintly. "There were two."

He dimly saw through streams of water, that something else had happened; that men were running over the rocks and collecting in a cleft, and stooping down to look, and that most of them turned away as soon as they had looked.

The old woman's was the only quiet figure of them all. She had not left her place upon the cliff, but stood bent and stiff, staring straight ahead. He thought he heard a girl's voice say:—

ELIZABETH STUART PHELPS

"Hush! Don't talk so loud. She doesn't know—it's Johnny; and he's been battered to jelly on the rocks."

"Mr. Bayard, sir," said Job, who had crawled up and got as far as his knees, "I wasn't wuth it."

"That's so," said a candid bystander with an oath.

"Then *be* worth it!" said Bayard in a loud voice. He seemed to have thrown all that remained to him of soul and body into those four words; as he spoke them, he lifted his dripping arms high above his head, as if he appealed from the drunkard to the sky; then he sank.

The gentlest hands in the crowd caught him, and the kindest hearts on the coast throbbed when the old captain called:—

"Boys! Stand back! Stir up the fire! Where's the dry blankets? There's plenty to 'tend to Johnny. Dead folks can bury their dead folks. Hurry up them dry clo'es an' that there Jamaiky ginger! This here's a livin' man. Just a drop, sir—here. I'll hold ye kinder easy. Can't? *What?*—Sho! . . . Boys, the parson's hurt."

At that moment a sound solemn and sinister reverberated from the tower of the lighthouse. The iron lips of the fog bell opened and spoke.

IX

C aptain Hap had reached the years when a trip to the Grand Banks is hard work, dory fishing off the coast a doubtful pleasure, and even yachting in an industrial capacity is a burden. He had a quick eye, a kind heart, a soft foot, and the gentle touch strangely enough sometimes to be found in hands that have hauled in the cod-line and the main-sheet for fifty years. In short, Captain Hap made an excellent nurse, and sometimes served his day and generation in that capacity.

Bayard lay on the straw mattress under the photograph of Leonardo's Christ, and thoughtfully watched Captain Hap. It was the first day that conversation had presented itself to the sick man in the light of a privilege; and he worked up to the luxury slowly through intervals of delicious silence.

"Captain Hap, I am quite well now—as you see. I must speak next Sunday."

"Call it Sunday arter," suggested Captain Hap.

"It was only a scratch on the head—wasn't it, Cap'n? And this cold. It *is* a bad cold."

"For a cold, yes, sir; quite a cold. You see, it anchored onto your lungs; there air folks that call such colds inflammation. That there cut on the head was a beautiful cut, sir; it healed as healthy as a collie dog's, or a year-old baby's. We'll have you round, now, sir, before you can say Cap'n Hap!"

"Cap'n Hap?"

"Well, sir?"

"You've done something for me—I don't know just what; whether it's my life that's saved, or only a big doctor's bill."

"Ask Mrs. Granite, sir, and that there handy girl of hers; we're all in it. You kept the whole crew on deck for a few days. You was a sick man—for a spell."

"Captain, I am a well man now; and there's one thing I will know. I've asked you before. I've asked when I was out of my head, and I've asked when I was in it, and I've never got an answer yet. *Now* I'm going to have it."

"Be you?" said Captain Hap. His small, dark, soft eyes twinkled gently; but they took on lustre of metal across the iris; as if a spark of iron or flint had hit them.

ELIZABETH STUART PHELPS

"It is time," said Bayard, "that I knew all about it."

"Meaning"—began the captain softly.

"Meaning everything," said Bayard impatiently. "The whole story. It's the best thing for me. I dream about it so."

"Yes, I've noticed your dreams was bad," replied the nurse soothingly.

"Captain, where's the Clara Em?"

"To the bottom," responded the fisherman cheerfully.

"And the men? The crew? Her captain? Job Slip? How many were drowned? Out with it, Cap'n! I'm not very easy to deceive, when I'm in my senses. You may as well tell me everything."

"Mebbe I mought," observed the captain. "Sometimes it's the best way. There wasn't but one of 'em drowned, sir,—more's the pity."

Bayard uttered an exclamation of shocked rebuke and indignation; but the old captain sat rocking to and fro in Mrs. Granite's best wooden rocking-chair, with the placid expression of those who rest from their labors, and are not afraid that their works should follow them.

"Fellars that'll take a new fisherman—a regular dandy like that—and smash her onto Ragged Rock, bein' in the condition those fellars were, ain't *worth* savin'!" said the seaman severely. "Your treasurer here, J. B. S. Bond, he says last time he come to see you, says he: 'The whole of 'em warn't *worth* our minister!'"

"I must speak to Mr. Bond about that," said the young man with a clerical ring in his voice. "It wasn't a proper thing for him to say.—Who was drowned, Captain Hap?"

"Only Johnny," replied the captain indifferently. "He was born drunk, Johnny was; his father was so before him; and three uncles. He ain't any great loss."

"Did you see Johnny's mother, Captain,—on the cliff, there,—that night?"

"I didn't take notice of her particular," replied Captain Hap comfortably. "I see several women round. There's usually a good many on the rocks, such times."

"Well, you've got me," said Bayard with a smiling sigh. "I'm a little too weak to play the parson on you yet, you Christian heathen—you stony-hearted minister of mercy!"

"Sho!" said the captain. "'Tain't fair to call names. I can't hit back; on a sick man."

"Very well," said Bayard, sinking back on his thin, small pillows. "Just go ahead and tell me the whole business, then. Where is Job Slip?"

"Off haddockin'."

"Sober?"

"So far. He's come over here half a dozen times, but the doctor wouldn't let him up to see you. His wife come, too. That woman, she'd kiss the popples underneath your rubber-boots."

"Where's Johnny's mother?"

"They took her to the Widders' Home yesterday. Some of 'em screeches all the way over. Folks say she never said nothing."

"What became of all those men—the crew and captain?"

"Why, they waited till ebb, just as I told you. Then they come ashore, the whole twelve on 'em. The crew they come first, and Cap'n Salt—that's Joe Salt—he follered after. There was some folks waited round to see 'em off—but it come up dreadful thick, spite of the breeze; so thick it had stems to it. You couldn't see the vessel, not a line of her, and 'twas kinder cold and disagree'ble. So most the folks went home. But they got ashore, every man-jack of 'em alive."

"Thank God!" breathed the sick man.

"Well," said the captain, "that's a matter of opinion. You've talked enough, sir."

"Just one more, Cap'n Hap! Just this! This I've *got* to know. What was it—exactly—that those men did? How did they come to be in such a plight? How in the world—that beautiful new boat—and an intelligent officer at the helm, Captain—how on earth did it come about?"

"The Clara Em was sot to sail," replied Captain Hap calmly. "That's about all. Her owners they were sot, and her cap'n he was sot. It was the sotness done it. They'd make the market first, you see, if they got the start—and it's a job gettin' your crew aboard, you know. Anything to get your crew. Drunk or sober, that isn't the point. Drunker they be, the easier to ship 'em. *See? Get your crew.* Get 'em anyhow! They was all full, every mother's son of 'em. Cap'n Joe, he was the only sober soul aboard, and that's the truth, and he knew it when he set sail. Yes—oh, yes. The storm was comin'. He knew it was breezin' up.—Oh, yes, of course. So he got some sober men off the wharves to help him at the sheets, and he put up every stitch. Yes, sir! Every stitch he had! And out he sails—with thirteen drunken men aboard—him at the wheel, and not a hand to help him. That's the English on't. The boat was d—drunk, beg your pardon, Parson! He driv right out the harbor, and it was a sou'easter, and blew quite a breeze o' wind, and you see he tacked, and

ELIZABETH STUART PHELPS

set in, and he was tackin' out, and it had breezed up consider'ble more'n he expected. So he drove right on the reef. That's about it."

"But why didn't he take in sail?"

"How was he goin' to do it with that crew? Why, he couldn't leave the wheel to tie a reef-point."

"But there was his anchor."

"Did you ever try to heave one of them big anchors? It takes four men."

"What a situation! Horrible!"

"Wall, yes; it was inconvenient—him at the wheel, and a dead drunk crew, thirteen of 'em, below. Why, they was too drunk to know whether they drowned or not."

"Can the boat be raised? Will she ever be good for anything?"

"Kindlin' wood," remarked the captain dryly.

"Captain Hap," asked Bayard feebly, "do things like this often happen?"

"Sometimes."

"Isn't this an extreme case?"

"Well, it don't happen every day."

"But things of this kind—do they occur often? Do you know of other cases?"

"Windover don't have the monopoly of 'em by no means," mused Captain Hap. "There was the Daredevil over on South Shore. She was launched about a year ago. She went on a trial spin one day, and everybody aboard was pretty jolly. They put all their canvas up to show her off. It was a nor'wester that day, and they driv her right before the wind. She jest plunged bows down, and driv straight to the bottom, the Daredevil did. Some said it was her name. But, Lord, rum done it."

"What do people say—how do they take it here in Windover, this case of the Clara Em? Weren't they indignant?"

"Wall, the insurance folks was mad."

"No, but the people—the citizens—the Christian people—how do they feel about it?"

"Oh, they're used to it," said Captain Hap.

Bayard turned wearily on his hard bed. He did not answer. He looked out and towards the sea. The engraved Guido over the study-table between the little windows regarded him. St. Michael was fighting with his dragon still.

"*He* never got wounded," thought the sick man.

"Captain," he said presently, "these rooms seem to be full of—pleasant things. Who sent them all?"

"Them geraniums and other greens? Oh, the ladies of the mission, every mother's daughter of 'em, married and single, young an' old. Jellies? Lord! Yes. Jellies enough to stock a branch grocery. What there *is* in the female mind, come to sickness, that takes it out in jellies"—mused the captain.

"I've taken solid comfort out of this screen," said Bayard gratefully. "I did suffer with the light before. Who sent that?"

"That's Jane Granite's idee," replied the captain. "She seems to be a clever girl. Took an old clo'es-horse and some rolls of wall paper they had in the house. They give fifteen cents a roll for that paper. It's kinder tasty, don't you think? 'Specially that cherubim with blue wings settin' on a basket of grapes."

"That reminds me. I see—some Hamburg grapes," said Bayard, with the indifferent air of a man who purposely puts his vital question last. He pointed to a heaping dish of hothouse fruit and other delicacies never grown in Windover.

The captain replied that those come from the Boston gentleman; they'd kept coming all along. He thought she said there was a card to 'em by the name of—

"Worcester?" asked the sick man eagerly.

That was it. Worcester.

"He hasn't been here, has he? The gentleman hasn't called to see me?"

The nurse shook his head, and Bayard turned his own away. He would not have believed that his heart would have leaped like that at such a little thing. He felt like a sick boy, sore and homesick with the infinite longing for the love of kin. It was something to know that he was not utterly forgotten. He asked for one of the Boston pears, and ate it with pathetic eagerness.

"There's been letters," said the captain; "but the doctor's orders are agin your seeing 'em this week. There's quite a pile. You see, its bein' in the papers let folks know."

"In the papers! *What* in the papers?"

"What do you s'pose?" asked the captain proudly. "A fellar don't swim out in the undertow off Ragged Rock to save a d—— fool of a drunken fisherman every day."

"I'll be split and salted!" added the fisherman-nurse, "if we didn't have to have a watchman here three nights when you was worst, to keep the reporters off ye. Thirteen Windover fellars volunteered for the job, and they wouldn't none of 'em take a cent for it. They said they'd set up forty nights for you."

"For *me*?" whispered the sick man. His eyes filled for the first time since the Clara Em went ashore on Ragged Rock. Something new and valuable seemed to have entered life as suddenly as the comfort of kin and the support of friends, and that bright, inspiriting atmosphere, which one calls the world, had gone from him. He had not expected that precious thing—the love of those for whom we sacrifice ourselves. He felt the first thrill of it with gratitude touching to think of, in so young and lovable a man, with life and all its brilliant and beautiful possibilities before him.

It was an April night, and sea and sky were soft in Windover.

A stranger stood in Angel Alley hesitating at a door, which bore above its open welcome these seven words:—

"The Church of the Love of Christ."

"What goes on here?" the gentleman asked of a bystander.

"Better things than ever went on here before," was the reply. "They've got a *man* up there. He ain't no dummy in a minister's choker."

The stranger put another question.

"Well," came the cordial answer, "he has several names in Angel Alley: fisherman's friend is one of the most pop'lar. Some calls him the gospel cap'n. There's those that prefers jest to say, the new minister. There's one name he *don't* go by very often, and that's the Reverend Bayard."

"He has no right to the title," murmured the stranger.

"What's that?" interposed the other quickly. The stranger made no reply.

"Some call him the Christ's Rest man," proceeded the bystander affably.

"That is a singular—ah—remarkable cognomen. How comes that?"

"Why, you see, the old name for this place was Seraph's Rest—it was the wust hell in Angel Alley—see? before he took it up an' sot to prayin' in it. So folks got it kinder mixed with the Love of Christ up on that sign there. Some calls the place Christlove for short. I heerd an I-talian call him the Christman t'other day."

The stranger took off his hat by instinct, it seemed unconsciously; glanced at the inscription above the door, and passed thoughtfully up the steep, bare stairs into the hall or room of worship.

The service was already in progress, for the hour was late, and the gentleman observed with an air of surprise that the place was filled. He looked about for a comfortable seat, but was forced to content himself with standing-room in the extreme rear of the hall. Crowds overflowed the wooden settees, brimmed into the aisles, and were packed, in serried rows as tight as codfish in a box, against the wall. The simile of the cod was forced upon the visitor's mind in more senses than one. A strong whiff of salt fish assailed him on every side. This was varied by reminiscences of glue factories, taking unmistakable form. An expression of disgust crossed the stranger's face; it quickly changed into that abstraction which indicates the presence of moral emotion too great for attention to trifles.

The usual New England religious audience was not to be seen in the Church of the Love of Christ in Angel Alley. The unusual, plainly, was. The wealth and what the "Windover Topsail" called the society of Windover were sparsely represented on those hard settees. The clean, sober faces of respectable families were out in good force; these bore the earnest, half-perplexed, wholly pathetic expression of uninfluential citizens who find themselves suddenly important to and responsible for an unpopular movement; a class of people who do not get into fiction or history, and who deserve a quality of respect and sympathy which they do not receive; the kind of person who sets us to wondering what was the personal view of the situation dully revolving in the minds of Peter and the sons of Zebedee when they put their nets to dry upon the shores of Galilee, and tramped up and down Palestine at the call of a stronger and diviner mind, wondering what it meant, and how it would all end.

These good people, not quite certain whether their own reputations were injured or bettered by the fact, sat side by side with men and women who are not known to the pews of churches. The homeless were there, and the hopeless, the sinning, the miserable, the disgraced, the neglected, the "rats" of the wharves, and the outcasts of the dens.

The stranger stood packed in, elbow to elbow between an Italian who served the country of his adoption upon the town waterworks, and a dark-browed Portuguese sailor. American fishermen, washed and shaven, in their Sunday clothes, filled the rear seats. Against the wall, lines of rude, red faces crowded like cattle at a spring; men of the sea and the coast, men without homes or characters; that uninteresting and dangerous class which we dismiss in two idle words as the "floating population." Some of these men were sober; some were not; others were hovering midway between the two conditions: all were orderly, and a few were listening with evidences of emotion to the hymn, in which by far the greater portion of the audience joined. A girl wearing a Tam o' Shanter and a black fur cape, and singing in a fine, untrained contralto, held her hymn-book over the settee to the Italian.

"Come, Tony! Pass it along!" she whispered, "I can get on without it. Make 'em pile in and sing along the wall, there!"

With rude and swelling cadence the fishermen sang:—

> *"I need Thee every hour,*
> *Most gracious Lord."*

Their voices and their hearts rose high on one of those plaintive popular melodies of which music need never be ashamed:—

> *"I need Thee, oh, I need Thee,*
> *Every hour I need Thee;*
> *Oh, bless me now, my Saviour"* . . .

The stranger, who had the appearance of a religious man, joined in the chorus heartily; he shared the book which the girl had given to the Italian, who came in a bar too late, and closed the stanza on a shrill solo,—

> *"I co—home to thee."*

This little accident excited a trifling smile; but it faded immediately, for the preacher had arisen. His appearance was greeted with a respect which surprised the stranger. The audience at once became grave even to reverence; the Italian cuffed a drunken Portuguese who was under the impression that responses to the service were expected of him; the girl in the Tam o' Shanter shook a woman who giggled beside her. A fisherman whispered loudly,—

"Shut up there! The parson ain't quite tough yet. Keep it quiet for him! Shut up there, along the wall!"

There is nothing like a brave deed to command the respect of seafaring men. Emanuel Bayard, when he plunged into the undertow after Job Slip's drunken, drowning body, swam straight into the heart of Windover. A rough heart that is, but a warm one, none warmer on the freezing coast, and sea-going Windover had turned the sunny side of its nature, and taken the minister in. The standards by which ignorant men judge the superior classes—their superb indifference to any scale of values but their own—deserve more study than they receive.

It had never occurred to Bayard, who was only beginning to learn to understand the nature of his material, that he had become in three weeks the hero of the wharves and the docks, the romance of Angel Alley, the admiring gossip of the Banks and Georges', the pride and wonder of the Windover fishermen. Quite unconscious of this "sea-change," wrought by one simple, manly act upon his popularity, he rose to address the people. His heart was full of what he was going to say. He gave one glance the length of the hall. He saw the crowds packed by the door. He saw the swaying nets, ornamented with globes and shells and star-fish, after the fashion of the fishing-town; these decorations softened the bare walls of the audience-room. He saw the faces of the fishermen lifting themselves to him and blurring together in a gentle glow. They seemed to him, as a great preacher once said of his audience, like the face "of one impressive, pleading man," whose life hung upon his words. He felt as if he must weigh them in some divine scales into which no dust or chaff of weakness or care for self could fall.

Something of this high consciousness crept into his face. He stood for a moment silent; his beautiful countenance, thin from recent suffering, took on the look by which a man represses noble tears.

Suddenly, before he had spoken a word, a storm of applause burst out—shook the room from wall to wall—and roared like breakers under his astonished feet. He turned pale with emotion, but the fishermen thundered on. He was still so weak that this reception almost overcame him, and involuntarily he stretched out both his hands. At the gesture the noise sank instantly; and silence, in which the sigh of the saddest soul in the room might have been heard, received the preacher.

His sensitive face, melted and quivering, shone down upon them tenderly. Men in drunken brawls, and men in drowning seas, and women in terrible temptation, remembered how he looked that night when the safe and the virtuous and the comfortable had forgotten.

The stranger back by the door put his hat before his face.

X

The preacher began to speak with a quietness in almost startling contrast to his own evident emotion, and to the excitement in the audience room. He made no allusion to the fact that this was his first appearance among his people since the wreck of the Clara Em, and the all but mortal illness which had followed his personal share in that catastrophe. Quite in his usual manner he conducted his Sunday evening service; a simple religious talk varied by singing, and a few words from the New Testament. Bayard never read "chapters;" a phrase sufficed, a narrative or a maxim: sometimes he stopped at a single verse. The moment that the fishermen's eyes wandered, the book closed. It was his peculiarity that he never allowed the Bible to bore his listeners; he trained them to value it by withholding it until they did. It was long remembered of him among the people of the coast that he made use of public prayer with a reserve and a power entirely unknown to the pulpits and the vestries. The ecclesiastical "long prayer" was never heard in Angel Alley. Bayard's prayers were brief, and few. He prayed audibly before his people only when he could not help it. It seemed sometimes as if his heart broke in the act.

On this evening, no prayer had as yet passed his lips; the stranger, with a slight frown, noticed this fact. But now, the preacher brushed aside his notes, and, clearing the desk, crossed his hands upon it, and leaned forward with a marked change of manner. Suddenly, without a hint of his purpose, the young minister's gentle voice rose into the tones of solemn arraignment.

"I came here," he said, "a stranger to this town and to its customs. It has taken me all this while to learn what your virtues and your vices are. I have dealt with you gently, preaching comfortable truths as I have been expected to preach them. I have worked in ignorance. I have spoken soft words. Now I speak them no more! Your sin and your shame have entered like iron into my soul. People of Windover! I accuse you in the name of Christ, whose minister I am!"

The expression of affectionate reverence with which his audience had listened to Bayard up to this moment now changed into a surprise that resembled fear. Before he had spoken ten words more, it became evident that the young preacher was directing the full force of his conscience and his intelligence to a calm and deliberate attack upon the liquor habit and the liquor traffic—one of the last of the subjects (as it is well known) conceded to be the business of a clergyman to meddle with in any community, and the very last which Windover had been trained to hear herself held to account for by her clerical teachers. At the hour when he came nearest to the adoration of those who adore without thought, when they saw him through the mist of romance, when the people, carried on a wave of hero-worship, lay for the first time at his feet, Bayard for the first time opened fire upon their favorite sin.

Shot after shot poured down from those delicate, curving lips. Broadside followed broadside, and still the fire fell. He captured for them the elusive statistics of the subject; he confronted them with its appalling facts; he pelted them with incidents such as the soul sickens to relate or to remember. He denied them the weak consolation of condoning in themselves a moral disease too well known to be the vice of the land, and of the times. He scored them with rebuke under which his leading men grew pale with alarm. Nothing could have been more unlike the conventional temperance address, yet nothing could have been more simple, manly, reasonable, and fearless.

"For every prayer that goes up to God from this room," he said, "for every hymn, for every sacred word and vow of purity, for every longing of a man's heart to live a noble life, there open fifty dens of shame upon this street to blast him. We are pouring holy oil upon a sea of mud. That is not good religion, and it is not good sense. We must prove our right to represent the Christian religion in Angel Alley. We must close its dens, or they ought to close our lips. I am ready to try," he added with his winning simplicity, "if you are. I shall need your help and your advice, for I am not educated in these matters as I ought to be. I was not taught how to save drunken men in the schools where clergymen are trained. I must learn now—we must learn together—as best we can. . . Oh, my people!" His voice passed from the tone of loving entreaty into that of prayer; by one of those moving transformations peculiar to himself, wherein those who heard him scarce could tell the moment when he ceased to speak to men and began to talk with God.

"People of the Church of the Love of Christ! Approach God, for He is close at heart. . . Thou great God! Holy, Almighty, Merciful! Make us know how to deal with sin, in our own souls, and in the lives of others. For the sake of Thy Son whose Name we dare to bear. Amen."

As the words of this outcry, this breath of the spirit, rose and ceased, the silence in the room was something so profound that a girl's sigh was heard far back by the door.

The hush was stung by a long, low, sibilant sound; a single hiss insulted that sacred stillness. Then a man purple to the brows, rose and went out. It was old Trawl, whose saloon had been a landmark in Angel Alley for fifty years.

The stranger, who had been more moved than it seemed he cared to show by what he had heard and seen, passed slowly with the crowd down the long stairs, and reached the outer air. As the salt wind struck in his face, a hand was laid upon his shoulder. The young minister, looking pale and tired, but enviably calm, drew the visitor's hand through his arm.

"I saw you, Fenton," he said quietly, "when you first came in. You'll come straight to my lodgings with me. . . Won't you?" he added wistfully, fancying that Fenton hesitated. "You can't know how much it will mean to me. I haven't seen anybody—why, I haven't seen a fellow since I came to Windover."

"You must lead rather an isolated life, I should think," observed Fenton with some embarrassment, as the two stood to hail the electric car that ran by Mrs. Granite's humble door.

"We'll talk when we get there," replied Bayard, rather shortly for him. "The car will be full of people," he added apologetically. "One lives in a glass bell here. Besides, I'm a bit tired."

He looked, indeed, exhausted, as the electric light smote his thin face; his eyes glowed like fire fed by metal, and his breath came short. He leaned his head back against the car window.

"You cough, I see," said Fenton, who was not an expert in silence.

"Do I? Perhaps. I hadn't thought of it." He said nothing more until they had reached his lodgings. Fenton began to talk about the wreck and the rescue. He said the usual things in the usual way, offering, perforce, the tribute of a man to a manly deed.

Bayard nodded politely; he would not talk about it.

Jane Granite opened the door for them. She looked at the minister with mute, dog-like misery in her young eyes.

"You look dead beat out, sir," she said. But Ben Trawl stood scowling in the door of the sitting-room; he had not chosen to go to the service, nor to allow her to go without him. Jane thought it was religious experience that made this such a disappointment to her.

"Ah, Trawl," said the minister heartily, "I'm glad to see you here."

He did not say, "I am sorry you were not at church," as Ben Trawl pugnaciously expected.

Bayard led his guest upstairs, and shut and locked the study door.

"There!" he said faintly. "Now, George Fenton, talk! Tell me all about it. You can't *think* how I am going to enjoy this! I wish I had an easy-chair for you. Will this rocker do? If you don't mind, I think I'll just lie down a minute."

He flung himself heavily upon the old carpet-covered lounge. Fenton drew up the wooden rocking-chair to the cylinder stove, in which a low fire glimmered, and put his feet on top of the stove, after the manner of Cesarea and Galilee Hall.

"Well," he began, in his own comfortable way, "I've accepted the call."

"I supposed you would," replied Bayard, "when I heard it was under way. I am glad of it!" he said cordially. "The First Church is a fine old church. You're just the man for them. They'll ordain you as easily as they swallow their native chowders. You came right over from their evening service to our place to-night? You must have hurried."

"I did," said the guest, with a certain air of condescension. "I wanted to hear you, you know—once, at least."

"When you are settled, you can't come, of course," observed Bayard quickly. "I understand that."

"Well—you see—I shall be—you know—in a very delicate position, when I become the pastor of that church."

Fenton's natural complacency forsook him for the instant, and something like embarrassment rested upon his easy face; he showed it by the way he handled Mrs. Granite's poker.

"It's 72° in this room already," suggested Bayard, smiling. "Would you poke that fire any more? . . . Oh, come, Fenton! I understand. Don't bother your head about me, or how I may feel. A man doesn't choose to be where I am, to waste life in considering his feelings; those are the least important items in his natural history. Just stick to your subject, man. It's *you* I want to hear about."

"Well," replied the guest, warming to the theme with natural enthusiasm, "the call was unanimous. Perfectly so."

"That must be delightful."

"Why, so it is—it is, as you say, delightful. And the salary—they've raised the salary to get me, Bayard. You see it had got out that I had refused—ah—hum—several calls. And they'd been without a man so long, I fancy they're tired of it. Anyhow, I'm to have three thousand dollars."

ELIZABETH STUART PHELPS

"That is delightful too," said Bayard cordially. He turned over on his old lounge, coughing, and doubled the thin, cretonne pillow under his head; he watched his classmate with a half-quizzical smile; his eyes and brow were perfectly serene.

"I shall be ordained immediately," continued Fenton eagerly, "and bring my wife. They are refitting the parsonage. I went in last night to see that the carpets and papers and all that were what they should be. I am going to be married—Bayard, I am going to be married next week."

"And that is best of all," said Bayard in a low voice.

"She is really a lovely girl," observed Fenton, "though somewhat limited in her experience. I've known her all my life—where I came from, in the western part of the State. But I think these gentle, country girls make the best ministers' wives. They educate up to the position rapidly."

Bayard made no answer to this scintillation; a spark shot over his soft and laughing eyes; but his lips opened only to say, after a perceptible pause,—

"Where is Tompkinton—he of the long legs and the army cape?"

"Settled somewhere near you, I hear; over across the Cape. He has a fine parish. He's to have two thousand—that's doing well for a man of his stamp."

"I don't think Tompkinton is the kind of man to think much about the salary," observed Bayard gravely. "He struck me as the other sort of fellow. What's become of Bent?"

"Graduates this summer, I suppose. I hear he's called to Roxbury. He always aimed at a Boston parish. He's sure to boom."

"And that brakeman—Holt? He who admired Huxley's 'Descent of Man'?"

"Oh, *he* is slumming in New York city. They say he is really very useful. He has some sort of mission work, there, at the Five Points. I'm told he makes a specialty of converted burglars."

"I haven't been able to follow any of the boys," said Bayard, coughing. "I can't very well—as I am situated. It does me good to hear something about somebody. Where's that round fellow—Jaynes? With the round glasses? I remember he always ate two Baldwins, two entire Baldwin apples."

"Gone West, I believe. He's admirably adapted to the West," replied Fenton, settling his chair in his old comfortable way.

"What an assorted lot we were!" said Bayard dreamily. "And what a medley we were taught! I haven't opened one of my note-books since I came here."

"Oh, in *your* work," said Fenton, "you don't need to read, I should think."

Bayard's eyes sought his library; rested lovingly on its full and well-used shelves; then turned away with the expression of one who says to a chosen friend: "We understand. Why need anything be said?" He did not otherwise reply.

"Were you ever ordained over your present charge?" asked his visitor suddenly, balancing the poker on the top curl of the iron angel that ornamented the cylinder stove. "How did you manage it? Did any of the—regular clergy—recognize the affair?"

"I was not ordained," replied Bayard, smiling contentedly. "I sought nothing of the kind. But a few of the country ministers wished us Godspeed. There was one dear old man—he was my moderator at that Council—he came over and put his hands on my head, and gave me the blessing."

"Oh—the charge to the pastor?"

"We didn't call it that. We did not steal any of the old phrases. He prayed and blessed me, that was all. He is a sincere, good man, and he made something impressive out of it, my people said. At all events they were satisfied. We have to do things in our own way, you know. We are experimenting, of course."

"I should say that was a pretty serious experiment you inaugurated to-night in your service. If you'll allow me to say so, I should call it very ill-advised."

"It *is* a serious experiment," replied Bayard gravely.

"Expect to succeed in it?"

"God knows."

"Bound to go on with it?"

"Till I succeed or fail."

"What do you propose? To turn temperance lecturer, and that sort of thing? I suppose you'll be switching off your religious services into prohibition caucuses, and so forth."

"I propose nothing of the kind. I am not a politician. I am a preacher of the Christian religion."

"I always knew you were eccentric, of course, Bayard. Everybody knows that. But I never expected to see you leading such a singular

ELIZABETH STUART PHELPS

life. I never took you for this sort of fanatic. It seems so—common for a man of your taste and culture, and there can be no doubt that it is unwise, from every point of view, even from your own, I should think. I don't deny that your work impressed me, what I saw of it to-night. Your gifts tell—even here. It is a pity to have them misapplied. Now, what was your motive in that outbreak to-night? I take it, it was the first time you had tackled the subject."

"To my shame— yes. It was the first time. I have had reasons to look into it, lately—that's all. You see, my ignorance on the subject was colossal, to start in. We were not taught such things in the Seminary. Cesarea does as well as any of them—but no curriculum recognizes Job Slip. Oh, when I think about it—Predestation, foreordination, sanctification, election, and botheration,—and never a lesson on the Christian socialism of our day, not a lecture to tell us how to save a poor, lost woman, how to reform a drunkard, what to do with gamblers and paupers and thieves, and worse, how to apply what we believe to common life and common sense—how to lift miserable creatures, scrambling up, and falling back into the mud as fast as they can scramble—people of no religion, no morals, no decency, no hope, no joy—who never see the inside of a church"—

"They ought to," replied Fenton severely. "That's their fault, not ours. And all seminaries have a course on Pastoral Theology."

"I visited sixteen of the dens of this town this last week," replied Bayard. "I took a policeman, and went through the whole thing. I don't blame them. I wouldn't go to church if I were they. I shall dream about what I saw—I don't know that I shall ever stop dreaming about it. It is too horrible to tell. I wouldn't even *speak* what I saw men and women *live*. The old sailors who have seen a good many ports, call it a hell of a town. My own idea is, that it isn't a particle worse than other places of its class. I fancy it's a fair, average seaport town. Six thousand seamen sail this harbor every year. I can't get at the number of dens they support; such figures are runaway lunatics, you understand; they have a genius for hiding; and nobody *wants* to find them. But put it low—call it two hundred—in this little town. If it isn't the business of a Christian church to shut them—whose is it? If it isn't the business of religious people to look after these fellows—whose is it? I say, religious people are answerable for them, and for their vices! The best people are responsible for the worst, or there's no meaning in the New Testament, and no sense in the Christian religion. Oh," said Bayard, with a sound that was more like a moan than a sigh, "if Christ could come into Angel Alley—just this one street! If He could take this little piece of a worldful of human woe—modern human misery, you understand, all the new forms and phases that Palestine knew nothing about—if He could sweep it clean, and show us how to do it *now*! Think, Fenton, think, how He would go to work—what that would be! . . . sometimes I think it would be worth dying for."

"It strikes me it is harder to guess than predestination,—what He would do if He were reincarnated," replied Fenton gravely.

"It had not struck me so," answered Bayard gently, "but there may be something in that."

"Now," continued Fenton, "take yourself. I fancy you believe—Do you suppose *you* are doing the kind of thing He would set about, if He were in your place?"

"How can I tell?" replied Bayard in a voice so low that it was scarcely articulate. "How can a man *know*? All I do know is, that I try. That is what—and that is all—I try to do. And I shall keep on trying, till I die."

He spoke with a solemnity which admitted of no light response, even from a worldly man. Fenton was not that, and his eyes filled.

"Well," he said, after a silence, "you are a good man, Emanuel Bayard. God go with you."

"And with you," replied Bayard, holding out his hand. "Our roads lie different ways. We shall not talk like this again."

"You won't mind that? You won't feel it," said Fenton uncomfortably, for he had risen to leave, and the conversation hung heavily on his heart, "if I don't run across your way, often? It would hardly do, you see. My people—the church—the circumstances"—

He brought the poker down hard upon the cerebrum of the iron angel, who resented the insult by tumbling over on the funnel; thence, with a slam, to the floor. Fenton picked up the ornament with a red face, and restored it to its place. He felt, as a man sometimes does, more rebuked than irritated by the inanimate thing.

"Good-by," said Bayard gently. It was all he said. He still held out his hand. His classmate wrung it, and passed, with bowed head, from his presence.

THE HAPPY WEATHER HELD OVER into the next day; and the harbor wore her celestial smile. The gentleness of summer clothed in the colors of spring rested upon the wooded coast beyond the long cliff-outline, upon the broken scallops of the beaches, and the moss-green piers of the docks, upon the waves swelling without foam, and the patched sails of the anchored fleet unfurled to dry. The water still held the blue and gray tints that betoken cold weather too recently past or too soon returning to be forgotten. But the wind was south; and the saxifrage was in bud upon the downs in the clefts of the broken rocks between the boulders.

Bayard was a weak and weary man that day,—the events of the previous evening had told upon him more than he would have supposed possible,—and he gave himself a luxury. He put the world and the evil of it from his heart and brain, and went out on Windover Point, to sun himself, alone; crawling along, poor fellow, at a sad pace, stopping often to rest, and panting as he pushed on. He had been an athletic lad, a vigorous, hearty man; illness and its subtle train of physical and mental consequences spoke in the voices of strangers to him.

"They will pass on," he thought.

Bayard was such a lovable, cordial, human man, that the isolation of his life in Windover had affected him more than it might have done a natural recluse. Solitude is the final test of character as well as of nature.

The romance of consecration has its glamour as well as the romance of love. Bayard had felt his way into this beautiful mist with a stout, good sense which is rare in the devotee, and which was perhaps his most remarkable quality. This led him to accept without fruitless resistance a lot which was pathetically alien to him. He was no gray-bearded saint, on whose leathern tongue joy had turned to ashes; to whom renunciation was the last throw left in the game of life. He was a young man, ardent, eager, buoyant, confiding in hope because he had not tested it; believing in happiness because he had not known it: full of untried, untamed capacity for human delight, and with the instinct (generations old) of a luxurious training toward human ease. He had cut the silken cords between himself and the world of his old habits, ambitions, and friends with a steady stroke; he had smitten the soft network like a man, and flung it from him like a spirit; but there were hours when he felt as if he were bleeding to death, inwardly, from sheer desolation.

"That call of George Fenton's upset me last night," he said aloud, as he sank down at the base of a big boulder in the warm sand. He sometimes talked to the sea; nothing else in Windover could understand him; he was acquiring some of the habits of lonely people who live apart from their own class. How impossible it would have been in Cambridge, in Boston, or in Cesarea to be caught talking aloud! His pale face flushed, and he drew his hat over it, thanking Heaven that rocks were deaf and the downs were dumb, that the sun would never tell, and the harbor was too busy to listen. He had lain there in the sand for some time, as motionless as a mollusk at low water.

"All a man needs is a little common rest," he thought. The April sun seemed to sink into his brain and heart with the healing touch that nothing human ever gives. He pushed his hat away from his face, and looked up gratefully, as if he had been caressed.

As he did so, he heard footsteps upon the crisp, red-cupped moss that surrounded the base of the boulder. He rose instinctively, and confronted a woman—a lady. She had been walking far and fast, and had glorious color. The skirt of her purple gown was splashed with little sticks and burrs and bits of moss; her hands were full of saxifrage. She was trying in the rising wind to hold a sun-umbrella over her head, for she wore the street or traveling dress of the town, and her little bonnet gave her as much protection from the sun as a purple butterfly whose wings were dashed with gold.

Oddly enough, he recognized the costume before he did the wearer; so incredible did he find it that she should stand there living, glowing, laughing,—a sumptuous beauty, stamped against the ascetic sky of Windover.

"*You!*" he cried.

"Oh, I did not expect—I did not think"—she stammered. He had never seen Helen Carruth disconcerted. But she blushed like a schoolgirl when she gave him, saxifrage and all, her ungloved hand.

XI

M other sent me!—I came down for her and father!" began Helen
Carruth abruptly. Then she thought how that sounded—as if
she need be supposed to apologize for or explain the circumstance that
she happened to find one of her father's old students sunning himself
upon a given portion of the New England coast; and she blushed again.
When she saw the sudden, upward motion of Bayard's heavy eyelids,
she could have set her pretty teeth through her tongue, for vexation at
her little *faux pas*. From sheer embarrassment, she laughed it off.

"I haven't heard anybody laugh like that since I came to Windover,"
said Bayard, drawing a long breath. "Do give me an encore!"

"Now, then, you are laughing at me!"

"Upon the word of a poor heretic parson—no. You can't think how it
sounds. It sinks in—like the sun."

"But I don't feel like laughing any more. I've got all over it. I'm afraid
I can't oblige you."

"Why not? You used to be good-natured, I thought—in Cesarea,
ages ago."

"You are enough to drive the laugh out of a faun," said the young lady
soberly. "Pray sit down again on your sand sofa. I did not know you had
been so ill. Put on your hat, Mr. Bayard. Good society does not require
ghosts to stand bareheaded at the seacoast in April."

"I don't move in good society any longer. I am not expected to know
anything about its customs. Sit down beside me, a minute—and I will.
No—stay. Perhaps you will take cold? I wish I had some wraps. My coat"—

"When *I* take *your* coat"—began the healthy girl. He had already
flung his overcoat upon the dry, warm sand. She gave it back to him.
Then she saw the color start into his pale face.

"Oh, forgive me!" she said quickly. "I did not mean—Mr. Bayard, I
never was ill in my life."

"Nor I, either, before now," pleaded Bayard rather piteously.

"Who called it the 'insolence of health'? I did not mean to be
impertinent, if you will take the trouble to believe me. I fail to grasp the
situation, that's all. I am simply obtuse—blunt—blunt as a clam."

She waved her sun-umbrella dejectedly towards the beach where a
solitary clam-digger, a bent, picturesque old man, was seeking his next
chowder.

"The amount of it is," said Miss Carruth more in her usual manner, "that I was taken a little by surprise. You used to look so—different. You are greatly changed, Mr. Bayard. Being a heretic does not agree with you."

"I have had a little touch of something they call pneumonia down here," observed Bayard carelessly. "I've been out only a few days."

She made no answer at first; Bayard was looking at the clam-digger, but he felt that she was looking at him. She had seated herself on the sand beside him; she was now quite her usual self; her momentary embarrassment had disappeared like a sail around the Point—a graceful, vanishing thing of whose motion one thinks afterwards. He did not suppose that she was there to sympathize with him, but he was vaguely aware of a certain unbridged gap in the subject, when she unexpectedly said,—

"You have not asked me what I came to Windover for."

"Windover does not belong to me, Miss Carruth; nor"—a ray of disused mischief sprang to his eyes. Did he start to say, "Nor you?" He might have been capable of it as far back as Harvard, or even in junior year at Cesarea. That flash of human nonsense changed his appearance to an almost startling extent.

"Why now," she laughed, "I think I could recognize you without an introduction."

"But you haven't told me why you *did* come to Windover."

"It doesn't signify. You exhibit no interest in the subject, sir."

"You are here," he answered, looking at her. "That fact preoccupied me."

This reply was without precedent in her experience of him; and she gave no sign, whether of pleasure or displeasure, of its effect upon her. She looked straight at the clam-digger, who was shouldering his basket laboriously upon his bent back, making a sombre, Millet sketch against the cheerful, afternoon sky.

"I came down to engage our rooms," she said lightly. "We are coming here, you know, this summer. We board at the Mainsail. I had to have it out with Mrs. Salt about the mosquito bars. Mother wouldn't come last year because the mosquito bars had holes, and let in hornets and a mouse. You understand," she added, with something of unnecessary emphasis, "we always come here summers."

"I understand nothing at all!" said Bayard breathlessly. "You were not here last summer, when I was candidating in the First Church."

"That, I tell you, was on account of the hornets and the mouse; the

ELIZABETH STUART PHELPS

mouse clinched it; he waked her walking up her sleeve one morning. So we went to Campo Bello the year after. But we *always* come to Windover."

"For instance, how many seasons constitute 'always'?"

"Three. This will be four. Father likes it above everything. So did mother before the mouse epoch. She got to feeling hornets in her shoes whenever she put them on. I wonder father never told you we always come to Windover."

"The Professor had other things in his mind when he talked to me,— second probation, and the dangers of modern German exegesis."

"Yes, I know. Dear papa! Windover isn't a doctrine."

"I wonder *you* never told me you always came to Windover."

"Oh, I left that to Father," replied the young lady demurely. "I did come near it, though, once. Do you remember that evening"—

"Yes," he interrupted; "I remember that evening."

"I mean, when you had taken me up the Seminary walk to see the cross. When you said good-by that night, I thought I'd mention it. But I changed my mind. You see, you hadn't had your call, then. I thought—I might—hurt your feelings. But we always *do* come to Windover. We are coming as soon as Anniversary is over. We have the Flying Jib to ourselves—that little green cottage, you know, on the rocks. What! Never heard of the Flying Jib? You don't know the summer Windover, do you?"

"Only the winter Windover, you see."

"Nor the summer people, I suppose?"

"Only the winter people."

"Father's hired that old fish-house for a study," continued Helen with some abruptness. "He says he can't stand the women on the Mainsail piazzas; you can hear them over at the Flying Jib when the wind sets our way; they discuss the desserts, and pick each other's characters to pieces, and compare Kensington stitches, and neuralgia. Father is going to bring down his article on 'The State of the Unforgiven after Death'— There!" she said suddenly, "that Millet sketch is walking into father's study with his basket on his back. The State of the Unforgiven will be a little—clammy, don't you think?"

Her eyes rippled like the bed of a brown brook in the sun. Bayard laughed.

"The dear Professor!" he said.

"If father weren't such an archangel in private life, it wouldn't be so funny," observed Helen, jabbing the point of her purple-and-gold changeable silk sun-umbrella into the sand; "I can't see what he wants the unconverted to be burned up *for*. Can you?"

"The State of the Unforgiven before Death is more than I can manage," replied Bayard, smiling; "I have my hands full."

"Do you like it?" asked Helen, with a pretty, puzzled knot between her smooth brows.

"Like what? I like this."

He looked at her; as any other man might—like those students who used to come so often, and who suddenly called no more. Helen had never seen that expression in his eyes. She dropped her own. She dug little wells in the fine, white sand with her sun-umbrella before she said,—

"I have to get the six o'clock train; you know I haven't come to stay, yet."

"But you are coming!" he exclaimed with irrepressible joyousness.

She made no answer, and Bayard's sensitive color changed.

"Do I like *what*?" he repeated in a different tone.

"Heresy and martyrdom," said Helen serenely.

"I regret nothing, if that is what you mean; no matter what it costs; no matter how it ends—no, not for an hour. I told the truth, and I took the consequences; that is all. How *can* a man regret standing by his best convictions?"

"He might regret the convictions," suggested Helen.

"Might he? Perhaps. Mine are so much stronger than they were when I started in, that they race me and drag me like winged horses in a chariot of fire."

His eyes took on their dazzling look; like fine flash-lights they shot forth a brilliance as burning as it was brief; then their calm and color returned to them. Helen watched the transfiguration touch and pass his face with a sense of something so like reverence that it made her uncomfortable. Like many girls trained as she had been, she had small regard for the priestly office, and none for the priestly assumptions. The recognition of a spiritual superiority which she felt to be so far above her that in the nature of things she could not understand it, gave her strong nature a jar: something within her, hitherto fixed and untroubled, shook before it.

Bayard, without apparent consciousness of the young lady's thoughts, or indeed of her presence for that moment, went on dreamily:—

"I was a theorizer, a dreamer, a theologic apprentice, a year ago. I knew no more of real life than—that silver sea-gull making for the lighthouse tower. I took notes about sin in the lecture-room. Now I study misery and shame in Angel Alley. The gap between them is as wide as the stride of that angel in Revelation—do you remember him?—who stood with one foot upon the land and one upon the sea. All I mind is, that I have so much more to learn than I need have had—everything, in fact. If I had been taught, if I had been trained—if it had not all come with that kind of shock which benumbs a man's brain at first, and uses up his vitality so much faster than he can afford to spare it—but I have no convictions that I ought to be talking like this!"

"Go on," said Helen softly.

"Oh, to what end?" asked Bayard wearily. "That ecclesiastical system which brought me where I am can't be helped by one man's rebellion. It's going to take a generation of us. But there is enough that I *can* help. It is the can-be's, not the can't-be's, that are the business of men like me."

"I saw you with that drunken man; he had his arms about you," said Helen with charming irrelevance. Her untroubled brows still held that little knot, half of perplexity, half of annoyance. It became her, for she looked the more of a woman for it.

"Job Slip? Oh, in Boston that day; yes. I got him home to his wife all right that night. He was sober after that for—for quite a while. I wish you had seen that woman!" he said earnestly. "Mari is the most miserable—and the most grateful—person that I know. I never knew what a woman could suffer till I got acquainted with that family. They have a dear little boy. His father used to beat him over the head with a shovel. Joey comes over to see me sometimes, and goes to sleep on my lounge. We're great chums."

"You *do* like it," said Helen slowly. She had raised her brown eyes while he was speaking, and watched his face with a veiled look. "Yes; there's no doubt about it. You do."

"Wouldn't you?" asked Bayard, smiling.

"No, I shouldn't."

She shook her head with that positiveness so charming in an attractive woman, and so repellent in an ugly one. "When they burn you at the stake you'll swallow the fire and enjoy it. You'll say, 'Forgive them, for they don't mean it, poor things.' I should say, 'Lord, punish them, for they ought to know better.' That's just the difference between us. Mother must be right. She always says I am not spiritual."

"I don't know but I should like to see that little boy, though," added Helen reluctantly; "and Mari—if she had on a clean apron."

"She doesn't very often. But it might happen. Why, you might go over there with me—sometime—this summer, and see them?" suggested Bayard eagerly.

"So you lay the first little smoking fagot, do you?—For me, too?"
She laughed.

"God forbid!" said Bayard quickly. Helen's voice had not been as light as her laugh; and her bright face was grave when he turned and regarded it. She gave back his gaze without evasion, now. She seemed to have grown indefinably older and gentler since she had sat there on the sand beside him. Her eyes, for the first time, now, it seemed, intentionally studied him. She took in the least detail of his changed appearance: the shabby coat, the patch on his boot, his linen worn and darned, the fading color of his hat. She remembered him as the best-dressed man in Cesarea Seminary; nothing but rude, real poverty could have so changed that fashionable and easy student into this country parson, rusting and mended and out-of-the-mode, and conscious of it to the last sense, as only the town-bred man of luxurious antecedents can be of the novel deprivation that might have been another's native air.

"I don't know that it is necessary to look so pale," was all she said. "I should think you'd tan here in this glare. I do. See!"

She held out her bare hands, and doubled them up, putting them together to scrutinize the delicate backs of them for the effect of an hour's Windover sun. Her dark purple gloves and the saxifrage lay in her lap. Bayard held the sun-umbrella over her. It gave him a curious sense of event to perform this little courtesy; it was so long since he had been among ladies, and lived like other gentlemen; he felt as if he had been upon a journey in strange lands and were coming home again. A blossom of the saxifrage fell to the hem of her dress, and over upon the sand. He delicately touched and took it, saying nothing.

"Does Mr. Hermon Worcester come and pour pitch and things on the bonfire?" asked Helen suddenly.

"I thought you knew," said Bayard, "my uncle has disinherited me. He is not pleased with what I have done."

"Ah! I did not know. Doesn't he—excuse me, Mr. Bayard. It is not my business."

"He writes to me," said Bayard. "He sent me things when I was sick.

ELIZABETH STUART PHELPS

He was very kind then. We have not quarreled at all. But it is some time since I have seen him. I am very fond of my uncle. He is an old man, you know. He was brought up so—We mustn't blame him. He thinks I am on the road to perdition. He doesn't come to Windover."

"I see," said Helen. She leaned her head back against the boulder and looked through half-shut lids at the dashing sea. The wind was rising.

"I must go," she said abruptly.

"May I take you over to the station?" he asked with boyish anxiety.

"Mr. Salt is going to harness old Pepper," she answered. Bayard said nothing. He remembered that he could not afford to drive a lady to the station; he could not offer to "take" her in the electric conveyance of the great American people. He might have spent at least three quarters of an hour more beside her. It seemed to him that he had not experienced poverty till now. The exquisite outline of his lip trembled for the instant with that pathos which would have smitten a woman to the heart if she had loved him. Helen was preoccupied with her saxifrage and her purple gloves. She did not, to all appearance, see his face at all, and he was glad of it.

He arose in silence, and walked beside her to the beach and towards the town.

"Mr. Bayard," said Helen, with her pleasant unexpectedness, "I owe you something."

All this while she had not mentioned the wreck or the rescue; she alone, of all people whom he had seen since he came out of his sickroom, had not inquired, nor exclaimed, nor commended, nor admired. Something in her manner—it could hardly be said what—reminded him now of this omission; he had not thought of it before.

"I owe you a recognition," she said.

"I cancel the debt," he answered, smiling.

"You cannot. I owe you the recognition—of a friend—for that brave and noble deed you did. Accept it, sir!"

She spread out her hands with a pretty gesture, as if she gave him something; she moved her head with a commanding and royal turn, as if her gift had value. He lifted his hat.

"I could have done no less then; but I might do more—now."

His worn face had lightened delicately. He looked hopeful and happy.

"A man doesn't put himself where I am, to complain," he added. "But I don't suppose you could even guess how solitary my position is. The right thing said in the right way gives me more courage than—people who say it can possibly understand. I have so few friends—now. If you allow me to count you among them, you do me a very womanly kindness; so then I shall owe *you*"—

"I cancel the debt!" she interrupted, laughing. "Didn't Father write to you?" she hurried on, "when you were so ill?"

"Oh, yes. The Professor's note was the first I was allowed to read. He said all sorts of things that I didn't deserve. He said that in spite of the flaws in my theology I had done honor to the old Seminary."

"Really? Father will wear a crown and a harp for *that* concession. Did he give you any message from me, I wonder?"

"He said the ladies sent their regards."

"Oh! Was that all?"

"That was all."

"It was not *quite* all," said Helen, after a moment's rather grave reflection. "But never mind. Probably Father thought the exegesis incorrect somewhere."

"Perhaps he objected to the context?" asked Bayard mischievously.

"More likely he had a quarrel in the Faculty on his mind and forgot it."

"If you had written it yourself"—suggested Bayard humbly. "But of course you had other things to do."

Helen gave him an inscrutable look. She made no reply. They passed the fish-house, and the old clam-digger, who was sitting on his overturned basket in the sun, opening clams with a blunt knife, and singing hoarsely:—

> *"The woman's ashore,*
> *The child's at the door,*
> *The man's at the wheel.*
>
> *"Storm on the track,*
> *Fog at the back,*
> *Death at the keel.*
>
> *"You, mate, or me,*
> *Which shall it be?*
> *God, He won't tell.*
> *Drive on to—!"*

ELIZABETH STUART PHELPS

"There is Mr. Salt," said Helen; for the two had come slowly up in silence to the old gate, (fastened with a rope tied in a sailor's knot), that gave the short cut across the meadow to the Mainsail summer hotel.

"He is watching for me. How sober he looks! Perhaps something dreadful has happened to Mrs. Salt. Wait a minute. Let me run in!"

She tossed her sun-umbrella, gloves, and saxifrage in a heap across Bayard's arm, and ran like a girl or a collie swaying across the meadow in the wind. In a few minutes she walked back, flushed and laughing.

"Pepper can't go!" she cried. "He's got the colic. He's swallowed a celluloid collar. Mr. Salt says he thought it was sugar. I must go right along and catch the car."

"You have eight minutes yet," said Bayard joyously, "and I can go too!"

The car filled up rapidly; they chatted of little things, or sat in silence. Jane Granite came aboard as they passed her mother's door. Bayard lifted his hat to her cordially; she was at the further end of the car; she got off at a grocery store, to buy prunes, and did not look back. She had only glanced at Helen Carruth. Bayard did not notice when Jane left.

The train came in and went out. Helen stood on the platform leaning over to take her saxifrage: a royal vision, blurring and melting in purple and gold before his eyes.

The train came in and went out; her laughing eyes looked back from the frame of the car window. The train went out. He turned away and went slowly home.

Jane had not returned, and Mrs. Granite was away. The house was deserted, and the evening was coming on cold. He climbed the steep stairs wearily to his rooms, and lighted a fire, for he coughed a good deal. He had to go down into the shed and bring up the wood and coal. He was so tired when this was done that he flung himself upon the old lounge. He looked slowly about his dismal rooms: at the top curl of the iron angel on the ugly stove; at the empty, wooden rocking-chair with the bones; at the paper screen, where the Cupid on the basket of grapes sat forever tasting and never eating impossible fruit; at the study-table, where the subscription list for his quarter's salary lay across the manuscript notes of his last night's sermon. The great Saint Michael on the wall eyed him with that absence of curiosity which belongs to remote superiority. Bayard did not return the gaze of the picture. He took something from his vest-pocket and looked at it gently, twisting it about in his thin hands. It was a sprig of saxifrage, whose white blossom was hanging its head over upon the dry, succulent stem. Bayard got up suddenly, and put the flower in a book upon his study-table.

As he did so, a short, soft, broken sound pattered up the stairs. The door opened without the preliminary of a knock, and little Joey Slip walked seriously in. He said he had come to see the minister. He sat down sedately and ceremoniously upon the carpet-lounge. He said Marm said to say Father's home from Georges' drunk as a fish. He put out his little fingers and patted Bayard on the cheek, as if the minister had been the child, and Joey the old, old man.

XII

It was night, and it was Angel Alley. One of the caprices of New England spring had taken the weather, and it had suddenly turned cold. The wind blew straight from the sea. It was going to rain. The inner harbor was full; in the dark, thick air bowsprits nodded and swung sleepily, black outlines against little glimmering swathes of grayish-yellow cut by the headlights of anchored vessels. Dories put out now and then from the schooners, and rowed lustily to the docks; these were packed with sailors or fishermen who leaped up the sides of the wharves like cats, tied the painter to invisible rings in black, slimy places, and scrambled off, leaving the dory to bob and hit the piers; or they cast the painter to the solitary oarsman, who rowed back silently to the vessel, while his gayer shipmates reeled, singing, over the wharves and disappeared in the direction of the town.

The sky was heavily clouded, and fog was stealing stealthily off the Point.

Angel Alley was full, that night. Half a dozen large fishermen were just in from Georges'; these had made their trip to Boston to sell their cargoes of halibut, haddock, or cod, and had run home quickly on a stiff sou'easter, or were unloading direct at their native wharves. The town overflowed with men of unmistakably nautical callings, red of face, strong of hand, unsteady of step; men with the homeless eye and the roving heart of the sea: Americans, Scotch, Swedes, Portuguese, Italians, Irish, and Finns swung up together from the wharves and swarmed over the alley, ready for a song, a laugh or a blow, as the case might be; equally prepared to smoke, to love, to quarrel, or to drink, liable to drift into a prayer-room or a bar-room, just as it happened, and there was small space to doubt which would happen; men whose highest aspiration was to find the barber and the boot-black; men who steered steadily home, thinking of their baby's laugh, and the wife's kiss; and men who turned neither to the right nor to the left, who lingered for neither men nor gods nor women, but pushed, with head thrust out like a dog's on the scent, straight on to the first saloon that gaped at them.

Open and secret, lawful and unlawful, these were of an incredible number, if one should estimate the size of the short street. Angel Alley overflowed with abomination, as the tides, befouled by the town, overflowed the reeking piers of the docks. In sailors' boarding-houses, in open bars, in hidden cellars, in billiard-rooms, in shooting-galleries, in dance-halls, and in worse, whiskey ran in rivers. At the banks of those black streams men and some women crawled and drank, flaunting or hiding their fiery thirst as the mood took them, and preying upon one another, each according to his power or his choice, as the chance of an evil hour decreed.

Girls with hard eyes and coarse mouths strutted up and down the alley in piteous numbers. Sights whose description cannot blot this page might have been detected in the shadows of the wharves and of the winding street. Men went into open doors with their full trips' earnings in their pockets, and staggered out without a penny to their shameful names. Fifty, seventy, a hundred dollars, vanished in the carouse of a single hour. One man, a foreigner, of some nationality unknown, ran up and down, wildly calling for the police. He had been robbed of two hundred dollars in a drunken bout, last night; he had but just come to such senses as nature may have given him, and to the discovery of his loss. His wife, he said, lived over in West Windover; she warn't well when he shipped; there was another baby,—seven young ones already,—and she couldn't get trust at the stores, the bills had run up so long.

"Lord!" he said stupidly; "s'pose I find 'em layin' round starved?"

He stoutly refused to go home. He swore he'd rather go to jail than face her. He sat down on the steps of old Trawl's, sobbing openly, like a child. A little crowd gathered, one or two voices jeered at him, and some one scolded him smartly, for no one moralizes more glibly than the sot in his intervals of sobriety.

"Oh, shut up there!" cried the girl Lena. "Ain't he miser'ble enough already? Ain't all of us that much?—Go home, Jean!" she urged kindly; "go home to Marie. She won't cuss you."

"She never cussed me *yet*," answered Jean doubtfully.

He got up and reeled away, wringing his stubbed hands. Lena walked up the alley, alone; her eyes were on the ground; she did not answer when one of the girls called her; she strolled on aimlessly, and one might almost say, thoughtfully.

"Better come in, Lena," said a voice above her. She looked up. The beautiful new transparency, which was still the wonder and admiration of the fishermen coming home from Georges' or the Banks, flashed out in strong white and scarlet lights the strange words, now grown familiar to Angel Alley:—

Beneath, in the broken, moving color stood the minister; his foot was on the topmost step of the long flight; he looked pale and tired.

"Isn't it better for you in here, than out there?" he asked gently. Lena gave one glance at his pitying eyes; then she followed that brilliance like a moth.

He stepped back and allowed her to precede him, as if she had been any other woman, the only difference being one which the girl was not likely to notice: the minister did not lift his hat to Lena. She hung her head and went in.

"They are singing to-night—practicing for their concert," he said. "Perhaps they might like the help of your voice."

She made no answer, and the preacher and the street girl entered the bright hall together.

It was well filled with well-behaved and decently dressed groups of men and women; these were informally scattered about the main room and the ante-rooms, for no service was in progress; the whole bore the appearance of a people's club, or social entertainment, whose members read or chatted, played games, or sang, as the mood took them.

A bowling-alley and a smoking-room adjoined; these last were often quite full and busy with fishermen and sailors; but that night the most of the people were listening to the singing. Music, Bayard had already learned, would lead them anywhere. At the first sound of the poor and pathetic melodeon, they had begun to collect around the net of harmony like mackerel round a weir. When Lena came into the room, the little choir were singing the old-fashioned, beautiful Ave Sanctissima which even Angel Alley knew. Lena dropped into an obscure seat, and remained silent for a time. Suddenly her fine contralto rang in,—

> "'Tis midnight on the sea.
> Ora pro nobis,
> We lift our souls to thee."

The minister, distant and pale, blurred before her eyes while she sang. He looked like a figure resting on a cloud in a sacred picture. He moved about among his people, tall, smiling, and shining. They looked at him with wistful, wondering tenderness. He passed in and out of the halls on errands whose nature no one asked. Occasionally he returned, bringing some huddling figure with him from the street; a homesick boy, a homeless man, a half-sodden fellow found hesitating outside of Trawl's den, midway between madness and sanity, ready for hell or heaven, and following Bayard like a cur.

DOWN THE DARK THROAT OF Angel Alley a man, that night, was doing a singular thing. He was a fisherman, plainly one of the recent arrivals of the anchored fleet; he was a sturdily built fellow with a well-shaped head; he had the naturally open face and attractive bearing often to be found among drinking men; at his best he must have been a handsome, graceful fellow, lovable perhaps, and loving. At his worst, he was a cringing sot. He wore, over his faded dark-red flannel shirt, the gingham jumper favored by his class; and it seemed he had lost his hat. This man was monotonously moving to and fro, covering a given portion of Angel Alley over and again, retracing his unsteady footsteps from point to point, and repeating his course with mysterious regularity. His beat covered the space between the saloon of old Trawl (which stood about midway of the alley) and the scarlet and white transparency, whose strange and sacred heraldry blazed, held straight out, an arm of fire, across the mouth of the street. Angel Alley, as we have explained, had, at the first, inclined to call the mission Christ's Rest, for reasons of its own; but even that half-godless reminder of a history better forgotten was growing out of date. The people's name for Emanuel Bayard's house of worship and of welcome was fast settling into one beautiful word—Christlove.

The fisherman in the jumper wavered to and fro between Christlove and the ancient grogshop. In the dark weather the figure of the man seemed to swing from this to that like a pendulum; at moments he seemed to have no more sense or sentience. He was hurled as if he were forced by invisible machinery; he recoiled as if wound by unseen springs; now his steps quickened into a run, as he wrenched himself away from the saloon, and faced the prayer-room; then they lagged, and he crawled like a crab to the rum-shop door. His hands were clenched together. Long before it began to rain his hatless forehead was wet.

His eyes stared straight before him. He seemed to see nothing but the two open doors between which he was vibrating. No one had happened to notice him, or, if so, his movements were taken for the vagaries of intoxication. A nerve of God knows what, in his diseased will began to throb, and he made a leap away from the saloon, and ran

     ELIZABETH STUART PHELPS

heavily towards the white and scarlet lights of the transparency; at the steps, he fell, and lay groveling; he could hear the singing overhead:—

> *"Ora pro nobis,*
> *We lift our souls to thee."*

He tried to climb up; but something—call it his muscle, call it his will, call it his soul; it does not signify—something refused him, and he did not get beyond the second stair. Slowly, reluctantly, mysteriously, his feet seemed to be dragged back. He put out his hands, as if to push at an invisible foe; he leaned over backwards, planting his great oiled boots firmly in the ground, as if resisting unseen force; but slowly, reluctantly, mysteriously, he was pulled back. At the steps of the saloon, in a blot of darkness, on the shadowed side, he sank; he got to his hands and knees like an animal, and there he crawled. If any one had been listening, the man might have been heard to sob,—

"It's me and the rum—God and the devil—Now we'll see!"

He rose more feebly this time, and struggled over toward the prayer-room; he wavered, and turned before he had got there, and made weakly back. Panting heavily, he crawled up the steps of the saloon, and then lurched over, and fell down into the blot whence he had come. There he lay, crying, with the arm of his brown gingham jumper before his eyes.

"Look up, Job!" said a low voice in the shadow at his side. Job Slip lifted his sodden face, swollen, red, and stained with tears. Instinctively he stretched up his hands.

"Oh, sir!" was all he said.

Bayard stood towering above him; he had his grand Saint Michael look, half of scorn and half of pity.

Job had not seen his face before since the night when it suddenly rose on a great wave, like that of another drowning man, making towards him in the undertow off Ragged Rock. Job put up his hands, now, before his own face. He told Mari, long afterwards, that the minister blinded him.

"Get up!" said Bayard, much in the tone in which he had said it the day he knocked Job down.

Job crawled up.

"Come here!" said the preacher sternly. He held out his white hand; Job put his wet and fishy palm into it; Bayard drew that through his own arm, and led him away without another word. Old Trawl came muttering to the door, and stood with his hand over his eyes, shutting out the glare of the bar-room within, to watch them. Ben looked over his shoulder, scowling. Father and son muttered unpleasantly together, as the minister and the drunkard moved off, and melted into the fine, dark rain.

Bayard led his man down towards the wharves. It was dark, there, and still; there was a secluded spot, which he knew of, under a salt-house at the head of a long pier but seldom used at night. The fine rain was uncertain, and took moods. As the two came down the larynx of the Alley, the drizzle had dripped off into a soft mist. Bayard heard Captain Hap across the street giving utterance to his favorite phrase:—

"It's comin' on thick; so thick it has stems to it."

The captain looked after the minister and the drunkard with disapproval in his keen, dark eyes.

"Better look out, Mr. Bayard!" he called, with the freedom of a nurse too recently dismissed not to feel responsible for his patient. "It ain't no night for you to be settin' round on the docks. You cough, sir! Him you've got in tow ain't worth it—no, nor twenty like him!"

"That's a fact," said Job humbly, stopping short.

"Come on, Job," Bayard answered decidedly.

So they came under the salt-house, and sat down. Both were silent at first. Job wiped off an old fish-keg with the sleeve of his jumper, and offered this piece of furniture to the minister; the fisherman perched himself on the edge of a big broken pile which reared its gray head above the wharf; the rising tide flapped with a sinister sound under his feet which hung over, recklessly swinging. Job looked down into the black water. He was man enough still to estimate what he had done, and miserable enough to quench the shame and fire in him together by a leap. Men do such things, in crises such as Job had reached, far oftener than we may suppose. Job said nothing. Bayard watched him closely.

"Well, Job?" he said at last; not sternly, as he had spoken at Trawl's door.

"I haven't touched it before, sir, not a drop till last night," said Job with sullen dreariness. "I was countin' on it how I should see you the fust time since—I thought of it all the way home from Georges'. I was so set to see you I couldn't wait to get ashore to see you. I took a clean jump from the dory to the landin'. I upset the dory and two men. . . Mr. Bayard, sir, the cap'n's right. I ain't wuth it. You'd better let me drownded off the Clara Em."

"Tell me how it happened," said Bayard gently. Job shook his head.

"You know's well's I, sir. We come ashore, and Trawl, he had one of his—runners to the wharf. Ben was there, bossin' the—job."

The minister listened to this profanity without proffering a rebuke. His teeth were set; he looked as if he would have liked to say as much, himself.

"There was a fellar there had made two hundred dollars to his trip. He treated. So I said I didn't want any. But I hankered for it till it seemed I'd die there on the spot before 'em. Ben, he sent a bar-boy after me come to say I needn't drink unless I pleased, but not to be onsocial, and to come along with the crowd. So I said, No, I was a goin' home to my wife and kid. When the fellar was gone, I see he'd slipped a bottle into my coat pocket. It was a pint bottle XXX. The cork was loose and it leaked. So I put it back, for I swore I wouldn't touch it, and I got a little on my fingers. I put 'em in my mouth to lick 'em off—and, sir, before God, that's all I know—till I come to, to-day. The hanker got me, and that's all I know. I must ha' ben at it all night. Seems to me I went home an' licked my wife and come away ag'in, but I ain't sure. I must ha' ben on a reg'lar toot. I'm a—drunken fool, and the quicker you let me go to—the better."

Job leaned over and gazed at the water quietly. There was a look about his jaw which Bayard did not like. He came out from under the salt-house and moved the keg close beside the broken pile.

"What were you doing when I found you? I've been looking for you everywhere—last night, and all day."

"I was havin' it out," said Job doggedly.

"Having?"—

"It lays between me and the rum, God and the devil. I was set to see which would beat."

"Why didn't you come straight over to see me?"

"I couldn't."

"*Couldn't* put your feet up those steps and walk in?"

"No, sir. I couldn't do it. I come over twenty times. I couldn't get no further. I *had* to come back to Trawl's. I HAD To Do It!"

Job brought his clenched hand down heavily on his knee.

"You can't onderstand, sir," he said drearily. "You ain't a drinkin' man."

"I sometimes wish I had been," said the minister unexpectedly. "I must understand these things."

"God forbid!" said Job solemnly. He stretched his shaking arm out with a beautiful gesture, and put it around Bayard, as if he were shielding from taint a woman or some pure being from an unknown world.

Tears sprang to the minister's eyes. He took the drunkard's dirty hand, and clasped it warmly. The two men sat in silence. Job looked at the water. Bayard looked steadily at Job.

"Come," he said at length, in his usual tone. "It is beginning to rain, in earnest. I'm not *quite* strong yet. I suppose I must not sit here. Take my arm, and come home to Mari and Joey."

Job acquiesced hopelessly. He knew that it would happen all over again. They walked on mutely; their steps fell with a hollow sound upon the deserted pier; the water sighed as they passed, like the involuntary witness of irreclaimable tragedy.

Suddenly, Bayard dropped Job's hand, and spoke in a ringing voice:—

"Job Slip, get down upon your knees—just where you stand!"

Job hesitated.

"Down!" cried Bayard.

Job obeyed, as if he had been a dog.

"Now, lift up your hands—so—to the sky."

As if the minister had been a cut-throat, Job obeyed again.

"Now pray," commanded Bayard.

"I don't know—how to," stammered Job.

"Pray! Pray!" repeated Bayard.

"I've forgot the way you do it, sir!"

"No matter how other people do it! This is your affair. Pray your own way. Pray anyhow. But *pray*!"

"I haven't done such a thing since I was—since I used to say: 'Eenty Deenty Donty,'—no, that ain't it, neither. 'Now I lay me?' That's more like it. But that don't seem appropriate to the circumstances, sir."

"Try again, Job."

"'Tain't no use, Mr. Bayard. I'm a goner. If I couldn't keep sober for you, I ain't ergointer for no Creetur I never see nor spoke to,—nor no man ever see nor spoke to,—a thousand fathoms up overhead."

Job lifted his trembling arms high and higher towards the dark sky.

"Pray!" reiterated Bayard.

"I can't do it, sir!"

"*Pray!*" commanded Bayard.

"Oh,—God!" gasped Job.

ELIZABETH STUART PHELPS

Bayard took off his hat. Job's arms fell; his face dropped into them; he shook from head to foot.

"There!" he cried, "I done it. . . I'll do it again. God! God! *God!*"

Bayard bowed his head. Moments passed before he said, solemnly,—

"Job Slip, I saved your life, didn't I?"

"You committed that mistake, sir."

"It belongs to me, then. *You* belong to me. I take you. I give you to God."

He dropped upon his knees beside the drunkard in the rain.

"Lord," he said, in a tone of infinite sweetness, "here is a poor perishing man. Save him! He has given himself to Thee."

"The parson did that, Lord," sobbed Job. "Don't give me no credit for it!"

"Save him!" continued Bayard, who seemed hardly to have heard the drunkard's interruption. "Save me this one man! I have tried, and failed, and I am discouraged to the bottom of my heart. But I cannot give him up. I will never give him up till he is dead, or I am. If I cannot do any other thing in Windover, for Christ's sake, save me this one drunken man!"

Bayard lifted his face in a noble agony. Job hid his own before that Gethsemane.

"Does the parson care so much—as *that*?" thought the fisherman.

The rain dashed on Bayard's white face. He rose from his knees.

"Job Slip," he said, "you have signed a contract which you can never break. Your vow lies between God and you. I am the witness. I have bound you over to a clean life. Go and sin no more.—I'll risk you now," added Bayard, quietly. "I shall not even walk home with you. You have fifteen rum-shops to meet before you get back to your wife and child. Pass them! They all stand with open doors, and the men you know are around these doors. You will not enter one of them. You will go straight home; and to-morrow you will send me written testimony from Mari, your wife,—I want her to write it, Job,—that you did as I bade you, and came home sober. Now go, and God go with you."

As Bayard turned to give the drunkard his hand, he stumbled a little over something on the dark pier. Job had not risen from his knees, but stooped, and put his lips to the minister's patched shoe.

"This is to sertify that my Husband come home last nite sober
and haint ben on a Bat sence, god bless you ennyhow.

MARIA SLIP

This legend, written in a laborious chirography on a leaf torn from a grocer's pass-book, was put into Bayard's hand at noon of the next day. Joey brought it; he had counted upon a nap on the study lounge, and was rather disappointed to find it occupied. Mrs. Granite said she had sent for Cap'n Hap; she said the minister's temperature had gone up to a hundred and twenty, and she should think it would.

XIII

Jane Granite came out of the kitchen door, and sat down in the back yard underneath the clothes-lines. She sat on the overturned salt-fish box that she kept to stand on and reach the clothes-pins,—Jane was such a little body. She looked smaller than usual that Monday afternoon, and shrunken, somehow; her eyes were red, as if she had been crying. She cried a good deal on Mondays, after Ben Trawl had come and gone on Sunday evenings.

The minister was quite himself again, and about his business. This fact should have given Jane the keenest gratification; whereas, in proportion as their lodger had grown well and cheerful, Jane had turned pale and sober. When he was really ill, her plain face wore a rapt look. For Captain Hap had remained on duty only a day or two; Mr. Bayard had not been sick enough to need professional nursing, this time, and it had since devolved wholly upon the women of the household to minister to his convalescent needs.

Happy Jane! She ran up and down, she flitted to and fro, she cooked, she ironed, she mended, she sewed, she read aloud, she ran errands, she watched for the faintest flicker in the changes of expression on his face: its dignity, its beauty, and its dearness for that one precious page out of her poor story were hers. All the rest of her life he belonged to other people and to other things: to the drunkards and the fishermen and the services; to his books and his lonely walks and his unapproachable thoughts; to his dreams of the future in which Jane had no more part than the paper Cupid on the screen, forever tasting and never eating impossible fruit; to his memories of a past of which Jane knew that she knew no more than she did of the etiquette at the palace of Kubla Khan in Xanadu.

Jane understood about Kubla Khan (or she thought she did, which answers the same purpose), for she had read the poem aloud to him one day while her mother sat sewing in the wooden rocking-chair. Jane was "educated," like most respectable Windover girls; she had been through the high school of her native town; she read not at all badly; Mr. Bayard had told her something to this effect, and Jane sang about the house all the rest of the day. Yes; Jane understood Kubla Khan.

Jane watched the luminous patience in the sick man's eyes,

"Where Alph, the sacred river, ran
Through caverns measureless to man."

She repeated the lines mechanically, with the bitter consciousness of the half-educated of being moved by something which it was beyond her power and her province to reconcile with the facts of her life. She sighed when the brilliant eagerness and restlessness of returning health replaced that large and gentle light. Bayard had asked her mother to let Jane keep his copy of that volume; he said he had two sets of Coleridge. He had written her name in it; how could he guess that Jane would lock the book away in her bureau drawer by day, and sleep with it under her pillow at night? He tossed her a rose of common human gratitude; it fell into a girl's heart,—a burning coal of ravenous longing,—and ate its way.

It was summer in Windover; and Jane's one beautiful leaf of life had turned. Mr. Bayard had long since been able to take care of himself; coughing still, and delicate enough, but throwing off impatiently, as the gentlest man does, in health, the little feminine restraints and devotions which he found necessary and even agreeable in illness. It would not be too much to say that Jane loved him as unselfishly as any woman ever had, or ever would; but in proportion as his spirits rose, hers sank. She reproached herself, poor child, that it did not make her perfectly happy to have the minister get well. Suffering and helpless, he had needed *her*. Busy and well, he thought of her no more. For that one time, that cruelly little time, she, Jane Granite, of all the women in the world, had known that precious right. To her, only to her, it had been given to serve his daily, common wants; she had carried up his tray, she had read or written tireless hours as his mood decreed, or she had sat in silent study of his musing face, not one lineament of which did muse of her.

But it was summer in Windover, and the minister was Jane's no more.

It was one of the last of the days of a celestial June. Bayard had lived the month of blossoms out eagerly and restlessly. His work had grown enormously upon his hands, and required an attention which told on every nerve. He had gone headlong into the depths of one of those dedications which do not give a man time to come up for air. His eye wore an elate, rapt look. His cheeks burned with a fine fever. His personal beauty that summer was something at which the very "dock-rats" on the wharves turned back to look. No woman easily forgot it, and how many secretly dreamed of it, fortunately the young man never knew. The best of men may work his share of heart-break, and the better he is the less he will suspect it.

Bayard was far too busy to think of women. For he did not exactly think of Helen Carruth; he felt her. She did not occupy his mind so far that he experienced the need of communication with her; he had never written her so much as a note of ceremony. After her brief scintillation before him on Windover Point that April afternoon, she had melted from his horizon. Nevertheless, she had changed the tint of it. Now and then in the stress of his prosaic, thankless, yet singularly enthusiastic work, there came to the young preacher that sense of something agreeable about to happen, which makes one wake up singing in the morning of one's hardest day's labor, or sends one to rest dreaming quietly in the face of the crudest anxiety. The devotee, in the midst of his orisons, was aware of the footstep of possible pleasure falling lightly, distant, doubtful, towards his cell. Some good men pray the louder for this sweet and perilous prescience. Bayard worked the harder.

And it was summer in Windover. The scanty green carpet of the downs had unrolled to its full, making as much as possible of its meagre proportions, atoning in depth of color for what it lacked in breadth and length: if the cliffs and boulders were grayer for the green, the grass looked greener for the gray. The saxifrage had faded, but among the red-cupped moss the checkerberry shot up tender, reddish leaves, the white violets scented the swamps, and the famous wild roses of the Cape dashed the bayberry thickets with pink. The late apple blossoms had blushed and gone, but the leaf and the hidden fruit responded to the anxious attention of the unenthusiastic farmer who wrenched his living out of the reluctant granite soil. In front of the hotels the inevitable geraniums blazed scarlet in mathematical flower-beds; and the boarding-houses convalesced from housecleaning in striped white scrim curtains and freshly painted blue wooden pumps. The lemonade and candy stores of "the season" sprouted with the white clovers by the wayside; and the express cart of the summer boarder's luggage blossomed with the lonely and uncomfortable hydrangea, bearing its lot in yellow jars on piazza steps. Windover Point wore a coquettish air of expectation, like a girl in her best dress who waits in a lane for an invisible admirer.

Windover Harbor was alive and alert. The summer fleets were out; the spring fleets were in. Bayard could hear the drop of anchors now, in the night, through his open windows; and the soft, pleasant splash, the home-coming and home-yearning sound which wakened the summer people, only to lull them to sleep again with a sense of poetic pleasure in a picturesque and alien life, gave to the lonely preacher of the winter Windover the little start of anxiety and responsibility which assassinates rest. He thought:—

"Another crew in! Is it Job? Or Bob? Or Jean? Will they go to Trawl's, or get home straight? I must be off at dawn to see to this."

On the little beach opposite Mrs. Granite's cottage the sea sighed in the night to answer him; ebbing, it lapped the pebbles gently, as if it felt sorry for the preacher, who had not known Windover as long as it had; it inhaled and exhaled long, soft breaths, in rhythm with which his own began to grow deep and quiet; and the start from a dream of drowning in the undertow off Ragged Rock would tell him that he had slept. More often, of late, the rising tide had replied nervously; it was fitful and noisy; it panted and seemed to struggle for articulation: for the June sea was restless, and the spring gales had died hard. The tints of the harbor were still a little cool, but the woodland on the opposite shore held out an arm of rich, ripe leaf; and the careening sails warmed to the sunrise and the sunset in rose and ochre, violet and pearl, opening buds of the blossom of midsummer color that was close at hand.

Bayard was in his rooms, resting after one of these unresting nights. He had set forth at daybreak to meet an incoming schooner at the docks. It had become his habit, whenever he could, to see that the fishermen were personally conducted past the dens of Angel Alley, and taken home sober to waking wife and sleeping child. In this laborious task Job Slip's help had been of incredible value. Job was quite sober now; and in the intervals between trips this converted Saul delighted to play the Paul to Bayard's little group of apostles. Yet Job did not pose. He was more sincere than most better men. He took to decency as if it had been a new trade; and the novel dignity of missionary zeal sat upon him like a liberal education. The Windover word for what had happened to Job was "re-formation." Job Slip, one says, is a reformed man. The best way to save a rascal is to give him another one to save; and Job, who was no rascal, but the ruin of a very good fellow, brilliantly illustrated this eternal law.

Bayard had come back, unusually tired, about noon, and had not left the house since his return. He was reading, with his back to the light, and the sea in his ears. The portière of mosquito netting, which

ELIZABETH STUART PHELPS

hung now at the door between his two rooms, was pushed aside that he might see the photographed Leonardo as he liked to do. The scanty furniture of his sleeping-room had been moved about during his recent illness, so that now the picture was the only object visible from the study where he sat. The mosquito portière was white. Mrs. Granite having ineffectually urged a solferino pink, Bayard regarded this portière with the disproportionate gratitude of escape from evil.

A knock had struck the cottage door, and Jane Granite had run to answer it. She was in her tidy, blue gingham dress, but a little wet and crumply, as was to be expected on a Monday. She had snatched up a white apron, and looked like an excellent parlor-maid. For such, perhaps, the caller took her, for practical tact was not his most obtrusive quality. He was an elderly man, a gentleman; his mouth was stern, and his eyes were kind. He carried a valuable cane, and spoke with a certain air of authority, as of a man well acquainted with this world and the other too. He asked for Mr. Bayard, and would send up his card before intruding upon him; a ceremony which quite upset little Jane, and she stood crimson with embarrassment. Her discomfort was not decreased by the bewildering presence of a carriage at the gate of her mother's garden. Beyond the rows of larkspur and feverfew, planted for the vase on Mr. Bayard's study-table, Mr. Salt's best carryall, splendid in spring varnish, loomed importantly. Pepper, with the misanthropy of a confirmed dyspeptic, drew the carryall, and ladies sat within it. There were two. They were covered by certain strange, rich carriage robes undreamed of by Mr. Salt; dull, silk blankets, not of Windover designs. The ladies were both handsomely dressed. One was old; but one—ah! one was young.

"Mr. Bayard is in, my dear." The voice of the caller rose over the larkspur to the carryall. "Will you wait, or drive on?"

"We'll drive on," replied the younger lady rather hurriedly.

"Helen, Helen!" complained the elder. "Don't you *know* that Pepper is afraid of the electric cars? I've noticed horses are that live in the same town with them."

Helen did not laugh at this, but her eyes twinkled irreverently. She wrapped herself in her old-gold silk blanket, and turned to watch the sea. She did not look at Mrs. Granite's cottage.

The dignified accents of the Professor's voice were now wafted over the larkspur bed again.

"Mr. Bayard asks if the ladies will not come up to his study, Statira? It is only one short flight. Will you do so?"

Simultaneously Bayard's eager face flashed out of the doorway; and before Helen could assent or dissent, her mother, on the young man's arm, was panting up between the feverfew and into the cottage. Helen followed in meek amusement.

The stairs were scarcely more than a ship's gangway. Mrs. Carruth politely suppressed her sense of horrified inadequacy to the ascent, and she climbed up as bravely as possible. Helen's cast-down eyes observed the uncarpeted steps of old, stained pine-wood. She was still silent when they entered the study. Bayard bustled about, offering Mrs. Carruth the bony rocking-chair with the turkey-red cushion. The Professor had already ensconced himself in the revolving study-chair, a luxury which had been recently added to the room. There remained for Helen the lounge, and Bayard, perforce, seated himself beside her. He did not remark upon the deficiency of furniture. He seemed as much above an apology for the lack of upholstery as a martyr in prison. His face was radiant with a pleasure which no paltry thought could poison. The simple occasion seemed to him one of high festivity. It would have been impossible for any one of these comfortable people to understand what it meant to the poor fellow to entertain old friends in his lonely quarters.

Helen's eyes assumed a blank, polite look; she said as little as possible at first; she seemed adjusting herself to a shock. Mrs. Carruth warbled on about the opening of the season at the Mainsail, and the Professor inquired about the effects of the recent gales upon the fishing classes. He avoided all perilous personalities as adroitly as if he had been fencing with a German radical over the authenticity of the Fourth Gospel. It was Bayard himself who boldly approached the dangerous ground.

"You came on Saturday, I suppose? I did not know anything about it till this minute."

"We did not come till night," observed Helen hurriedly. "Mother was very tired. We did not go out anywhere yesterday."

"The Professor did, I'll be bound," smiled Bayard. "Went to church, didn't you, Professor?"

"Ye—es," replied Professor Carruth, hesitating. "I never omit divine service if I am on my feet."

"Did you hear Fenton?" asked Bayard with perfect ease of manner.

"Yes," more boldly from the Professor, "I attended the First Church. I like to recognize The Denomination wherever I may be traveling. I always look up my old boys, of course, too. It seems to be a prosperous parish."

ELIZABETH STUART PHELPS

"It *is* a prosperous parish," assented Bayard heartily. "Fenton is doing admirably with it. Did you hear him?"

"Why yes," replied the Professor, breathing more freely. "I heard Fenton. He did well—quite well. He has not that scope of intellect which—I never considered him our *ablest* man; but his theology is perfectly satisfactory. He preached an excellent doctrinal sermon. The audience was not so large as I could have wished; but it seemed to be of a superior quality—some of your first citizens, I should say?"

"Oh, yes, our first people all attend that church. You didn't find many of *my* crowd there, I presume?"

Bayard laughed easily.

"I did not recognize it," said the Professor, "as a distinctly fishing community—from the audience; no, not from that audience."

"Not many of my drunkards, for instance, sir? Not a strong salt-fish perfume in the First Church? Nor a whiff of old New England rum anywhere?"

"The atmosphere was irreproachable," returned the Professor with a keen look.

Bayard glanced at Helen, who had been sitting quietly on the sofa beside him. Her eyes returned his merriment.

"Father!" she exclaimed, "Mr. Bayard does not recant. He is proud of it. He glories in his heresy. He is laughing at his martyrdom—and at us. I think you'd better 'let up' on him awhile."

"Let up, Helen? Let up?" complained her mother. "That is a very questionable expression. Ask your father, my dear, if it is good English. And I'm sure Mr. Bayard will be a *gentlemanly* heretic, whatever he is."

Helen laughed outright, now. Bayard joined her; and the four drew breath and found themselves at their ease.

"For my part," said Helen unexpectedly, "I should like to see Mr. Bayard's church—if he would stoop to invite us. . . I suppose," she added thoughtfully, "one reason saints don't stoop, is for fear the halo should tumble off. It must be so inconvenient! Don't you ever have a stiff neck, Mr. Bayard?"

"Why, *Helen!*" cried Mrs. Carruth in genuine horror. She hastened to atone for her daughter's rudeness to a young man who already had enough to bear. "I will come and bring Helen myself, Mr. Bayard, to hear you preach—that is, if you would like to have us."

"Pray don't!" protested Bayard. "The Professor's hair would turn black again in a single night. It won't do for you to recognize an outlaw like me, you know. Why, Fenton and I haven't met since he came here; unless at the post-office. I understand my position. Don't feel any delicacy about it. *I* don't. I can't stop for that! I am too busy."

The Professor of Theology colored a little.

"The ladies of my family are quite free to visit any of the places of worship around us," he observed with some dignity. "They are not bound by the same species of ecclesiastical etiquette"—

"We must be going, Mother," said Helen abruptly. Her cheeks were blazing; her eyes met Bayard's with a ray of indignant sympathy which went to his head like wine. He felt the light, quick motion of her breath; the folds of her summer dress—he could not have told what she wore—fell over the carpet lounge; the hem of the dress touched his boot, and just covered the patch on it from sight. He had but glanced at her before. He looked at her now; her heightened color became her richly; her hand—she wore a driving-glove—lay upon the cretonne sofa pillow; she had picked a single flower as she came up Mrs. Granite's garden walk. Bayard was amused to see that she had instinctively taken a deep purple pansy with a heart of gold.

A little embarrassed, Helen held out the pansy.

"I like them," she said. "They make faces at me."

"This one is a royal creature," said Bayard. "It has the face of a Queen."

"Mr. Bayard," asked Mrs. Carruth, with the air of starting a subject of depth and force, "do you find any time to analyze flowers?"

"So far—hardly," replied Bayard, looking Helen straight in the face.

"I used to study botany when I was a young lady—in New York," observed Mrs. Carruth placidly; "it seems to me a very wholesome and refining"—

"Papa!" cried Helen, "Pepper is eating a tomato can—No, it's a piece of—It is an apron—a gingham apron! The menu of that horse, Mr. Bayard, surpasses anything"—

"It is plainly some article belonging to the ladies of the house," said Bayard, laughing.

He had started to rescue the apron, when Jane Granite was seen to run out and wrench that portion of her wardrobe from Pepper's voracity.

"That," observed Mrs. Carruth, "is the maid, I presume?"

"It is Miss Granite, my landlady's daughter," replied Bayard with some unnecessary dignity. Poor little Jane, red in the face, and raging at the heart, stood, with the eyes of the visitors upon her, contending with

Pepper, who insisted on retaining the apron strings, and had already swallowed one halfway.

Quick to respond to the discomfort of any woman, Bayard ran down to Jane's relief.

"It blew over from the lines," said Jane. She lifted to him her sad, grateful eyes. She would have cried, if she had ventured to speak. Helen, from the window, looked down silently.

When Bayard came upstairs again, his visitors had risen to leave, in earnest. Helen avoided his eyes. He felt that hers had taken in every detail of his poor place: the iron angel on the ugly stove; the Cupid and the grapes upon the paper screen; the dreary, darned, brown carpet; the barren shades; the mosquito-net portière; the whole homeless, rude, poverty-smitten thing.

"You have a fine engraving of Guido's Saint Michael, here," observed Professor Carruth, taking out his glasses.

"And I notice—don't I see another good picture through the gauze portière?" asked Mrs. Carruth modestly.

"That is Leonardo's Christ," said the Professor promptly, at a look. "It really makes a singular, I may say a beautiful, impression behind that white stuff. I never happened to see it before with such an effect. Look, Helen! It seems like a transparency—or a cloud."

A devout expression touched Helen's face, which had grown quite grave. She did not answer, and went downstairs behind her mother, very quietly.

Jane Granite had disappeared. Pepper was engaged in a private conflict with such portions of her wardrobe as he had succeeded in swallowing; Mrs. Carruth mounted heavily into the carryall, and Helen leaped after her. Then it appeared that the Professor had forgotten his cane, and Bayard ran back for it. As he came down, he caught a glimpse of Jane Granite in the sitting-room. She was crying.

"That is my Charter Oak cane," observed the Professor anxiously; "the one with the handle made from the old ship Constitution. I wouldn't have mislaid it on any account."

"Father would rather have mislaid me," said Helen with an air of conviction. Her mother was inviting Mr. Bayard to call on them at the Flying Jib. Helen said nothing on this point. She smiled and nodded girlishly, and Pepper bore them away.

Bayard came back upstairs three steps at a time. The sitting-room door was shut, and it did not occur to him to open it. He had quite forgotten Jane. He closed his study-door softly, and went and sat down on the carpet lounge; the pansy that she had dropped was there. He looked for it, and looked at it, then laid it gently on his study-table. He took up the cretonne pillow where her hand had lain, then put it softly down.

"I must keep my head," thought the young man. He passed his hand over his too brilliant eyes, and went, with compressed lips, to his study-table.

But Jane Granite went out in the back yard, and sat down under the clothes-lines, on the salt-fish box. The chewed apron was in her hand. The clothes flapped in the rising wind above her head. She could not be seen from the house. Here she could cry in peace.

She was surprised to find, when she was seated there, that she did not want to cry. Her eyes, her throat, her lips, her head, seemed burning to ashes. Hot, hard, wicked wishes came for the first time in her gentle life to Jane. That purple-and-gold woman swam giddily between her and the summer sky.

Jane had known her at the first look. Her soul winced when she recognized the stranger of the electric car. Mr. Bayard had thought Jane did not notice that lady that April day. Jane had by heart every line and tint and detail of her, from the gold dagger on her bonnet to the dark purple cloth gaiter of her boots; from her pleased brown eyes, with the well-bred motion of their lids, to the pretty gestures that she made with her narrow, gloved hand. Jane looked at her own wash-day dress and parboiled fingers. The indefinable, undeniable fact of the stranger's personal elegance crushed the girl with the sense of helpless bitterness which only women who have been poor and gone shabby can understand. The language of dress, which is to the half-educated the symbol of superiority, conveyed to Jane, in advance of any finer or truer vocabulary, the full force of the situation.

"She is different," thought Jane.

These three words said it all. Jane dropped her face in her soaked and wrinkled fingers. The damp clothes flapped persistently about her neat, brown head, as if trying to arouse her with the useless diversion of things that one is quite used to. Jane thought of Ben Trawl, it is true, but without any distinct sense of disloyalty or remorse. She experienced the ancient and always inexplicable emotion not peculiar to Jane: she might have lived on in relative content, not in the least disturbed by any consciousness of her own ties, as long as the calm eyes she worshiped

ELIZABETH STUART PHELPS

reflected the image of no other woman. Now something in Jane's heart seemed to snap and let lava through.

Oh, purple and gold, gall and wormwood, beauty and daintiness, heart-ache and fear! Had the Queen come to the palace of Kubla Khan? Let Alph, the sacred river, run! Who was she, Jane Granite, that she should stem the sweeping current?

". . . Crying *again*? This is a nice way to greet a fellar," said roughly a sudden voice in Jane's dulled ear.

Ben Trawl lifted the damp clothes, strode through between the poles, and stood beside his promised wife. His face was ominously dark.

XIV

It is not so hard to endure suffering as to resist ease. The passion for martyrdom sweeps everything before it, as long as it is challenged by no stronger force. Emanuel Bayard had lived for a year upon the elixir of a spiritual exaltation such as has carried men to a glowing death, or through a tortured life without a throb of weakness. He had yet to adjust his nature to the antidote of common human comfort.

Like most of the subtler experiences of life, this came so naturally that, at first, he scarcely knew it by sight or name.

It was not a noteworthy matter to show the courtesies of civilized life to the family of his old Professor. Bayard reminded himself of this as he walked down the Point.

It was quite a week before he found leisure to attend to this simple, social obligation. His duties in Angel Alley had been many and laborious; it did not occur to him to shorten a service or an entertainment; to omit a visit to the wharves when the crews came in, or to put by the emergency of a drunkard's wife to a more convenient season because he had in view that which had grown so rare to the young man, now—the experience of a personal luxury. Like a much older and more ascetic man than he was, he counted the beads on his rosary of labors conscientiously through. Then he hurried to her.

Now, to women of leisure nothing is so incomprehensible as the preoccupation of a seriously busy man. Bayard had not counted upon this feminine fact: indeed, he lived in a world where feminine whim was an element as much outside his calculation as the spring fashions of the planet Uranus. He was quite at a loss when Miss Carruth received him distantly.

The Flying Jib was, as to its exterior, an ugly little cottage run out on the neck of the jutting reef that formed the chief attraction of the Mainsail Hotel. The interior of the Flying Jib varied from a dreary lodge to a summer home, according to the nature of the occupants. It seemed to Bayard that season absurdly charming. He had lived so long out of his natural world, that the photographs and rugs, the draperies, the flowers, the embroidery, the work-baskets, the bric-a-brac, the mere presence of taste and of ladies, appeared to him at first essential luxury. He looked about him with a sigh of delight, while Mrs. Carruth went to call her daughter, who had gone over to the fish-house study with the

ELIZABETH STUART PHELPS

Professor, and who could be seen idling along home over the meadow, a stately figure in a pale, yellow summer dress, with a shade hat, and pansies on it.

As we say, that young lady at first received Bayard coolly. She sauntered into the little parlor with her hands full of sweet-briar, nodded to him politely, and excused herself at once to arrange her flowers. This took her some time. Mrs. Carruth entertained him placidly. Helen's eyes saw but did not seem to see the slightest motion of his nervous hand, each tone of expression that ran over his sensitive face. He had looked so eager and happy when she came; almost boyishly thirsting for that little pleasure! She had that terrible inability to understand the facts of his life or feeling which is responsible for most of the friction between two half-attracted or half-separating human beings. But when she saw the light die from his eyes, when she saw that hurt look which she knew quite well, settle about the lower part of his face, Helen was ashamed of herself. Mrs. Carruth was mildly introducing the subject of mosquito bars; theirs, she said, were all on the second story; the supply didn't go round, and the Professor objected to them; so the hornets—

"Mother," said Helen, "I wonder if Mr. Bayard wouldn't like to have us show him the clam study?"

"Your father said he should be at work on the 'State of the Unforgiven after Death,'" replied Mrs. Carruth. "I don't know that we ought to disturb him; do you think we ought, Helen?"

"He was whittling a piece of mahogany for the head of a cane when I left him," said Helen irreverently; "he stole it out of the cabin of that old wreck in the inner harbor. Do you think a Professor of Theology could be forgiven after death for sneak-thieving, Mr. Bayard?"

She abandoned the idea of visiting the clam study, however, and seated herself with frank graciousness by their visitor. Mrs. Carruth having strolled away presently to keep some elderly tryst among the piazza ladies of the hotel, the young people were left alone.

They sat for a moment in sudden, rather awkward silence. Helen looked like a tall June lily, in her summer gown; she had taken her hat off; her hair was a little tumbled and curly; the wind blew in strong from the sea, tossing the lace curtains of the Flying Jib like sails on a toy boat. The scent of the sweet-briar was delicately defined in the room. Bayard looked at her without any attempt to speak. She answered his silent question by saying, abruptly:—

"You know you'll *have* to forgive me, whether you want to, or not."

"Forgive you?"

"Why, for being vexed. I *was* a little, at first. But I needn't have been such a schoolgirl as to show it."

"If you would be so kind as to tell me what I can possibly have done to—deserve your displeasure—" began Bayard helplessly.

"If a man doesn't understand without being told, I've noticed he *can't* understand when he is told. . . Why didn't you wait till next fall before you came to see us, Mr. Bayard?"

"Oh!" said Bayard. His happy look came back to his tired face, as if a magic lantern had shifted a beautiful slide. "Is *that* it?"

He laughed delightedly. "Why, I suppose I must have seemed rude—neglectful, at any rate. But I've noticed that if a woman doesn't understand without being told, she makes up for it by her readiness of comprehension when she is told."

"What a nice, red coal!" smiled Helen. "The top of my head feels quite warm. Dear me! Isn't there a spot burned bald?"

She felt anxiously of her pretty hair.

"Come over and see my work," said Bayard, "and you'll never ask me again why I didn't do anything I—would so much rather do."

"I never asked you before!" flashed Helen.

"You did me an honor that I shall remember," said Bayard gravely.

"Oh, please don't! Pray forget it as soon as you can," cried Helen, with red cheeks.

"You can't know, you see you *can't* know, how a man situated as I am prizes the signs of the simplest human friendship that is sincere and womanly."

So said Bayard quietly. Helen drew a little quick breath. She seemed reconciled now, to herself, and to him. They began to talk at once, quite fast and freely. Afterwards he tried to remember what it had all been about, but he found it not easy; the evening passed on wings; he felt the atmosphere of this little pleasure with a delight impossible to be understood by a man who had not known and graced society and left it. Now and then he spoke of his work, but Helen did not exhibit a marked interest in the subject.

Bayard drew the modest inference that he had obtruded his own affairs with the obtuseness common to missionaries and other zealots; he roused himself to disused conversation, and to the forgotten topics of the world. It did not occur to him that this was precisely what she intended. The young lady drew him out, and drew him on. They chatted about Cesarea and Beacon Street, about Art, Clubs, Magazine literature, and the Symphony Concerts, like the ordinary social human being.

"You see I have been out of it so long!" pleaded Bayard.

"Not yet a year," corrected Helen.

"It seems to me twenty," he mused.

"You don't go to see your uncle, yet?"

"I met him once or twice down town. I have not been home, yet. But that would make no difference. I have no leisure for—all these little things."

He said the words with such an utter absence of affectation that it was impossible either to smile or to take offence at them. Helen regarded him gravely.

"There were two or three superb concerts this winter. I thought of you. I wished you had come in"—

"Did you take that trouble?" he asked eagerly.

"I don't think I ever heard Schubert played better in my life," she went on, without noticing the interruption. "Schoeffelowski does do The Serenade divinely."

"I used to care for that more than for any other music in the world, I think," he answered slowly.

"I play poorly," said Helen, "and I sing worse, and the piano is rented of a Windover schoolgirl. But I have got some of his renderings by heart—if you would care for it."

"It is plain," replied Bayard, flushing, "that I no longer move in good society. It did not even occur to me to ask you. I should enjoy it—it would rest me more than anything I can think of. Not that that matters, of course—but I should be more grateful than it is possible for you to understand."

Helen went to the piano without ado, and began to sing the great serenade. She played with feeling, and had a sweet, not a strong voice; it had the usual amateur culture, no more, but it had a quality not so usual. She sang with a certain sumptuous delicacy (if the words may be conjoined) by which Bayard found himself unexpectedly moved. He sat with his hand over his eyes, and she sang quite through.

"Komm beglücke mich?
Komm beglücke mich!"

Her voice sank, and ceased. What tenderness! What strength! What vigor and hope and joy, and—forbid the thought!—what power of loving, the woman had!

"Some lucky fellow will know, some day," thought the devotee. Aloud, he said nothing at all. Helen's hands lay on the keys; she, too, sat silent. It was beginning to grow dark in the cottage parlor. The long, lace curtain blew straight in, and towards her; as it dropped, it fell about her head and shoulders, and caught there; it hung like a veil; in the dim light it looked like—

She started to her feet and tossed it away.

"Oh!" he breathed, "why not let it stay? Just for a minute! It did nobody any harm."

"I am not so sure of that," thought Helen. But what she said, was,—

"I will light the candles."

He sprang to help her; the sleeve of her muslin dress fell away from her arm as she lifted the little flicker of the match to the tall brass candlestick on the mantel. He took the match from her, and touched the candle. In the dusk they looked at each other with a kind of fear. Bayard was very pale.

Helen had her rich, warm look. She appeared taller than usual, and seemed to stand more steadily on her feet than other women.

"Do you want me to thank you?" asked Bayard in a low voice.

"No," said Helen.

"I must go," he said abruptly.

"Mother will be back," observed Helen, not at her ease. "And Father will be getting on with the Unforgiven, and come home any minute."

"Very well," replied Bayard, seating himself.

"Not that I would keep you!" suggested Helen suddenly.

He smiled a little sadly, and this time unexpectedly rose again.

"I don't expect you to understand, of course. But I really ought to go. And I am going."

"Very well," said Helen stiffly, in her turn.

"I have a—something to write, you see," explained Bayard.

"You don't call it a sermon any more, do you? Heresy writes a 'something.' How delicious! Do go and write it, by all means. I hope the Unforgiven will appreciate it."

"You are not a dull woman," observed Bayard uncomfortably. "You don't for an instant suppose I *want* to go?"

Helen raised her thick, white eyelids slowly; a narrow, guarded light shone underneath them. She only answered that she supposed nothing about it.

"If I stay," suggested Bayard, with a wavering look, "will you sing The Serenade to me—all over again?"

"Not one bar of it!" replied Helen promptly.

"You are the wiser of us two," said Bayard after a pause.

The tide was coming in, and gained upon the reef just outside the cottage windows, with a soft, inexorable sound.

"I am not a free man," he added.

"Return to your chains and your cell," suggested Helen. "It is—as you say—the better way."

"I said nothing of the kind! Pardon me."

"Didn't you? It does not signify. It doesn't often signify what people *say*—do you think?"

"Are you coming to see my people—the work? You said you would, you know. Shall I call and take you, some day?"

"Do you think it matters—to the drunkards?"

"Oh, well," said Bayard, looking disappointed, "never mind."

"But I do mind," returned Helen, in her full, boylike voice. "I want to come. And I'm coming. I had rather come, though, than be taken. I'll turn up some day in the anxious seat when you don't expect me. I'll wear a veil, and an old poke bonnet—yes, and a blanket shawl—and confess. I defy you to find me out!"

"Miss Carruth," said the young preacher with imperiousness, "my work is not a parlor charade."

Helen looked at him. Defiance and deference battled in her brown eyes; for that instant, possibly, she could have hated or loved him with equal ease; she felt his spiritual superiority to herself as something midway between an antagonism and an attraction, but exasperating whichever way she looked at it. She struggled with herself, but made no reply.

"If I am honored with your presence," continued Bayard, still with some decision of manner, "I shall count upon your sympathy. . . God knows I need it!" he added in a different tone.

"And you shall have it," said Helen softly.

It was too dark to see the melting of her face; but he knew it was there. They stood on the piazza of the cottage in the strong, salt wind. Her muslin dress blew back. The dim light of the candle within scarcely defined her figure. They seemed to stand like creatures of the dusk, uncertain of each other or of themselves. He held out his hand; she placed her own within it cordially. How warm and womanly, how strong and fine a touch she had! He bade her good-night, and hurried away.

That "something" which is to supersede the sermon was not written that night. Bayard found himself unable to work. He sat doggedly at his desk for an hour, then gave it up, put out his light, and seized his hat again. He went down to the beach and skirted the shore, taking the spray in his face. His brain was on fire; not with intellectual labor. His heart throbbed; not with anxiety for the fishing population. He reached a reef whence he could see the Mainsail Hotel, and there sat down to collect himself. The cottage was lighted now; the parlor windows glimmered softly; the long, lace curtains were blowing in and out. Shadows of figures passed and repassed. The Professor had settled the state of the Unforgiven, and had come back from the clam study; he paced to and fro across the parlor of the Flying Jib; a graceful figure clung to his theologic arm, and kept step with him as he strode.

Presently she came to the low window, and pushed back the lace curtain, which had blown in, half across the little parlor. She lifted her arms, and shut the window.

The waves beat the feet of the cliff monotonously; like the bars of a rude, large music which no man had been able to read. Bayard listened to them with his head thrown back on the hard rock, and his hat over his eyes. Even the gaze of the stars seemed intrusive, curious, one might say impertinent, to him. He desired the shell of the mollusk that burrowed in the cleft of the cliff.

The tide was rising steadily. The harbor wore its full look; it seemed about to overflow, like a surcharged heart. The waves rose on; they took definite rhythm. All the oldest, sweetest meanings of music— the maddest and the tenderest cries of human longing—were in the strain:—

> *"Komm beglücke mich?*
> *Beglücke mich!"*

Those mighty lovers, the sea and the shore, urged and answered, resisted and yielded, protested and pleaded, retreated and met, loved and clasped, and slept. When the tide came to the full, the wind went down.

ELIZABETH STUART PHELPS

XV

Dear Mr. Bayard,

I have been thinking since I saw you. I have health,
and a summer. What can I do to help your work? I haven't a
particle of experience, and not much enthusiasm. But I
am ready to try, if you are willing to try me. I don't think
I'm adapted to drunkards. I don't know which of us would
be more scared. He would probably run for the nearest
grogshop to get rid of me. Aren't there some old ladies who
bother you to death, whom you could turn over to me?

Yours sincerely,
Helen Carruth

This characteristic note, the first that he had ever received from her,
reached Bayard by mail, a few days after his call at the cottage of the
Flying Jib.

He sat down and wrote at once:—

My Dear Miss Carruth,

There is an old lady. She doesn't bother me at all, but I am
at my wits' end with her. She runs away from the institution
where she belongs, and there's no other place for her. At
present she is inflicting herself on Mrs. Job Slip, No. 143
Thoroughfare Street, opposite the head of Angel Alley. Her
mind is thought to be slightly disordered by the loss of her son,
drowned last winter in the wreck of the Clara Em. Mrs. Slip
will explain the circumstances to you more fully. Inquire for
Johnny's mother. If the old woman ever had any other name,
people have forgotten it, now. I write in great haste and stress
of care. It will not be necessary to traverse Angel Alley to
reach this address, which is quite in the heart of the town, and
perfectly safe and suitable for you. I thank you very much.

Yours sincerely,
Emanuel Bayard

Helen frowned a little when she read this. No Bishop of a diocese,
dictating the career of a deaconess, no village rector, guiding some

anxious and aimless visiting young lady through the mild dissipations of parish benevolence, could have returned a more business-like, calm, even curt, reply.

The position of a man who may not love a woman and must not invite her to marry him—or, to put it a little differently, who must not love and cannot marry—is one which it seems to be asking too much of women to understand. At all events they seldom or never do. The withdrawals, the feints, the veils and chills and silences, by which a woman in a similar position protects herself, may be as transparent as golden mist to him whom she evades; but the sturdy retreat of a masculine conscience from a too tender or too tempting situation is as opaque as a gravestone to the feminine perception.

Accustomed to be eagerly wooed, Helen did not know what to make of this devotee who did not urge himself even upon her friendship. She had never given any man that treasure before. Like all high-minded women who have not spent themselves in experiments of the sensibilities, Helen regarded her own friendship as valuable. She would have preferred him to show, at least, that he appreciated his privilege. She would have liked him to make friendship as devotedly as those other men had made love to her.

His reserve, his distance, his apparent moodiness, and undoubted ability to live without seeing her except when he got ready to do so, gave her a perplexed trouble more important than pique.

Without ado or delay, she took the next electric car for Mrs. Slip's.

Bayard received that afternoon, by the familiar hand of Joey Slip, this brief rejoinder:—

Dear Mr. Bayard,

This experienced boy seems to be on intimate terms with you, and offers to take my report, which stands thus: Johnny's mother is in the Widows' Home. Shall I write you details?

Truly yours,
H. C.

"Run on down to the Mainsail Hotel, Joey," said the minister, writing rapidly. "Find the lady—there will be a good many ladies—and hand her this."

"Pooh!" retorted this nautical child with a superior air, "Vat ain't nuffin! She's good-lookin' nuff to find off Zheorges in a fog-bank."

ELIZABETH STUART PHELPS

Thus ran the note:—

When Bayard reached her mother's piazza the next evening, Helen was in the middle of the harbor.

"My daughter is considered a good oarswoman, I believe," said the Professor with a troubled look. "I know nothing about these matters myself. I confess I wish I did. I have not felt easy about her; she has propelled the craft so far into the stream. I am delighted to see you, Mr. Bayard! I will put another boat at your service—that is—I suppose you understand the use of oars?"

"Better than I do Verbal Inspiration, Professor!" replied Bayard, laughing. "She is rather far out, and the tide has turned."

He ran down the pier, and leaped into the first boat that he could secure. It happened to be a dory.

"Can you overtake her?" asked her father with a keen look.

"I can try," replied the young man, smiling.

The Professor heaved a sigh, whether of relief or of anxiety it would not be easy to say, and stood upon the pier watching Bayard's fine stroke. Mrs. Carruth came clucking anxiously down, and put her hand upon her husband's arm. Bayard looked at the two elderly people with a strange affectionateness which he did not analyze; feeling, but not acknowledging, a sudden heart-ache for ties which he had never known.

The sun was sinking, and the harbor was a sea of fire. A sea of glass it was not, for there was some wind and more tide. Really, she should not have ventured out so far. He looked over his shoulder as he gained upon her. She had not seen him, and was drifting out. Her oars lay crossed upon her lap. Her eyes were on the sky, which flung out gold and violet, crimson and pale green flame, in bars like the colors of a mighty banner. The harbor took the magnificence, and lifted it upon the hands of the short, uneasy waves.

The two little boats, the pursuing and the pursued, floated in one of those rare and unreal splendors which make this world, for the moment, seem a glorious, painless star, and the chance to live in it an ecstasy.

By the island, half a mile back, perhaps, Jane Granite in a dory rowed by the younger Trawl, silently watched the minister moving with strong strokes across the blazing harbor. Drifting out, with beautiful pose and crossed hands, was the absorbed, unconscious woman whom his racing oars chased down.

Between the glory of the water and the glory of the sky, he gained upon her, overtook her, headed her off, and brought up with a spurt beside her. Jane saw that the minister laid his hand imperiously upon the gunwale of the lady's boat; and, it seemed, without waiting for her consent, or even lingering to ask for it, he crept into the cockle-shell, and fastened the painter of his dory to the stern. Now, between the color of the sky and the color of the sea, the two were seen to float for a melting moment—

"Where Alph, the sacred river, ran."

"Ben," said Jane, "let us put about, will you? I'm a little chilly."

"Ben?" said Jane again, as they rowed under the dark shadow of the island. "Ben?" with a little loyal effort to make conversation such as lovers know, "did you ever read a poem called Kubla Khan?"

"I hain't had time to read sence I left the grammar school," said Ben. "What's up with you, anyhow?" he added, after a moment's sullen reflection.

He looked darkly over Jane's head towards the harbor's mouth. At that moment Bayard was tying the painter of the dory to the stern of the shell. Jane did not look back. A slight grayness settled about her mouth; she had the protruding mouth and evident cheek-bones of the consumptive woman of the coast.

"D—— him!" said Ben Trawl.

BAYARD HAD INDEED CROSSED INTO Helen's boat without so much as saying, By your leave. Her eyes had a dangerous expression, to which he paid no sort of attention.

"Didn't you know better than to take this shell—so far—with the tide setting out?" he demanded. "Give me those oars!"

"I understand how to manage a boat," replied the young lady coldly. She did not move.

"Give me those oars!" thundered Bayard.

She looked at him, and gave them.

"Don't try to move," he said in a softer voice. "It's the easiest thing in the world to upset these toys. If you had taken a respectable ocean dory—I can't see why they don't provide them at the floats," he complained, with the nervousness of an uneasy man. "I can manage perfectly where I am. Sit still, Miss Carruth!"

She did not look at him this time, but she sat still. He put about, and rowed steadily. For a few moments they did not exchange a word. Helen had an offended expression. She trailed her hand in the water with something like petulance. Bayard did not watch her.

Captain Hap crossed their course, rowing home in an old green dory full of small bait—pollock and tinkers. He eyed Bayard's Harvard stroke with surprised admiration. He had seldom seen a person row like that. But he was too old a sailor to say so. As the minister swerved dexterously to starboard to free the painter of his tender from collision with the fisherman, Captain Hap gave utterance to but two words. These were:—

"Short chops!"

"Quite a sea, yes!" called Bayard cheerily.

Captain Hap scanned the keel-boat, the passenger, and the dory in tow, with discrimination.

"Lady shipwrecked?" he yelled, after some reflection.

"No, sir," answered Helen, smiling in spite of herself; "captured by pirates."

"Teach ye bet-ter!" howled Captain Hap. "Hadn't oughter set out in short cho-ops! Hadn't oughter set out in a craft like that nohow! They palm off them eggshells on boarders for bo-o-oats!"

Helen laughed outright; her eyes met Bayard's merrily, and, if he had dared to think so, rather humbly.

"I was very angry with you," she said.

"I can't help that," replied Bayard. "Your father and mother were very anxious about you."

"Really?"

"Naturally. I was a chartered pirate, at any rate."

"But I was in no sort of danger, you know. You've made a great fuss over nothing."

"Take these oars," observed Bayard. "Just let me see you row back to the float."

Helen took the oars, and pulled a few strokes strongly enough. The veins stood out on her soft forehead, and her breath came hard.

"I had no idea the tide was so strong to-night. The wind seems to be the wrong way, too," she panted.

"It was blowing you straight out to sea," observed Bayard quietly.

"Shall I take the oars?" he added.

She pulled on doggedly for a few moments. Suddenly she flung them down.

"Why, we are not making any headway at all! We are twisting about, and—going out again."

"Certainly."

"It is that heavy dory! You can't expect me to row two boats at once."

"The dory does make some difference. But very little. See—she doesn't draw a teaspoonful of water. Shall I take the oars?"

"If you please," said Helen meekly.

She gave them up without looking at him, and she was a trifle pale from her exertion. Her hat was off, and the wind made rich havoc of her pretty hair. She was splashed with spray, and her boating-dress was quite wet. Bayard watched her. The sun dropped, and the color on the harbor began to fade.

"I suppose you came for the report?" she asked suddenly. "I stayed in all the afternoon. I couldn't be expected to wait indefinitely, you know!"

"I could not possibly set the hour. I am much overworked. I should beg your pardon," said Bayard in his gentlest way.

"You *are* overworked," answered Helen, in her candid voice. "And I am an idle, useless woman. It wouldn't have hurt me a bit to wait your leisure. But I'm not— . . . you see. . . I'm not used to it."

"I must remind you again, that I no longer move in good society," said Bayard, looking straight at her. "You must extend to me as much tolerance as you do to other working men."

"Yes," returned Helen; "we always wait a week for a carpenter, and ten days for the plumbers. Anyhow, Johnny's mother is in the Widows' Home. She's as snug as a clam in a shell. She says she won't run away again till I've been to see her."

"How in the world did you manage?" asked Bayard admiringly.

"Oh, I don't just know," replied Helen, clasping her hands behind her head; "I made myself lovely, that's all."

"That might be enough, I should fancy," ventured the young man under his breath.

"I took her shopping," said Helen.

"Took her *shopping*!"

ELIZABETH STUART PHELPS

"Why, yes. She wanted to buy some mourning. She said Johnny's father had been dead so long, her black was all worn out. She wanted fresh crape. So I took her round the stores, and got her some."

"Bought her crape?"

"Yes. I got her a crape veil—oh, and a bonnet. She's the happiest mourner you ever saw. She went back to the Widows' Home like a spring lamb. She wore a chocolate calico dress with red spots on it, and this crape veil. You can't think how she looked! But she's perfectly contented. She'll stay awhile now. She says they wouldn't give her any mourning at the Home. She said that was all she had 'agin' 'em.'"

"Oh, these widows!" groaned Bayard. "We got two starving women in there by the hardest work, last spring, and one left in a week. She said it was too lonesome; she wanted to live with folks. The other one said it 'depressed' her. A Windover widow is a problem in sociology."

"Johnny's mother is the other kind of woman; I can see that," replied Helen. "She sits by herself, and puts her face in her hands. She doesn't even cry. But she takes it out in crape. You can't think how happy she is in that veil."

"Your political economy is horrible," laughed Bayard, "but your heart is as warm as"—

"I saw Mari and Joey," interrupted Helen, "and Job Slip. I stayed two hours. Job was as sober as you are. They invited me to dinner. I suppose they were thankful to be rid of that poor old lady."

"Did you stay?"

"Of course I did. We had pork gravy, and potatoes—oh, and fried cunners. I sat beside Joey. I believe that child is as old as She. He's a reincarnation of some drowned ancestor who went fishing ages ago, and never came back. Did you ever notice his resemblance to a mackerel?"

"I hadn't thought of it in that light. I see now what it was. It takes you to discover it!"

"Johnny's mother looks like a cod, poor thing!" continued Helen. "I don't wonder. I should think she would. I'm sure I should in her place."

"You are incorrigible!" said Bayard, laughing in spite of himself. "And yet—you've done a better morning's work than anybody in Windover has done here for a month!"

"I'm going to take tea with Johnny's mother next week," observed Helen—"at the Widows' Home, you know. But I've promised to take Joey to the circus first."

"You are perfectly refreshing!" sighed Bayard delightedly.

"Mr. Bayard," said Helen, with a change of manner as marked yet as subtle as the motion of the wave that fell to make way for the next, against the bobbing bows of the empty dory, "I had a long talk with Job Slip."

"You say you found him sober?"

"As sober as a Cesarea trustee. But the way that man feels to you is something you haven't an idea of. I thought of that verse, you know, about love 'passing the love of women.' It is infatuation. It is worship. It is enough to choke you. Why, I cried when I heard him talk! And I don't cry, you know, very often. And I'm not ashamed to own it, either. It made me feel ashamed to be alive—in such a world—why, Mr. Bayard!" Helen unclasped her hands from the back of her head, and thrust them out towards him, as if they were an argument.

"Why, I thought this earth was a pleasant place! I thought life was a delightful thing! . . . If the rest of it is like this town—Windover is a world of woe, and you are one of the sons of God to these unhappy people!"

She said this solemnly, more solemnly than he had ever heard her say anything before. He laid down his oars, and took off his hat. He could not answer, and he did not try.

She saw how much moved he was, and she made a little gesture, as if she tossed something that weighed heavily, away.

"You see," she interposed, "I've never done this kind of thing. I'm not a good Professor's daughter. I didn't like it. I went through an attack of the missionary spirit when I was fifteen, and had a Sunday-school class—ten big boys; all red, and eight of them freckled. We were naming classes one Sunday, and my boys whistled 'Yankee Doodle' when the superintendent prayed, and then asked if they might be called the lilies of the valley. I told them they weren't fit to be called red sorrel. So after that I gave them up. I've never tried it since. I'm of no more use in the world—in this *awful* world—than the artificial pansies on my hat."

Helen picked up her straw hat from the bottom of the boat, and tied it on her head, with a little sound that was neither a laugh nor a sigh.

It was growing dark, fast. They were nearly at the float, now. Bayard laid down his oars. The headlights were leaping out all over the harbor. The wind had gone down with the sun. Boats crept in like tired people, through the sudden calm, to anchor for the night. The evening steamer came in from the city, and the long waves of her wake rolled upon the beach, and tossed the little boats. The sea drew a few long, deep breaths.

ELIZABETH STUART PHELPS

"The trouble with me, you see," said Helen, "is just what I told you. I am not spiritual."

"You are something better—you are altogether womanly!" said the young preacher quickly.

He seized his oars, and rowed in, as if they were shipwrecked. The old clam-digger was hauling his lobster-pots straight across their course. As Bayard veered to avoid him, he could be heard singing:—

"The woman's ashore,
The child's at the door,
The man's at the wheel.

"Storm on the track,
Fog at the back,
Death at the keel.

"You, mate, or me—
Which shall it be?"—

The old clam-digger stopped, when he saw the lady in the boat. It was now quite dark. Bayard and Helen were the last people to land at the float. He gave her his hand in silence. She stood by, while he helped the keeper of the float up with the two boats. He coughed a little as he did so, and she said, rather sharply:—

"Tim! you should keep two men here, to do that work."

Tim apologized, grumbling, and the two walked on up the pier together; still alone. At the door of the cottage, she asked him, rather timidly, if he would come in. But he excused himself, and hurried away.

When he found himself far from the hotel, and well on the way to his lodgings, Bayard drew the long breath of a man who is escaping danger. He experienced a kind of ecstatic terror. He thought of her—he thought of her till he could think no more, but fell into an ocean of feeling, tossing and deep. It seemed to have no soundings. He drowned himself in it with a perilous delight.

What would a lonely fate be, if a woman capable of understanding the highest, and serving it, capacious for tenderness, and yielding it, a woman warm, human, sweet, and as true as one's belief in her, should pour the precious current of her love into a long life's work? Why, a man would be a god! He would climb the inaccessible. He would achieve the undreamed and the unknown. He would not know where consecration ended, and where heaven began.

"He would be a freer man than I am," thought Bayard, as he passed, between the larkspurs and the feverfew, up Mrs. Granite's garden.

Mrs. Granite met him at the door; she held a kerosene lamp high in one hand; with the other she handed to him a soiled and crumpled bit of paper.

"A boy left it here, sir, not ten minutes ago, and he said you was to read it as soon as you came home. I don't know the boy. I never saw him before, but it seemed to be something quite partikkelar."

Bayard held the message to the lamp and read:—

A pore man in distres would take it kindly of the minester to mete him as sune as possibel to-nite to Ragged Rock. i am a miserbul Drunkhard and i want to Knock Off. i heer when folks talk with you they stop Drinkin. i wish youde talk to me so I would stop

Yours
JACK HADDOCK

XVI

B ayard re-read this message thoughtfully. He could hardly have told why it perplexed him. Up and down the shores and streets of Windover no cry of misery or of guilt had ever yet lifted itself to him in vain. Such appeals were common enough. Often it would happen that a stranger would stop him in the street, and use much the same naïve language: "I hear when you talk to folks they stop drinking. I wish you'd talk to me." Contrary to his custom in such matters, he showed this slip of paper to Mrs. Granite.

"Mr. Bayard, sir," she said, with that prompt feminine fear which sometimes takes the place of reliable good sense, "don't you go a step!"

Bayard did not reply. He turned away musing, and paced up and down between the larkspurs. True, the place was lonely, and the hour late. But the vagaries of disgraced men are many, and nothing was more possible than that some fisherman, not wholly sober, and not half drunk, should take it into his befuddled brain that an interview with the minister located at a safe distance from nagging wife, crying child, or jeering messmate, or, let us say, far removed from the jaws of Trawl's door, should work the magic or the miracle for which the morally defective are always waiting.

"I see no reason why I should not comply with this request," he said decidedly.

"Mr. Bayard, sir," urged Mrs. Granite, "it's a thing I don't like to be her who tells you, but it's time somebody did. There's them in this town wouldn't stop at nothing, they have that feeling to you."

"To *me*?" cried Bayard, opening his hazel eyes as wide as a child's.

"Rum done it," stammered Mrs. Granite, instinctively using the three familiar words which most concisely covered the ground. "It's your temperance principles. They ain't pop'lar. They affect your standing in this community."

This was the accepted phrase in Windover for all such cases made and provided. It was understood to contain the acme of personal peril or disgrace. To talk to a man about "your standing in this community" was equivalent to an insult or a scandal. Poor Mrs. Granite, an affectionate and helpless parrot, reëchoed this terrible language, and trembled. She felt as if she had said to the minister, Your social ruin is complete for all time, throughout the civilized world.

"Not that it makes any difference to *us*," sobbed Mrs. Granite; "we set just as much by you. But your standing is affected in this community. There's them that hates you, sir, more shame to 'em, more'n the Old Boy himself. Mr. Bayard, Mr. Bayard, don't you go to Ragged Rock alone, sir, this time o' night to meet no tom-fool of a drunkard anxious about his soul. He don't own such a thing to his name! All he's got is a rum-soaked sponge, he's mopped up whiskey with all his born days!"

"Your drinks (if not your metaphors) are getting a little mixed, dear Mrs. Granite," laughed Bayard.

"*Sir?*" said Mrs. Granite.

"But still I must say, there is some sense in your view of the case— Ah, here's Jane; and Ben with her. We'll put the case to—No. I have it. Mrs. Granite, to please you, I will take Ben Trawl along with me. Will that set you at rest?—Here, Trawl. Just read this message, will you? Something about it looks a little queer, and Mrs. Granite is so kind as to worry about me. What do you make of it?"

"Oh, you've got home so soon, have you?" said Trawl rather sullenly.

In the evening his eyebrows met more heavily than ever across his forehead; they looked as if they had been corked for some ugly masquerade. He glanced from under them, coldly, at the minister; read the note, and was about to tear it into strips.

"I'll take it, thank you," said Bayard quietly, holding out his hand.

"Mr. Bayard," said Jane, who had not spoken before, "I hope you will pay no attention to this message."

She spoke in a voice so low as to be almost inarticulate.

"Oh, I'll go with him, if he's afraid," said Trawl, with that accent which falls just so far short of a sneer that a man may not decently notice it.

"I incline to think it is wise to take a witness to this adventure," replied Bayard serenely. "But I need not trouble you, Mr. Trawl. Pray don't exert yourself to oblige me."

"It's no exertion," said Ben, with a change of tone. "Come along!"

He strode out into the street and Bayard, after a moment's hesitation, did the same, shutting the garden gate behind him. Jane Granite opened it, and followed them for a little way; she seemed perplexed and distressed; she did not speak, but trotted silently, like a dog, in the dark.

"Go back!" said Trawl, stopping short. Jane slunk against a fence, and stopped.

"Go back, I say!" cried Trawl.

"It is natural that she should want to come. She feels anxious about you," observed Bayard kindly.

"Go back to your mother, and stay there!" commanded Trawl, stamping his foot.

Jane turned and obeyed, and vanished. The two men walked on in silence. They came quickly through the village and down the Point, turning thence to cross the downs that raised their round shoulders, an irregular gray outline against the sky. Bayard glanced back. It looked black and desolate enough ahead of him. Below and behind him the life of the summer-seekers stirred softly, like the figures in a gay game, or old-fashioned walking-dance. The hotels blazed cheerfully; the piazzas were full and merry; in the parlors people were playing and singing. He could not see the lights of the Flying Jib from where he stood; this disappointed him, and he walked on. The music from the Mainsail piano followed him. There was a parlor concert—a woman's voice—a soprano solo—ah! The great serenade!

"Komm, beglücke mich!"

The strain seemed to chase him, like a cry, like an entreaty, almost like a sob. His heart leaped, as if soft arms had been thrown around him. He stopped and listened, till the song had ceased.

"That is good music," he said aloud, not knowing what he said, but oppressed by the dogged silence which his escort maintained.

"Good enough," said Ben roughly. The two walked on, and neither said anything more. It was now quite dark and still around them. The rough, broken surface of the rocky downs made traveling difficult; but both men were familiar with the way, and lost no time upon it. The sky was cloudy, and the sea was dark. The ebbing tide met the deserted beach with a sigh. The headlights in the harbor looked far off, and of the town not a glimmer could be seen. Ben strode on in sullen silence. Bayard watched him with some discomfort, but nothing like a sensation of fear had yet reached his nerves.

"This fellow chose a lonely place for a pastoral visit," he observed at length, as they approached the little beach made memorable by the wreck of the Clara Em.

"Wanted to stump you," said Ben, with an unpleasant laugh. "Wanted to dare you, you know—to see if you'd show game. It's a way they have, these toughs who meddle with parsons. They like to make out a big story, and tell it round the saloons. Probably the whole thing's a put-up job."

"That is more than possible, of course. But I'd rather investigate three put-up jobs than neglect one real need of one miserable man. That is my business, you see, Ben. Yours is to ruin people. Mine is to save them. We each attend to our own affairs, that's all."

"D—— you!" cried Ben, suddenly facing about. "That's just it! You don't attend to your own affairs! You meddle with mine, and that's what's the matter! I'll teach you to mind your own business!"

Before Bayard could cry out or move, he felt the other's hands at his throat.

XVII

Bayard stood so still—with the composure of a man not without athletic training, determined to waste no strength in useless struggle—that Trawl instinctively loosened his clutch. Was the minister strangling? This was not Ben's immediate purpose. His fingers relaxed.

"Ah," said Bayard quietly, "so you are Jack Haddock."

"I wrote that note. You might have known it if you hadn't been a—fool."

"I might have known it—yes; I see. But I took you for a decent fellow. I couldn't be expected to suspect you were—what you are. Well, Mr. Trawl, perhaps you will explain your business with me in some less uncomfortable manner."

He shook Ben off with a strong thrust, and folded his arms.

"Come," he said. "Out with it!"

"My game's up," replied Ben between his teeth. "I can't do what I set out to, now. There's too many witnesses in the case."

"You meant to push me off Ragged Rock, perhaps?" asked Bayard quietly. "I hadn't thought of that. But I see—it would not have been difficult. A man can be taken unawares in the dark, and as you say, there would have been no witnesses."

"You come home too soon," growled Ben. "I counted on getting away and bein' here to welcome you, and nobody the wiser; d—— them two women! I supposed you'd stay awhile with your girl. A man would, in our kind of folks. Lord! you don't seem to belong to *any* kind of folks that I can see. I don't know what to make of you.—you!—you!—you! I'd like to see you go yellin' and bub—ble—in' down to your drownin'! I'm heavier'n you be, come to the tug. I could do it now, inside of ten minutes."

"And hang for it in ten months," observed Bayard, smiling.

"I could get a dozen men to swear to an alibi!" cried Trawl. "You ain't so popular in this town as to make that a hard job. You've got the whole liquor interest ag'in' you. Lord! the churches would back 'em, too, that's the joke of it!"

He laughed savagely.

Bayard made no reply. He had winced in the dark at the words. They were worse than the grip at his throat.

"When you get ready, Ben, suppose you explain what you have against me?" he suggested, after an uncomfortable pause.

"You've took my girl!" roared Ben.

"Your girl? *Your* girl?"

Bayard gasped, from the sheer intellectual shock of the idea.

"You've made love to her, behind my back! You've turned her head! She ain't no eyes left in her for anybody but you,—you! And I've ben keepin' company with her for four years. You've got my girl away from me, and you'd oughter drown for it. Drownin' 's too good for you!"

"Look here, Ben," said Bayard. "Are you drunk?"

"We don't drink—me, nor my father. And you know it. We ain't such—fools!"

"It is a waste of the English language to add," observed the preacher, with an accession of his natural dignity, which was not without its effect upon Ben Trawl, "that I have never regarded Miss Granite—for a moment—in the extraordinary light which you suggest. It seems to me unnecessary to point out to you the unnaturalness—I may be frank, and say the impossibility—of such a supposition."

"—you!" raved Ben, "ain't she good enough for you, then?"

"Ben Trawl," said the minister imperiously, "this nonsense has gone far enough. If you have nothing more reasonable to say to me, we may as well stop talking, for I'm going home. If you have, I'll stay and hear it out."

Bayard calmly seated himself upon the base of Ragged Rock, and took off his hat.

"What a warm, pleasant night it is!" he said in a tone so changed that Ben Trawl stared.

"Plucky, anyhow," thought Ben. But he said: "I ain't got half through yet. I've got another score ag'in' you. You've took the girl, and now you're takin' the business."

"Ah," replied the preacher; "that's another matter."

"You own up to it, do you?—you!"

"Assuredly," answered Bayard. "I am doing my best to ruin your business. It is a pleasure to hear you admit it. It has gone further than I supposed."

"It *has* gone further 'n you suppose!" echoed Ben malignantly, "and it *will* go further 'n you suppose! Me and Father have stood it long enough. There's them that backs us that you never give one of your—holy thoughts to. I give you warning on the spot, Mr. Bayard. You stop just where you be. Meddle with our business one inch further, and you'll hear from the whole liquor interest of Windover. We'll blow you into eternity if you don't let us alone."

"I should count that," replied the preacher gently, "the greatest honor of my life."

"Anyhow," said Ben in a calmer tone, "if you don't let our business be, we'll ruin yourn."

"That is quite possible," returned Bayard; "but it won't be without a big tussle."

"You don't believe me," sneered Ben; "you think we ain't up to it."

"Do you suppose, Ben," asked the preacher quietly, "that an educated man would deliberately choose the course that I have chosen to pursue in this town without informing himself on all branches of the subject that he is handling? Do you suppose I don't know what the liquor interest is capable of when attacked by Christian temperance? There hasn't been an outrage, a persecution, a crime,—no, not a murder committed in the name of rum and the devil against the cause of decency and sobriety in this country for years, that I haven't traced its history out, and kept the record of it. Come up to my study, and see the correspondence and clippings I have collected on this matter. There are two shelves full, Ben."

"Lord!" said Ben. His jaw dropped a little. He felt the inferiority of the ignorant man before education, the weakness of moral debility before moral vigor. He turned and took a few steps towards the town. The minister followed him amiably, and the two strode on in silence.

"He don't scare worth a cent," thought Ben. Aloud he said:—

"So you're goin' to fight us, be you?"

"Till I die," answered Bayard solemnly; "and if I die!"

"You won't take no warnin' then?" asked Ben with a puzzled air.

"Neither from you, Ben, nor from any other man."

"The worse for you, then!" returned Ben in an ugly tone.

"I'll risk it," replied Bayard serenely.

"There's them that says you're goin' to fight it out at the polls," said Ben, more sullenly now than savagely. "Folks says you're goin' to get away Father's license."

"I hadn't thought of it till this minute!" exclaimed the preacher. "But it would be a good idea."

Ben made an inarticulate noise in his throat. Bayard instinctively thrust out his elbow; he thought for the moment that Ben would spring upon him out of sheer rage. They were out on the open downs, now; but still only the witness of the sky and sea and rocks remained to help him.

"Look here," said Ben, suddenly stopping. "Are you going to tell of me?"

"That you were so uncivil as to put your hands on my throat, Ben?—I haven't decided."

"Not that *I* care a—!" muttered Ben. "But Jane"—

"I shall never mention any circumstance of this—rather unpleasant evening—which would bring Miss Granite's name into publicity," replied the preacher quickly. "She is a good, modest girl. She should be sheltered and cared for. You might better toss a woman off Ragged Rock—as you intended to do by me—than to turn the gossip of Windover loose upon her."

"It *is* a hell of a town, if you come to that," said Ben with calm conviction.

"She is much too good for you, Ben Trawl," remarked Bayard quite politely, as if he were offering the other a glass of lemonade.

"Lord!" groaned Ben, writhing under the minister's manner. "Don't you suppose that's the worst on't?"

"I think I'll cut across here towards the hotel," observed Bayard pleasantly. "We seem to have talked out, for this time. Good-night, Ben."

"Say," said Ben, "why don't you spout temperance to me? Why ain't you talked religion? Why ain't you set out to convert me? I give you chance enough!"

"You are an intelligent man," replied the preacher; "you know what you are about. I don't waste sacred powder on useless shot."

"Queer Dick, you," mused Ben. "It's just as I said. You don't belong to *any* kind of folks I ever see before. I can't make you out."

"Next time you want to murder me, Ben," called the minister cheerily, "don't try anonymous traps! Show up like a man, and have it out in the open air!"

He walked on towards the beach. Ben watched him for a perplexed and sullen moment, then took his course thoughtfully in the direction of the town.

When the two men had disappeared from the dark map of the downs, a woman's figure swiftly and quietly crossed it. Jane Granite had followed the minister like the spaniel that she was, and, hidden in the shadows of Ragged Rock, thinking to save him, God knew how, from Heaven knew what fate, had overheard the interview from beginning to end.

ELIZABETH STUART PHELPS

XVIII

A fiery July was followed by a scorching August. There was a long drought, and simooms of fine, irritating dust. The gasping town and inland country flocked to the coast in more than the usual force. The hotels brimmed over. Even Windover fanned herself, and lay in hammocks lazily, watching for the two o'clock east wind to stir the topsails of the schooners trying under full canvas to crawl around the Point. In Angel Alley the heat was something unprecedented; and the devil shook hands with discomfort as he is fain to, and made new comrades.

Bayard was heavily overworked. He gave himself few pleasures, after the fashion of the man; and the summer people at the Point knew him not. He was not of them, nor of their world. Afterwards, he recalled, with a kind of pain lacking little of anguish, how few in number had been his evenings in the cool parlor of the cottage, where the lace curtains blew in and out through the purple twilight, or on the impearled harbor, in the dory, when the sun went down, and he drifted with her between earth and heaven, between light and reflection, in a glamour of color, in alternations of quiet, dangerous talk, and of more dangerous silence; brief, stolen hours when duty seemed a dimming dream, and human joy the only reality, the sole value, the decreed and eternal end of life. Upon this rare and scanty substitute for happiness he fed; and from it he fled.

Between his devotions and his desertions the woman stood mute and inscrutable. And while they still moved apart, saying, "The summer is before us," lo, the petals of the Cape roses had flown on the hot winds, the goldenrod was lifting its sword of flame on the undulating gray downs, and the summer was spent.

And yet, at every march and countermarch in the drill of duty, he was aware of her. It could not be said that she ever overstepped the invisible line which he had elected to draw between them; though it might be said that she had the fine pride which did not seem to see it. Helen had the quiet, maidenly reserve of an elder and more delicate day than ours. To throw her young enthusiasm into his work without obtruding herself upon his attention, was a difficult procedure, for which she had at once the decorum and the wit.

At unexpected crises and in unthought-of ways he came upon her footprints or her sleight-of-hand. Helen's methods were purely her own. She followed neither law nor gospel; no rules or precedents controlled her. She relieved what suffering she chose, and omitted where she did elect; and he was sometimes astonished at the common sense of her apparent willfulness. She had no more training in sociological problems than the goldenrod upon the bosom of her white gown; yet she seldom made a serious mistake. In a word, this summer girl, playing at charity for a season's amusement, poured a refreshing amount of novelty, vigor, ingenuity, and feminine defiance of routine into the labors of the lonely man. His too serious and anxious people found her as diverting as a pretty parlor play. A laugh ran around like a light flame whenever she came upon the sombre scene. She took a bevy of idle girls with her, and gave entertainments on which Angel Alley hung, a breathless and admiring crowd. She played, she sang, she read, she decorated. Pictures sprang on barren walls; books stood on empty shelves; games crowded the smoking-room; a piano replaced the painstaking melodeon; life and light leaped where she trod, into the poor and unpopular place. The people took to her one of the strong, loyal fancies of the coast. Unsuspected by her, or by himself, she began, even then, to be known among them as "the minister's girl." But this hurt nobody, neither herself nor him, and their deference to her never defaulted. In the indulgence of that summer's serious mood, Helen seldom met, he was forced to suspect that she purposely avoided, the preacher. Often he entered a laughing home from which she had just vanished. Sometimes—but less often—he found that she had preceded him where death and trouble were. Their personal interviews were rare, and of her seeking, never.

"She is amusing herself with a novelty," he thought. Then came the swift, unbidden question, If this is her beautiful whim, what would her dedication be?

Since, to play at helping a man's work, though at the tip of the sceptre by which he held her back, meant sense and sympathy, fervor and courage like this, what would it be to the great and solemn purpose of his life, if she shared it, crowned queen?

It was an August evening, sultry and smoky. Forest fires had been burning for a week on the wooded side of the harbor, and the air was thick. It was Sunday, and the streets and wharves and beaches of Windover surged with vacuous eyes and irritable passions. The lock-ups were full, the saloons overflowed. The ribald song and excessive oath of the coast swept up and down like air currents. There had been several accidents and some fights. Rum ran in streams. It was one of the stifling evenings when the most decent tenement retains only the sick or the helpless, and when the occupants of questionable sailors' boarding-houses and nameless dens crawl out like vermin fleeing from fire. It was one of the nights when the souls of women go to perdition, and when men do not argue with their vices. It was one of the nights when ease and cool, luxury and delicacy, forget the gehenna that they escape; and when only the strong few remember the weakness of the many.

Upon the long beach of fine white sand which spanned the space between the docks and the cliffs of the wooded coast, there gathered that evening a large and unusual crowd. Angel Alley was there en masse. The wharves poured out a mighty delegation. Dories put out from anchored vessels whose prows nodded in the inner harbor, and their crews swarmed to the beach in schools, like fish to a net.

A few citizens of another sort, moved, one might say, from curiosity, innocent or malicious, joined themselves to the fishermen and sailors. Their numbers were increased by certain of the summer people from the Point, drawn from their piazzas and their hammocks by rumors of a sensation. An out-of-door service, said to be the first of its kind conducted by the remarkable young preacher of such excellent family and such eccentric career, was not without its attractions even on the hottest evening of the season. There might have been easily eight hundred or a thousand people facing the light temporary desk or pulpit which had been erected at the head of the beach for the speaker's use.

The hour was early, and it would have been very light but for the smoke in the air, through which the sun hung, quivering and sinister, with the malevolent blood-red color of drought and blasting heat.

"Statira," in a low tone said the puzzled voice of the Professor of Theology, "this is—I must say—really, a most extraordinary gathering. It quite impresses me."

"I have read something somewhere it reminds me of," mused Mrs. Carruth, with a knot between her placid brows. "Where was it, Haggai?—Helen! Helen! What have I read that is like this? I can't think whether it is George Eliot, or Fox's Book of Martyrs. Perhaps it is the Memoirs of Whitefield; but certainly"—

"Possibly," suggested Helen, "it may have been the New Testament."

"That's it! You have it!" cried Mrs. Carruth, with mild relief. "That's the very thing. How extraordinary! It *is* the New Testament I have got into my head."

The Professor of Theology changed color slightly, but he made no answer to his wife. He was absorbed in watching the scene before him. There were many women in the crowd, but men predominated in proportion significant to the eye familiar with the painfully feminine character of New England religious audiences. Of these men, four fifths were toilers of the sea, red of face, uncertain of step, rough of hand, keen of eye, and open of heart,—

"Fearing no God but wind and wet."

The scent of bad liquor was strong upon the heavy, windless air; oaths rippled to and fro as easily as the waves upon the beach, and (it seemed) quite as much according to the laws of Nature. Yet the men bore a decent look of personal respect for the situation. All wore their best clothes, and most were clean for the occasion. They chatted among themselves freely, paying small heed to the presence of strangers, these being regarded as inferior aliens who did not know how to man a boat in a gale.

The fisherman's sense of his own superior position is, in any event, something delightful. In this case there was added the special aristocracy recognized in Angel Alley as belonging to Bayard's people. Right under the ears of the Professor of Theology uprose these awful words:—

"D—— them swells. He don't care a—for them. We get along up to Christlove without 'em, don't we, Bob? The parson's own, anyhow. He can't be bothered with the likes o' them."

"Look a' Job Slip yonder! See the face of him, shaved like a dude. That's him, a-passin' round hymn-books. Who'd believe it? *Job!* Why, he ain't teched a—drop sence he swore off! Look a' that young one of his taggin' to his finger! That's his wife, that bleached-out creetur in a new bunnet. See the look of her now!"

"It's a way women have,—lookin' like that when a man swears off," replied a young fellow, wriggling uncomfortably. "It kinder puts my eyes out—like it was a lamp turned up too high."

He winked hard and turned away.

"Ben Trawl! Hello, Trawl! *You* here? So fond of the minister as this?"

"I like to keep my eye on him," replied Ben Trawl grimly.

Captain Hap, distributing camp-chairs for the women of the audience, turned and eyed Ben over his shoulder. The Captain's small, keen eyes held the dignity and the scorn of age and character.

ELIZABETH STUART PHELPS

"Shut up there!" he said authoritatively. "The minister's comin'. Trot back to your grogshop, Ben. This ain't no place for Judases, nor yet for rummies."

"Gorry," laughed a young skipper; "he ain't got customers enough to okkepy him. They're all here."

Now there sifted through the crowd an eager, affectionate whisper.

"There! There's the preacher. Look that way—See? That tall, thin fellar—him with the eyes."

"That's him! That's him. That long-sparred fellar. Three cheers for him!" shouted the mate of a collier, flinging up his hat.

A billow of applause started along the beach. Then a woman's voice called out:—

"Boys, he don't like it!" and the wave of sound dropped as suddenly as it rose.

"He comes!" cried an Italian.

"So he does, Tony, so he does!" echoed the woman. "God bless him!"

"He comes," repeated Tony. "Hush you, boys—the Christman comes!"

The Professor of Theology pressed the tips of his scholarly fingers upon his aging eyes.

It was some moments before he commanded himself, and looked up.

Bayard stood bareheaded in the color of the red sun. He was pale, notwithstanding the warmth of the evening, and had a look so worn that those who loved him most felt unspoken fear like the grip of a hand at their hearts. The transparence, the delicacy of his appearance,—bathed in the scarlet of the murky sunset, as he was,—gave him an aspect half unreal. He seemed for the moment to be a beautiful phantom rising from a mist of blood. A hush, half of reverence, half of awe, fell upon all the people; it grew so still that the lazy breath of the shallow wave at that moment spent upon the beach, could be heard stirring through the calm.

Suddenly, and before the preacher had spoken any word, the impressive silence was marred by a rude sound. It was a girl's coarse laugh.

Then there was seen upon the beach, and quite apart from the throng, a little group of nameless women, standing with their backs to the sacred scene. Some one—Job Slip, perhaps, or Captain Hap—started with an exclamation of horror to suppress the disturbance, when the preacher's lifted hand withstood him. To the consternation of his church officers, and to the astonishment of his audience, Bayard deliberately left the desk, and, passing through the throng, which respectfully divided before him to left and right, himself approached the women.

"Lena! . . . *Magdalena!*"

He said but that word. The girl looked up—and down. She felt as if an archangel from the heavens, commissioned with the rebuke of God, had smitten her with something far more terrible—the mercy of man.

"You disturb us, Lena," said the preacher gently. "Come."

She followed him; and the girls behind her. They hung their heads. Lena scrawled she knew not what with the tip of her gaudy parasol upon the beach. Her heavy eyes traced the little pebbles in the sand. For her life, she thought, she could not have lifted her smarting lids. Till that moment, perhaps, Lena had never known what shame meant. It overwhelmed her, like the deluge which one dreams may foretell the end of the world.

The street girls followed the preacher silently. He conducted them gently through the throng, and seated them quite near the desk or table which served him as a pulpit. Some of his people frowned. The girls looked abashed at this courtesy.

Bayard ignored both evidences of attention to his unexpected act, passing it by as a matter of course, and without further delay made signs to his singers, and the service began.

WAS IT MAGIC OR MIRACLE? Was it holiness or eloquence? Did he speak with the tongue of man or of angel? Where was the secret? What was the charm? Not a man or woman of them could have answered, but not a soul of them could have gainsaid the power of the preacher; the Professor of Theology least of all. This learned man stood the service out, upon the beach, behind the camp-chairs of his wife and daughter, and knew neither fatigue nor the critical faculty, till the beautiful worship drew to its end.

Bayard's manner was quiet, finished, and persuasive; it must have appealed to the most fastidious oratorical taste; any instructor in homiletics might have seen in it a remarkable illustration of the power of consecrated education over ignorance and vice. But Bayard's thought threw off ecclesiastical form as naturally as the gulls, arising from the harbor in the reddening sunset, tossed off the spray from their wings. No class of men are more responsive to originality than sea-going men. Of the humdrum, the commonplace, they will naught. Cant they scorn, and at religious snobbery they laugh.

It would be difficult to say what it was in Emanuel Bayard that most attracted them: whether his sincerity or his intellect, his spirituality or his manliness; or that mystical charm which comes not of striving, or of prayer, or of education—the power of an elect personality. Perhaps it would be nearer the truth to say that the fishermen loved him because he loved them. The idea is older than the time of this biography, but it will bear repeating.

The red sun dipped, and the hot night cooled. Dusk purpled on the breathless water, and on the long beach. A thousand restless people grew as gentle as one. The outlines of the preacher's form softened into the surrounding shadow; the features of his high face melted and wavered. Only his appealing voice remained distinct. It seemed to be the cry of a spirit more than the eloquence of a man. It pleaded as no man pleads who has not forgotten himself, as no man can plead who is not remembered of God. Fishermen stood with one foot on the beach, and one on their stranded dories, like men afraid to stir. Rude, uncomfortable men in the heart of the crowd thrust their heads forwards with breath held in, as still as figure-heads upon a wreck. The uplifted eyes of the throng took on an expression of awe. It grew dimmer, and almost dark. And then, when no one could see the pathos of his face, they knew that he was praying for their souls. Some of the men fell upon their knees; but the heads of others got no lower than their guilty breasts, where they hung like children's. The sound of stifled sobbing mingled with the sigh of the waves.

The unseen singers, breathing upon the last words of the prayer, chanted a solemn benediction. The tide was rising slowly, and the eternal Amen of the sea responded. Suddenly a lantern flashed—and another—and light and motion broke upon the scene.

Rough men looked into one another's wet faces, and were not ashamed. But some held their hats before their eyes. The girls in the front chairs moved away quietly, speaking to no person. But Lena separated herself from them, and disappeared in the dark. Job Slip had not arisen from his knees, and Mari, his wife, knelt by him. The woman's expression was something touching to see, and impossible to forget. Captain Hap held a lantern up, and Bayard's face shone out, rapt and pale.

"Behold the Christman!" said the Italian, repeating his favorite phrase in a reverent whisper.

The Professor of Theology heard it again; and repetition did not weaken its effect upon the Orthodox scholar. He removed his hat from his gray head. His wife held her delicate handkerchief to her eyes. Helen, struggling with herself, was pale with emotion. The Professor tried to speak.

"It is not," he said, "precisely a doctrinal discourse, and his theology"—

The Professor checked himself. "It is written," he said, "that the common people heard HIM gladly. And it must be admitted that our dear young friend, His servant, seems to command that which—men older and—sounder than he, would give their lives—and fame—to—"

But there he choked, and tried to say no more.

THERE OUGHT TO HAVE BEEN a moon that night, and the electric jets at the crest of the beach had not been lighted. By the special request of the preacher, or by the forethought of the police, in view, perhaps, of the unusual size of the crowd, the lights now sprang out.

The throng dispersed slowly. The dark sea formed a sober background to the mass of quietly moving figures. The fishermen, with one foot on their dories, leaped in, and pushed off; scattered crews gathered gently, and rowed soberly back to their schooners. Groups collected around the preacher, waiting their turns for a word from his lips, or a touch from his hand. It was evident that he was very tired, but he refused himself to no one.

The summer people walked away softly. They passed through Angel Alley on their way to take the electric car. They looked up thoughtfully at the illuminated words swinging over their heads in fire of scarlet and white:—

"THE LOVE OF CHRIST."

As she passed by the door of the mission, Helen was recognized by some of the women and children, who surrounded her affectionately, begging for some little service at her hands. It seemed to be desired that she should play or sing to them. While she stood, hesitating, between her father and her mother, Bayard himself, with a group of fishermen around him, came up Angel Alley.

"I will see that she is safely taken home, Professor, if you care to let her stay," he said. "We won't keep her—perhaps half an hour? Will that do? The people like to hear her sing; it helps to keep them out of the street."

"Mr. Bayard will look after her, Haggai," replied Mrs. Carruth wearily. "I see no objections, do you?"

Mrs. Carruth was very tired. Not to give a sober Monday to all the drunkards of Angel Alley would she have felt that she could stay another hour in that mob. She never saw such sights in Cesarea; where charity took a mild, ladylike form, consisting chiefly of missionary barrels, and Dorcas societies for the families of poor students who had no business to have married.

The Professor took her away. He wanted to tell his heretic graduate what he had thought about that service on the beach; indeed, he made one effort to do so, beginning slowly:—

"My dear Bayard, your discourse this evening"—

"To h—— with 'em!" cried Captain Hap in a thunderous sea-voice, at that moment. "Mr. Bayard! Mr. Bayard, sir! Come here! Here's them two Trawlses a-tryin' to toll Job Slip into their place! Mr. Bayard! Mr. Bayard!"

Mr. Bayard held out his hand to his Professor, and, smiling, shook his head. Then he vanished down the Alley. He had lingered only to say these words in Helen's ear:—

"Go into the chapel and stay there till I come for you. Look after Lena—will you? I want her kept inside. Get her to singing with you, if you can."

He called back over his shoulder:—

"I will bring her home, Mrs. Carruth, in half an hour. I will row her home, myself. I have a boat here."

Professor Carruth stood for a moment watching the thronged, bright doorway into which his daughter had disappeared. The fishermen and the drunkards, the Windover widows in their crape and calico, the plain, obscure, respectable parishioners, and the girls from the street moved in together beneath the white and scarlet lights. Helen's voice sounded suddenly through the open windows. She sang:—

> *"I need Thee every hour.*
> *Stay Thou near by."*

"Hello, Bob," said a voice in the street. "That's the minister's hymn." Groups of men moved over from the grogshop to the chapel door. They collected, and increased in numbers. One man struck into the chorus, on a low bass,—

> *"Stay near me, O my Saviour."*

Another voice joined; and another. Up and down the street the men took the music up. From Angel Alley without, and Christlove within, the voices of the people met and mingled in "the parson's hymn."

The Professor of Theology glanced at the illuminated words above his head.

"It is growing chilly. I am sure you will take cold," complained his wife. With bared, gray head the Professor walked out of Angel Alley, and his old wife clung silently to his arm. She felt that this was one of the moments when Mr. Carruth should not be spoken to.

Bayard brought Helen home as he had promised; and it was but a little beyond the half of the hour when his dory bumped against the float. He rowed her over the dim harbor with long, skillful strokes; Helen fancied that they were not as strong as they might have been; he seemed to her almost exhausted. They had exchanged but a few words. Midway of the harbor she had said abruptly,—

"Mr. Bayard, I cannot keep it to myself! I must tell you how what you said this evening on the beach—how that service made me feel."

"Don't!" said Bayard quickly. Helen shrank back into the stern of the dory; she felt, for the moment, terribly wounded.

"Forgive me!" he pleaded. "I didn't feel as if I could bear it—that's all."

"I am not in the habit of making a fool of myself over ministers," replied Helen hotly. "I never told one I liked his sermon, yet, in all my life. I was going to say—I meant to say—I *will* say!" she cried, sitting up very straight, "Mr. Bayard, you are better than I am; truly, infinitely, solemnly better. I've never even *tried* to be what you *are*. You've done me good, as well as Job, and Lena, and the rest. I *won't* go away without saying it,—and I'm going away this week. . . There!"

She drew a long breath and leaned back.

Bayard rowed on for some moments in inscrutable silence. It was too dark to see the expression of his face. When he spoke, it was in a half-articulate, tired way.

"I did not know. Are you coming back?"

"I am going to Campo Bello with the Rollinses," replied Helen briefly. "I don't expect to come back again this year."

"I wonder I had not thought of it," said Bayard slowly. "I did not," he added.

"The people will miss you," he suggested, after a miserable pause.

"Oh, they will get used to that," said Helen.

ELIZABETH STUART PHELPS

"And *I?*" he asked, in a tone whose anguish smote suddenly upon her ears, like a mortal cry. "What is to become of *me?*"

"You'll get used to it, too," she said, thrusting out her hands in that way she had.

His oars dropped across his knees.

Before either of them could speak or think or reason, he had caught one of her outstretched hands. It lay, warm, soft, quivering,—a terrible temptation in the grasp of the devotee.

He could have devoured it—her—soul and body; he could have killed her with kisses; he could have murdered her with love.

Instead, he laid Helen's hand down gently. He did not so much as lift it to his starving lips. He laid it down upon her own lap quite solemnly, as if he relinquished something unspeakably precious. He took up his oars, and rowed her home.

Neither had spoken again. Helen's heart beat wildly. She dared not look at him. Under the solitary lantern of the deserted float she felt his strong gaze upon her, and it looked, not with the eyes of angels, but with the eyes of a man.

"Oh, my dear, I love you!" he breathed in a broken voice.

Saying this, and only this, he led her to her father's door, and left her.

XIX

The mosquito-net portière swayed softly in the night wind. Emanuel Bayard sat in his study and looked about the poor place, gasping, like a man who has received or given a mortal hurt. The marred face of the great Christ looked through the coarse, white gauze; it seemed to scrutinize him sternly; he bowed his head before the gaze of the picture.

The gradual descent from a spiritual height to a practical level is, at best, a strain under which the godliest nature quivers; but Bayard experienced the shock of a plunge. From the elation of the past hour to the consternation of the present moment was a long leap.

He closed his eyes to see the blood-red sunset unfurling its flag over the broad beach; he opened them to see Mrs. Granite's kerosene lamp smoking on the study-table of grained pine wood. The retina of his soul suffered an adjustment as abrupt and as severe. But an hour ago, a thousand people had hung swaying upon the breath that went forth from between his lips; their upturned faces offered him that most exquisite of flatteries—the reverence of a great audience for an orator who has mastered them. We should remember that—the religious orator stands, both in privilege and in peril, apart from his kind. He may suffer at once the subtlest of human dangers, and the deepest of human joys. Bayard trembled yet with the exaltation of that solemn hour.

Midway between earth and heaven, commissioner between man and his Maker, he had stood transcendent, well-nigh translated. He had floated in the adoration of his people; he had been to them one of the sons of God; he had held their bare souls in his hand.

While his head whirled with the suffocation of the incense, he had stumbled. He had made the misstep which to a lofty soul may give more anguish than guilt to the low. He had fallen from the heights of his own faith in himself, sheer over, and below the ideal which those upon whose worshiping love he lived trustfully cherished of him.

An hour ago, he was a man of God. Now he called himself less than a man among men.

Bound by every claim of spiritual and of human honor to preserve the strong silence by which a man protects a woman from himself, and himself from her, he had weakly, to his high view it seemed he had ignobly, broken it. He had declared love to a woman whom he could not ask to be his wife. To crown the pity of it and the shame, he had turned on his heel, and left her—so!

"I have done a thing for which I would have thrashed a man who had done as much by a sister of mine!" said this young apostle between his teeth. It did not occur to him that he might be liable to overestimate the situation. Religious exaltation exposes a sensitive nature to mental and spiritual excess as dangerous in its way as physical dissipation. Bayard stood in that great desert known only to fine souls, where the noblest side of a man seems to take up arms against him; and where the very consecrated weapons by which he has battled his way to purity, unselfishness, and peace turn themselves like sentient foes and smite him. He seemed to stand unarmed and defenceless before forces of evil whose master he had been so long, that he looked upon their defiant faces with more astonishment than fear.

"This is an insurrection of slaves," he thought. He looked blindly about his dreary room.

"Down!" he said, as if he had been speaking to dogs.

And now—what? It seemed to his quivering sensibility a proof that he had fallen to a far depth, that the first, bare instinct of his anguish was not to say, "What is my duty in this thing?" but, "How shall I bear it?"

With that automatism of Christian habit which time and trouble may teach the coldest scoffer to respect, Bayard's hand groped for his Bible. We have seen this touching movement in the sick, the aged, the bereaved, and in the utterly alone; and who of us has been so poor in spirit as to do it irreverence? In so young a man this desolate instinct had a deep significance.

Bayard's Bible opened at the New Testament, whose worn pages moved apart, at a touch, like lips that would answer him.

As he took the book something fell from it to the floor. He stooped, holding his finger between the open leaves, and picked the object up. It was a flower—a pressed flower—the saxifrage that he had gathered from the hem of her dress on the sand of the beach, that April day.

The Bible fell from his knee. He snatched the dead flower to his lips, and kissed it passionately.

"There was another, too," he hungrily said. "There was a pansy. She left it on the sofa pillow in this room. The pansy! the pansy!"

He took up the Bible, and searched feverishly. But he could not find the pansy; the truth being that Jane Granite had seen it on the study-table, and had dusted it away.

He laid the Bible down upon the table, and seized the saxifrage. He kissed it again and again; he devoured it over and over; he held it in the palm of his hand, and softly laid his cheek upon it. . .

Behind the white gauze, the Christ on the wall looked down. Suddenly Bayard raised his haggard face. The eyes of the picture and the eyes of the man met.

"Anything but this—everything but this—Thou knowest." Aloud, Bayard uttered the words as if he expected to be heard.

"Only *this*—the love of man for woman—how canst THOU understand?"

Bayard arose to his full height; he lifted his hands till they touched the low, cracked ceiling; it seemed to him as if he lifted them into illimitable heaven; as if he bore on them the greatest mystery and the mightiest woe of all the race. His lips moved; only inarticulate whispers came from them.

Then his hands fell, and his face fell into them.

BAYARD WENT TO HER LIKE a man, and at once. At an hour of the morning so early that he felt obliged to apologize for his intrusion, his sleepless face appeared at the door of her father's cottage.

He had no more idea, even yet, what he should say to her than the Saint Michael over his study-table. He felt in himself a kind of pictorial helplessness; as if he represented something which he was incapable of expressing. His head swam. He leaned back on the bamboo chair in the parlor. Through the soft stirring of the lace curtains he watched a fleet start out, and tack across the harbor. He interested himself in the greenish-white sails of an old schooner with a new suit on. He found it impossible to think coherently of the interview which awaited him.

A hand fell on the latch of the door. He turned—ah!

"Good-morning, Professor," said Bayard, rising manfully. His pale face, if possible, turned a shade whiter. It seemed to him the fitting sequel to his weakness that he should be called to account by the girl's father. "I have deserved it," he thought.

"Ah, Bayard, this is too bad!" said the Professor of Theology, cordially holding out his hand. "You have just missed my daughter. I am sure she will regret it. She took the twenty minutes past seven train."

"Took the *train*?" panted Bayard.

"She has gone to join some friends of ours—the Rollinses, at Campo Bello. She did not intend to leave for some days; but the mood took her, and off she started. I think, indeed, she went without her breakfast. Helen is whimsical at times. Do be seated! We will do our poor best to take my daughter's place," pursued the Professor, smiling indulgently; "and I'm especially glad of this opportunity, Bayard, to tell you how much I was impressed by your discourse last night. I don't mind saying so at all."

"Thank you, Professor," said Bayard faintly.

"It was not theology, you know," observed the Professor, still smiling; "you can't expect me to admit that it was sound, Bayard. But I must say, sir, I *do* say, that I defy any council in New England to say it was not Christianity!"

"Thank you, Professor," repeated Bayard, more faintly than before. He found it impossible to talk about theology, or even Christianity. The Professor felt rather hurt that the young man took his leave so soon.

He had thought of inviting him into the clam study, and reading some extracts from the essay on the State of the Unforgiven after Death.

Bayard went back to his own rooms, and wrote to her; if he could have done so, he would have followed her to Campo Bello by the next boat. The pitiable fact was, that he could not raise the money for the trip. It occurred to him to force the occasion and borrow it—of his treasurer, of George Fenton, of his uncle; but he dismissed these fantasies as madness, and swiftly wrote:—

I hurried to you at the first decent moment this morning; but I was not early enough by an hour.

The reason why I do not—why I cannot follow you, by the next train, perhaps you will understand without my being forced to explain. I take the only method left to me of justifying myself—if it is possible for me to do that—in your eyes.

I dare not believe—I dare not hope, that what I have done can mean any more to *you* than passing embarrassment to a friendship whose value and permanence shall not be disturbed by my weakness if I can help it.

I love you. I ought not to have told you so. I did not mean to tell you so.

But I love you! A man situated as I am has no right to declare his feeling for a woman like yourself. This wrong have I done—not to you; I do not presume to dream that I could thereby in any way wrong *you*—but to myself, and to my love for you. It was my sacred secret; it is now your absolute possession. Do with it—and with me—as you will.

EMANUEL BAYARD

He dispatched this note by the first mail to Campo Bello, and waited in such patience as he could command for such answer as she chose to make him. He waited a miserable time. At the end of that week came a letter in her strong, clear hand. He shut himself into his rooms, turned the key, and read:—

MY DEAR MR. BAYARD

I am not quite sure that I entirely understand you. But I believe in you, altogether; and what I do not understand, I am proud to take on trust.

The love of a man like yourself would be a tribute to any woman. I shall count it the honor of my life that you have given it to me. And I shall be, because of it, all the more and always,

Your loyal friend,
HELEN CARRUTH

This composed and womanly reply did not serve to quell the agitation in which Bayard had awaited it. He read and re-read, studied and scrutinized the few self-contained words with a sense of helplessness which equaled his misery. His position seemed to him intolerable. Something undignified about it cut the proud fellow to the quick. He had thought himself prepared for any natural phase in the lot which he had elected. In the old language which the devotees of ages have instinctively used, and which to each solitary heart seems a figure of speech as new as its own anguish, Bayard had believed himself able to "bear his cross." He had now to learn that, in the curious, complex interplay of human life, a man may not be able even to wear his burden alone, and drop decently under it when the time comes. Suppose, as the cross-bearer crawls along in blood and dust, that the arm of the coarse wood strikes and bruises the delicate flesh of a woman's shoulder?

Suppose—oh, suppose the unsupposable, the maddening!

Suppose she might have been led, taught by his great love to love him? What then?

Because a man had a duty to God, had he none to a woman? After a night of sleepless misery, he wrote again:—

Is there no way in which I can see you—if only for a moment? Shall you be in Boston—if you are not coming to Windover—on your return home? This is more than I can bear.

Yours utterly,
E. B.

And Helen answered:—

MY DEAR FRIEND
Mother wrote me yesterday that she needed my help in packing. We go back to Cesarea on the 9th, and I shall therefore be in Windover for the twenty-four hours preceding our start... Do not suffer so! I told you that I trusted you. And I always shall.

Yours faithfully,
H. C.

It was a chilly September evening. The early dark of the coming autumn leaned from a clouded sky. The goldenrod and asters on the side of the avenue looked dim under the glimmer of the hotel lights; and the scarlet petals of the geraniums in the flower-beds were falling. In the harbor the anchored fleets flung out their headlights above a tossing sea. There was no rowing. The floats were deserted.

The guests, few now, and elect, of the sort that know and love the September Windover, clustered around the fireplace in the big parlor of the Mainsail. On the piazza of the Flying Jib the trunks stood strapped for the late evening porter and the early morning train. Bayard heard Helen's voice in the rooms overhead, while he sat, with whirling brain, making such adieus as he could master to Professor and Mrs. Carruth. He thought that the Professor looked at him with unwonted keenness; he might have called it sternness, if he had given himself time to reflect upon it. Reflect he did not, would not. He asked distinctly for Miss Helen. Her mother went to call her, and did not return. Professor Carruth lingered a few moments, and excused himself. The proofs of the article on the Unforgiven had come by the evening mail; he had six galleys to correct that night. He shook hands with Bayard somewhat abstractedly, and went over to the clam study, swinging a lantern on his thin arm to light the meadow path.

"It is too cold for Father over there, to-night," said Helen immediately, when she and Bayard were left alone. "I don't think he ought to go. The Unforgiven are always up to some mischief. I would accept the doctrine of eternal punishment to get rid of them. I'm glad they've got as far along towards it as proof-sheets."

"Am I keeping your father out of this warm room?" asked Bayard with his quick perception. He glanced at the open fire on the hearth. "That won't do!" he said decidedly, rising.

"Oh, I didn't mean *that*!" cried Helen, flushing.

"It is true, all the same, whether you meant it or not," returned Bayard. "I shall stay but a few moments. Would you mind putting on something warm, and walking with me—for a little? We can go over to the clam study and get him."

"Very well," said Helen somewhat distantly.

She wore a summer traveling-dress of purple serge, fastened at the throat with a gold pansy. A long, thick cape with a hood lay upon the sofa.

"Mother's waterproof will do," she said. She wrapped it quickly around her, and they started out. Something in the utter absence of vanity which led a girl at such a moment to wear the most unbecoming thing that she could put hands on, roused a keen throb of admiration in Bayard. Then he remembered, with a pang, the anomaly of the situation. Why should she *wish* to make herself beautiful to him? What had he done—great heavens! what *could* he do, to deserve or to justify the innocent coquetries of a beloved and loving woman?

Helen pulled the hood of the cloak far over her head. And yet, what a look she had! The severity and simplicity of her appearance added to the gravity of her face a charm which he had never seen before. How womanly, how strong, how rich and ripe a being! He drew her hand through his arm authoritatively. She did not resent this trifling act of mastery. His fingers trembled; his arm shook as she leaned upon it. They struck out upon the meadow path in the dark, and, for a moment, neither spoke. Then he said:—

"I have something to say to you. I shall wait till we have sent the Professor back."

"That will be better," said Helen, not without embarrassment. They came to the clam study, and he waited outside while she said:—

　　　　　ELIZABETH STUART PHELPS

"Come, Papa! Put the Unforgiven in your pocket, and go back to the fire! Mr. Bayard and I are going to walk."

The Professor meekly obeyed, and Helen locked the door of the fish-house, and put the key in her pocket.

"I shall give it to Mr. Salt to-night," she said. "We start at 7.20. Pepper is going to take us over."

These trivial words staggered Bayard's self-control.

"You always leave—so—early!" he stammered.

"Does that make it any worse?" she asked, trying to smile. It was not a very successful smile, and Bayard saw it. They were approaching the electric arc that lighted the entrance to the beach. The cold, light lay white on her face. Its expression startled him.

"Everything makes it worse!" he groaned. "It is as bad as it can be!"

"I can see how it might have been worse," said Helen.

"That's more than I can do. What do you mean?"

"I would rather not tell you," replied Helen with gentle dignity.

"Tell me what you mean!"

He turned about and lifted her averted face; he touched her with the tip of one trembling finger under the chin.

"I prefer not to tell you, Mr. Bayard."

She did not flush, nor blush. Her eyes met his steadily. Something in them sent the mad color racing across his face.

"Forgive me! I have no right to insist—I forgot—I have none to anything. I have no right to hear—to see—*anything*. God have mercy upon me!"

He put out his shaking hand, and gently covered with it her uplifted eyes; veiling from his own gaze the most sacred sight on earth. It was a beautiful act, and so delicately done that Helen felt as if a spirit had touched her.

But when she came to herself, and gave him her eyes again, with their accustomed, calm, feminine disguise, she saw no spirit, but the passionate face of a man who loved her and despaired of her as she had seen no man love or despair before.

"I cannot even ask for the chance to *try*," he cried. "I am as much shut out as a beggar in the street. I ought to be as dumb before you as the thousand-years' dead! And yet, God help me—I am a live man and I love you. I have no right to seek a right—I wrong you and myself by every word I say, by every moment I spend in your presence. Good-by!" he said with cruel abruptness, holding out his hand.

Helen did not take it. She turned her back to the great arc, and looked out to sea. Her figure, in its hooded cloak, stood strongly against the cold, white light. The tide rose upon the deserted beach insistently. The breakers roared on the distant shore.

"You must see—you must understand," he groaned. "I am a poor man—poorer than you ever took the trouble to think. A heretic, unpopular, out of the world, an obscure, struggling fellow, slighted, forgotten—no friends but a handful of fishermen and drunkards—and living on—what do you suppose my salary is?"

"It never occurred to me to suppose," said Helen, lifting her head proudly.

"Five hundred dollars a year; to be collected if possible, to be dispensed with if necessary."

He jerked the words out bitterly. His fancy, with terrible distinctness, took forbidden photographs by flashlight. He saw this daughter of conventional Cesarea, this child of ease and indulgence, living at Mrs. Granite's, boarding on prunes and green tea. He saw her trying to shake down the coal fire on a January day, while he was out making parish calls; sitting in the bony rocking-chair with the turkey-red cushion, beside the screen where the paper Cupid forever tasted uneaten fruit. He saw the severe Saint Michael looking down from the wall on that young, warm woman-creature. He saw her sweep across the old, darned carpet in her purple robes, with gold at her throat and wrists. He saw her lift her soft arms. He saw—Now he put his hands before his own eyes.

"Oh, do not suffer so!" said Helen, in a faltering voice. "Do not, do not mind it—so much! It—it breaks my heart!"

These timid, womanly words recalled Bayard to himself.

"Before I break your heart," he cried, "I ought to be sawn asunder!

". . . Let us talk of this a little," he said in a changed tone. "Just a word. You must see—you *must* understand my position. What another man would say, in my place, I cannot say—to any woman. What I would die for the right to ask, I may not ask."

"I understand," said Helen almost inaudibly.

She still stood with her back to the light, and her face to the sea.

"I love you! I love you!" he repeated. "It is *because* I love you—Oh, do you see? *Can* you see?"

Helen made no reply. Was it possible that she dared not trust herself, at that moment, to articulate? Her silence seemed to the tortured man more cruel than the bitterest word which ever fell from the lip of a proud and injured woman.

Now again the camera of his whirling brain took instantaneous negatives. He saw himself doing what other men had done before him: abandoning a doubtful experiment of the conscience to win a woman's love. He saw himself chopping the treadmill of his unpopular, unsuccessful work to chips; a few strong blows would do it; the discouraged people would merge themselves in the respectable churches; the ripples that he had raised in the fishing-town would close over, and his submerged work would sink to the bottom and leave no sign. A few reformed drunkards would go on a spree; a few fishermen would feel neglected for awhile: the scarlet and white fires of the Church of the Love of Christ would go out on Angel Alley. In a year Windover would be what Windover was. The eye of the great Christ would gaze no more upon him through the veil of coarse gauze; while he—free—a new man—with life before him, like other men, and the right to love— like any other man—

"*That*," he said solemnly, as if he had spoken aloud, "is impossible. There could be only that one way. I cannot take it."

"No," she said, lifting her head, as if he had explained it all to her; "no. You could never do *that*. I would not have you do that for—for all that could happen—for—" she faltered.

"Great God!" thought Bayard, "and I cannot even *ask* her how much she cares—if she could ever learn or try to love me."

He felt suddenly a strange weakness. He leaned against a boulder for support, coughing painfully. It seemed to him as if he were inwardly bleeding to death.

"Oh!" cried Helen, turning about swiftly and showing her own white face. "You are not well—you suffer. This will not—must not—I cannot bear it!" she said bravely, but with a quivering lip. "Give me your arm, Mr. Bayard, and let us get home."

He obeyed her in silence. He felt, in truth, too spent to speak. They got back to the door of the cottage, and Helen led him in. Her father was not in the parlor, and her mother had gone to bed. The fire had fallen to embers. Helen motioned him to an easy-chair, and knelt, coaxing the blaze, and throwing on pine wood to start it. She looked so womanly, so gentle, so home-like, and love-like, on her knees in the firelight there, caring for the comfort of the exhausted man, that the sight was more than he could bear. He covered his eyes.

"The fire flares so, coming in from the dark," he said.

She stepped softly about, and brought him wine and crackers, but he shook his head.

"My little tea-urn is packed," she said, smiling, trying to look as if nothing had happened. "I would have made you such a cup of tea as you never tasted!"

"Spare me!" he pleaded. "Don't you suppose I know that?"

He rose manfully, as soon as he could. She stood in the firelight, looking up. A quiver passed over her delicate chin. He held out his hand. She put her strong, warm clasp within it.

"I told you that I trusted you," she said distinctly. "Believe me, and go in peace."

"I don't know another woman in the world who would!" cried Bayard.

"Then let me be that only one," she answered. "I am proud to be."

He could not reply. They stood with clasped hands. Their eyes did not embrace, but comradeship entered them.

"You will let me write?" he pleaded, at last.

"Yes."

"And see you—sometimes."

"Yes."

"And trust me—in spite of all?"

"I have said it."

"My blessing isn't worth much," he said brokenly, "but for what it is—Oh, my Love, God go with you!"

"And stay with you!" she whispered.

He laid her hand gently down, and turned away. She heard him shut the door, and walk feebly, coughing, up the avenue. He looked back, once. He saw her standing between the lace curtains with her arms upraised, and her hand above her eyes, steadily looking out into the dark.

XX

S o Emanuel Bayard entered into his Wilderness. Therein he was tempted like other men of God who renounce the greatest joy of life for its grandest duty. There he thirsted and hungered, and put forth no hand towards the meat or drink of human comfort; there he contended with himself, and hid his face, for he went into solitary places, and prayed apart, asking for that second strength which sustains a man in the keeping of the vow that he has not feared to take upon his soul— not knowing, till God teaches him, how easy it is to recognize, and how hard to hold, "the highest when we see it."

WINTER DREW ITS YOKE OF ice about the shrinking shoulders of the Cape; the fleets huddled in the harbor; the fishermen drowned on the Grand Banks; Windover shivered and shriveled, and looked with wincing, winking eyes upon the blinding horizon of the winter sea; the breakers broke in white fire upon the bar; Angel Alley drank and cursed to keep warm; and the young preacher's delicate face, patiently passing in and out beneath the white and scarlet lights of the chapel of Christlove, gathered a snowdrift of its own with the whitening of the year.

His work, like most service sustained in consecration and in common sense by one pure and strong personality, grew upon his hands; not steadily, but by means of much apparent failure.

The fame of the heretic missionary had gone abroad as such things do. It was no uncommon thing for members of the strictest sect of the Orthodox churches to stand half curious, half deferent, and wholly perplexed by what they saw and heard, and calculating the prospects of an experiment which the observer was, as a rule, too wise a man or too good a woman not to respect.

It even happened now and then that some distinguished clergyman was seen jammed between a fisherman and a drunkard in the crush by the door; taking notes of the sermon, studying the man and his methods with the humility characteristic of large men, and seldom imitated by little ones.

The Reverend George Fenton was not, but would have liked to be, one of these eminent and docile clerical visitors at the chapel of Christlove. He dared not leave his congregation, decorously scattered to listen to a sound theology, in the pews of the old First Church, to elbow his unnoticed way among the publicans and sinners who thronged his classmate's mission; but he often wished he could. He asked himself anxiously: "What is the secret? How does the man do it?" Sometimes he envied his heretic friend the drunkards, and sailors, the reckless girls, and most of all the fishermen, sacred in the canon and to the imagination of the church,—the fishermen, once the chosen friends of Our Lord.

Bayard even fancied that Fenton looked at him a little wistfully; and that he spoke with him oftener and lingered longer when they met upon the streets of the sad and tempted town whose redemption both men, each in his own way, desired and sought, with a sincerity which this biography would not intimate was to be found only in the heart of its subject, and hero. For the Reverend George Fenton was no hypocrite, or Pharisee; the prevailing qualities of his class not being of this sort. No one rated him more generously than his heretic classmate; or looked more gently upon the respectable, dreary effort to save the world by an outgrown method, which the conformer dutifully and comfortably sustained.

"I heard a Boston man call you the Father Taylor of Windover," one day abruptly said the clergyman to the missionary, upon the post-office steps. "Boston could no farther go, I take it. I hear your audience has outgrown your mission-room. That must be a great encouragement; you must consider it a divine leading," added Fenton, with the touch of professional slang and jealousy not unnatural to better men than he. "But you must remember that we, too, are following the Master in our way; it's a pretty old and useful way."

Then up spoke Captain Hap, who stood at Bayard's elbow.

"It's jest about here, Mr. Fenton. You folks set out to *foller* Him; but our minister, he *lives* like Him. There's an almighty difference."

Another day, Fenton, with his young wife on his arm, came down Angel Alley with the air of a tourist inspecting the points of interest in a new vicinity.

"Bayard!" he exclaimed; "you look as white as a Cesarea snowdrift. You are overworked, man. What can I do, to help you?—If there *is* anything," he added with genuine concern, "you'd let me know, wouldn't you?"

"Probably not, Fenton," replied Bayard, smiling.

"I mean it," urged the other, flushing.

"If you do, the time may come," said Bayard dreamily.

He glanced at his old friend,—the rosy, well-fed man; at the round face destitute of the carving of great purpose or deep anxiety; at the pretty girl with the Berkshire eyes who looked adoringly over the sleek elbow to which she clung. These two well-meaning, commonplace people seemed ennobled and beautified, as commoner far than they may be, by their human love and happiness. Bayard, in his shabby clothes, with his lonely face, watched them with a certain reverence.

He thought—but when did he *not* think of Helen?

He wrote; she answered; they did not meet; he worked on patiently; and the winter went. Bayard drowned himself in his work with the new and conscious ardor of supreme renunciation. He thought of the woman whom he loved, as the diver at the bottom of the sea, when the pumps refuse to work, thinks of sky and shore and sun, of air and breath.

ONE BLEAK, BRIGHT FEBRUARY NIGHT, Bayard came out from his mission, and looked about Angel Alley anxiously.

Bob was within, and Tony and Jean were safe; Job Slip was sober, and Tom, Dick, and Harry were accounted for. But Lena—Lena had not been seen at Christlove for now many weeks.

The waywardness of the girl had long been sore at Bayard's heart, and the step which he took that night was the result of thought and deliberate purpose. Afterwards he was glad to remember that he had acted on no one of those mere sentiments or impulsive whims which are the pitfalls of a philanthropic life.

The hour was not early, decent people were scattering to their homes, and Windover was giving herself over to the creatures of the night. It was a windy night, and the snow blew in cold, white powder from the surface of drifts called heavy for the coast, and considered a sign of "a spell of weather."

There was a full moon; and the harbor, as one looked down between the streets, showed in glints and glimpses, bright and uneasy. The bellow of the whistling-buoy nine miles out, off the coast, was audible at firesides. The wind sped straight from Cape Cod, and was as icy as death.

It was one of the nights when the women of Windover grow silent, and stand at the window with the shade raised, looking out between their hands, with anxious, seaward eyes. "God pity the men at sea!" they say who have no men at sea. But those who have say nothing. They pray. As the night wears on, and the gale increases, they weep. They do not sleep. The red light on the Point goes out, and dawn is gray. The buoy shrieks on malignantly. It "comes on thick"; and the fog-bell begins to toll. Its mighty lips utter the knell for all the unburied drowned that are, and have been, and are yet to be. Windover listens and shudders. It is one of the nights when the sheltered and the happy and the clean of life bless God for home, for peace, for fire and pillow. It is one of the nights when the soul of the gale enters into the soul of the tempted and the unbefriended, and with it seven devils worse than the first. It was one of the nights when girls like Lena are too easy or too hard to find.

Bayard sought her everywhere. She was not to be seen in Angel Alley, and he systematically and patiently searched the town. With coat-collar turned up, and hat turned down, he tried to keep warm, but the night was deadly bleak. It came on to be eleven o'clock; half past; and midnight approached. He was about to abandon his quest when he struck a trace of her, and with redoubled patience he hunted it down. He had taken no one with him in his search for Lena; in truth, he knew of no person in all that Christian town who would have wished to share that night's repulsive errand if he had asked it. He recognized this fact with that utter absence of bitterness which is the final grace and test of dedication to an unselfish end.

"Why should I expect it?" he thought gently. "Duty is not subject to a common denominator. This is mine and not another's."

A policeman gave him, at last, the clew he needed; and Bayard, who had returned on his track to Angel Alley, halted before the door of a house at the end of a dark court, within a shell's-throw of the wharves. His duty had never led him before into precisely such a place, and his soul sickened within him. He hesitated, with his foot on the steps.

"Better stay outside, sir," suggested the policeman.

Bayard shook his head.

"Shan't I go with you, sir? You don't know what you're about. Better have an officer along."

"Stay here, within call, will you?" answered Bayard. "That will do. The law can't do my errand."

"Nor nothin' else in this town but *that*," returned the officer, touching his helmet.

He pointed up the Alley where the large letters of the solemn white and scarlet sign blazed all night before the chapel of Christlove. The fishermen could see it from their schooners' decks as they dropped anchors; and it shone strangely in their weather-beaten faces as they pushed past—or sank into—the doors of the dens that lined the street.

Bayard's eye followed the officer's finger, lighting with that solemn radiance peculiar to himself; and with this illumination on his face he entered the place whose ways take hold on death.

The officer waited without. In an incredibly short time the minister reappeared. He was not alone. Lena followed him with hanging head.

"Thank you, Sergeant," said Bayard quietly, touching his hat, "I shall need you no longer."

He turned, with the girl beside him, and crossed the Alley. The officer, with a low whistle, lingered a moment, and watched the astounding pair. In the full moonlight, in the sight of all whom it did or did not concern, Bayard walked up and down the street with Lena. It was now near to the stroke of midnight. The two could be seen conversing earnestly. Lena did not raise her eyes. The minister watched her eagerly. They paced up and down. Men staggering home from their sprees stood stupidly and stared at the two. Old Trawl came to his door and saw them, and called Ben, who looked, and swore the mighty oath of utter intellectual confusion. The minister nodded to Ben, and spoke once or twice to some sailor who awaited salutation; but he suffered no interruption of his interview with the girl. In the broad moonlight he continued quietly to walk up and down Angel Alley, with the street-girl at his side.

"Lena," Bayard had begun, "I have been trying to help the people in this Alley for almost a year and a half, and I have met with nothing to discourage me as much as you do. Some men and women have grown better, and some have not changed at all. You are growing worse."

"That's so," assented Lena. "It's as true as Hell."

"I begin to think," replied the minister, "that it must be partly my fault. It seems to me as if I must have failed, somehow, or made some mistake—or you would be a better girl, after all this time. Do you think of anything—Come, Lena! Give your best attention to the subject—Do you think of anything that I could do, which I have not done, to induce you to be a decent woman?"

"I tried, for you!" muttered Lena. "I tried; you know I did!"

"Yes, I know you did; and I appreciated it. You failed, that was all. You are discouraged, and so am I. Now, tell me! What else can I do, to make a good girl of you? For it's got to be done, you see," he added firmly. "I can't have this any longer. You disgrace the chapel, and the people, and me. It makes me unhappy, Lena."

"Mr. Bayard! Mr. Bayard!" said Lena with trembling lip, "I'll go drown in the outer harbor. I ain't fit to live. . . if *you* care. I didn't suppose you *cared*."

"You are not fit to die, Lena," returned Bayard gently. "And I do care. I have always thought you were born to be a fine woman. There's something I like about you. You are generous, and brave, and kind-hearted. Then see what a voice you have! You might have been a singer, Lena, and sung noble things—the music that makes people purer and better. You might have" . . .

"Oh, my God!" cried Lena; "I was singin' in that—in there—to-night. They're always after me to sing 'em into damnation."

"Lena," said Bayard in a thrilling tone, "look into my face!"

She obeyed him. High above her short stature Bayard's delicate countenance looked down at the girl. All the loathing, all the horror, all the repulsion that was in him for the sin he suffered the sinner to see for the first time. His tender face darkened and quivered, shrinking like some live thing that she tormented.

"Oh," wailed Lena, "am I like *that*—to you? Is it as bad as *that*?"

"It is as bad as that," answered the minister solemnly.

"Then I'll go drown," said Lena dully; "I might as well."

"No," he said quietly. "You will not drown. You will live, and make yourself a girl whom I can respect."

"Would you *ever* respect me—*respect* ME, if I was to be—if I was to do what you say?" asked Lena in a low, controlled tone.

"I should respect you from my soul," said Bayard.

"Would you—would you be willing to—would you feel ashamed to shake hands with me, Mr. Bayard,—if I was a different girl?"

"I will shake hands with you now," returned the minister quietly, "if you will give me your word of honor that you will never, from this hour"—

"I will never, from this hour, so help me God!" said Lena solemnly.

"So help her, God!" echoed Bayard.

He lifted his hand above her head, as if in prayer and blessing; then gently extended it. The girl's cold, purple fingers shook as he touched them. She held her bare hand up in the moonlight, as if to bathe it in whiteness.

"Mr. Bayard, sir," she said in her ordinary voice, "it is a bargain."

ELIZABETH STUART PHELPS

Bayard winced, in spite of himself, at the words; but he looked at Lena's face, and when he saw its expression he felt ashamed of his own recoil.

"Very well," he answered, adopting her business-like tone, "so it is. Now, then, Lena! What next? What are you going to do? Have you any home—any friends—anywhere to turn?"

"I have no friend on all God's earth but you, sir," said Lena drearily, "but I guess I'll manage, somehow. I can mostly do what I set out to."

"Your mother?" asked Bayard gently.

"She died when my baby was born, sir. She died of the shame of it. I was fifteen year old."

"*Oh!* and the—the man? The father of your child?"

"He was a gentleman. He was a married man. I worked for him, in a shop. *He* ain't dead. But I'd sooner go to hell than look to him."

"I'd about as soon you would"—the minister said in his heart. But his lips answered only,—"You poor girl! You poor, poor, miserable girl!"

Then, for the first time, Lena broke down, and began to cry, there, on the streets, in the sight of every one.

"I must find you work—shelter—home—with some lady. I will do whatever *can* be done. Rely on me!" cried Bayard helplessly.

He began to realize what he had done, in undertaking Lena's "case" without the help of a woman. Confusedly he ran over in his mind the names of the Christian women whom he knew, to whom he could turn in this emergency. He thought of Helen Carruth; but an image of the Professor's wife, her mother, being asked to introduce Lena into the domestic machinery of a Cesarea household, half amused and half embittered him. He remembered the wife of his church treasurer, a kindly woman, trained now to doing the unexpected for Christ's sake.

"I will speak to Mrs. Bond. I will consider the matter. Perhaps there may be some position—some form of household service," he ventured, with the groping masculine idea that a domestic career was the only one open to a girl like Lena.

Then Lena laughed.

"Thank you, sir. But I ain't no more fit for housework than I be for a jeweler's trade, or floss embroidery, or a front pew in Heaven. There ain't a lady in Christendom would put up with me. I wouldn't like it, either," said Lena candidly. "There's only one thing I would like. It's just come over me, standin' here. I guess I'll manage."

"I shall wish to know," observed Bayard anxiously, "what you are going to do, and where you will be."

"I'll take a room I know of," said Lena. "It ain't in Angel Alley. It's a decent place. I'll get Johnny's mother to come along o' me. She's dead sick of the Widders' Home. She's kinder fond of me, Johnny's mother is, and she can take in or go out, to help a bit. Then I'll go over to the powder factory."

"The powder factory?" echoed the puzzled pastor.

"The gunpowder factory, over to the Cut," said Lena. "They're kinder short of hands. It ain't a popular business. The pay's good, and Lord, *I* shouldn't care! The sooner I blow up, the safer I'll be. I guess I'd like it, too. I always thought I should."

"Very well," said the minister helplessly. "That may answer, till we can find something better."

It was now past twelve o'clock, and the night was growing bitterly cold. Bayard said good-night to Lena, and they separated opposite Trawl's door.

He went shivering home, and stirred up his fire. He was cold to the heart. That discreet afterthought which is the enemy of too many of our noble decisions, tormented him. He turned to his books, and taking one which was lying open upon the study-table read:—

"He spoke much about the wrongs of women; and it is very touching to know that during the last year of his life he frequently went forth at night, and endeavored to redeem the fallen women of Brighton." . . .

It was not three days from this time that Captain Hap approached the minister on the Alley, with a sober and anxious face. He held in his hand a copy of the "Windover Topsail." His rough finger trembled as it pressed the paragraph which he handed in silence for Bayard to read:—

"We regret to learn that a certain prominent citizen of this place who has been laboring among the sailors and fishermen in a quasi-clerical capacity, is so unfortunate as to find his name associated with a most unpleasant scandal arising out of his acquaintance with the disreputable women of the district in which he labors. We wish the Reverend gentleman well out of his scrape, but may take occasion to suggest that such self-elected censors of our society and institutions must learn somehow that they cannot touch pitch and not be defiled, any more than ordinary men who do not make their pretensions to holiness."

"Well?" said Bayard, quietly returning the paper.

Job Slip had joined them, and read the paragraph over the Captain's shoulder. Job was white to the lips with the virile rage of a man of the sea.

"I've shipped here, and I've coasted there, and I've sailed eenymost around the world," slowly said Captain Hap. "I never in my life—and I'm comin' on seventy-five year old—I never knew no town I wouldn't d'ruther see a scandal a-goin' in, than this here. It's Hell let loose on ye," added the Captain grimly.

"Find me the fellar that put up that job!" roared Job Slip, rolling up his sleeves.

"He ain't fur to seek," answered the Captain with a short laugh.

"He's the devil and all his angels smithered into one!" raved Job.

"That's drawrin' of it mild," said Captain Hap.

"This—low—matter does not trouble me," observed Bayard, smiling with genuine and beautiful remoteness.

"Excuse me, sir," said Captain Hap; "that's all you know!"

XXI

C aptain Hap was wiser in his generation than the child of light. Before a week had gone by, Bayard found himself the victim of one of the cruelest forms of human persecution—the scandal of a provincial town.

Its full force fell suddenly upon him.

Now, this was the one thing for which he was totally unprepared; of every other kind of martyrdom, it seemed to him, he had recognized the possibility: this had never entered his mind.

He accepted it with that outward serenity which means in a man of his temperament the costliest expenditure of inward vitality, and, turning neither to the right nor to the left, kept on his way.

Averted looks avoided him upon the streets. Cold glances sought him in Angel Alley. Suspicion lurked in eyes that had always met him cordially. Hands were withdrawn that had never failed to meet his heartily. His ears quivered with comments overheard as he passed through groups upon the business streets. The more public and the more respectable the place, the worse his reception. He came quickly into the habit of avoiding, when he could, the better portions of the town.

Before he had time to determine on any given course of conduct, he felt himself hunted down into Angel Alley, like other outcasts.

The Reverend Mr. Fenton in this crisis did what appealed to him as a praiseworthy deed. He came down to the chapel, and, in the eyes of Angel Alley sought his classmate boldly. Give him the credit of the act; it meant more than we may readily distinguish.

Men who conform, who live like other men, who think in the accustomed channels, are not to be judged by the standard which we hold before our heroes. He held out his hand to Bayard with some unnecessary effusion.

"My dear fellow!" he murmured, "this is really—you know—I came to—express my sympathy."

"Thank you, Fenton," said Bayard quietly.

He said nothing more, and Fenton looked embarrassed. He had prepared himself at some length to go into the subject. He felt that Bayard's natural indiscretion needed the check which it had probably now received, for life. But he found himself unable to say anything of the kind. The words shriveled on his tongue. His own eyes fell before

Bayard's high look. A spectator might have thought their positions to be reversed; that the clergyman was the culprit, and the slandered missionary the judge and patron. Fenton was uncomfortable, and, after a few meaningless words, he said good-morning, and turned away.

"Of course," he observed, as he went down the long steps of the mission, "you will meet this slander by some explanation, or change of tack? You will adapt your course hereafter to the circumstances?"

"I shall explain nothing, and change nothing," answered Bayard calmly. "I should do the same thing over again to-morrow, if I had it to do. I have committed no imprudence, and I shall stoop to no apology. I doubt if there are six civilized places in this country where an honest man in my position, doing my work, would have been subjected to the consequences which have befallen a simple deed of Christian mercy such as has been done by scores of better men than I, before me. Why, it has not even the merit—or demerit—of originality! I did not invent the salvation of the Magdalene. That dates back about two thousand years. It takes a pretty low mind to slander a man for it."

This was the only bitter thing he was heard to say. It may be pardoned him. It silenced the Reverend Mr. Fenton, and he departed thoughtfully from Angel Alley.

As Bayard looked back upon these lonely days, when the fury of the storm which swept about his ears had subsided, as such social tornadoes do, he perceived that the thing from which he had suffered most keenly was the disapproval of his own people. Wrong him they did not, because they could not. They might as easily have smirched the name and memory of the beloved disciple. But criticise him they did, poor souls! Windover gossip, the ultimatum of their narrow lives, seemed to them to partake of the finalities of death and the judgment. The treasurer of the society was troubled.

"We must reef to the breeze! we must reef to the breeze!" he repeated mournfully. "But, my dear sir, you must allow me to say that I think it would have been better seamanship to have avoided it altogether."

"What would you have had me do, Mr. Bond?" asked Bayard, looking rather pale. "I am sorry to disappoint *you*. The love and trust of my own people is all I have," he faltered.

"Some witness, for instance," suggested Mr. Bond. "To be sure, you did call on the police, I am told."

"All Angel Alley was my witness," returned Bayard, recovering his self-possession.

"Some woman, then—some lady?"

"Name the woman. I thought of summoning your wife. Should you have let her go on such an errand, on such a night, at such an hour, and under such conditions?"

"I ought to have let her go," answered the officer of the heretic church, honestly. "I'm not sure that I should."

He looked perplexed, but none the less troubled for that, and sighed as he shook hands with his pastor. Mrs. Bond took her husband's arm, and walked away with him. "I would have done it, John," she said. But she was crying; so was Mrs. Granite. Jane's face was white and scared. Captain Hap was very sober. Job Slip was significantly silent. Rumor had it, that a fight was brewing between Job and the Trawls. Job's anger, if thoroughly aroused, was a serious affair. Bayard felt the discomfort and annoyance of his people acutely. He went away alone, and walked up and down the winter coast, for miles and hours, trying to regain himself in solitude and the breath of the sea. For some time he found it impossible to think coherently. A few words got the ring of his mind, and shook it:—

"From that time many of His disciples went back, and walked no more with Him."

USUALLY IN SUCH A SITUATION, some one trivial occurrence fixes itself upon the sore imagination of a man and galls him above all the really important aspects of his misfortune. This trifle came to Bayard in the reception of a letter from the girl herself.

> DEAR SIR, MR. BAYARD
> My hart will brake to think I cause you shame for savin
> of a poor girl. I see that peece in the paper. It aint far to gess
> who done it. If it wasnt for disgrasin you Ide kill Ben Trawl
> tonite. I wouldnt mind hangin. I know how Ide do it too.
> But dont you trubble I wont shame you no more. I'll clare
> out all-together. So good-bye and God bless you Sir.
>
> This is from, Yours respictfully,
> LENA

Bayard's reply to Lena's note was to go straight to the gunpowder factory, and speak with the girl. The superintendent stood by, and overheard him say, in a commanding tone:—

ELIZABETH STUART PHELPS

"Lena, you will not leave this town. You will come to the chapel as usual. You will sing with us next Sunday. You will pay no attention to anything that you hear, or see. You will never suffer yourself even to *suppose* that any base, low mind or tongue can injure your pastor. You will do as I bid you, and you will become the woman you promised to. You will do this with my help or without it. Anything may happen to a person. Nothing can undo a promise."

"Mr. Bayard, sir," said Lena, forcing back her tears, for she was not a crying girl, "I'm a girl of my word, and I ain't goin' back on you. But there's one thing I've got to say. Mebbe I shouldn't have another chance, bein' things are as they be. I *did* want to ask you, Mr. Bayard, sir, if I was to be a good girl long enough,—as long as you should set the time to make me fit,—do you suppose, Mr. Bayard, you would ever feel so as if you could touch your hat to me—same as you do to decent girls?"

The superintendent of the powder factory brushed his hand across his eyes. Bayard was much moved.

The dark, little figure of the girl, in her working-clothes, standing stolidly at her post in the most dangerous of the deadly trades, wherein no "hand" can insure his life, blurred before the minister. He thought how little life could mean to Lena, at its kindest and best.

"When the time comes," he said gently, "I shall lift my hat to you."

"That's worth while," said Lena in her short, forcible way. She turned and went back to her work.

The factory seemed to throb with the struggle of imprisoned death to burst its bars. Bayard came out into the air with the long breath which the bravest man always drew when he left the buildings.

These incidents (which are events to the solitary, missionary life) were but two days old when Joey Slip climbed the minister's stairs, sobbing dolorously.

Rumor was running in Windover that Job was drunk again. Neither the child nor the wife could say if truth were in it, for neither had seen the man since yesterday. But Mari had dispatched the boy to the minister with the miserable news. With a smothered exclamation which Joey found it impossible to translate, Bayard snatched the child's hand, and set forth. His face wore a terrible look. He reached the wharves in time to come directly upon Job, the centre of a ring of jeering roughs. Muddy, wet, torn, splashed with slime from the docks, hatless and raving, Job was doing his maudlin best to fight Ben Trawl, who stood at a safe distance, smiling with the cynicism of a rumseller who never drinks.

Job—poor Job, the "reformed man"; Job, who had fought harder for his manhood than most sober men ever fight for anything from the baby's crib to the broadcloth casket; Job, the "pillar" of Christlove mission, the pride and pet of the struggling people; Job, the one sure comfort of his pastor's most discouraged hour,—Job stood there, abased and hideous.

He had lived one splendid year; he had done one glorious thing; he had achieved that for which better men than he should take off their hats to him. And there—Bayard looked at him once, and covered his face.

Job recognized him, and, frenzied as he was, sunk upon his knees in the mud, and crawled towards the minister, piteously holding up his hands. One must have been in Job's place, or in Bayard's, to understand what that moment was to these two men.

In the paltry scenes of what we call the society of the world, there are no actors who should criticise, as there are few who can comprehend the rôles of this plain and common tragedy.

With the eyes of a condemning angel, Bayard strode into the group, and took Job home.

"It's clear D. T.," said Captain Hap between his teeth.

Bayard sent for a doctor, who prescribed chloral, and said the case was serious. Mari put on a clean apron, and dusted up the rooms, and reinforced the minister, who proceeded to nurse Job for thirty-six hours. Captain Hap went home. He said he'd rather tie a slipknot round the fellar's neck, and drawr it taut.

But when Job came to himself, poor fellow, the truth came with him. Job had been the blameless victim of one of those incredible but authenticated plots which lend blackness to the dark complexion of the liquor trade.

Job was working ashore, it seemed, for a week, being out of a chance to ship; and he had been upon the wharves, salting down fish, and came out at his nooning, with the rest, for his lunch. There was a well, in a yard, by the fish-flakes, and a dipper, chained, hung from the pump.

It came Job's turn to drink from the dipper. And when he had drunk, the devil entered into him. For the rim of the dipper had been maliciously smeared with rum. Into the parched body of the "reformed man" the fire of that flavor ran, as flame runs through stubble in a drought.

The half-cured drunkard remembered putting down his head, and starting for the nearest grogshop on a run, with a yell. From that moment till Bayard found him, Job remembered nothing more. Such

ELIZABETH STUART PHELPS

episodes of the nether world are not rare enough to be doubted, and this one is no fiction.

"I'm in for it, now," groaned Job. "Might as well go to h—— and done with it."

Then Bayard, haggard from watching, turned and looked on Job. Job put his hands before his face.

"Oh, *sir*!" he cried. "But you see, there ain't a wharf-rat left in Windover as 'u'd trust me now!"

"Take my hand, Job," said the minister slowly.

Job took it, sobbing like a baby.

"Now climb up again, Job!" said Bayard in a strong voice. "I'm with you!"

Thus went the words of the shortest sermon of the minister's life. To the end of his days, Job Slip will think it was the greatest and the best.

Captain Hap, penitent, but with no idea of saying so, came up the tenement stairs. Mari and Joey sat beside the fire. Mari was frying chunks of haddock for supper. Joey was singing in a contented little voice something that he had caught in the mission:—

> *"Veresawidenessin Godsmer—cy*
> *Likevewidenessof vesea. . .*
> *ForveloveofGod is bwoard—er*
> *Vanvemeazzerof mansmine*
> *Anve heartof veE—ter—nal*
> *Ismoswonderfully kine."*

"Hear the boy!" cried Mari, laughing for the first time for many black days.

"What in the world is he singin'?" asked Joey's father.

"Why, I'm sure it's as plain as can be," said Joey's mother,—

> *"'There's a wideness in God's mercy,*
> *Like the wideness of the sea.'*

Then he says:—

> *"'For the love of God is broader*
> *Than the measure of man's mind,*
> *And the heart of the Eternal*
> *Is most wonderful and kind.'*

Oh, ain't he the clever boy?"

"We'll see," said Job unexpectedly, putting his feet to the floor. "I ain't a-goin' to have the little fellar ashamed of his father, see if I be!"

"All the same," observed Captain Hap dryly, "I wouldn't go on the street to-night, if I was you. I'll stay along of you a spell. The minister's beat out. There's enough goin' on yet to capsize a soberer man than you be, Job. The fellar that did this here ain't a-goin' to stop at rims of dippers. No, sir! . . . Job Slip! Don't you tech nothin'; not *nothin'* outside of your own house, this six month to come! Not a soda, Job! Not a tumbler o' milk! Not a cup o' coffee! Not a swaller o' water! No, nor a bite of victuals. You'll be hunted down like a rat. There's bread buttered with phosphorus layin' round loose for ye most anywheres. Everybody knows who done this. 'T ain't no use to spile good English callin' bad names. He won't stop at nothin' partikkelar to drawr you under."

"But why?" asked Bayard. "Why should he hound down poor Job so?"

"To spite you, sir," replied the captain without hesitation.

In the dead silence which followed the captain's words, Joey's little voice piped up again:—

> *"Be hushed my dark spew—it*
> *Ve wussvatcancome*
> *But shortens vy zhour—nee*
> *Anhastingsme home."*

Joey stole up merrily, and patted out the tune with his little fingers on the minister's pale cheek.

"He says," began Mari proudly,

> *"'Be hushed, my dark spirit,*
> The worst that can come'"—

But Captain Hap, who was not in a pious mood, interrupted the maternal translation.

"Folks say that they've got into their—heads their license is in genooine danger. Confine yourself to prayin' an' singin', an' they don't deny that's what you're hired for. Folks say if you meddle with city politics, there ain't an insurance company in New England 'u'd take a policy on your life, sir. You might as well hear what's goin' on, Mr. Bayard. I don't suspicion it'll make no odds to you. I told 'em you wouldn't tech the politics of this here town with a forty-fathom grapplin'-iron,—no, nor with a harbor-dredger!"

"You're right there, Captain," returned Bayard, smiling.

"Then 'tain't true about the license?" asked the captain anxiously.

"I have nothing to conceal in the matter, Captain," answered Bayard after a moment's silence. "There are legalized crimes in Angel Alley which I shall fight till I die. But it will be slow work. I don't do it by lobbying. I have my own methods, and you must grant me my own counsel."

"The dawn that rises on the Trawls without their license," slowly said the captain, "that day, sir, you may as well call on the city marshal for a body-guard. You'll need it!"

"Oh, you and Job will answer, I fancy," replied Bayard, laughing.

He went straight home and to bed, where he slept fitfully till nearly noon of the next day. He was so exhausted with watching and excitement, that there is a sense of relief in thinking that the man was granted this one night's rest before that which was to be befell him.

For, at midnight of the succeeding night, he was awakened by the clang of the city bells. It was a still night, there was little wind, and the tide was calm at the ebb. The alarm was quite distinct and easily counted. One? two? three? Six? One—two—three. Six. Thirty-six. Thirty-six was the call from the business section of the town. This alarm rang in for the board of trade, Angel Alley, the wharves, and certain banks and important shops.

"A fire on the wharves, probably," thought Bayard; he turned on his pillow; "the fire-boat will reach it in three minutes. It is likely to be some slight affair."

One—two—three. Six. One—two—three. Six. *One-two. One-two.* The sounding of the general alarm aroused him thoroughly. He got to the window and flung open the blinds. In the heart of the city, two miles away, a pillar of flame shot straight towards the sky, which hung above it as red as the dashed blood of a mighty slaughter.

At this moment a man came running, and leaned on Mrs. Granite's fence, looking up through the dark.

"Mr. Bayard! Mr. Bayard!" he called loudly.

"Bob! Is that you? What is it? Where is it?"

"It's in Angel Alley, sir."

"Be there in a minute, Bob."

"But, Mr. Bayard, sir—there's them as think you're safer where you be. Job Slip says you stay to home if you love us, Mr. Bayard!"

"Wait for me, Bob," commanded Bayard. "I'm half dressed now."

"But, Mr. Bayard, Mr. Bayard—you ain't got it through your head—I said I wouldn't be the man to tell you, and I wish to gollyswash I'd stuck to it."

"Bob! It isn't the *Mission*?"

"Oh, sir—yes! They've set us afire!"

"Now, Bob," said the minister, suddenly shooting up in the dark at Bob's side, with coat and vest over his arm, "run for it! Run!"

THE BUILDING WAS DOOMED FROM the first. The department saw that, at a glance, and concentrated its skill upon the effort to save the block.

The deed had been dexterously done. The fire sprang from half a dozen places, and had been burning inwardly, it was thought, for an hour before it was discovered. The people had been too poor to hire a night-watchman.

"We trusted Providence," muttered Captain Hap. "And this is what we get for it!"

The crowd parted before the minister when he came panting up, with Bob a rod behind. Bayard had got into his coat on the way, but he had not waited for his hat. In the glare, with his bared head and gray-white face, he gathered an unearthly radiance.

He made out to get under the ropes, and sprang up the steps of the burning building.

"No, sir!" said the chief respectfully; "you can't get in, now. We've saved all we could."

"There are some things I *must* have. I can get at them. I've done this before. Let me in!" commanded the minister.

All the coherent thought he had at that moment was that he must save some of the pictures—Helen's pictures that she had given to the people. In that shock of trouble they took on a delirious preciousness to him.

"Let me into my own chapel!" he thundered. But the chief put his hand upon the preacher's breast, and held it there.

"Not another step, Mr. Bayard. The roof will fall in five minutes. Get back, sir!"

He heard his people calling him; strong hands took hold of him; pitying faces looked at him.

ELIZABETH STUART PHELPS

"Come, Mr. Bayard," some one said gently. "Turn away with us. Don't see it go."

He protested no more, but obeyed quietly. For the first time since they had known him, he faltered, and broke before his people. They led him away, like a wounded man. He covered his face when the crash came. The sparks flew far and hot over the wharves, and embers followed. The water hissed as it received them.

At the first gray of dawn, the minister was on the ground again. Evidently he had not slept. There was a storm in the sky, and slow, large flakes of snow were falling. The crowd had gone, and the Alley was deserted. Only a solitary guardian of the ruins remained. Bayard stood before them, and looked up. Now, a singular thing had happened. The electric wire which fed the illuminated sign in front of the mission had not been disconnected by the fire; it had so marvelously and beautifully happened; only a few of the little colored glass globes had been broken, and four white and scarlet words, paling before the coming day, and blurring in the snow, but burning steadily, answered the smothered tongues of fire and lips of smoke which muttered from the ruins.

As day opened, the people began to collect upon the spot. Expressions of awe or of superstition were heard, as they looked up and read, serene and undisturbed against the background of the rising storm,—

THE LOVE OF CHRIST

XXII

Immediately upon the destruction of the chapel, two things happened. The first, was a visit from Mr. Hermon Worcester. Nothing could have been more unexpected; and when Bayard, coming into his lodgings one dreary afternoon, found his uncle in the bony rocking-chair, the young man was much moved.

Mr. Worcester, not untouched by the sight of his nephew's emotion, held out an embarrassed hand. Bayard took it warmly. He had learned the lesson of loneliness so thoroughly, that he was ill prepared for the agitation of this little, common, human incident.

"You are ill, Manuel!" cried the elder man. "Good heavens, how you have changed! I had no idea—You should have told me!" he added, with the old autocratic accent. "I ought to have been informed. . . And *this* is how you live!"

Hermon Worcester looked slowly about him. His eye fell on the paper screen, the mosquito-net portière, the iron angel on the stove, the hard lounge, the old carpet, the stained wall-paper; he scrutinized the bookcase, he glanced at the Saint Michael. When he saw the great Christ, he coughed, and turned his face away; got up uneasily, and went into the bedroom, where he fell to examining the cotton comforters.

"At least," he said sharply, "you could have sent for your own hair mattress! Nobody has slept on it, since"—

He broke off, and returned to the skeleton rocking-chair, with an expression of discomfiture so serious that Bayard pitied him. He hastened to say:—

"Oh, I have done very well, very well indeed, Uncle. A man expects to rough it, if he chooses to be a home missionary. Give yourself no concern—now."

If there were an almost uncontrollable accent on the last word, Mr. Hermon Worcester failed to notice it. Something in that other phrase had arrested his Orthodox attention. A home missionary? A home missionary. Was it possible to regard this heretic boy in that irreproachable light?

To the home missions of his denomination Mr. Worcester was a large and important contributor. Now and then an ecclesiastical Dives is to be found who gives a certain preference to the heathen of his own land before those of India, Africa, and Japan; Mr. Worcester had always been one of these illuminated men. Indeed, Japan, Africa, and India had been known to reflect upon the character of his Christianity for the reason that his checks were cashed for the benefit of Idaho, Tennessee, and the Carolinas.

To this hour it had not occurred to Mr. Worcester that the heathen of Windover could be properly rated as in the home missionary field. Even the starving pastors in the northern counties of Vermont might have gratefully called for yearly barrels of his old clothes; but Windover? Why, that was within two hours of Boston! And, alas, the Vermont ministers were always "sound." In Idaho, Tennessee, and the Carolinas, where was a corrupt theology to be found?

But that phrase had lodged in some nick of Mr. Worcester's mind; and he could no more brush it off than one can brush away a seed out of reach in the crevice of a rock. He regarded his nephew with a certain tolerance, warmly tinged by compassion.

"The boy is a wreck," he said to himself. "Manuel will die if this goes on. He might have expected it. And so might I."

The old man's face worked. He spoke, crossly enough. Bayard remembered that he always used to be cross when he was touched.

"What's to happen now? Ready to give it up, Manuel?"

"I am ready to begin all over again," replied Emanuel, smiling.

His voice had the ring that his uncle knew too well; when he was a little fellow, and bound to do a thing whether or no, he spoke in that tone, and always with that engaging smile.

"Who pays for this phœnix?" asked the man of business brusquely. "I passed by your place. It is a fine heap of ashes. A curious sight I saw there, too. That sign you hang out—those four words."

Bayard nodded.

"It *is* a pleasant accident. The department says it is almost unprecedented. Oh, we shall crawl up somehow, Uncle! I don't feel *very* anxious. The town hall is already hired for temporary use. There is great excitement in the city over the whole affair. You see, it has reached the proportions, now, of a deadlock between the rum interest and the decent citizens. Our treasurer is circulating some sort of a paper. I think he hopes to collect a few hundreds—enough to tide us over till we can float off. I don't know just how it is all coming out. Of course we can't expect the help that an ordinary church would get in a similar trouble."

"I'm glad if you recognize that fact, Manuel," replied Mr. Worcester uncomfortably. In his heart he was saying, "The boy has his mother's splendid Worcester pride. He'll perish here, like a starving eagle on a deserted crag, but he won't *ask* me!"

"You need a new building," observed Mr. Worcester, with that quiet way of putting a startling thing which was another Worcester quality. "You seem to have made—from your own point of view, of course—what any man of affairs would call a success here. Of course, you understand, Manuel, that I cannot approve of your course. It has been the greatest grief of my life."

Bayard hastened to observe that his comprehension of this point was not limited.

"From *your* point of view, not mine, Manuel, I should, as a man of business, suggest that a new building—your own property—something to impress business men, you know; something to give material form to that—undoubtedly sincere and—however mistaken—unselfish, religious effort that you have wasted in this freezing hole. . . I wonder, Manuel, if you could put the draughts on that confounded box-burner with the angel atop? I don't know when I've been so chilly!"

Bayard hastened to obey this request, without intimating that the draughts were closed to save the coal. This species of political economy was quite outside of his uncle's experience, and yet, perhaps, the man of business had more imagination than his nephew gave him credit for; he said abruptly:—

"Look here, Manuel, I've got to get the seven o'clock train home, you know, and I'd best do the errand I came on, at once. You know those old Virginia mines of your mother's? There was a little stock there, you remember? It went below zero. Hasn't been heard of for twenty years. But it remained on the inventory of the estate, you know. Well, it's come up. There's a new plant gone in—Northern enterprise, you know—and the stock is on the market again. There is only a trifle, a paltry two thousand, if well handled. It's yours, you see, whatever there is of it. I came down to ask if you would like to have me force a sale for you."

"Two thousand dollars!" cried Bayard, turning pale. "Why, it would almost build me—at least, it would furnish a new chapel. We had about so much of inside property—library, piano, pictures, settees, hymn-books, and all that—it is all a dead loss. Unfortunately, Mr. Bond had never insured it—we were so poor; every dollar tells!"

"Then he was a very bad man of business for a church—for a—missionary officer!" cried Mr. Worcester irritably; "and I hope you'll

ELIZABETH STUART PHELPS

do nothing of the kind. You could spend that amount on your personal necessities inside of six months, and then not know it, sir! You are—I hope, Manuel," sternly, "that you will regard my wish, for once, in one respect, before I die. Don't fling your mother's money into the bottomless pit of this unendowed, burnt-out, unpopular enterprise! Wait awhile, Manuel. Wait a little and think it over. I don't think, under the circumstances," added Mr. Worcester with some genuine dignity, "that it is very much to ask."

"Perhaps it is not," replied Bayard thoughtfully. "At least, I will consider it, as you say."

Four days after, an envelope from Boston was put into Bayard's hand. It contained a typewritten letter setting forth the fact that the writer desired to contribute to the erection of the new chapel in Windover known by the name of Christlove, and representing a certain phase of home missionary effort—the inclosed sum. It was a bank draft for twenty-five hundred dollars. The writer withheld his name, and requested that no effort be made to identify him. He also desired that his contribution be used, if possible, in a conditional character, to stimulate the growth of a collection sufficient to put the building and the mission behind it, upon a suitable basis.

The following day Mr. Worcester sent to Bayard by personal check the remnant of his mother's property. This little sum seemed as large, now, to the Beacon Street boy, as if he had been reared in one of the Vermont parsonages to which his uncle sent old overcoats; or, one might say, as if he had never left the shelter of that cottage under the pine grove in Bethlehem, where his eyes first opened upon the snow-girt hills. Self-denial speaks louder in the blood than indulgence, after all; and who knew how much of Bayard's simple manliness in the endurance of privation he owed to the pluck of the city girl who left the world for love of one poor man, and to become the mother of another?

Bayard had scarcely adjusted his mind to these events when he received from Helen Carruth this letter:—

My Dear Mr. Bayard,

My little note of sympathy with your great trouble did not deserve so prompt an answer. I thank you for it. I could not quite make up my mind to tell you, in the midst of so much care and anxiety, what I can delay no longer in saying"—

Bayard laid down the letter. The room grew black before his starting eyes.

"There is another man," he thought. "She is engaged. She cannot bear to tell me."

Sparks of fire leaped before his eyeballs. Black swung into purple—into gray—light returned; and he read on:—

"If I flatter myself in supposing that you might mind it a little, why, the mistake hurts nobody, neither you nor me; but the fact is we are not coming to Windover this summer. We sail for Europe next week.

"Father has decided quite suddenly, and there is nothing to be done but to go. It is something to do with Exegesis, if you please! There is a mistake in Exegesis, you know,—in the New Version. It seems to me a pretty Old Version by this time, but father has always been stirred up about it. He has been corresponding with a German Professor for a year or two on this burning subject. I have an inarticulate suspicion that, between them, they mean to write the New Testament over again. Could they do another Version? How many Versions *can* be versed?

"I never graduated, you know; I never even attended a Cesarea Anniversary in my life (and you can't think how it shocked the Trustees at dinner, and *that* was such fun, so I kept on not going!), and I can't be expected to fathom these matters. Anyhow, it is mixed up with the Authenticity of the Fourth Gospel, and the Effect of German Rationalism upon the Evangelical Faith. It is a reason full of capital letters and Orthodoxy,—and go he will. He won't leave mother behind, for he is one of the men who believe in living with their wives; he's just as dependent on his womenkind when he's engaged in a theological row, as a boy who's got hurt at football; and I've got to go to take care of the two of them. So there it is! I think there is a convention in Berlin—an Exegetical Something—anyhow, there's a date, and live up to it we must. He has sublet the Flying Jib to the Prudential Committee of the A. B. C. F. M.—I mean to one of it, with six grandchildren. Think how they'll punch their fists through our lace curtains! I wish you'd go down and tell

ELIZABETH STUART PHELPS

Mr. Salt they shan't have my dory. Couldn't you manage to use it yourself? And I—I can't take Joey Slip to the circus, nor sit down in sackcloth on the ashes of Christlove Chapel to help you.

"Truly, dear friend, I *meant* to help this summer. And I am disappointed, if you care to know it.

Yours faithfully,
HELEN CARRUTH

"I forgot to say that father has doubled up his lectures, and the Trustees have given him the whole summer term. This, I believe, is in view of the importance of the quarrel over the Fourth Gospel. We sail in the Scythia a week from Saturday."

IT WAS EARLY AFTERNOON OF the next day, when Helen, standing in her window to draw the shades, glanced over automatically at the third-story northwest corner front of Galilee Hall. The room had long since been occupied by a middler with blue spectacles and a peaked beard; a long-legged fellow, who was understood to be a Hebrew scholar, and quite Old School, and was expected to fill a large parish without offending the senior deacon. Privately, Helen hated the middler. But the eye that had learned to wander at sunset across the Seminary "yard" to the window blazing in gold and glory, had slowly unlearned the lesson of its brief and pleasant habit. Even yet, on blue-white winter days, when life stood still to freeze on Cesarea Hill, Helen found herself drearily looking at the glittering glass—as one looks at the smile on a face from which the soul has fled.

It was still many hours to sunset, and the early April afternoon fell gustily and gray upon the snows of Cesarea. It was not a sunny day, and Cesarea was at her worst. Helen idly watched a figure splashing through two feet of slush "across lots" over the Seminary grounds from the Trustees' Hotel.

"A post-graduate," she thought, "back on a visit. Or, more likely, a minister without a pulpit, coming to Cesarea after a parish, or places to supply. Probably he has seven children and a mother-in-law to support. If he's 'sound' he'll come to Father—no—yes. Why, *yes!*"

She drew suddenly back from the window. It was Emanuel Bayard.

He waded through the slush as quickly as so tired a man could. He had walked from the station, saving his coach fare, and had made but feint of being a guest at the hotel, where he had not dined. He was not quite prepared to let Helen know that he had lunched on cold johnny-cake and dried beef, put up by Mrs. Granite in a red cotton doily, and tenderly pinned over by Jane with a safety-pin.

He lifted his eyes to the gloomy landscape for illumination, which it denied him. He knew no more than the snow professor what he should do, what he should say, no, nor why he had lapsed into this great weakness, and come to Cesarea at all. He felt as if he might make, indeed, a mortal mistake, one way or the other. He pleaded to himself that he must see her face once more, or perish. Nature was mightier than he, and drove him on, as it drives the strongest of us in those reactions from our strenuous vow and sternest purpose, for which we have lacked the simple foresight to provide in our plan of life.

There was a new snow professor, by the way, comfortably melting before the pump beside the Academy commons. He had been considered sounder than any of his predecessors, and had been supplied with a copy of St. Augustine's Confessions, which he perused with a corncob pipe between his lips of ice. A Westminster catechism ornamented his vest pocket. He was said to have slumped beautifully, when the thaw came.

Bayard shot a tolerant smile at the snow professor's remains, as he came up the steps.

Helen herself answered his ring. Both of them found this so natural that neither commented upon this little act of friendliness.

The Professor was at his lecture; and Mrs. Carruth was making her final appearance at certain local Cesarea charities; principally, to-day, at the Association for Assisting Indigent Married Students with blankets and baby-clothes. Helen explained these facts with her usual irreverence, as she ushered her visitor into the parlor.

"If I had a fortune," she observed, "I would found a society in Cesarea for making it a Penal Offence for a Married Man to Study for the Ministry without a Visible Income. The title is a little long, don't you think? How could we shorten it? It's worse than the Cruelty to Animals thing. Mr. Bayard?—why, Mr. Bayard!"

When she saw the expression of his face, her own changed with remorseful swiftness.

"You are perfectly right," he said with sudden, smiting incisiveness. "You are more than right. It is the greatest act of folly of my life that I am here."

ELIZABETH STUART PHELPS

He stood still, and looked at her. The despair she saw in his eyes seemed to her a measureless, bottomless thing.

"I *had* to come," he said. "How could I let you go, without—you *must* see that I had to look upon your face once more. Forgive me—dear!"

Her chin trembled, at the lingering of that last, unlooked-for word.

"I have tried," said Bayard slowly. "*You* won't misunderstand me if I say I have tried to do the best I can, at Windover; and I have failed in it," he added bitterly, "from every point of view, and in every way!"

"As much as that," said Helen, "happened to the Founder of the Christian religion. You are presumptuous if you expect anything different."

"You are right," answered Bayard, with that instinctive humility which was at once the strongest and the sweetest thing about him. "I accept your rebuke."

"Oh," cried Helen, holding out her hands, "I *couldn't* rebuke you! I"—she faltered.

"You see," said Bayard slowly, "that's just the difference, the awful, infinite difference. All His difficulties were from the outside."

"How do you know that?" asked Helen quickly.

"I don't," replied Bayard thoughtfully. "I don't know. But I have been accustomed to think so. Perhaps I am under the traditions yet; perhaps I am no nearer right than the other Christians I have separated myself from. But mine, you see—my obstacles, the things that make it so hard—the only thing that makes it seem impossible for me to go on—is within myself. You don't suppose He ever loved a woman—as I—love you? It's impossible!" cried the young man. "Why, there are times when it seems to me that if the salvation of the world hung in one scale, and you in the other—as if I—" He finished by a blinding look. Her face drooped, but did not fall. He could see her fingers tremble. "It was something," he went on dully, "to see you; to know that I—why, all winter I have lived on it, on the knowledge that summer was coming—that you—Oh, *you* can't know! *You* can't understand! I could bear all the rest!" he cried. "This—this—"

His sentence broke, and was never completed; for Helen looked up into his face. It was ashen, and all its muscles were set like stiffening clay. She lifted her eyes and gave them to him.

"I do understand. . . I *do*," she breathed. "Would it make you any happier if you knew—if I should tell you—of course, I know what you said; that we can't. . . but would it be any easier if I should tell you that I have loved you all the time?"

XXIII

To the end of her life Helen will see the look on Emanuel Bayard's face when she had spoken these words.

With more of terror than delight, the woman's nature sprang, for that instant, back upon itself. Would she have recalled what she had said? It is possible; for now she understood how he loved her, and perceived that she had never understood what a man's love is.

Yet, when he spoke, it was with that absence of drama, with that repression amounting almost to commonplace, which characterize the intensest crises of experience.

"*Do* you?" he said. "*Have* you?"

And at first that was all. But his voice shook, and his hand; and his face went so white that he seemed like a man smitten rather by death than by love.

Helen, in a pang of maiden fright, had moved away from him, and retreated to the sofa; he sank beside her silently. Leaning forward a little, he covered his eyes with one hand. The other rested on the cushion within an inch of her purple dress; he did not touch her; he did not touch it. Helen felt sorry, seeing him so troubled and wrung; her heart went out in a throb of that maternal compassion which is never absent from the love of any woman for any man.

"Oh," she sighed, "I meant to make you happy, to give you comfort! And now I have made you unhappy!"

"You have made me the happiest of all miserable men!"

He raised his head, and looked at her till hers was the face to fall.

"Oh, don't!" she pleaded. "Not like *that*!"

But he paid no heed to this entreaty. The soul of the saint and the heart of the man made duel together; and the man won, and exulted in it, and wondered how he dared; but his gaze devoured her willfully. The first embrace of the eyes—more delicate, more deferent, and at once less guarded than the meeting of hands or clasp of arms—he gave her, and did not restrain it. Before it, Helen felt more helpless than if he had touched her. She seemed to herself to be annihilated in his love.

"Happy?" he said exultingly, "you deify me! You have made a god of me!"

"No," she shook her head with a little teasing smile, "I have made a man of you."

"Then they are one thing and the same!" cried the lover. "Let me hear you say it. Tell it to me again!"

She was silent, and she crimsoned to the brows.

"You are not sure!" he accused her. "You want to take it back. It was a madness, an impulse. You don't mean it. You do not, you have not loved me. . . How *could* you?" he added humbly. "You know I never counted on it, never expected, did not trust myself to think of it—all this while."

She lifted her head proudly.

"I have nothing to take back. It was not an impulse. I am not that kind of woman. I have been meaning to tell you—when you gave me the chance. I love you. I have loved you ever since—"

She stopped.

"Since when? How long have you loved me? Come! Speak! I *will* know!" commanded Bayard deliriously.

"Oh, what is going to be gained if I tell you?" Helen gave him a prisoner's look. She turned her head from side to side rebelliously, as if she had flown into a cage whose door was now unexpectedly shut.

"I meant to make you happy. All I say seems to make everything worse. I shall tell you nothing more."

"You will tell me," he said in a tone of calm authority, "all I ask. It is my affair whether I am happy or wretched. Yours is to obey my wish: because you love me, Helen."

His imperious voice fell to a depth of tenderness in which her soul and body seemed to sink and drown.

"I have loved you," she whispered, "ever since that night,—the first time I saw you here, in my father's house."

"Now, sir!" she added, with her sudden, pretty willfulness, "make the most of it. I'm not ashamed of it, either. But I shall be ashamed of *you* if—this—if after I've said it *all*, it doesn't make you happy. . . That's all I care for," she said quietly. "It is all I care for in this world."

"Oh, what shall we do?" pleaded Bayard.

"You have your work," said Helen dreamily, "and I your love."

Her voice sank to a whisper.

"Is that enough for you?" demanded the man. "I shall perish of it, I shall perish!"

Something in his tone and expression caused Helen to regard him keenly. He looked so wasted, so haggard, that her heart stood still, and said to her,—"This is truer than he knows."

"No," she answered with a sweet, womanly composure, "it is not enough for me."

"And yet," he said with the brutality of the tormented, "I cannot, I must not, ask you to be my"—

She put the tips of her fingers to his lips to check the word. He seized her hand and held it there; then, for he came to himself, he relinquished it, and laid it down.

"Dear," said Helen, "I shouldn't mind it. . . to be poor. I want you to understand—to know how it is. I have never felt. . . any other way. It shall be just as you say," she added with a gentleness which gave a beautiful dignity to her words. "We need not. . . do it, because I say this. But I wanted you to know—that I was not *afraid* of a hard life with you."

"Oh, you cannot understand," he groaned. "It is no picturesque poverty you would have to meet. It would mean cold, hunger, misery you've never thought of, cruel suffering—for you. It would mean all that a man has no right to ask a woman to endure for him, *because* he loves her. . . as I love you."

"I could starve," said Helen.

"God help us!" cried the man. Nothing else came to his dry lips.

Then Helen answered him in these strong and quiet words: "I told you I would trust you, and I shall do it to the end. When you are ready for me, I shall come. I am not afraid—of anything, except that you should suffer and that I could not comfort you. If you never see the way to think it right. . . I can wait. I love you; and I am yours to take or leave."

"This," whispered Bayard reverently, for he could have knelt before her, "is a woman's love! I am unworthy of it—and of you."

"Oh, there is the other kind of woman," said Helen, trying rather unsuccessfully to smile. "This is only *my* way of loving. I am not ashamed of it."

"Ashamed of it? It honors you! It glorifies you!"

He held out his arms; but she did not swerve towards them; they dropped. She seemed to him encompassed in a shining cloud, in which her own celestial tenderness and candor had wrapped and protected her.

"Love me!" he pleaded. "Love me, trust me, till we can think. I must do right by *you*, whatever it means to *me*."

"We love each other," repeated Helen, holding out her hands, "and I trust you. Let us live on that a little while, till we—till you"—

But she faltered, and her courage forsook her when she looked up into his face. All the anguish of the man that the woman cannot share, and may not understand, started out in visible lines and signs upon his features; all the solemn responsibility for her, for himself, and for the unknown consequences of their sacred passion; the solitary burden, which it is his to wear in the name of love, and which presses hardest upon him whose spirit is higher and stronger than mere human joy.

But at this moment a sound was heard upon the stone steps of the Queen Anne house. It was the footfall of the Professor himself, returning from his closing lecture of the series on Eschatology. Mrs. Carruth pattered behind him with short, stout steps. She had wound the affairs of the Association for Assisting Indigent Married Students with Blankets, to a condition in which they could run along without her till the exegetical trip to the German Professor's in Berlin should be over, and the slush of Cesarea should know her again.

XXIV

The summer slid, Bayard knew not how. They separated as so many confused lovers do in the complicated situations of our later life; wherein we love no longer in the old, outright, downright way, when men and women took each other for better, for worse, and dared to run the risk of loving, without feeling responsible for the consequences. We are past all that; and whether it is the worse or the better for us, who shall say?

At least, these two had the healthy ring to their love; in that great and simple feeling was no delinquency or default. Bayard did not hesitate or quibble—one day a lover, the next a prudential committee, after the fashion of such feeble mathematicians as go by the name of men, to-day. He was incapable of calculating his high passion; there was no room in his soul or body for a doubt to take on lease of life. He loved her; as the greatest of women might be proud and humble to be loved; as the smallest would be vain to be.

He loved her too much to make her miserable; and he knew, with that dreary, practical perception of the truth sometimes but rarely granted to men of the seer's temperament, that he could not make her happy. Between love and joy a dead wall shut down; it seemed to him to reach from the highest heavens to the waters under the earth. What elemental chaos could rend it? What miracle was foreordained to shatter it? Would the busy finger of God stretch out to touch it?

"God knows," he wrote her. "And He purposes, I am fain to believe, if He purposes anything we do or suffer. The hour may come, and the way *might* clear. More incredible things have happened to men and women loving less than we. If I can, I claim you when I can. Oh, wait for me, and trust me! Life is so short; it is not easy. Sometimes madness enters into me, to fling all these cold, these cruel considerations, these things we call honor, unselfishness, chivalry, to the gales. . . Then I come to myself. I will not wrong you. Help me to bear to live without you till I see your face again."

Helen wrote him noble letters; brave, womanly, and as trustful as the swing of the earth in its orbit. It is not too much to say that few women in her place would have shown the strong composure of this ardent girl. The relation between acknowledged lovers unbetrothed is one whose difficulty only an inspired delicacy can control. Helen's clear eyes held no shadows. The dark wing of regret for a moment's weakness never brushed between her heart and this Sir Galahad who loved her like man and spirit too. Few women reared as she had been would have trusted the man as she did; we may add that fewer men would have deserved it.

Emanuel Bayard did. Her heart knew him for one of the sons of light, who will not, because he cannot, cause the woman whom he loves an hour's regret that she has believed in him utterly and told him so. Now, the value of a woman's intuition in most of the problems or relations of life cannot be overestimated; when she loves, it is the least reliable of her attributes or qualities. Helen in her composed way recognized this fact perfectly, but it gave her no uneasiness.

"My own perception might fail me," she wrote. "You could not. It is not my own sense of what is best to do that I am trusting, in this: it is you."

When he read these words, he put the paper to his lips, and laid his face upon it, and covered it from the sight even of his own eyes.

The date of Professor Carruth's return was set for early October. In September Bayard received from Helen the news that her mother had met with an accident—a fall; an arm was broken, and, at the age of the patient, the surgeon forbade the voyage. The Professor would get back to his lecture-room, as he must. The two ladies were indefinitely delayed in Berlin.

THE WINTER PROVED A BLEAK one, and went with Bayard as was to be expected. The devotee had yet to learn how a woman's absence may work upon a lover; but of this, since he had no right to do so, he did not complain. Headlong, fathoms down into his work he leaped, and with the diver's calm he did the diver's duty. The new chapel progressed after the manner of its kind. Bayard had peremptorily insisted upon the severest economy of plan, demanding a building which should be a "shelter for worship," he said, and nothing more. Not a waste dollar went into architecture. Not a shingle went into debt. No mortgage desecrated the pulpit of Christlove Church. He built what he could pay for, and nothing more. The dedication of the building was expected to take place in the spring.

Meanwhile, his audiences grew upon his hands; and Windover First Church looked darkly at Windover town hall. Orthodoxy, decorum, property, position, gazed at gaping pews, and regretted that "these temperance movements estranged themselves from the churches."

Obscurity, poverty, religious doubt, sin and shame and repentance jammed the aisles to hear "the Christman" interpret decency and dignity and the beauty of holiness. He spoke to these, not with the manner of preachers, but with the lips and heart of a man. Week after week strange, unkempt, unlettered seamen poured in; they stood sluggishly, like forming lava, to listen to him. Certain of his audiences would have honored Whitefield or Robertson. Bayard's soul seemed that winter alight with a sacred conflagration. He prayed and wrought for Windover as a tongue of flame goes up to the sky—because it was the law of life and fire. It is pathetic to think, now, how it would have comforted the man if he had known how much they loved him—these undemonstrative people of the sea, for whom he gave himself. The half of it was never told him. Censure, and scorn, and scandal, and the fighting of foes in the dark, he knew. The real capacity for affection and loyalty which existed in the rough, warm heart of Windover he sometimes thought he understood. He did not see—as we see now—that he had won this allegiance.

This was the more obscure to him because the tension between himself and the liquor interests of Windover was growing quietly into a serious thing, and heavily occupied his attention. And here we know that he was seldom deceived or blinded.

His methods were deliberate, his moves were intelligent, he ran no stupid risks, he measured his dangers, he took them in the name of good citizenship and good Christianity, and strode on to their consequences with that martial step characteristic of him. Of this chapter of the winter's story, he wrote little or nothing to Helen. She heard how the chapel grew, how the library gathered, and the smoking-room was fitted; about the hope of a gymnasium, the vision of a bowling-alley, the schedule for lectures and entertainments; all his dreams and schemes to give homeless and tempted men shelter and happiness under the rising roof of Christlove;—all the little pleasures and hopes of the missionary life she shared, as Helen had it in her to share the serious energy of a man's life. Upon the subject of the dangers he was silent. The extent to which these existed she could not measure; for Helen belonged to those social and religious circles into whose experience the facts in the remote lives of that worthy class of people known as temperance agitators do not enter. She had no traditions to enlighten her, and her own joyous nature vaguely filled in the darker outlines of her lover's life. How should the summer girl understand the winter Windover? She thought of Bayard's real situation with little more vividness than if he had been a missionary in Darkest Africa. Pleasant sketches of Job Slip and Joey, little reminiscences of Captain Hap, and Lena, pretty, womanly plans for replacing the burned furniture and decorations flitted across the leisurely continental tour by which she escorted her mother homewards. Mrs. Carruth was now quite recovered, but had developed the theory that the dangers of a midwinter voyage were lessened by every week's delay. As a result, the two ladies engaged passage in February, at the height of the gales.

It was a bitter winter. Two hundred Windover fishermen were drowned; and poverty of the dreariest kind sat sullenly in the tragic town. Bayard worked till he staggered for the women and children whom the sea bereft. Afterwards a cry went up out of scores of desolated homes which told what the man had been and done in Windover, when the gales went down.

One night, a short time before Helen was to sail, there happened to Bayard one of those little mysteries which approach us so much oftener than we recognize them, that we have never properly classified them; and may be long yet in doing so.

He had been in his own rooms since noon; for there was a heavy snowstorm on, and he was conscious of obvious physical inability to brave the weather unless the call of duty should be louder than a certain oppression on his lungs, which he had been forced of late to recognize more often than usual. It was a gray day at Mrs. Granite's. Jane was sad, and coughed. Her mother had cried a good deal of late, and said that "Jane was goin' off like her Aunt Annie before her."

Ben Trawl came sullenly and seldom, now, to see the reluctant girl.

Mrs. Granite thought if Jane could go to her Aunt Annie's second cousin Jenny in South Carolina, for a spell, she would be cured; but Mrs. Granite said climate was only meant for rich folks; she said you lived and died here in Windover, if your lungs was anyways delicate, like frozen herring packed into a box. She was almost epigrammatic—for Mrs. Granite.

Bayard had been sitting in his study-chair, writing steadily, while his mind, with his too sensitive sympathy, followed the fortunes of these poor women who made him all the home he knew. It was towards six o'clock, and darkening fast. The noise on the beach opposite the cottage was heavy; and the breakers off Ragged Rock boomed mightily.

Snow was falling so thickly that he could not see the water. The fog-bell was tolling, and yells of agony came from the whistling-buoy. It was one of the days when a man delicately reared winces with a soreness impossible to be understood unless experienced, from life in a place and in a position like his; when the uncertain value of the ends of sacrifice presents itself to the mind like the spatter from a stream of vitriol; when the question, Is what I achieve worth its cost? burns in upon the bravest soul, and gets no answer for its scorching.

Bayard laid down his pen and paper, and looked patiently out of the window; putting his empty hand in his pocket as he did so.

His eyes gazed into the curtain of the whirling snow. He wondered how far out to sea it extended; how many miles of it dashed between himself and Helen. It was one of the hours when she seemed to fill the world.

The snowflakes took on fantastic shapes—so! That was the way she held out her white hands. The soft trailing of her gown sounded in the room. If he turned his head, should he see her standing, a vision in purple and gold, smiling, warm, and sweet? It would be such a disappointment not to find her! Rather believe that he should, if he would, and so not stir.

Suddenly his hand in his own pocket struck an object whose character he did not at the moment recall. He drew it out and looked at it. It was the key of his old home in Beacon Street.

For three years, perhaps, he had not thought of his uncle's words: "Keep your latch-key. You will want to use it, some day."

Bayard regarded the latch-key steadily. The senseless thing burned his palm as if it were trying to articulate.

He never sought to explain to himself, and I see no reason why we should explain for him, the subtile meaning which went from the metal to the man.

The key said, "Go!"

And Bayard went. He made such efforts as all cool-headed people make, to buffet the inexplicable, and to resist an unreasonable impression. But, after an hour's protest with himself, he yielded to the invisible summons.

"It is a long while since I have seen my uncle," he reasoned. "This may be as good a time as any other to look him up."

He dressed for the storm, and took the nine o'clock train to Boston. It was blowing a blizzard when he arrived in town; and eleven o'clock. He took a carriage and drove to his uncle's house. The lights were out on the front of the house, and the servants asleep. Bayard stood a moment irresolute. The folly of his undertaking presented itself to him with emphasis, now he was there. He could not tell when he had yielded to any of that class of highly wrought emotions which we call presentiments, or "leadings." Impatient with himself, and suddenly vividly aware that Mr. Hermon Worcester was a man who particularly objected to being disturbed in his sleep, Bayard was about to call the cab back to take him away, when he perceived that the driver had started off, and was laboring heavily up Beacon Street, with the snow to the hubs of the wheels. (Who has ever fathomed the inscrutable mind of the Boston cabman who has to be snowed under, before he will get on runners?) Resisting no longer, Bayard softly put his key in the lock.

It creaked a little, for it had grown rusty in the Windover salts, but the boy's key turned in the man's hand, and admitted him loyally into his old home.

The hall was dark, and the house still. He brushed off the snow in silence, and stood wondering what to do next. He felt mortified at his own lack of good sense.

Why was he here? And what reason could he give for this stupendous foolishness? He dripped on the Persian rugs awhile, and, finding neither enlightenment nor consolation in this moist occupation, proceeded to take off his overcoat and hang it on his own nail on the mahogany hat-tree under the stairs. When had such a shabby overcoat put that venerable piece of furniture to the blush? Never, if one excepted the case of the Vermont clergyman who had been known to take a lunch with his benefactor, and who received a barrel of old clothes the following week. Bayard hung up his wet hat, too, in the old place, took off his shoes, and crept upstairs in his stockings, as he had done—how many hundred nights, coming home from Cambridge, late, in college days?

His uncle's door was closed, but to his surprise, he found the door of his own room open. He crept in. It seemed warm and pleasant—how incredibly pleasant and natural! The register seemed to be open. Oh, the luxury of a furnace! The wet and tired man crawled up, feeling his way in the familiar dark, and got down by the register. He remembered where the safety-matches used to be, that struck, and made no sound. Groping, he found them, in their paper match-box, set within the old bronze one. He struck one, softly, and looked about. In the little flare he saw that the room was just as it had always been. Nothing was changed or disturbed, except that his books had gone to Mrs. Granite's. His bed lay turned back, open for the night, as it always was; the big, soft pillow, the luxurious mattresses, the light warmth of the snowy blankets, invited him. His mother's picture hung over the head of his bed. Those old pipes and silk menus and college traps and trifles were crossed on the wall by the bureau; his gun was there, and his fishing-rods.

Bayard was about to yield to his weariness, and crawl into his own bed, thinking to see his uncle in the morning, as a sane man should, when his attention was attracted by a slight sound in Mr. Worcester's room, and something about it struck the young man unpleasantly.

Without noise he opened the door of the bath-room intervening between his own and his uncle's apartments. Then he perceived a crack of light at the threshold of Mr. Worcester's closed door.

As he stood uncertain, and troubled, the sound which he had heard was repeated. It seemed to resemble the effort of difficult breathing, and was accompanied by a slight groan.

Then a thick voice called,—

"Partredge?"

"Partredge always did sleep like the dead," thought Bayard. "I hope he doesn't neglect my uncle, now he is growing old."

"Nancy?" summoned the voice again.

Nancy always woke easily and good-naturedly. But Nancy heard nothing now. Bayard, afraid to shock the old man by so astounding an appearance, was moving quickly and quietly to find the servants, when something caused him to change his purpose. Apparently, Mr. Worcester had tried to reach the bell—it was one of the old-fashioned kind, with a long, embroidered bell-handle—he had partly crossed the room, when Bayard intercepted the fall, and caught him.

The gas was lighted, and recognition was instant. Without shock, it seemed without surprise, Hermon Worcester lay back in the young man's arms, and smiled pleasantly into his face.

"I *thought* you would use the latch-key—some night," he said with difficulty. "You've chosen the right one, Manuel. The servants did not hear—and—I'm afraid I'm not—quite—well, my boy."

After this, he said nothing; but lingered for three days, without evident suffering, and with evident content, making signs that Manuel should not leave him; which he did not, to the end.

Hermon Worcester passed on serenely, in the Faith, and the prominence and usefulness thereof; though the last prayer that he heard on earth came from the lips of the affectionate heretic in whose arms he died.

Bayard had been so long out of the world and the ways of it, that it did not occur to him, till he received the summons of the family lawyer, that he would be required to be present at the reading of his uncle's will.

"As the nearest of kin, my dear sir," suggested the attorney, "the occasion will immediately concern you, doubtless."

Bayard bowed, in silence. He did not think it necessary to explain to the attorney that he had been, for a long time, aware of the fact of his disinheritance.

"Possibly Uncle may have left me his library," he thought, "or the furniture of my old room."

He had, indeed, received the library. The rest of Hermon Worcester's fortune, barring the usual souvenirs to relatives, had been divided between Mr. Worcester's favorite home missionary associations and Cesarea Seminary, of which he had been, for thirty years, trustee.

The house on Beacon Street, with its contents, went unreservedly, "and affectionately," the testator had expressed it, to his nephew, Emanuel Bayard.

"I think," observed the lawyer at the first decent opportunity, "that Mr. Worcester intended, or—hoped that you might make your plans of life in accordance with such circumstances as would enable you to keep, and to keep up, the homestead."

"But of course," added the attorney, shrewdly reading Bayard's silent face, "that might be—as you say—impossible."

"I said nothing," replied Bayard in a low voice.

"The place is yours, without conditions," pursued the lawyer, with polite indifference. "It can be sold, or converted into income—rented, if you please, if ever unfortunately necessary. It would seem a pity. It would bring so little. But still, it could, of course, be done."

"What do you call a little?" asked Bayard.

"Oh, enough for a small fresh-water Professor or retail grocer to get along on, if he knew how," replied the Back Bay lawyer carelessly.

He mentioned the figures.

The house was old, and in need of repair; the furniture out of date, and worn. The probable values were not large, as the attorney said. To the pastor from Angel Alley their possession seemed to represent the shock of nature involved in a miracle.

XXV

H elen was to sail for Boston the following Saturday. It lacked three days of that date. It being out of the question to reach her, now, by letter, Bayard cabled to her:—

> Will meet you arrival steamer. Future clear before me. I await you.
>
> E. B.

To this impulsive message he found himself expecting a reply. The wan missionary had burst into a boyish and eager lover. Oh, that conscientious, cruel past! He dashed it from him. He plunged into the freedom of his heart. In honor—in his delicate honor—he could win her, now.

Helen did not answer the cable message. A hundred hindrances might have prevented her; yet he had believed she would. He thought of her ardent, womanly candor, her beautiful courage, her noble trust. It did not occur to him that a woman has two natures, this for the unfortunate and that for the fortunate lover. One he had tasted; the other he had yet to know.

He vibrated restlessly to and fro between Windover and Boston, where his presence was urgently required in the settlement of his uncle's affairs. A snowstorm set in, and increased to a gale. Ten days passed, somehow. The steamer was due in twenty-four hours. She did not arrive.

Bayard had lived in Windover long enough to acquire the intelligent fear of the sea which characterizes the coast; and when the next day went, and another, and the boat was admitted at headquarters to be three days overdue, he suffered the unspeakable. It had been nothing less than a terrible midwinter gale. Wrecks lined the coast; glasses scoured it; watchers thronged it; friends besieged the offices of the steamship company. The great line which boasted that it had never lost a life held its stanchest steamer three days—four days overdue.

It was like him that he did not overlook his duty in his trouble, but stood to his post, and remembered the little service appointed for that most miserable evening when he was expected to be with his people. Those who were present that night say that the scene was one impossible to forget. Looking more like death than life, the preacher prayed before them "to the God of the sea."

Now, for the first time, he felt that he knew what Windover could suffer. Now the torment of women all their lives watching for returning sails entered into his soul; those aged men looking for the sons who never came back; the blurred eyes peering off Windover Point to see the half-mast flag on the schooner as she tacked up the bay; the white lips that did not ask, when the boat came to anchor, "Which is it?" because they dared not—all this, now, he understood.

His personal anguish melted into the great sum of misery in the seaport town.

"If she comes back to me," he thought, "how I shall work for them—my poor people!"

Now, for the first time, this devout, unselfish man understood that something else than consecration is needed to do the best and greatest thing by the human want or woe that leans upon us. Now that he took hold on human experience, he saw that he had everything to learn from it. The knowledge of a great love, the lesson of the common tie that binds the race together—these taught him, and he was their docile scholar.

Five days overdue! . . . Six days. Bayard had gone back to Boston, to haunt the offices and the docks. Old friends met him among the white-lipped watchers, and a classmate said:—

"Thank God, Bayard, *you* haven't wife and child aboard her."

He added:—

"Man alive! You look like the five days dead!"

Suddenly, the stir ran along the crowd, and a whisper said:—

"*They've sighted her! . . . She's in!*"

Then came the hurrah. Shouts of joy reëchoed about him. But Bayard's head fell upon his breast in silence. At that moment he was touched upon the arm by a beautiful Charter Oak cane, and, looking up, he saw the haggard face of the Professor of Theology.

"I was belated," thickly articulated the Professor with dry lips. "I came straight from the lecture-room. It is the course on the 'Nature of Eternal Punishment,'—a most important course. I felt it my duty to be at my desk. But—Bayard, I think I shall substitute to-morrow my lecture (perhaps you may recall it) on the 'Benevolence and Beneficence of God.'"

The two men leaped into the tug together, and ploughed out to the steamer.

Helen was forward, leaning on the rail. Her thick steamer-dress blew like muslin in the heavy wind. Her eyes met Bayard's first—yes, first. Her father came in second, but his were too dim to know it.

"Mother is in the cabin, dear Papa!" cried Helen; "we have to keep her warm and still, you know."

His daughter's precious kiss invited him, but the old man put Helen gently aside, and dashed after his old wife.

For that moment Helen and Bayard stood together. Before all the world he would have taken her in his arms, but she retreated a little step.

"Did you get my message?" he demanded.

"Yes."

"Did you answer it?"

"No."

"Why not?"

"I thought it would do just as well when I got here."

"And you might have been—you might never have got here at all!" cried Bayard fiercely.

"Have you been anxious?" asked Helen demurely.

He did not think it was in her to coquette with a man in a moment like that, and he made her no reply. Then Helen looked full in his face, and saw the havoc on it.

"Oh, you poor boy!" she whispered; "you poor, poor boy!"

THIS WAS IN THE AFTERNOON; and he was compelled to see her carried off to Cesarea on her father's arm, without him. There was no help for it; and he waited till the next day, unreconciled and nervous in the extreme. He had been so overworn and overwrought, that his mind took on feverish fancies.

"Something may happen by to-morrow," he thought, "and I shall have never—once"—

He rebuked even his own thought, even then, for daring to dream of the touch of her lips. But the dream rode over his delicacy, and rushed on.

At an early hour the next day he went to Cesarea, and sought her in her father's house. It was a cold, dry, bright day. Cesarea shivered under her ermine. The Professor's house was warm with the luxurious, even warmth of the latest modern heater, envied by the rest of the Faculty, in the old-fashioned, draughty houses of the Professors' Row. Flowers in the little window conservatory of the drawing-room breathed the soft air easily, and were of rich growth and color. Helen was watering the flowers. She colored when she saw him, and put down the silver pitcher which she had abstracted from the breakfast-room for the purpose of encouraging her lemon verbena, that had, plainly, missed her while she was abroad. She wore a purple morning-gown with plush upon it. She had a royal look.

"How early you have come!" she said half complainingly.

He paid no attention to her tone, but deliberately shut the door, and advanced towards her.

"I have come," he said, "to *stay*; that is—if you will let me, Helen."

"Apparently," answered Helen, taking up the pitcher, "I am not allowed a choice in the matter."

But he saw that the silver pitcher shook in her hand.

"No," he said firmly, "I do not mean to give you any choice. I mean to take you. I do not mean to wait one hour more."

He held out his arms, but suspended them, not touching her. The very air which he imprisoned around her seemed to clasp her. She trembled in that intangible embrace.

"It will be a poor man's home, Helen—but you will not suffer. I can give you common comforts. I cabled to you the very hour that I knew. . . Oh, I have trusted your trust!" he said.

"And you *may* trust it," whispered Helen, suddenly lifting her eyes.

His, it seemed to her, were far above her—how blinding beautiful joy made them!

Then his starved arms closed about her, and his lips found hers.

THE PROFESSOR OF THEOLOGY SAT in his study. The winter sun struck his loaded shelves; the backs of his books inspected him tenderly. At the western window, on the lady's desk which was reserved for Mrs. Carruth, her sewing-basket stood. The Professor glanced at it contentedly. He had never been separated from his wife so long before, and they had been married thirty-five years. She had unpacked that basket and taken it into the study that morning, with a girlish eagerness to sit down and darn a stocking while the Professor wrote.

"This is a great gratification, Statira," he had said.

Mrs. Carruth had gone out, now, to engage in the familiar delights of a morning contest with the Cesarea butcher, and the Professor was alone when Emanuel Bayard sturdily knocked at the study door.

The Professor welcomed the young man with some surprise, but no uncertain warmth. He expressed himself as grateful for the prompt attention of his former pupil, on the joyful occasion of this family reunion.

"And it was kind of you, Bayard, too—meeting the ladies on that tug. I was most agreeably surprised. I was wishing yesterday—in fact, it occurred to me what a comfort some young fellow would have been whom I could have sent down, all those anxious days. But we never had a son. Pray sit down, Mr. Bayard. . . I am just reading the opinions of Olshausen on a most interesting point. I have collected valuable material in Berlin. I shall be glad to talk it over with you. I found Professor Kammelschkreiter a truly scholarly man. His views on the errors in the Revised Version are the most instructed of any I have met."

"Professor," said Bayard stoutly, "will you pardon me if I interrupt you for a minute? I have come on a most important matter. I am sorry to seem uncivil, but the fact is I—I cannot wait another moment, sir. . . Sir, I have the honor to tell you that your daughter has consented to become my wife."

At this truly American declaration, the Professor of Theology laid down his copy of Olshausen, and stared at the heretic missionary.

"*My* daughter!" he gasped, "*your* wife?—I beg your pardon," he added, when he saw the expression of Bayard's face. "But you have taken me altogether by surprise. I may say that such a possibility has never—no, never once so much as occurred to me."

"I have loved her," said Bayard tenaciously, "for three years. I have never been able to ask her to marry me till now. I think perhaps my uncle meant to make it possible for me to do so, but I do not know. I am still a poor man, sir, but I can keep her from suffering. She does me the undeserved honor to love me, and she asked me to tell you so."

The Professor had risen and was pacing the study hotly. His face was rigid. He waved his thin, long fingers impatiently at Bayard's words.

"Scholars do not dwell upon paltry, pecuniary facts like parents in lower circles of society!" cried the Professor with superbly unconscious hauteur. "There would have lacked nothing to my daughter's comfort, sir, in any event—if the right man had wooed her. I was not the father to refuse him mere pecuniary aid to Helen's happiness."

"And I was not the lover to ask for it," observed Bayard proudly.

"Hum—m—m," said the Professor. He stopped his walk across the study floor, and looked at Bayard with troubled respect.

"I will not take her from you at once," urged Bayard gently; "we will wait till fall—if I can. She has said that she will become my wife, then."

His voice sank. He spoke the last words with a delicate reverence which would have touched a ruder father than the Professor of Theology.

"Bayard," he said brokenly, "you always were my favorite student. I couldn't help it. I always felt a certain tenderness for you. I respect your intellectual traits, and your spiritual quality. Poverty, sir? What is *poverty*? But, Bayard, *you are not sound*!"

Against this awful accusation Bayard had no reply; and the old Professor turned about ponderously, like a man whose body refused to obey the orders of his shocked and stricken mind.

"How can I see my daughter, *my* daughter, the wife of a man whom the Ancient Faith has cast out?" he pleaded piteously.

He lifted his shrunken hands, as if he reasoned before an invisible tribunal. His attitude and expression were so solemn that Bayard felt it impossible to interrupt the movement by any mere lover's plea. Perhaps, for the first time, he understood then what it meant to the old man to defend the beliefs that had ruled the world of his youth and vigor; he perceived that they, too, suffered who seemed to be the inflicters of suffering; that they, too, had their Calvary—these determined souls who doggedly died by the cross of the old Faith in whose shelter their fathers and their fathers' fathers had lived and prayed, had battled and triumphed. Bayard felt that his own experience at that moment was an intrusion upon the sanctuary of a sacred struggle. He bowed his head before his Professor, and left the study in silence.

But Helen, who had the small reverence for the theologic drama characteristic of those who have been reared upon its stage, put her beautiful arms around his neck and, laughing, whispered:—

"Leave the whole system of Old School Orthodoxy to me! I can manage!"

"You may manage him," smiled Bayard, "but can you manage *it*?"

"Wait a day, and see!" said Helen.

He would have waited a thousand for the kiss with which she lifted up the words.

The next day she wrote him, at Windover, where he was dutifully trying to preach as if nothing had happened:—

"Papa says I have never been quite sound myself, and that he supposes I will do as I please, as I always have."

There followed a little love-letter, so deliciously womanly and tender, that Bayard did not for hours open the remainder of his mail. When he did so, he read what the Professor of Theology had written, after a night of prayer and vigil such as only aged parents know.

"My Dear Bayard," the letter said,
    "Take her if you must, and God be with you both! I cannot find it in my heart to impose the shadow of my religious convictions upon the happiness of my child. I can battle for the Truth with men and with demons. I cannot fight with the appeal of a woman's love. I would give my life to make Helen happy, and to keep her so. Do you as much!

Yours sincerely,
Haggai Carruth

"P.S.—We will resume our discussion on the views of Professor Kammelschkreiter at some more convenient season."

XXVI

E arly June came to Windover joyously that year. May had been
a gentle month, warmer than its wont, and the season was in
advance of its schedule.

Mrs. Carruth, found paling a little, and thought to be less strong
since her accident abroad, had been ordered to the seaside some three
or four weeks before the usual flitting of the family. Helen accompanied
her; the Professor ran down as often as he might, till Anniversary Week
should set him free to move his ponderously increasing manuscript on
the "Errors in the Revised Version" from Cesarea to the clam study.
The long lace curtains blew in and out of the windows of the Flying
Jib; Helen's dory glittered in two coats of fresh pale-yellow paint upon
the float; and Helen, in pretty summer gowns of corn color, or violet,
or white, listened on the piazza for the foot-ring of her lover. She was
lovely that spring, with the loveliness of youth and joy. Bayard watched
her through a mist of that wonder and that worship which mark the
highest altitudes of energy in a man's life. It was said that he had never
wrought for Windover, in all his lonely time of service there, as he did
in those few glorified weeks.

It is pleasant to think that the man had this draught of human
rapture; that he tasted the brim of such joy as only the high soul in the
ardent nature knows.

Helen offered him her tenderness with a sweet reserve, alternating
between compassion for what he had suffered, and moods of pretty,
coquettish economy of his present privilege, that taunted and enraptured
him by turns. He floated on clouds; he trod on the summer air.

Their marriage was appointed for September: it was Helen's wish to
wait till then; and he submitted with such gentleness as it wrung her
heart, afterwards, to remember.

"We will have one perfectly happy summer," she pleaded. "People
can be lovers but once."

"And newly wed but once," he answered gravely.

"Dear," said Helen, with troubled eyes, "it shall be as you say. *You*
shall decide."

"God will decide it," replied the lover unexpectedly.

His eyes had a look which Helen could not follow. She felt shut out
from it; and both were silent.

Her little dreams and plans occupied hours of their time together. She was full of schemes for household comfort and economy, for serving his people, for blessing Windover. She talked of what could be done for Job Slip and Mari, Joey, Lena, Captain Hap and Johnny's mother, Mrs. Granite and poor Jane. Her mind dwelt much upon all these children of the sea who had grown into his heart. "Jane," she said, "should have her winter in the South." She spoke of Jane with a reticent but special gentleness. They would rent the cottage; they would furnish the old dreary rooms.

Helen did not come to her poor man quite empty-handed. The Professor had too much of the pride of total depravity left in him for that. "I shall be able to buy my own gowns, sir, if you please!" she announced prettily. "And I am going to send Mrs. Granite—with Jane—to her aunt Annie's cousin Jenny's (was that it?) in South Carolina, next winter, to get over that Windover cough. We've got to go ourselves, if *you* don't stop coughing. No? We'll see!"

"I *shall* stop coughing," cried Bayard joyously.

She did not contradict him, for she believed in Love the Healer, as the young and the beloved do. So she went dreaming on.

"I came across a piece of gold tissue in Florence; it will make such a pretty portière in place of that old mosquito-net! And we'll make those dismal old rooms over into"—

And Bayard, who had thought never to know Paradise on earth, but only to toil for Heaven, closed her sentence by one ecstatic word.

The completion of the chapel, still delayed after the fashion of contractors, was approaching the belated dedication day of which all Windover talked, and for which a growing portion of Windover interested itself. Bayard was over-busy for a newly betrothed man. His hours with Helen were shortened; his brief snatches of delight marked spaces between days of care. Erected upon the site of the burned building, the new chapel rose sturdily in the thick and black of Angel Alley. The old, illuminated, swinging sign remained,—"for luck," the fishermen said. It was to be lighted on the day when the first service should be held in the new Christlove.

There came a long, light evening, still in the early half of June. Bayard was holding some service or lecture in the town, and had late appointments with his treasurer, with Job Slip, and Captain Hap. He saw no prospect of freedom till too late an hour to call on Helen, and had gone down to tell her so; had bade her good-night, and left her. She had

ELIZABETH STUART PHELPS

gone out rowing, in the delicious loneliness of a much loved and never neglected girl, and was turning the bow of the dory homewards. She drifted and rowed by turns, idle and happy, dreamy and sweet. It was growing dark, and the boats were setting shorewards. One, she noticed (a rough, green fishing-dory from the town), lay, rudely held by a twist of the painter, to the cliffs, at the left, below the float. The dory was empty. A sailor hat and an old tan-colored reefer lay on the stern seat. Two girls sat on the rocks, sheltered in one of the deep clefts or chasms which cut the North Shore, talking earnestly together. One of them had her foot upon the painter. Neither of them noticed Helen; she glanced at them without curiosity, rowed in, tossed her painter to the keeper of the float, and went up to the house. Her father was in Windover that night; he and her mother were discussing the inconceivable prospect of an Anniversary without entertaining the Trustees; they were quite absorbed in this stupendous event. Helen strolled out again, and off upon the cliff.

She had but just tossed her Florentine slumber-robe of yellow silk upon the rocks, and thrown herself upon it, when voices reached her ear. Eavesdropping is an impossible crime on Windover Point, where the cliffs are common trysting-ground; still, Helen experienced a slight discomfort, and was about to exchange her rock for some less public position, when she caught a word which struck the blood to her heart, and back again, like a smart, stinging blow.

The voices were the voices of two girls. The stronger and the bolder was speaking.

"So I come to tell you. Do as you please. If *you* don't let on, I shall."

"Lena!" groaned the other, "are you sure? Isn't there some mistake?"

"Not a—chance of any," replied Lena promptly. "Do you s'pose I'd thrust myself upon you this way, and tell for nothin'? Lord, *I* know how decent girls feel, bein' seen with the likes of me. That's why I set it after dark, and never come nigh your house. Besides, *he's* there. I warn't a-goin' to make no talk, you better believe, Jane Granite. I've seen enough o' that."

"Mr. Bayard says you are a—good girl, now," faltered Jane, not knowing what to say. "I'm sure he wouldn't want me to be ashamed to be seen with you—now. And I—I'm much obliged to you, Lena. Oh, Lena! what ever in the world are we going to do?"

"Do?" said Lena sharply; "why, head 'em off; that's all! It only needs a little horse sense, and—to care enough. I'd be drownded in the mud in the inner harbor in a land wind—I'd light a bonfire in the powder factory, and stand by it, if that would do him any good. I guess you would, too."

Jane made no answer. She felt that this was a subject which could not be touched upon with Lena. It was too dark to see how Jane looked.

"Why," said the other, "you're shaking like a topsail in a breeze o' wind!"

"How do you mean? What is your plan? What do you mean to have me do?" asked Jane, whose wits seemed to have dissolved in terror.

"Get him out of Windover," coolly said Lena; "leastways for a spell. Mebbe it'll blow by. There ain't but one thing I know that'll do it. Anyhow, there ain't but one person."

"I can't think what you can mean!" feebly gasped Jane.

"*She* can," replied Lena tersely. Jane made a little inarticulate moan. Lena went on rapidly.

"You go tell her. That's what I come for. Nothin' else—nor nobody else—can do it. That's your part of this infernal business. Mine's done. I've give you the warnin'. Now you go ahead."

"Oh, are you *sure*?" repeated Jane weakly; "isn't it *possible* you've got it wrong, somehow?"

"Is it possible the dust in the street don't hear the oaths of Windover!" exclaimed Lena scornfully. "Do you s'pose there ain't a black deed doin' or threatenin' in Angel Alley that *I* don't know? I tell you his life ain't worth a red herrin', no, nor a bucketful of bait, if them fellars has their way in this town! . . . It's the loss of the license done it. It's the last wave piled on. It's madded 'em to anything. It's madded 'em to murder. . . Lord," muttered Lena, "if it come to that, wouldn't I be even with 'em!"

She grated her teeth, like an animal grinding a bone; took her foot from the painter, sprang into the fishing-dory, and rowed with quick, powerful strokes into the dark harbor.

Helen, without a moment's hesitation, descended the cliff and peremptorily said:—

"Jane, I heard it. Tell me all. Tell me everything, this minute."

Jane who was sobbing bitterly, stopped like a child at a firm word: and with more composure than she had yet shown, she gave her version of Lena's startling story.

Lena was right, she said; the rum people were very angry with Mr. Bayard: he had got so many shops shut up; and other places; he had shut up so much in Angel Alley this year. And now old Trawl had lost his license. Folks said a man couldn't make a decent living there any longer.

"That's what Ben said," observed Jane, with a feeble sense of the poignancy of the phrase. "A man couldn't make an honest living there, now. But there's one thing," added Jane with hanging head. "Lena don't know it. I couldn't tell *Lena*. God have mercy on me, for it's me that helped it on!"

"I do not understand you, Jane," replied Helen coldly; "how could you injure Mr. Bayard, or have any connection with any plot to do him harm?"

"I sent Ben off last Sunday night," said Jane humbly. "I sent him marching for good. I told him I never could marry him. I told him I couldn't stand it any longer. I told him what I heard on Ragged Rock— that night—last year."

"What did you hear on Ragged Rock?" asked Helen, still distant and doubtful.

"Didn't the minister ever tell you?" replied Jane. "Then I won't."

"Very well," said Helen, after an agitated silence, "I shall not urge you. But if Mr. Bayard's life is in *real* danger—I cannot believe it!" cried the sheltered, happy woman. Such scenes, such possibilities, belonged to the stage, to fiction; not to New England life. The Professor's daughter had a healthy antagonism in her to the excessive, the too dramatic. Her mind grasped the facts of the situation so slowly that the Windover girl half pitied her.

"You don't see," said Jane. "You don't understand. You ain't brought up as we are."

"If Mr. Bayard is in danger—" repeated Helen. "Jane!" she cried sharply, thinking to test the girl's sincerity and judgment, "should you have come and told me what Lena said, if I had not overheard it?"

"Miss Carruth," answered Jane, with a dignity of her own, "don't you know there is not one of his people who would not do *anything* to save Mr. Bayard?"

Through the dark Jane turned her little, pinched face towards this fortunate woman, this other girl, blessed and chosen. Her dumb eyes grew bright, and flashed fire for that once; then they smouldered, and their spaniel look came on again.

"You ought to speak differently to me," she said. "You should feel sorry for me, because it's along of Ben. I tried to keep it up—all this while. I haven't dared to break with him. I thought if I broke, and we'd been keeping company so long, maybe he might do a harm to Mr. Bayard. Then it come to me that I couldn't, couldn't, *couldn't* bear it, not another time! And I told him so. And Ben, he swore an awful oath to me, and cleared out. And then Lena came and told."

"What was it Ben swore?" asked Helen, whose sanguine heart was beginning to sink in earnest. "This is no time for being womanly, and—and not saying things. If it takes all the oaths in the catalogue of Angel Alley, it is my right to know what he said, and it is your duty to tell me!"

"Well," said Jane stolidly, "he said: 'Damn him to hell! If we ain't a-goin' to be married, he shan't, neither!'"

"Thank you, Jane," said Helen gently, after a long silence. She held out her hand; Jane took it, but dropped it quickly.

"Do you know the details? The plan? The plot—if there is a plot?" asked Helen, without outward signs of agitation.

"Lena said they said Christlove should never be dedicated," answered Jane drearily. "Not if they had to put the parson out of the way to stop it."

"*Oh!*"

"That's what Lena said. She thought if Mr. Bayard could be got out of town for a spell, right away, Lena thought maybe that would set 'em off the notion of it. I told her Mr. Bayard wouldn't go. She said you'd see to that."

"Yes," said Helen softly, "I will see to that."

Jane made no reply, but started unexpectedly to her feet. The two girls clambered down from the cliff in silence, and began to walk up the shore. At the path leading to the hotel, Jane paused and shrank away.

"How you cough!" said Miss Carruth compassionately. "You are quite wet with this heavy dew. Do come into the cottage with me."

She put her hand affectionately on the damp shoulder of Jane's blue and white calico blouse.

The hotel lights reached faintly after the figures of the two. Jane looked stunted and shrunken; Helen's superb proportions seemed to quench her. The fisherman's daughter lifted her little homely face.

"I don't suppose," she faltered, "you'd be willing to be told. But mother and me have done for him so long—he ain't well, the minister ain't—there's ways he likes his tea made, and we het the bricks, come cold weather, for him—and—all those little things. We've tried to take good care of Mr. Bayard! It's been a good many years!" said Jane piteously. It was more dreadful to her to give up boarding the minister,

ELIZABETH STUART PHELPS

than it was that he should marry the summer lady in the gold and purple gowns.

"I suppose you and he will go somewhere?" she added bitterly.

"We shan't forget you, Jane," said Helen gently.

The calico blouse shoulder shook off the delicate hand that rested upon it.

"I won't come in," she said. "I'll go right home."

Jane turned away, and walked across the cliffs. The hotel lights fell short of her, and the darkness swallowed her undersized, pathetic figure, as the mystery of life draws down the weak, the uncomely, and the unloved.

Jane went home, and unlocked her bureau drawer. From beneath the sachet-bag, on which her little pile of six handkerchiefs rested precisely, she drew out an old copy of Coleridge. The book was scented with the sachet, and had a sickly perfume; it was incense to Jane. She turned the leaves to find "Alph, the sacred river;" then shut the book, and put it back in the bureau drawer. She did not touch it with her lips or cheek. She handled it more tenderly than she did her Bible.

LEFT TO HERSELF, HELEN FELT the full force of the situation fall upon her, in a turmoil of fear and perplexity. The whole thing was so foreign to her nature and to the experience of her protected life, that it seemed to her more than incredible. There were moments when she was in danger of underrating the facts, and letting the chances take their course—it seemed to her so impossible that Jane and Lena should not, somehow, be mistaken.

Her mind was in a whirlwind of doubt and dismay. With a certain coolness in emergencies characteristic of her, she tried to think the position out, by herself. This futile process occupied perhaps a couple of hours.

It was between eleven and twelve o'clock when the Professor, with a start, laid down his manuscript upon the Revised Version. For the door of the clam study had opened quietly, and revealed his daughter's agitated face.

"Papa," she said, "I am in a great trouble. I have come to you first—to know what to do—before I go to him. I've been thinking," she added, "that perhaps this is one of the things that fathers are *for*."

Like a little girl she dropped at his knee, and told him the whole story.

"I couldn't go to a man, and ask him to marry me, without letting you know, Papa!" said the Professor's daughter.

The Professor of Theology reached for his Charter Oak cane as a man gropes for a staff on the edge of a precipice. The manuscript chapter on the Authenticity of the Fourth Gospel fell to the floor. The Professor and the cane paced the clam study together feverishly.

The birds were singing when Helen and her father stopped talking, and wearily stole back to the cottage for an hour's rest.

"You could go right home," said the old man gently. "The house is open, and the servants are there. I am sure your mother will wish it, whenever she is acquainted with the facts."

"We won't tell Mother, just yet, Papa—not till we must, you know. Perhaps Mr. Bayard won't—won't take me!"

The Professor straightened himself, and looked about with a guilty air. He felt as if he were party to an elopement. Eager, ardent, boyishly sympathetic with Helen's position, quivering with that perfect thoughtfulness which she never found in any other than her father's heart, the Professor of dogmatic Orthodox Theology flung himself into the emergency as tenderly as if he had never written a lecture on Foreordination, or preached a sermon on the Inconceivability of Second Probation.

It was he, indeed, and none other, who summoned Bayard to Helen's presence at an early hour of the morning; and to the credit of the Department, and of the ancient Seminary in whose stern faith the kindest graces of character and the best graciousness of manner have never been extinguished, be it said that Professor Haggai Carruth did not once remind Emanuel Bayard that he was meeting the consequences of unsoundness, and the natural fate of heresy. Nobly sparing the young man any reference to his undoubtedly deserved misfortune, the Professor only said:—

"Helen, here is Mr. Bayard," and softly shut the door.

HELEN'S HEARTY COLOR WAS QUITE gone. Such a change had touched her, that Bayard uttered an exclamation of horror, and took her impetuously in his arms.

"Love, what ails you?" he cried with quick anxiety.

Arrived at the moment when she must speak, if ever, Helen's courage and foresight failed her utterly. She found herself no nearer to knowing what to say, or how to say it, than she had been at the first moment

ELIZABETH STUART PHELPS

when she heard the girls talking on the rocks. To tell him her fears, and the grounds for them, would be the fatal blunder. How could she say to a man like Bayard: "Your life is in danger. Come on a wedding-trip, and save yourself!" Yet how could she quibble, or be dumb before the truth!

Following no plan, or little, preached part, but only the moment's impulse of her love and her trouble, Helen broke into girlish sobs, the first that he had ever heard from her, and hid her wet face against his cheek.

"Oh," she breathed, "I don't know *how* to tell you! But I am so unhappy—and I have grown so anxious about you! I don't see. . . how I can bear it. . . as we are." . . .

Her heart beat against his so wildly, that she could have said no more if she had tried. But she had no need to try. For he said:—

"*Would* you marry me this summer, dear? It would make me very happy. . . I have not dared to ask it."

"I would marry you to-morrow." Helen lifted her head, and "shame departed, shamed" from her sweet, wet face. "I would marry you to-day. I want to be near you. I want. . . if anything—whatever comes."

"Whatever comes," he answered solemnly, "we ought to be together—now."

Thus they deceived each other—neither owning to the tender fault—with the divine deceit of love.

Helen comforted herself that she had not said a word of threat or danger or escape, and that Bayard suspected nothing of the cloudburst which hung over him. He let her think so, smiling tenderly. For he knew it all the time; and more, far more than Helen ever knew.

XXVII

The Professor threw himself into the situation with a fatherly tenderness which went to Bayard's heart; but the theologian was disconcerted by this glimpse into real life. He had been so occupied with the misery of the next world that he had never investigated the hell of this one. He was greatly perplexed.

"As man to man, Bayard," he said, "you must tell me the exact amount of truth in those womanly alarms which agitate my daughter's heart, and to which I allowed myself to yield without, perhaps, sufficient reflection. I find it difficult to believe that any harm can actually befall you in a New England town. That Windover would really injure you? It seems to me, in cool blood, incredible."

"*Windover* would not," replied Bayard, smiling. "They don't love me, but they don't mob a man for that. *Windover* won't harm me. Did you ever hear a phrase, common along the coast, here, Professor—'*Rum done it*'?"

The Cesarea Professor shook his head. "I am not familiar with the phrase," he urged; "it lacks in grammar"—

"What it gains in pith," interrupted Bayard; "but it sums up the situation. A business that thrives on the ruin of men is not likely to be sensitive in the direction of inflicting unnecessary suffering. I have successfully offended the liquor interests of the whole vicinity. The new chapel represents to them the growth of the only power in this town which they have found reason to fear. That's the amount of it."

"But the—churches, Bayard—the Christian classes? The ecclesiastical methods of restraining vice?"

"The ecclesiastical methods do not shut up the saloons," said Bayard gently. "Angel Alley is not afraid of the churches."

"I am not familiar with the literature of the temperance movement," observed the Professor helplessly. "It is a foreign subject to me. I am not prepared to argue with you."

"You will find some of it on my library shelves," said Bayard; "it might interest you some time to glance at it."

"When my manuscript on the New Version is completed, I shall take pleasure in doing so," replied the Professor politely; "but the point *now* is, just what, and how much do you fear from the state of things to which you refer? Helen is a level-headed girl. I take it for granted that she has not wrought herself into a hysterical fright without basis. I have acted on my knowledge of my daughter's nature. I understand *that*, if I am uninstructed in the temperance agitation."

"Helen has not been misinformed, nor has she overestimated anything," returned Bayard quietly.

"Is it a mob you fear?"

"Possibly; but probably nothing of the kind. My chief danger is one from which it is impossible to escape."

"And that is?"—

"Something underhanded. There is a personal element in it."

Bayard rose, as if he would bring the conversation to a check.

"There is nothing to be done," he said, "nothing whatever. Everything shall go on, precisely as it is arranged. I shall not run from them."

"You do not think wise to defer the dedication—for a time?"

"Not an hour! The dedication will take place a week from Sunday."

The Professor was silent. He found it a little difficult to follow the working of this young man's mind.

"And yet," he suggested anxiously, "after the marriage—to-morrow—you will take the temporary absence, the little vacation which your friends advise? You will not think better of that, I hope, for Helen's sake?"

"I shall leave Windover for a week, for Helen's sake," replied Bayard gravely.

In his heart he thought that it would make but little difference; but she should have it to remember that everything had been done. He would not be foolhardy or obstinate. The sacred rights of the wife over the man had set in upon his life She should be gratified and comforted in every way left to the power of that love and tenderness which God has set in the soul abreast of duty and honor. He would give the agitation in Angel Alley time to cool, if cool it could. He would give himself—oh, he would give himself—

Helen, in the next room, sat waiting for him. She ran her fingers over the keys of the piano; her foot was on the soft pedal; she sang beneath her breath,—

> *"Komm beglücke mich?*
> *. . . Beglücke mich!"*

Bayard sought her in a great silence. He lifted her tender face, and looked down upon it with that quiver on the lower part of his own which she knew so well; which always meant emotion that he did not share with her. She did not trouble him to try to have it otherwise. She clung to him, and they clasped more solemnly than passionately.

Around the bridegroom's look in Bayard's face, the magic circle of the seer's loneliness was faintly drawn.

If God and love had collided—but, thank God! He and Love were one.

"Lord, I have groped after Thee, and to know Thy will, and to do it if I could. I never expected to be happy. Dost Thou mean this draught of human joy for *me*?"

So prayed Bayard, while her bright head lay upon his breast with the delicate and gentle surrender of the girl who will be wife before another sun goes down.

Out upon the piazza of the Flying Jib the Professor was entertaining visitors, by whose call the lovers were not disturbed. The Reverend George Fenton had unexpectedly and vaguely appeared upon the scene. He was accompanied by a lean, thoughtful man, with clerical elbows and long, rustic legs, being no other than Tompkinton of Cesarea and the army cape. Professor Carruth had taken his two old students into the confidence of the family crisis. The Reverend Mr. Fenton looked troubled.

"I had a feeling that something was wrong. I have been impressed for days with a sense that I ought to see Bayard—to help him, you know—to offer him any assistance in my power. He is in such a singular position! He leads such a singular life, Professor! It is hard for a man situated as I am, to know precisely what *to* do."

"The only thing that can be done for him, just now, that I see," suggested the Professor dryly, "is to find him a supply for Sunday. His marriage to my daughter will, of necessity, involve a short absence from his missionary duties."

"I wish I could preach for him!" cried Fenton eagerly. "I should like nothing better. I should love to do so much for him. He never has any supplies or vacations, like the rest of us. Now I think of it, nobody has been near his pulpit for three years, to help him out—I mean nobody whom *we* should recognize. I've half a mind to consult my committee. The First Church"—

"*I* will preach for Bayard," interrupted Tompkinton with his old, slow manner. "My church is so small—we are not important across the Cape, there—it is not necessary for me to consult my committee. I will preach for him with all my heart; in the evening at all events—all day, if the Professor here will find me a supply of some sort."

"Thank you, gentlemen," observed the Professor quietly; "I will accept your offer, Tompkinton, for the evening. I shall myself occupy Mr. Bayard's pulpit in Windover town hall on Sunday morning."

"*You*, Professor?"

Fenton turned pale. Tompkinton gave that little lurch to his shoulders with which, for so many years, he had jerked on the army cape in cold weather. Tompkinton was well dressed, now, well settled, well to do, but the same simple, manly fellow. There was the gentleman in this grandson of the soil, this educated farmer's boy; and an instinct as true as the spirit of the faith which he preached in the old, unnoticed ways, and with the old, unobserved results. Tompkinton spent his life in conducting weekly prayer meetings, in comforting old people in trouble, and in preaching what he had been taught, as he had been taught it. But he was neither a coward nor a cad for that.

"If I had had a little time to think of this," protested Fenton. "My committee are, to a man, opposed to this temperance movement, and our relation to Bayard is, of course,—you must see, Professor,—peculiar! But perhaps"—

"Oh, Tompkinton and I can manage," replied the Professor, not without a twinkle in his deep eyes. "I don't suppose the First Church has ever heard of us, but we will do our humble best."

Now, as the event fell out, the Professor and Tompkinton changed their programme a little; and when the time came to do Bayard this fraternal service,—the first of its kind ever offered to him by the clergymen of the denomination in which he was reared,—the Professor drove across the Cape in the hot sun, ten miles, to fill the Reverend Mr. Tompkinton's little, country pulpit, and Tompkinton took the morning service for his classmate.

In the evening the Professor of Theology from Cesarea Seminary occupied the desk of the heretic preacher in Windover town hall. The hall was thronged. George Fenton preached to yawning pews; for the First Church, out of sheer, unsanctified curiosity, lurched over, and sixty of them went to hear the distinguished Professor. Bayard's own people were present in the usual summer evening force and character.

The Professor of Theology looked uncomfortably at the massed and growing audience. He was sixty-eight years old, and in all his scholarly and Christian life he had never stood before an audience like this. He opened his manuscript sermon,—he had selected a doctrinal sermon upon the Nature of the Trinity,—and began to read it with his own distinguished manner.

The audience, restrained at first by the mere effect of good elocution and a cultivated voice, were respectful for awhile; they listened hopefully; then perplexedly; then dully. Sentence after sentence, polished, and sound as the foundations of Galilee or Damascus Hall, fell softly from the lips of the Cesarea Professor upon the ears of the Windover fishermen. Doctrine upon doctrine attacked them, and they knew it not. Proof-text upon proof-text bombarded them in vain.

The Professor saw the faces of his audience lengthen and fall; across the rude, red brows of the foreign sailors wonder flitted; then confusion; then dismay. Drunkards and reformed men and wretched girls, and the homeless, wretched people of a seaport town, stood packed in rows before the Professor of Theology, and gaped upon him. Restlessness struck them, and began to run from man to man.

"Shut up there!" whispered Job Slip, punching a big Swede. "Be quiet, can't ye, for common manners! You'll disgrace Mr. Bayard!"

"Be civil to the old cove, for the parson's sake!" commanded Captain Hap, hitting a Finn, and stepping on the toes of a Windover seiner, who had presumed to snicker.

"Why don't he talk English then?" protested the fisherman.

A dozen men turned and left the hall. Half a dozen followed. Some girls giggled audibly. A group of Norwegians significantly shuffled their feet on the bare floor.

The Professor of Theology laid down his manuscript. It occurred to him, at last, that his audience did not understand what he was saying. It was a dreadful moment. For the first time in his honored life he had encountered the disrespect of a congregation which he could not command. He laid down his sermon on the Nature of the Trinity, and looked the house over.

"I am afraid," he said distinctly, "that I am not retaining the interest of this congregation. I am not accustomed to your needs, or to the manner in which your pastor presents the Truth to you. But for his sake, you will listen to me, I am sure."

"Lord, yes," said the seiner in an audible whisper; "we'd listen to Bunker Hill Monyment for *him*."

This irreverence did not, happily, reach the ears of the Professor of Theology, who, with his famous ease of manner, proceeded to say:—

ELIZABETH STUART PHELPS

"My discourse is on the Nature of the Trinity; and I perceive that my thoughts on this subject are not your thoughts, and that my ways of expression are not your ways, and that an interpreter is needed between this preacher and his audience. . . I have been thinking, since I stood at this desk, about the name which you give to the beautiful new chapel which your pastor will dedicate for you, God willing, next Sunday"—

From a remote corner of the hall a sound like that of a serpent arose, and fell. The Professor did not or would not hear it (no man could say which), and went firmly on.

"Christlove you call your chapel, I am told. You may be surprised to know it, but the fact is that the sermon which I have been preaching to you, and the thing which the tender and solemn name of your chapel signifies, are one and the same."

"I don't see how he figgers that," muttered the seiner.

"I will try to show you how," continued the Professor, as if he had heard the fisherman.

He abandoned his manuscript on the Trinity, and plunged headlong— not in the least knowing how he was to get out again—into a short extempore talk upon the life of Christ. The fishermen listened, for the old preacher held to it till they did; and as soon as he had commanded their respect and attention, he wisely stopped. The service came to a sudden but successful end; and the exhausted Professor thoughtfully retired from his first, his last, his only experience in the pulpit of the Unsound. The most depressing part of the occasion was that his wife told him it was the best sermon she had heard him preach in thirty years.

But Bayard and Helen knew these things not, nor thought of them. They had been married, as it was decided, upon that Saturday, the day before. Helen's father married them. There was no wedding party, no preparation. Helen had a white gown, never worn before; Jane Granite sent some of her mother's roses, and Mrs. Carruth, who distinguished herself by abnormal self-possession, fastened one of the roses at Helen's throat. It was thought best that Windover should know nothing of the marriage until the preacher and his bride had left the town; so it was the quietest little wedding that love and the law allow.

And Bayard and Helen went to her old home in the glory and the blossom of the Cesarea June. And the great cross came out upon the Seminary green, for the moon was up that week.

"It used to divide us," she whispered; "it never can again."

She wondered a little that he did not answer; but that he only held her solemnly, in the window where they stood to see the cross.

Helen's happy nature was easily queen of her. She had begun to feel that her anxiety for Bayard's sake was overstrained. Tragic Windover slipped from her consciousness, almost from her memory. She felt the sacred right of human joy to conquer fate, and trusted it as royally as she had trusted him. In spite of himself, he absorbed something of her warm and brilliant hopefulness. When she gave herself, she gave her ease of heart. And so the worn and worried man came to his Eden.

XXVIII

Helen's happy heart proved prophet; so they said, and smiled. For there was no mob. Sunday dawned like a dream. The sun rode up without cloud or fire. The sea carried its cool, June colors. The harbor wore her sweetest face. The summer people, like figures on a gay Japanese fan, moved brightly across the rocks and piers; Bayard and Helen looked out of the windows of the Flying Jib, and watched them with that kindness of the heart for the interests of strangers which belongs to joy alone. A motionless fleet lay in the harbor, opening its silvery wings to dry them in the Sunday sun.

The fishermen had hurried home by scores to witness the dedication. Everybody had a smile for the preacher's bride,—the boarder on the rocks, the fisherman from the docks.

Every child or woman to whom she had ever done a kindness in her inexperienced, warm-hearted fashion, remembered it and her that day. She wore the unornamented cream-white silk dress in which she had been married; for Bayard asked it.

"The people will like to see you so," he said. "It will give them a vision."

All the town was alive and alert. The argument of success, always the cogent one to the average mind, was peculiarly effective in Windover. People who had never given the mission a thought before, and people who had given it many, but never a kindly one, looked at the doors of the new chapel, smothered in wild Cape roses for the solemn gala, and said: "That affair in Angel Alley seems to prosper, spite of everything. There may be something in it, after all."

It was expected that the churches themselves, though reserved on the subject, would be better represented at Christlove that evening, than they cared to be; for the young people were determined to see the dedication, and would pair off in scores to Angel Alley, leaving their elders behind, to support the ecclesiastical foundations in decorum and devotion, as by the creed and confession bound.

The attendance of other audiences was not encouraged, however, by the pastor in Angel Alley; his own would more than fill the chapel. All the little preparations of the people went on quietly, and he brought them, as it was his will to do, without weariness or worry, to the evening. He wished the dedication of his chapel to be free from the fret and care which turn so many of our religious festivals into scrambles,—I had almost said, shambles, for the harm they do to exhausted women, and to careworn men.

The day passed easily. Bayard himself, though moving under deep excitement, gave no evidence of it. He was as quiet as the Saint Michael in the picture, whose foot was on the dragon, and whose head was in the skies.

The day passed uneventfully. The evening was one of Windover's fairest and most famous. The sky gave the ethereal colors of transparent rose-clouds, and the harbor returned them delicately. There was a slight, watery line in the northwest, but the oldest sailors scarcely noticed it. Nothing had happened in any way to hinder the movement of the ceremonial, or to mar its success. There was no mob, nor threat of any. There was no mass, no riot, no alarm. Angel Alley was decorous—if one might say so, obtrusively decorous. Captain Hap, and Job Slip, the special police, and the officers of the mission looked out of narrow lids at Angel Alley, and watched guardedly.

Not a misdemeanor disturbed the calm of this, to all appearance, now law-abiding—nay, law-adoring street. Saloon after saloon that Bayard had closed presented locked front doors to the thirstiest sailor who swaggered from the wharves in search of what he might swallow. Nameless dens that used to flourish the prosperity of their sickening trade were shut.

Old Trawl's door was barred. The Trawls themselves were invisible. There would be no mob. So said the treasurer of the chapel. So said the Windover police. So thought the anxious Professor, and his tearful wife. So said Helen, sparkling with the pretty triumph of love and joy.

"Dear! You see we were mistaken. They *do* love you here, in rough old Windover—bless it, after all! We were too anxious—I was worried; I own it, now. I was afraid because you were so precious to me. And I could not be with you. . . if anything. . . went wrong. But *now*"—

"Now," he said, "nothing *can* go wrong. For you are mine, and I am yours, and this is forever."

"I am glad to hear you speak so cheerfully," she said, catching at the lighter note in the chord of his words.

He did not answer her; and when she looked up, she was surprised at the solemn expression of his face.

"Love," he said, "it is time to go. Kiss me, Helen, before we start."

They stood at the window in her own little room in the summer cottage.

The tide was rising, and it gained quietly upon the beaches and the pier. Bayard looked out upon the sea, for a moment, out to the uttermost horizon's purple curve. Then he took his wife to his heart, and held her there; within a clasp like that, no woman speaks, and Helen did not.

The Professor and his wife passed down Angel Alley. The Reverend Mr. Tompkinton and that dear old moderator, the very Orthodox but most Christian minister who had always done a brother's deed by the heretic pastor when he could, followed the great Professor. These officers of the evening's ceremony entered the chapel, and—not staying to leave Mrs. Carruth in a front pew, but leading her with them—passed on to the platform.

Whispers buzzed about.

"The minister! Where's the minister? Has anything happened to Mr. Bayard?"

For the chapel was already full. Captain Hap trotted impatiently down the aisle. Job Slip looked at the policeman in the vestibule in a worried way. But the officer stolidly signaled that all was well; and Captain Hap and Job Slip and scores of watchers breathed again.

The congregation increased quietly. Angel Alley was unprecedentedly still. The audience was serious and civil. All of Bayard's own people were there—many citizens of Windover—and the young folks from the churches, as expected.

Then, came the throng from the wharves. Then, came the crowd from the streets. Then, came the rough, red faces from foreign ports, and from the high seas, and from the Grand Banks, and Georges'. There came all the homeless, neglected, tossed, and tempted people whom Bayard loved, and who loved him. There came the outcast, and the forgotten, and the unclean of heart and body. There came the wretches whom no one else thought of, or cared for. There came the poor girls who frequented no other house of worship, but were always welcomed here. There came the common people, who heard him gladly; for to them he spoke, and for them he lived.

The preacher walked down Angel Alley with his wife, in her white dress, upon his arm. The Alley was thronged with spectators who did not or who could not enter the chapel. Two policemen stepped forward to escort the minister, but he waved them back. He and Helen walked quietly to the chapel steps, and were about to enter, when a slight disturbance in the crowd, at their immediate side, caused Bayard to look around. A girl was struggling with an officer, to get near enough to speak to the minister.

"Get back there!" commanded the policeman. "Keep back, I say! This is no place nor time for the likes of *you* to pester the minister!"

"Let her come!" ordered Bayard authoritatively. For it was Lena. The girl was pale, and her handsome eyes had a ferocious look.

"I've got something to tell him," announced Lena with calm determination. "It's important, or I wouldn't bother him, is it likely? I ain't no such a fool nor flat."

She approached, at Bayard's beck, and said a few words in a tone so low that even the wife upon his arm did not understand them.

"Lena still feels a little anxious," said Bayard aloud, distinctly. "Have you any wishes to express, Helen?"

But Helen, smiling, shook her head. She felt exalted and not afraid. She would have gone with him to death; but she did not think about death. She did not believe that his angels would suffer a pebble of Windover to dash against him; nor that a curl of his gold-brown head would come to harm. His mood ruled her utterly. His own exaltation, his beauty, his calm, his spiritual power, made clouds before her eyes, on which he moved as a god.

So they entered the chapel, together. As they did so, Bayard turned, and looked back. Before all the people there, the preacher lifted his hat to Lena, and passed on.

The girl's dark face dropped upon her breast, as if she made obeisance before him; then she lifted it with the touching pride of lost self-respect regained. Her lips moved. "He thinks I'm fit, at last," said Lena.

The preacher and his young wife passed through the rose-wreathed door, and into the chapel. Roses were there, too; their pale, pink lamps burned all over the chapel, wherever hand could reach, or foot could climb. This was the decoration chosen to welcome the June bride to Windover—the people's flower, the blossom of the rocks and downs.

It was a pleasant chapel. The library, the gymnasium, the bowling-alley, opened from the prayer-room. Pictures and books and games and lounging-places for tired fellows were part of Bayard's Christianity. Many a fisherman, smoking in the room below, where an oath turned a man out, and a coarse phrase was never heard, would listen to the singing of old hymns, above him, and lay his pipe down, and wonder what the music meant, and catch a line he used to hear his mother sing, and so steal up to hear the rest; and sing the loudest of them all, perhaps, before the hymn was done.

Bayard moved up among his silent people, to his place. His wife went with him, and he led her to her mother's side, at his right hand.

"In any event," he thought, "I could reach her in a moment."

His eyes sought hers for that instant. She neither blushed nor paled, but had her sweet composure. In her bridal white, she looked like the lily of his life's work, the angel of his worried heart. It seemed to him as if peace and hope came with her, as purity and honor dwelt in her presence. He felt happier and stronger for knowing that she was so near him, now, and, with a brightening brow he gave the signal for opening the evening's service.

It was a short and pleasant service. The great Professor, cordially recognized by the rough audience that he had not allowed to conquer him last Sunday, contributed his most distinguished manner, his best good sense, and the least possible evidence of his theology to the dedicating hour. The old moderator and the pastor's classmate from across the Cape added their heartiest help. Most of the congregation omitted to notice that the clergymen from the city were not present. They were not missed. Who could say if they had been invited to dedicate Emanuel Bayard's chapel? He had pulled along without them for three years. He was incapable of resentment, but it was still possible that habit had its way with the missionary, and that, in his hour of success he had simply forgotten them, as in his time of distress and failure they had forgotten him. Who could blame him?

But all the little trouble of the past had melted from his mind and heart; both were clear and happy when he rose, at last, to address his people. His delicate lips had but parted to speak to them, when there started such a storm of welcome from the fishermen as well-nigh swept his self-possession from him. He was not prepared for it, and he seemed almost disturbed. From aisle to aisle, from wall to wall, the wind of sound rose and rolled upon him. At last it became articulate, and here and there words defined themselves.

"God bless him!"

"Bless our dear young parson!"

"Windover fishermen stand by him every time!"

"Blessin's on him, anyhow!"

"Christlove's good enough for us!"

But when he smiled upon them, they grew quiet, as they had done once before—that evening after the wreck and rescue off Ragged Rock; for these two were the only occasions when the applause of his people had got the better of their pastor.

When he began to speak, it was not without emotion, but in a voice so low that the house had to hold its breath to hear him.

He began by thanking the fishermen of Windover for their trust and their friendship. Both, he said, he valued, and more than they would ever know. Of his own struggles and troubles, of the bitter years that he had toiled among them, he said no word. He spoke of the kindness of Windover, not of its neglect. He spoke of the strength and the goodness of the city, rather than of its weakness and its error. He spoke of the warm heart of the people, of their readiness to help any need which they understood, and in whose claim they believed. He told how generous they were in emergencies. "You give money," he said, "more lavishly than any town I have ever known. When the gales have struck, and the fleets gone down, and when, with widows and orphans starving on my heart and hands, I have asked for bread, Windover has never given them a stone. Your poor have spent themselves utterly upon your poorest, and your rich have not refused. Windover gives gloriously," said Bayard, "and I am glad and proud to say so."

Their faults, he told them, they had, and he was not there to condone what he had never overlooked. One, above the rest, they had to answer for; and what that was—did he need to name?

"It is not your sin alone," he said firmly. "It is the sin of seaport towns; it is the sin of cities; it is the sin of New England; it is the sin of the Nation;—but *it is the sin of Windover*, and my business is with Windover sins. I have fought it since I came among you, without an hour's wavering of purpose, and without an hour's fear of the result; and at all costs, at any cost, I shall fight it till I go from you. For God has set me among you, not to minister to your self-satisfaction, but to your needs."

Bayard paused here, and regarded his people with a long look. Their faces blurred before him for a moment, for his heart was full. He saw them all, in the distinctness with which the public speaker perceives familiar sights; every trifle upon the map of his audience started out.

He saw Captain Hap, anxious and wrinkled, doing usher's duty by the door—Captain Hap, neither pious nor godless, but ready to live for the parson or to die for him, and caring little which; the good fellow, true with the allegiance of age and a loyal nature—dear Captain Hap!

ELIZABETH STUART PHELPS

Bayard saw Job Slip, pale with the chronic pallor of the reformed drunkard—poor Job, who drank not now, neither did he taste; but bore the thirst of his terrible desert, trusting in the minister and God Almighty,—in the succession of the phrase.

Mari was there, incapable and patient, her face and figure stamped with the indefinable something that marks the drunkard's wife. And Joey, serious and old—little Joey! Bob was there, and Jean, and Tony, and all the familiar faces from the wharves. Mrs. Granite, in her rusty black, sat tearfully in a front settee, with Jane beside her. Jane looked at the minister, before all the people, as she never ventured to look at home. But nobody noticed Jane. Bayard did but glance at her pinched, adoring face; he dared not dwell upon it.

Ben Trawl was not to be seen in the audience. But Lena was. She stood the service through, for she had come in too late to find a seat; she stood behind Johnny's mother, who wore Helen's crape bonnet and veil, poor old lady, with a brown bombazine dress. Lena had a worried look. She did not remove her eyes from the preacher. Lena sang that day, when the people started "the minister's hymn,"—

> *"I need Thee every hour,*
> *Stay Thou near by."*

Her fine voice rose like a solo; it had a certain solitariness about it which was touching to hear.

> *"Temptations lose their power*
> *When Thou art nigh."*

The melody of the hymn died away into the hush in which Bayard rose again, for it came to his heart to bless his people and his chapel in one of his rare prayers.

"Lord," he said, "Thou art the God of the sea and its perils; of the land and its sorrow. Draw near to these sea-people who tread upon the shore of Thy mercy. I dedicate them to Thee. Father, take them from my hands! Lift them up! Hold them, that they fall not. Comfort their troubles. Forgive their sins. Take them! Take my people from my heart! . . . Lord, I consecrate this house of worship, for their sakes, and in Christ's name, and for Christ's love, to Thee, and to Thy service. . . Father! Thou knowest how I have loved this people." . . .

Bayard's voice broke. It was the only time—in all those years. His prayer remained unfinished. The sobs of his people answered him; and his silence was his benediction upon them.

The audience moved out quietly. It was now dark. The lights in the chapel had been noiselessly lighted. The jets of the illuminated words above the door were blazing.

The Professor and the clergymen and Helen's mother stepped apart and out into the street; none of them spoke to Bayard, for his look forbade them. The Professor of Theology was greatly moved. Signs of tears more natural than evangelical were on his aged face. Bayard, lingering but a moment, came down the aisle with his wife upon his arm.

"Love," she whispered, "it is over, and all is well."

"Yes," he answered, smiling, "it is over, and it is well."

They came down and out upon the steps. Bayard stood uncovered beneath the white and scarlet lights, which spelled the words,—

"THE LOVE OF CHRIST."

He gave one glance down Angel Alley. It was packed; his people were massed to protect him. Beyond them, marshaled into the darkness and scarcely distinguishable from it, hovered certain sullen groups of frowning men. Not a hand was raised. Not a cry was heard. No. There was to be no mob. He had to meet, not violence, but mute and serried Hate.

She clung to his arm with a start. She looked up into his face. Its more than earthly radiance hushed the cry upon her lips. He was transfigured before her. For that moment, all the people—they who loved and they who loved him not—saw him glorified, there, beneath the sacred words whose pure and blazing fires seemed to them the symbol of his soul.

Then, from the darkest dark of Angel Alley a terrible oath split the air. Something struck him; and he fell.

XXIX

Half a thousand men gave chase; but the assailant had escaped to the common shelter of the coasting town. He had taken to the water.

It was now quite dark; clouds had gathered; the wind had risen suddenly; thunder was heard. A fierce gust tore the dust of Angel Alley, and hurled it after the fleeing criminal; as if even the earth that he trod rejected him. In this blinding and suffocating whirlwind the pursuers stumbled over each other, and ran at haphazard. The police swept every skulking-place, dividing their forces between the Alley and the docks. But their man, who was shrewd enough, had evaded them; it was clear that he had marked out an intelligent map of escape, and had been able to follow it.

The baffled police, thinking at least to pacify the angry people behind them, kept up that appearance of energy, with that absence of expectation, for which their race is distinguished.

An officer who was stealthily studying the docks far to the westward, and alone, suddenly stopped. A cry for help reached him; and it was a woman's cry. The voice kept up an interrupted iteration:—

"Police! Help!—Murder! Sergeant!—Help! Help!" as if choked off, or strangled in the intervals.

The sergeant, following the sound as well as he could, leaped down the long, empty wharf from whose direction the cry seemed to come, and peered over the slimy edge. The storm was passing noisily up the sky, and the darkness was of the deepest.

Out of its hollow a girl's voice uprose:—

"Sergeant! Sergeant! He's drowning me! But I've got him!" and bubbled away into silence.

At that moment there was lightning; and the outlines of two figures struggling in the water could be distinctly seen. These two persons were Lena and Ben Trawl. They seemed to have each other in a mutual death-grip. The girl's hands were at the man's throat. He dashed her under and under the water. But her clutch did not relax by a finger. He held her down. But Lena held on.

"After I've strangled you!" gasped Lena.

"—you," muttered the man. "Drown, then!"

Her head went under; her mouth filled; this time she could not struggle up; her ears rang; her brain burst. But the little fingers on the big throat clutched on. Then she felt herself caught from above—air came, and breath with it—and Ben swore faintly.

"Undo your hands, Lena," said the sergeant. "We've got him. You don't want to hang him before his time."

Another flash of lightning revealed the sea and sky, the docks and the officers, and Ben, purple and breathing hard, stretched upon the wharf. Lena heard the snap of the handcuffs upon his wrists; and then she heard and saw no more.

The sergeant touched the girl's dripping and unconscious figure with a respect never shown to Lena in Windover police circles before.

"She might not come to, yet," he said; "she's nigh enough to a drowned girl. Get a woman, can't you, somebody?"

"The man's all we can manage," replied a brother officer. "Get him to the station the back way—here! Give a hand there! Quick! We'll have lynch-law here in just about ten minutes, if you ain't spry. Hark! D'ye hear that?"

A muffled roar came down the throat of Angel Alley. It grew, and approached. It was the cry of all Windover raging to avenge the Christian hero whom it learned, too late, to honor.

"Anyhow, he'll hang for it," muttered Lena, when she came to herself in her decent room. Johnny's mother was moaning over her. Lena pushed the old woman gently away, and commanded the retreating officer,

"Say, won't he? Out with it!"

"Well," replied the officer in a comfortable tone, "a good deal depends. Liquor men ain't skerce in this county. He'd get twenty witnesses to swear to an alibi as easy as he'd get one."

"Let 'em swear," said Lena. "I see him do it. I saw him heave the stone."

"That might alter the case, and again it mightn't," replied the officer; "it would depend on the value of the testimony—previous reputation, and so on."

Lena groaned.

"But I caught him by the arm! I stood alongside of him. I was watching for it. I thought I'd be able to stop him. I'm pretty strong. I grabbed him—but he flung me off and stamped on me. I see him heave the rock. See! There's the mark, where he kicked me. Then he ran, and I after him. I can swear to it before earth and heaven. I see him fling that rock!"

"You see," observed the officer, "it ain't a case of manslaughter just yet. The minister was breathing when they moved him."

THEY CARRIED HIM TO HIS own rooms, for it was not thought possible to move him further. He had not spoken nor stirred, but his pulse indicated that a good reserve of life remained in him. The wound was in the lung. The stone was a large and jagged one, with a cruel edge. It had struck with malignant power, and by one of those extraordinary aims which seem to be left for hate and chance to achieve.

His wife had caught him as he fell. She had uttered one cry; after that, her lips had opened only once, and only to say that she assented to her father's proposal for the removal of her husband to Mrs. Granite's house, and that she entreated them to find some gentle method of transportation over the rough road. For Windover was a town of many churches, but of no hospital.

Oddly, the only quite coherent thought she had was of a man she had heard about, a carpenter, who fell from a staging on the other side of the Cape. He was put into an express cart and driven home, a seven-mile gallop, over the rudest road in the State, to his wife; naturally, he was dead when he got there. Bayard had been called to see the widow.

Captain Hap stepped up (on tiptoe, as if he had been in a sick-room), and whispered to the surgeon who had been summoned to Angel Alley.

"That will do," said the surgeon; "it has never been tried, that I know of, but it is worth trying—most modern ideas are—if practicable."

"The fishermen hev cleared the car, the company has cleared the track, and the motor man is one of his people," said Captain Hap; "an' there's enough of us to carry him from here to heaven so—so lovin'ly he'd never feel a jolt."

The old captain made no effort to wipe the tears which rained down his wrinkled cheeks. He and Job Slip, with Mr. Bond and Bob and Tony, took hold of the stretcher; they looked about, to choose, out of a hundred volunteers, the sixth strong hand.

The Reverend George Fenton, agitated and trembling, forced his way through the parting crowd, and pleaded piteously to be allowed to offer his assistance in carrying his wounded classmate.

"I have never lifted a hand to help him since I came to Windover," cried Fenton in the voice of a man who would rather that the whole world heard what he said and knew how he felt. "Let me have this chance before it is too late! . . . I'm not worthy to touch his bier," added Fenton brokenly.

They gave way to his pleading, and it was done as he asked. Thus the wounded man was carried gently to the electric car—"the people's carriage." The fishermen, as the captain said, had captured it; they stood with bowed heads, as the stretcher passed through them, like children, sobbing. Throngs of them followed the slowly moving car, which carried Bayard tenderly to his own door. It was said afterwards that scores of them watched all night outside the cottage, peering for some sign of how it fared with him; but they were so still that one might hardly tell their figures from the shadows of the night.

The wind had continued to rise, but the thunder had passed on, and the shower was almost over when Bayard's bearers lifted him across the threshold of Mrs. Granite's door. At that moment one belated flash ran over earth and sea and sky. It was a red flash, and a mighty one. By its crimson light the fishermen saw his face for that last instant; it lay turned over on the stretcher quietly, towards his wife. The red color dyed her bridal white, and the terrible composure of her attitude was revealed; her hand was fast in his; she seemed to communicate, God knew how, with the unconscious man.

The flash went out, and darkness fell again.

"Then God shut the door," muttered an old and religious fisherman who stood weeping by the fence, among the larkspurs.

THE WIND WENT DOWN, AND the tide went out. Bayard's pulse and breath fell with the sea, and the June dawn came. The tide came in, and the wind arose, and it was evening. Then he moaned, and turned, and it was made out that he tried to say, "Helen?—was Helen hurt?" Then the soul came into his eyes, and they saw her.

HE DID NOT SINK AWAY that day, nor the next, and the evening and the morning were the third day in the chamber where death and life made duel for him.

He suffered, it is hard to think how much; but the fine courage in his habit of living clung on. The injury was not, necessarily, a fatal one. The great consulting surgeon called from Boston said. "The patient may live." He added: "But the vitality is low; it has been sapped to the roots. And the lung is weak. There has been a strain sometime; the organ has received a lesion."

Then Job Slip, when he heard this, thought of the minister's cough, which dated from that battle with the surf off Ragged Rock. And the value of his own cheap life, bought at a price so precious, overwhelmed the man. He would have died a hundred deaths for the pastor. Instead, he had to do the harder thing. It was asked of him to live, and to remember.

In all those days (they were eight in number) Jane Granite's small, soft eyes took on a strange expression; it was not unlike that we see in a dog who is admitted to the presence of a sick or injured master. God was merciful to Jane. The pastor had come back. To live or to die, he had come. It was hers again to work, to watch, to run, to slave for him; she looked at the new wife without a pang of envy; she came or went under Helen's orders; she poured out her heart in that last torrent of self-forgetful service, and thanked God for the precious chance, and asked no more. She had the spaniel suffering, but she had the spaniel happiness.

FOR SEVEN DAYS AND NIGHTS he lay in his shabby rooms, a royal sufferer. The Christ above his bed looked down with solemn tenderness; in his moments of consciousness (but these were few) he glanced at the picture.

Helen had not left his room, either day or night. Leaning upon one arm on the edge of the narrow bed, she watched for the lifting of an eyelid, for the motion of a hand, for the ebbing or the rising of a breath. Sometimes he knew her, and seemed to try to say to her how comforting it was to him to have her there, in the dreary old rooms, where he had dreamed of her sumptuous presence; where they meant to begin their life and love together.

But he could not talk. She found herself already anticipating the habit of those whom the eternal silence bereaves, recalling every precious phrase that his lips had uttered in those last days; she repeated to herself the words which he had said to her on Sunday morning,—

"Nothing *can* harm us now, for you are mine, and I am yours, and this is forever."

As the seventh day broke he grew perceptibly stronger. Helen yielded to her father's entreaties, and for a moment absented herself from the sick-room—for she was greatly overworn,—to drink a breath of morning air. She sat down on the step in the front door of the cottage. She noticed the larkspur in the garden, blue and tall; bees were humming through it; the sound of the tide came up loudly; Jane Granite came and offered her something, she could not have said what; Helen tried to drink it, but pushed the cup away, and went hurriedly upstairs again.

A cot had now been moved in for her beside Bayard's narrow bed. She sat down on the edge of it, between her father and her husband. The Professor stirred to step softly out.

"Dear Professor!" said Bayard suddenly. He looked at the Christ on the wall, and smiled. "We meant—the same thing—after all," he whispered.

Then he put his hand in his wife's, and slept.

It came on to be the evening of the eighth day. He had grown stronger all the day, but he suffered much.

"Folks are keepin' of him back by their prayers," said the religious, old fisherman, who leaned every day upon the garden fence. "He can't pass."

But Job Slip and Captain Hap, who sat upon the doorsteps, listening from dawn to dark for any sign from Bayard's room, said nothing at all.

It came to be evening, and the tide had risen with the wind. The sea called all night long. Helen sat alone with her husband.

He did not wander that night, but watched her face whenever he was not asleep.

"Kiss me, Helen," he sighed at midnight.

She stooped and kissed him, but her lips took the air from him, and he struggled for it.

"You poor, poor girl!" he said.

The wind went down, and the tide went out. The dawn came with the ebb. Bayard fell into a sleep so gentle that Helen's heart leaped with hope. She stole out into the study. Captain Hap was there; his shoes were off; he stepped without noise. The sunrise made a rose-light in the rooms.

"It is real sleep," breathed Helen. "Don't wake him, Captain."

But when the old sailor-nurse would have taken her place for the morning watch, she shook her head. She went back and lay down on the cot beside her husband; he moved his hand, as if he groped for hers, and she was sorry that he had missed it for a moment.

"It shall not happen again," she thought.

Then exhaustion and vigil overcame her, for she had watched for many nights; and thinking that she waked, she slept.

When she came to herself it was broad, bright day. Her hand had a strange feeling; when she tried, she could not move it, for he held it fast. There were people in the room,—her father, her mother, Captain Hap. She stirred a little, leaning towards her husband's pillow.

"Dear, are you better this morning?"

But some one came up, and gently laid a hand upon her eyes.

XXX

Job Slip went down to the water, and it was dark. He walked apart, and took himself into that solitary place on the wharves which he remembered, where he had knelt in the rain, one night, and said, "God," for Mr. Bayard.

A mackerel keg was there—the same one, perhaps; he overturned it, and sat down, and tried to understand. Job had not been able to understand since Mr. Bayard was hurt.

Thought came to him slowly, and with pain like that caused by the return of congested blood to its channels.

"He is dead," said Job. "Lord A'mighty, he ain't alive. Seems I couldn't get it into my head. They've killed him. He's goin' to be buried."

Job clenched his gnarled hands together, and shook them at the sky; then they dropped.

"Seems like shakin' fists at *him*," thought Job. "I ain't a-goin' to. S'posen he's up yander. That's the idee. Lord A'mighty, what do you mean by it? You didn't stop to think of us reformed men, did you, when you let this happen? . . . For Christ's sake. Amen," added Job, under the impression that he had been giving utterance to a prayer.

"Mr. Bayard?" called Job aloud. He slipped off the keg and got upon his knees. As he changed his position, the fisherman vaguely noticed the headlight of the schooner on which he was to have taken his trip, that night. "There goes the Tilly E. Salt," said Job, interrupting himself; "she's got to weigh without me, this time. I'm guard of honor for the—the—I can't *say* it!" groaned Job. "It's oncredible him bein' in a—him put in a—Lord, he's the livin'est man I ever set my eyes on; he CAN'T die! . . . Mr. Bayard? *Mr. Bayard, sir?*"

Job paused, as if he expected to be answered. The water dashed loudly against the old pier. The distant cry of the buoy came over the harbor. The splash of retreating oars sounded faintly somewhere, through the dark.

"He's livin' along," said Job, after some thought. "He can't get fur out of Angel Alley. He wouldn't be happy. He'd miss us, someways; he's so used to us; he's hoverin' in them hymn-toons and that gymnasium he set so much by. I'll bet he is. He's lingerin' in us poor devils he's spent three year makin' men of. . . He's a-livin' *here*."

Job struck his own broad breast, and then he struck it again. A shudder passed over his big frame; and then came the storm. He had not wept before, since Mr. Bayard died. The paroxysm wearied and weakened him, and it was the piteous fact that these were the next words which passed the lips of the half-healed drunkard.

"God A'mighty, if I only had a drink!"

Two hours afterwards, Job Slip came up the wharves; he came as he went, alone; he walked with a steady step; he held his head high in the dark. He whispered as he walked:—

"I didn't—no, I didn't do it. . . Bein' left so—I've alwers had you, sir, before, you know. It makes a sight o' difference when a man hain't anybody but God. He's a kinder stranger. I didn't know, one spell there— but I was goin' under. . . You won't desert a fellar, will you—yander? I'll do you credit, sir, see if I don't. I won't disgrace you, ——d if I will!"

At that moment Job shied suddenly, like a horse, clear from one side of the wharf to the other. He cried aloud,—

"Why, why, what's here? What's got me?" Fingers touched him, but they were of flesh; little fingers, but they were warm, and curled confidingly in Job's big hand.

"Joey? *You?* Little Joey! Why, father's sonny boy! You come just in the right time, Joey. I was kinder lonesome. I miss the minister. I ain't—just feelin' right."

"Fa—ther," said Joey pleasantly; "Marm said to find you, for she said she fought you'd need you little boy."

"And so I do, my son, and so I do!" cried Job.

With Joey's little fingers clasped in his, Job walked up Angel Alley, past the doors of the dens that were closed, and the doors that were open still; and if the ghost of the dear, dead minister had swept visibly before Job and Joey, no man could have tempted or disturbed them less.

In his own chapel, in Angel Alley, Bayard lay in state. It was such state as the kings of the earth might envy, and its warriors and its statesmen and its poets do not know. It was said that his was the happiest dead face that ever rebuked the sadness of the living; and the fairest that they who wept for him had ever seen. Death had not marred his noble beauty; and in death or life there was no comelier man. All the city thronged to show him reverence who had lived among them baffled, doubted, and sick at heart; and it appeared that those who had done the least for him then, would have done most for him now: the people of ease; the imitators; the conformers, and the church members who never questioned their own creeds or methods; the summer strangers playing at life upon the harbor coast, and visitors from a distance where the preacher had his fame.

But when these superior and respectable persons crowded to give their tardy tribute to him, they were told that there was no room for them in the chapel; nay, they could scarcely find footing in the dust of Angel Alley. For they were held back by the sacred rights of "nearest mourners"; and Bayard's mourners claimed him. It was said that hundreds of sunburnt men had stood waiting in the street since midnight for the opening of the doors, and the chance to enter. Then, there had passed up the steps of Christlove Chapel the great mass of the neglected and the poor, the simple and the sodden and the heart-broken, and those who had no friends but only that one man; and God had taken him. The fishermen of Windover, and the poor girls, the widows of Windover, and her orphaned children, the homeless, foreign sailors, and the discontented laborers from the wharves poured in; and the press was great.

He lay among them regally, wrapped in his purple pall. And he and Helen knew that her bridal roses withered forever out of mortal sight upon his breast. But she had given him up at this last hour to his people; he was theirs, and they were his, and what they willed they did for him, and she did not gainsay them. They covered him with their wild flowers, after the fashion of the Cape; and clumsy sailors brought big, hothouse bouquets flaring on wires and splashed with tears, "to give the minister." And his dead heart, like his living one, was found large enough to hold them all.

One poor girl brought no flowers to Bayard's burial. Lena brought only sobs instead, and watered his pall with her tears, and hid her face, and passed on, with her hands before it.

Now, around the bier there stood a guard of honor strange to see; for it was chosen from the Windover drunkards whom the pastor had saved and cured. Among them, Job Slip stood proudly in command at the minister's head: the piteous type of all that misery which Bayard had died to lessen, and of that forgotten manliness which he had lived to save.

There was no dirge sung at Christlove Chapel when he was borne from it. A girl's voice from a darkened corner of the gallery started "the minister's hymn," but trembled, and broke quite down. So the fishermen took it up, and tried to sing,—

But they, too, faltered, for they needed him too much; and in silence, trying not to sob, with bared, bowed heads they passed out gently (for his spirit was upon them), thinking to be better men.

ONE OF THE SUMMER PEOPLE, a stranger in the town, strolling on the beach that day, was attracted by an unusual and impressive sight upon the water, and asked what that extraordinary display of the signs of public mourning meant.

An Italian standing by, made answer,—

"The Christman is dead."

He tried to explain further, but choked, and pointed seaward, and turned away.

For, from every main in the harbor, as far as eye could see, the flags of Windover floated at half-mast. The fishermen had done him this honor, reserved only for the great of the earth, and for their own dead mates; and most sacred for these last.

A Note About the Author

Elizabeth Stuart Phelps (1844–1911) was an American early feminist author and intellectual. Phelps advocated for women's rights, clothing reform, and animal rights, often finding herself surrounded in controversy because of it. Having published multiple best-sellers, Phelps was a well-known author and was the first woman to present a lecture series at Boston University. She wrote in several genres, including children's and spiritualist literature. Phelps often challenged traditional Christian beliefs and the expected domestic role of women in her writing. By the end of her career, Phelps published fifty-seven volumes of fiction, poetry, and essays, as well multiple novels.

A Note from the Publisher

Spanning many genres, from non-fiction essays to literature classics to children's books and lyric poetry, Mint Edition books showcase the master works of our time in a modern new package. The text is freshly typeset, is clean and easy to read, and features a new note about the author in each volume. Many books also include exclusive new introductory material. Every book boasts a striking new cover, which makes it as appropriate for collecting as it is for gift giving. Mint Edition books are only printed when a reader orders them, so natural resources are not wasted. We're proud that our books are never manufactured in excess and exist only in the exact quantity they need to be read and enjoyed.

bookfinity™

Discover more of your favorite classics with Bookfinity™.

- Track your reading with custom book lists.
- Get great book recommendations for your personalized Reader Type.
- Add reviews for your favorite books.
- AND MUCH MORE!

Visit **bookfinity.com** and take the fun Reader Type quiz to get started.

Enjoy our classic and modern companion pairings!

Classic & Modern

9 781513 279930